The Philotimo Affair

J.M. Cottrell

Raider Publishing International

New York   London   Johannesburg

Front cover photograph by Jonathan Copeland from the collection of Ni Wayan Murnis, www.murnis.com

Back cover photograph of Chapultepec Castle by Harald Sund from "Mexico City" by John Cottrell, Time-Life Books, 1979.

ISBN: 1-935383-97-3
Published By Raider Publishing International
www.RaiderPublishing.com
New York London Johannesburg

Printed in the United States of America and the United Kingdom

PREFACE

Though real events have sometimes closely mirrored invention, this is strictly a work of fiction. The principal characters are not based on real-life counterparts, and any similarity with living persons is entirely coincidental.

At the same time, the backgrounds are largely authentic, and in this respect my greatest debt of gratitude is owed to Roberto and Guadalupe Donadi, who gave invaluable support during my many months of research in Mexico City. To that enchanting couple - my most sincere thanks. In addition, I am indebted for expert advice to Dr Roger Berrett (forensic science) and John Beith (firearms).

Posthumously, I should also thank José López Portillo, President of Mexico (1976-82), who unwittingly sowed the first seed for this book. During a formal, tape-recorded interview, while flying to Guadalajara aboard his presidential airliner *Quetzalcoatl 11,* I asked him about his plans to combat corruption in his country, to which he gave the inspiring reply, "Corruption? What corruption?"

Subsequently, by way of spectacular mismanage-ment and profligate borrowing, Portillo took his country from boom to bust. Like so many holders of his omnipotent office, he ended his six-year term as a billionaire and spent years living in luxury abroad. When he finally returned to Mexico City, he became contemptuously known as *"El Perro"* (The Dog), with citizens barking on his rare appearances in public.

No apology is made for highlighting here the extraordinary degree of corruption and pettifogging bureaucracy in Mexico City. On the other hand, I would emphasise my profound admiration for the tens of millions of underprivileged citizens who display such remarkable resilience, exuberance and cynical good humour in enduring the trials and tribulations of life in the most densely populated conurbation of the western world.

To them this book is dedicated.

i

CAST OF CHARACTERS

The following characters are purely fictional and any similarity to characters either living or dead is strictly coincidental.

THE RAMÍREZ FAMILY

Fernando Luis Ramírez........................Ex- professional boxer
María Ramírez.............................Wife (deceased) of Fernando
Antonio Ramírez............Eldest son of Fernando, metalworker
Ricardo Ramírez ....Second son of Fernando,
video/TV store owner
Julio Ramírez..........Third son of Fernando, professional boxer
Manuel Gustavo Ramírez .... Fourth son of Fernando,
unemployed carpenter
Alfredo Ramírez ....Youngest son (deceased) of Fernando
Ester Ramírez...............Daughter of Fernando, bank employee
Marta Ramírez.................Daughter of Fernando, cleaning lady
Anita Herrera ....Married daughter of Fernando

THE TUNAMAN FAMILY

Kemal Tunaman...................... Turkish ambassador to Mexico
Raife Tunaman......................... First wife (deceased) of Kemal
María Dolores Tunaman........................ Second wife of Kemal
(*See Castillo Family*)
Yasemin Stephanopoulos..................Eldest daughter of Kemal
and Raife (*See Stephanopoulos Family*)
Nilufer...........................Younger daughter of Kemal and Raife
Serta..............................Husband of Nilufer, airline executive
Melissa ....Daughter of Nilufer and Sertac
Deniz... Son of Nilufer and Sertac

THE CASTILLO FAMILY

Don José Castillo........................Former Governor of Oaxaca,
hotel tycoon
Felipe Castillo.......................................Eldest son of Don José
Rosa Castillo.. Wife of Felipe

María Dolores.............................Eldest daughter of Don José,
                                        wife of Kemal Tunaman
Yolanda Martínez.......................Second daughter of Don José
Roberto Martinez ....Husband of Yolanda,
                                        Mexican Finance Minster
Esperanza Velázquez................Youngest daughter of Don José
Guillermo Velázquez............................Husband of Esperanza,
                                        hotel assistant manager
Jaime Velázquez.....................Son of Esperanza and Guillermo

THE STEPHANOPOULOS FAMILY
Stavros Stephanopoulos....... Greek shipping and media tycoon
Elena Stephanopoulos..................................... Wife of Stavros
Nicholas Stephanopoulos...... Son of Stavros and Elena, lawyer
Yasemin Stephanopoulos............................. Wife of Nicholas
                                        (*See Tunaman Family*)
Georgios Stephanopoulos............Son of Nicholas and Yasemin
Christina Stephanopoulos.........Daughter of Stavros and Elena

GOVERNMENT & LAW ENFORCEMENTS OFFICIALS IN MEXICO CITY
Enrique Pérez.. President of Mexico
Roberto Martínez...Finance Minister
Gen Juan Delgado........................Mexico City Chief of Police
Cor Ignacio Torres..........Colonel in Mexico City police force
Cor Salvador Hernández...................... Colonel in Mexico City
                                        police force
Capt Hidalgo...................................Mexico City police captain
José Rodríguez...Procurador General
Emilio Ortega............................PA to the Procurador General
Sebastián Fidel Barraza................................ PGR Comandante
José Ibarra ....PGR Subcomandante
Luis Enrique Montaño ....PGR chief detective
Alvaro Reyes..PGR detective
Arturo Contreras .... Deputy Attorney General
Rufino Cordero............Director General of Migration Services
Jesús Moreno......................Sergeant in the Presidential Guard
Eduardo Jiménez..................................Presidential guardsman

AMERICANS IN MEXICO CITY
James Henderson ...........................U.S. ambassador to Mexico
Ricky Henderson ....Son of U.S. ambassador
Mark Ballantyne.............................. U.S. marine/bodyguard

iv

Brad McClellan..Veteran CIA agent
Wade Hellman...CIA station chief
Jim Pollard ....CIA agent
Robert Carruthers .... FBI 'Legal attache' agent
Regina Marke ....Secretary/interpreter for
Nicholas Stephanopoulos

AMERICANS IN WASHINGTON AND LANGLEY, VIRGINIA

Sam Carmichael..U.S. President
Arthur Stephenson.....................................U.S. Vice-President
James Hathaway .... Secretary of State
Melvin J. Holmes..Attorney General
Charles Fairbrother...............................Secretary of Defense
Bill "Skerry" Butler ....National Security Advisor
Adm. George Stanton.................................. Retiring Director,
Central Intelligence
Brig. Lawrence Holt..................................... Deputy Director,
....Central Intelligence
William J. Stanleigh............CIA Deputy Director (operations)
Arthur Madison ....CIA national intelligence officer
(terrorism)
James Chester-Allen .... CIA NIO (Turkish Affairs)
Marjorie Featherstone ....CIA Deputy NIO (Turkish Affairs)
Henry Strachan...Director of the FBI
William Prentice ....FBI assistant director (Investigations)
Garfield Saunders, Jr..................U.S. senator for Massachusetts
William Force..U.S. Senator

CHARACTERS IN MIAMI

Lou Klein ....FBI agent
Angela Cruz..FBI undercover agent
Tony Morelli.. Boxing trainer
Diego Anaya.. Ex-cornerman
Arto Kamber ....Armenian jeweller
Sofi Kamber... Wife of Arto
Rita Kamber ....Sister of Arto
Sertak "Seto" Kamber.................Armenian jeweller (deceased)
Zabel (née Anbaroglu) Kamber......... Wife (deceased) of Sertak
Hagob Vartanyan...............Armenian financier, uncle of Zabel

CHARACTERS IN ACAPULCO

Lt Gen Ernesto Torres.................................... Chief of Police

Cor Carlos Rivas.................................Deputy Chief of Police
Com Luis González...Commander of
the Zorros Force
Jorge Barrientos..........................Corporal in Acapulco Police
Javier Zavala .... Assistant manager, Esmeralda Hotel
Dr Zaragoza...................Director of the Miguel Alemán Clinic
Señorita Orozco.............................Secretary to Dr. Zaragoza
Felix Calderón ....Guard at the Miguel Alemán Clinic
Francisco Domínguez..Security chief,
Miguel Alemán Clinic
Julia Philpotts..U.S. lawyer
Josefina .... Nanny to Jaime Velázquez
Brig. Gen. Antonio Cordero Reyes...............Army commander

MEXICAN PRESS & TV PERSONNEL

Alfredo Gómez......................*El Informador* gossip columnist
Miguel Ramos.................................. Editor of *El Informador*
Emiliano Vargas............................Reporter on *El Informador*
Isabel del Río ....*Channel 13 News* presenter
Señora Alvarez ....PA to Isabel del Río
Francisco Romero....................Producer of *Channel 13 News*
Félix Ortiz...................................Crime reporter on *Excelsior*
Juan Serra .... Photographer on *Excelsior*
Vicente Cabañas...............................Editor of *Excelsior*
Teresa 'Pepita' de Terreros.............................. TV astrologer

MISCELLANEOUS CHARACTERS

Erkan Gursoy...President of Turkey
Christos Andriopoulou......................Prime Minister of Greece
Mirka Kirillis...................Personal Secretary to Andriopoulou
Gastón Pérez .... Former Attorney General,
brother of Mexican President
Cholita Pérez...................................... Wife of Gaston Pérez
Viktor Gondicas.............Greek cultural attaché in Mexico City
Selim Suman ....Prime Minister of Turkey
Jennifer Morrow..............Mistress of Stavros Stephanopoulos
Mehmet Haybat.............. PA to Ambassador Kemal Tunaman
Ignacio Galván...Convicted thief
Professor Leonidas Kritikos........................... Director of the
Acropolis Museum
Kostas Bandanidis..........................Greek supermarket tycoon
Selim Atasoy ....Turkish author
Evangelina Arantes de Pérez.............Wife of President Pérez

vi

Don Carlos Velázquez .... Mexican steel magnate
Miguel Bernal García.......................... Mexican bank president
Enrique Mérida .... Mayor of Iztapalapa
Dr Sánchez Becerra........... Mexican obstetrician/gynaecologist
Louise Fontaine....................................... Air France stewardess
Ramón "El Tanque" Alvarez .... Champion boxer
El Nuevo Santo.. Champion wrestler
Médico de la Muerte .... Wrestler
Señora Sable.. Wrestling sceptator
Rodrigo Monteagudo.......... Manager/trainer of El Nuevo Santo
Consuelo Gutiérrez.................... Girl friend of Manuel Ramírez
Señor Gutiérrez... Father of Consuelo
Arturo Menéndez................................... Bolivian-born lawyer
Jaime Muzquiz .... Mexico City taxi driver
Alfonso Puentes .... Mexico City taxi driver
Ramón Alvarez............................. Mexican light-heavyweight
boxing champion
Juanita...................................... Maid at Apartamentos Orleáns
Elvira Mendoza .... Personal maid to Dolores Tunaman
Jesús Suarez... Crank telephone caller
José Santiago .... Crank telephone caller
Conchita... Mexican medium
Dr Armando Morelos..................................... Mexican surgeon
Leonor Contreras .... Senior mistress of General Delgado
Lupita Linares .... Second mistress of General Delgado
Carmen, Isabel and Teresa .... Friends of Dolores Tunaman
Marcos .... Professional magician
Chico.. Professional clown
Manuela............................. Bank clerk, neighbour of Rodrigo
Eugenia............................... Bank clerk; neighbour of Rodrigo
Carlos García .... Iztapalapa garage mechanic
Martha .... Flatmate of Regina Marke

The Mexican, whether young or old, criollo or mestizo, general or labourer or lawyer, seems to me to be a person who shuts himself away to protect himself; his face is a mask and so is his smile.

Octavio Paz (*The Labyrinth of Solitude*)

The Philotimo Affair

J.M. Cottrell

PART 1
La Muerte

CHAPTER 1

Dawn, Sunday, January 25, Mexico City

"*La suerte es como la muerte.*"

Manuel spoke the words softly and deliberately, his broad, sensual mouth stretching on the final syllable into a frozen, teeth-flashing grin. It was a curious grin, patently strained, conveying at once a sense of primitive savagery and intense delight; the expression, one might imagine, of a cannibal discovering some surprisingly tasty morsel in his stew. Manuel savoured the phrase, repeated the words, again slowly, and caressing them with a conscious rolling of the *r*'s.

"*La suerte es como la muerte.*"

He couldn't recall exactly when he had first heard the saying, but it must have been before his seventh birthday when *mamá* was still alive. She had given him twenty-five pesos to buy his first lottery ticket. The reason for her extravagance was forgotten, yet he could still vaguely remember sobbing into her skirt— the one with the multi-coloured flowers that she nearly always wore— and explaining how he had roamed the streets in vain to find a *lotería* who had all the number 7's. Without those magic numbers, he had babbled on, all hope was lost, and she had laughed and kissed his tears, and had said in her sweetly lilting voice, "Manuelito, *la suerte es como la muerte*. Luck is like death. It can come at any time, any place. The lucky numbers, my little one, are written in heaven, not in your head."

Years later, in moments of stress, he was to find comfort by echoing her words. And never more so than now.

His fatalism reaffirmed, Manuel levered himself into a more upright squatting position with his back hard against the parapet wall. Then, once again, he raised the semi-automatic sniping rifle from his lap, pointed it skywards and, with the butt pressed hard into his right shoulder, fixed the telescopic sight on a make-believe target and gently squeezed the trigger. There was a dull metallic click.

3

One more time he used the yellow rag to wipe down the stock and barrel; then, after gently stroking it over the telescopic sight, he threw the rag away. Beside him, on the stone floor, was a clip holding twenty cartridges. Bored with rehearsals, he inserted the magazine into the slot directly in front of the trigger guard and laid the rifle at his right side. The safety catch remained off.

Chinguen a su madre, he thought. *Fuck the whole human race!*

At that moment, for the first time, he became aware of welcome warmth from an unseen morning sun. Twisting into a crouching position, he stretched up to peer over the stone parapet that encircled his lofty perch. There was no sight or sound of life except for a brace of wood pigeons flitting by, and so he stood upright and stretched his arms as though lifting heavy weights.

His perch was atop a two-tiered, windowed tower, some sixty feet high and rising into a rounded turret from its square base section. Here, he occupied a circle of concrete 25 feet in diameter, with a bare flagstaff in the centre and beside it an arched hatchway opening out from a wide stairwell. Directly below him was the flat roof garden of Chapultepec Castle and, two floors beneath, spacious terraces fringed far and wide by the peaks of giant *ahuehuete* trees that rose from the slope of a hill some two hundred feet high.

Beyond the hill, mainly westward, lay the thousand-acre pleasure-paradise of the *Bosque de Chapultepec*, almost one-mile long and one mile at its widest. And beyond the lake-dotted park, stretching into seeming infinity, was the deranged sprawl of suburbs, satellites and shantytowns that made up the bulk of the most densely populated conurbation in the western world. Mexico City.

He took a deep breath of the morning air, and reflected that it was going to be a beautiful day. Momentarily, as he surveyed the panorama, he forgot the hazards ahead and responded to a rare urge to assert his own identity.

"Remember me, *papá*? Yes, it's Manuel. Okay, Manuelito. Little Manuel. I was always little, wasn't I? You old bastard. Well, I'm not so little now, eh? Look at me. I'm on top of the world. King of the castle. *El Presidente.*"

For a few minutes Manuel was daydreaming, his arms akimbo on the turret wall, his chin resting on overlapped hands. Not unusually, his random thoughts focussed on his father: a one-time light-heavyweight boxer, all muscle turned to flab, and bearing an enormous potbelly sustained, on all but forty days a year, by prodigious quantities of *pulque* and tequila.

Manuel recalled how, every Lent, out of sheer bloody-mindedness, the old man - a self-professed pagan - unfailingly took the pledge to confound everyone who called him a slave to the bottle. It would be the same again in three months' time. *Weird! How the fuck could he do it?*

Then, glancing down, his eyes were attracted by the flashing of his most precious possession: the gold Omega wristwatch that told him both time and date: 0710, Sunday, January 25.

The time alerted him to his immediate needs. He reached down to a dark-green haversack that was lying open on the grey blanket that had been used to wrap the rifle. From it, he extracted a large pair of binoculars and began to scan the view to the west, finally focussing far across the trees on a section of the park reserved for barbecue parties.

He was right. Sure enough, confirming that he was not alone, some paper chains and multi-coloured balloons had been freshly strung between trees to mark off a great square of grass. Hadn't he done just the same thing so many years ago, going out at dawn to help Ricardo and Julio stake out the best spot for Alfredo's birthday party?

He could not see anyone there. Perhaps they had left to fetch supplies of food and drink. But, as was to be expected, they had picked the perfect place, close by the adventure playground and, most valuably, beside a number of tree stump seats and an array of barbecues permanently fixed in concrete.

How clearly he could picture the scene ahead. Within a few hours, that reserved square of grass would be alive with dozens of children, and with friends and relatives organising games. There would be prizes and dancing and feasting, and, as always, the inevitable climax of blindfolded children swinging sticks at *piñatas* suspended from trees and then screaming with delight as the clay pots within papier-mâché figures finally disintegrated and disgorged their contents: candy, fruit, peanuts, sticks of sugar cane, and perhaps some plastic toys.

It was *mamá's* favourite scene. As she always used to say, "What does it matter if we are a family of thirteen crowded into two small rooms? Didn't Our Lady make sure that we have all the space that we need? In the park, we are

5

more lucky than kings and queens in their palaces. We can invite as many friends as we like. We don't get the furniture messed, and we can always be sure of fine weather."

Manuel grinned at the thought of those happy, carefree days in the sun. And then he remembered the reality. How *papá* had brought a black cloud over the last party. It had begun as a bit of good-humoured fun, his using their only *piñata* as a punch bag, and playfully tapping it to and fro. But, of course, that was never enough for *papá*. He could not resist showing off his strength, and finally, with one mighty right-hook, he had smashed the *piñata* to smithereens. Soon after, he collapsed into such a deep-drunken stupor that they had to carry him all the way to the car park.

There were no more parties in Chapultepec Park. Before the next birthday, *mamá* was dead. Without her, the family began to fall apart, and, without her, no one noticed when poor Alfredo, just ten-years-old, took to that bloody glue.

Manuel gritted his teeth and spat out the word introducing his new line of thought, *Cabrónes! They are to blame. All the fucking capitalists! It is just like papá always said. The great revolution was all for nothing. It is still a world of thousands of haves and millions of have-nots, still a world without justice and honour. Why should a few bastards have billions of pesos, more than anyone can ever hope to spend? Why can't the people share equally in the great riches of this beautiful land? Fuck the politicians and the capitalists. Fuck all of them.*

Manuel Gustavo Ramírez was twenty-two years old; in his features a mestizo rather more Indian than Spanish. He had high cheekbones, a straight nose, and thick, black brows above small, narrow eyes. Yet his skin was relatively light in colour, and he was marked as an urbanite by his grooming: pencil-thin moustache, long, neatly trimmed sideburns, and dark, off-the-shoulder hair slicked down with Vaseline. In dress, he was positively a city-dweller: clean, white trainers, blue denim trousers, and an olive-green shirt beneath a thickly lined zip-jacket of dark-brown leather.

A smart appearance was important to Manuel - not out of pure vanity but as a calculated part of his pursuit of sexual conquests. In this pursuit, born of a need to boost his machismo, he was not unusual among Mexican men. But it belied his true nature. Essentially, though he would never

6

admit it, he was an incurable romantic who yearned for a permanent, one-woman relationship. Instead, with one disastrous exception, he had been limited to passionate encounters that blazed from the onset and burst into brilliant light only to fizz out abruptly, like a Roman candle reaching its zenith over the Zócalo on Independence Day.

Manuel's strike-rate was high, and he kept the score. He might lack the charisma to have lasting impact on the young women he misguidedly placed on a pedestal. But there could be no denying his appeal to older ladies. His success with matronly tourists in Acapulco had proven that. He had a disarming smile, and a certain boyish vulnerability in his manner, which stirred the maternal instinct. His non-threatening physique was a further advantage. He was of only average height, without any sign of muscular power. But the slight, slim-waisted body was supremely lithe, seemingly devoid of one ounce of surplus fat.

No amount of eating seemed to add to Manuel's weight or stature. However, he saw this as more a curse than a blessing. He could never forget what *papá* used to say, "Look at the boy - not enough meat for a Chihuahua's dinner." And then always that raucous laugh, and the playful punch on his shoulder, as though the old man had made his little joke for the very first time.

To be sure, *Mamá* had often reassured her youngest surviving son that he was beautiful. But no matter. Manuel had always longed for *Papá's* approval, and even now— despite Julio's worldly guidance— he was still too immature to grasp that all of his father's loud-mouthed judgments and views were based on personal prejudices and values that had not changed one iota in more than forty years.

Superficially, Manuel was every inch his mother's son. Neither in looks nor manner did he remotely resemble his sire: a veritable bull of a man who had fathered thirteen children— including two stillborn— and who, though rarely physically cruel, and never when sober, had always dominated his household by the sheer force of his egocentric personality.

In thought, however, Manuel had more in common with his father than he ever knew. He had absorbed the old man's muddled and essentially bitter left-wing views. Like his father, also, he dwelt largely in the past and the future, brooding already over what might have been and fantasising about the shape of things to come. For the son, so young, this

7

represented a fatal, premature weakness. For the father, once wholly a man of action, it was a natural progression into old age.

Fernando Luis Ramírez was now sixty-five years old, a dinosaur lingering on in Tepito, the once-infamous quarter of central Mexico City that had been likened in his youth to New York's "Hell's Kitchen", a concrete jungle renowned as the nation's most fertile breeding ground of hungry fighters.

He not only lived mainly in the past, but also on the past. To be precise, on the events, over forty years ago, of his one never-to-be-forgotten day of an otherwise undistinguished life; the day, enshrined in Mexican boxing legend, when he had fought Ramón "*El Tanque*" Alvarez for the vacant national light-heavyweight championship.

The story of that extraordinary fight - never to be briefly told - had kept Fernando in free drinks ever since. No matter that the regulars in his local *pulqueria* had heard the story a hundred times or more. It was the way Fernando told it that counted. Given enough drinks, and never before, he would talk his way through a wild action-replay of the fight that was unwittingly hilarious— a confused medley of shadow-boxing, ducking, weaving, jabbing and much puffing as he attempted to play the parts of both fighters and the referee. No two performances were ever exactly the same, and his cronies would lay bets on whether he would finish the fight before collapsing into a drunken heap.

Either way, the final outcome was always the same: Fernando ended the evening legless and eventually arrived home draped over the shoulders of his two drinking *compadres*. On these occasions, his family needed no explanation, and knew that none would be given. The old man would sleep soundly until noon the next day and then awake without the faintest recall of the events of the night before.

Three decades ago, when the entire Ramírez household was crammed into a two-roomed apartment, such drunken paralysis had had its compensations: for *mamá* an undisturbed night, for the family a breakfast refreshingly free of Fernando's overpowering presence.

But now the household numbered only three: the old man and his two youngest daughters, both in their late twenties and anxiously unattached. His four other girls were married, each with a home and children of their own. Four of his five sons— Antonio, Ricardo, Julio and Manuel— had long since gone their own way, and one— mentally retarded after a year of sniffing glue— had been killed in a road accident.

For all the survivors the greatest loss was *mamá*. Unforgettable *mamá*. Fifteen years ago she had died, but in the hearts and minds of her children she lived on, her memory never fading. Indeed, never a day passed without her being recalled, for they saw her in spirit at every turn: in the ubiquitous image, dark and serene, of the Virgin of Guadalupe.

The children had not known a morning when *mamá* had missed her prayers at the little family shrine to Our Lady. And all her days, totally sustained by her faith, she had borne her heavy burdens with that same saint-like serenity, never complaining, never losing patience, never showing favour in bestowing her love and compassion. Each son and daughter was made to feel special to *mamá*. Each one deeply cherished her memory. And secretly Fernando wept for her, too.

Manuel slumped down once more on the turret floor, leant his head back against the stone wall, and gazed upward at the clear blue sky. It was warm enough now to discard the zip-jacket that had barely given adequate protection throughout the long, chilly night. He rolled it up and stuffed it in his haversack after removing a litre-bottle of tequila.

The bottle was almost empty. For the moment, he wished he had brought a thermos of coffee instead. Still, the tequila had saved him last night when he had feared he would never get to sleep. And now he was glad to have one last swig to steady his nerves.

The interminable waiting, he realised, was really bugging him now. His gold digital watch flashed, "0730," and he calculated that fourteen and a half hours had passed since he had slipped into the tower, just before the closing of the castle museum on Saturday night.

That night, when darkness came, he had soon lost all sense of time, drifting along with his random thoughts until falling into deep sleep. But now, following the dawn, he was conscious of every passing minute, of every flashing second that was taking him nearer and nearer to his moment of truth. With the light of day had come a fresh, uncomfortable awareness of reality. The reality was that henceforth he needed to stay down, undercover.

From this time on, the park would steadily become vibrant with life as Mexicans in their mounting thousands, and tourists in their hundreds, arrived to taste its myriad pleasures.

Within a few hours there would be activity all around - people strolling, cycling, boating, roller skating, watching open-air theatricals, listening to concerts, picnicking, playing football, volleyball and chess, and screaming on the wild roller coaster ride of the gigantic *Montaña Rusa.*

0730. In an hour and a half, *El Castillo* itself would be open to visitors. A few would make the 15-minute climb on foot, by way of spiralling pathways. The great majority would lazily mount the hill by way of a bus service, now provided free of charge and making obsolete the antiquated six-passenger elevator he remembered riding as a boy into the heart of the castle.

Manuel reflected cynically on the scene: the hordes of Mexican people wandering sheep-like through ornate salons and marble halls, through a world of crystal-chandeliered magnificence which might have belonged to another planet, so far was it removed from their everyday lives.

They called the place *El Museo Nacional de Historia,* as though it were all in the past, the walls covered with the portraits of the viceroys of New Spain, sixty-one of them, all solemn and beady-eyed, who had ruled Mexico with a rod of iron for three hundred years; the rooms crowded with luxurious mementoes of Maximilian and Carlota, bloody foreigners absurdly-styled emperor and empress of Mexico; the relics of Don Porfirio Díaz, the greatest and— to Manuel— the most loathsome dictator of all.

But he knew better. Tutored by his father, he had learnt to view the museum not simply as a depository of the past, but as "a mirror of the present, a monument to the never-ending, fucking exploitation of the masses by the bastards in power".

Mierda! How that old bugger could talk! It was like Julio said, if papá had been as fast with his fists as he was with his tongue he'd have been a world champion for sure. Manuel could still hear him now - playing the tour guide with a perverse style all of his own as he led them round the castle museum, gesticulating extravagantly, sometimes obscenely, and all the while pouring out the mishmash of history that he, in turn, had learnt from his father.

"Now there's a fine sight - the old carriage that Juárez had as a travelling office when those bloody French invaders forced him to flee from city to city. What a man! Our first and last truly democratic president. Think of it, Manuelito, a

10

barefoot Zapotec Indian shepherd-boy taking over all this splendour. But he knew what it was worth. Bugger all! He wouldn't live in a European palace while his people were starving. And he didn't spend one single peso on this fucking place. Not like that cabrón Don Porfirio. Go upstairs, and you can see how he spent a million pesos on fucking. Ha! Ha!

"See, there's his ridiculous bedchamber - five times the size of our apartmen. And that was just for sleeping. When he wanted to bury his chilli pepper, he stepped next door to that fancy bedroom of Doña Carmen. Who needs it? All this Victorian rubbish.

"Yeah, that was the great Díaz. Selfish bastard! D' you know how he celebrated a hundred years of Mexican independence in 1910? Threw a party costing 20 million pesos and had twenty carloads of champagne consumed in an all-night binge. Now I ask you, what kind of drink is that for a Mexican on Mexico's Day? Bloody French-loving faggot! Lived like an emperor for donkey's years while his people were dying of hunger. Good fucking riddance.

"Ah yes, viva la revolución. There they are, muchachos, all around the walls - Madero, Villa, Zapata, Carranza. Obregón, Calles and the rest. See their banners flying with those slogans, LAND AND LIBERTY. THE LAND IS FOR ALL. Huh! They had their revolution all right. Took us round in a full bloody circle, right back to where we fucking started."

Manuel thought of the popular saying: *If Benito Juárez were alive today, he would die.* Yeah! Die of a broken heart to see all his dreams of equality and justice distorted into a sham of democracy. Okay, so we've got television and videos and McDonald's, and a fat new upper-middle-class beneath the millionaire élite. But what else had changed? The overwhelming majority were still at the bottom of the heap, multiplying in their millions on the garbage of an industrialised society. And they called it "progress".

He again thought about what *papá* used to say - about all the double-dealing foreigners who had plundered this beautiful land: the Spaniards raping and brainwashing an entire civilisation, the French expansionists, and not least the American gringos who, by force and by guile, had taken half of all Mexico, and the richest half at that.

The foreigners were *cabrónes*. Especially the gringos, like cock-happy Clinton, who had sucked Mexico into a free

11

trade zone and then, with huge loans, had landed the country so heavily into debt that Mexico was now virtually the fifty-first American state.

But, like *papá* said, at least those bastards were true to the interests of their nations, their own people. The real villains, the unforgivable sinners, were the *malinchistas*: those Mexicans who, out of self-interest, conspired with foreigners to betray their own kind.

La Malinche! Manuel thought of the Serpent-Lady who had betrayed all her people by lying down with the conquistador Cortés, and who had given her name to all the Mexican quislings that followed.

And, as always, by association, his mind automatically locked into Consuelo Gutiérrez. His own little *Malinche*. He wanted to forget, to obliterate her from his memory. But there was no escape. She haunted him still. He loved her. He hated her. And now he even feared her.

The curse of Consuelo! She had become his personal *bruja,* a witch from whom there was no escape. He blamed her for all his recent misfortunes... and his greatest misfortune to come. For what else but the mind-shattering deception of that bewitching whore could have stampeded him to this place... to meet a terrifying destiny that was now only a few hours away?

CHAPTER 2

0800 hours, Sunday, January 25

The Paseo de la Reforma, modelled by command of Emperor Maximilian on the Champs Elysée, is one of the most magnificent boulevards in the world. Flanked by skyscrapers, and punctuated with monuments set in the six *glorietas* or circles of its main intersections, the great eight-lane avenue bisects Mexico City's central zone from the northeast to the south-west where it leads up to *La Fuente de la Diana Cazadora*, the last intersection before it turns into and cuts across the northern side of Chapultepec Park.

From the rooftop garden of the new Turkish embassy, two blocks north of the central Independence Monument, Ambassador Kemal Tunaman had a clear view between high-rise buildings of the westernmost monument, Diana the Huntress. In the 1950s, a puritanical mayor had outraged popular taste by clothing the sylphlike huntress in a pair of sculpted panties. But later, after years of public protest, she was restored to her natural condition - a handsome bronze figure, surmounting in refreshing nakedness the spectacular fountain near the main approach to the park.

Tunaman, however, had no interest in the fanciful attributes of Diana. On this, his last Sunday morning in Mexico City, he swung his tripod-fixed telescope towards the southeast and began scanning the far-distant horizon. Within a few seconds he had found his objective and, beaming with satisfaction, he locked the scope into position. "Hey, Dolly," he called out. "Come and look at this. You may never see it again."

There was no reply. In the far corner of the patio, seated at a long onyx table within the shade of flowering bougainvillaea, a dark, chub-faced woman ruffled the newspaper she was reading and glared back at him with a look of icy disdain.

At once the ambassador recognised his error, and

13

gently smiled. "Sorry, my dear."

Unusually, in his excitement, he had forgotten one of his wife's golden rules: never, ever, to address her by the nickname that was sometimes used by visiting Americans. At social functions, protocol demanded she accept such familiarity without hint of resentment. To everyday acquaintances, however, she made her feelings crystal clear. Her name was Dolores— to be precise, Doña María Dolores Castillo de Tunaman— eldest daughter of Don José Castillo, former governor of Oaxaca and millionaire-owner of hotels in Cancún, Acapulco and Guadalajara.

"Dolores." The ambassador, now standing at his wife's side, placed a hand on her shoulder. "Don't you want to take one last look? They're there, as clear as the day you first showed them to me."

"No, thank you, Kemal," she replied in a condescending tone. "It's nothing new to me." Then, for emphasis, she turned over a page of her *Excelsior.*

"But..." Tunaman shrugged resignedly and returned to his telescope to take one more look at the imposing, snow-clad peaks of Popocatépetl and Iztaccíhuatl, some forty miles away.

Somehow - and not only because he was about to be transferred from Mexico City - he felt certain he would never see the twin volcanoes again. And so he lingered over the view; at the same time trying to visualise that magic moment when Cortés and his *conquistadores,* climbing the pass between the volcanoes, had first looked down in wonder on the glistening waters of Lake Texcoco to behold in the hazy distance the dazzling island-metropolis of Tenochtitlán.

The capital of the Aztec empire was, according to accounts he had read, a city even richer and more beautiful than Venice; a majestic array of palaces and pyramidal temples, interspersed with broad plazas and exotic gardens, and divided from its mainland suburbs by three great causeways. What had the guidebook said, something about its buildings gleaming spotless white in the brilliant crystalline air?

He smiled to himself. That was hardly the picture now. Here was the smog capital of the world, a metropolis— nicknamed *Makesicko City*— so polluted that middle-aged citizens gave away their advancing years by recalling how they used to see the volcanoes with their naked eyes.

As Kemal had reflected before: leaving aside arctic wastes, arid deserts and impenetrable jungles, it was difficult to imagine a more unfavourable site for the most densely populated metropolis of the western world. It was as though a group of lunatic developers had pooled their resources to build the modern capital of Mexico. Their chosen site was on a volcanic belt ever subject to frequent Earth tremors; on filled-in lakes, with a subsoil so spongy that historic buildings sank at a rate of one foot every year, and the whole city shook in an earthquake like a bowl of jelly; at more than seven thousand feet above sea level, necessitating water to be pumped up at enormous expense, and in a great mountain-rimmed cauldron that trapped pollution largely created by the exhausts of some four million motorcars and made all the worse by factories perversely concentrated in the north, so that prevailing winds carried industrial fumes back over the urban mass. The result was the mad, illogical conurbation of Mexico City; a capital swollen to near bursting-point with some twenty-five million souls, more than a quarter of the nation's inhabitants, jammed into one per cent of the country's land.

But now, as he unlocked the scope and ranged it over the stately, sun-pierced greenery of Chapultepec Park and the glittering white marbles amid a still, silent Reforma, Kemal the romantic saw the city in a new heartwarming light: as a maiden revealed in pristine beauty and glory after casting off her weekday, workaday *sarape* of smog.

Gone was the city that former mayor Carlos Hank González had called a "labyrinth of anxiety". Gone the city whose angst-driven mentality showed in the desperation of commuters struggling to enter already jam-packed Metro trains, in the foot-shuffling impatience of long-queuing bus travellers, in the cold-blooded, horn-hooting aggression of traffic-snarled motorists.

Soon the city would come alive again, but awakening to an entirely different pace and mood as its teeming millions were set free from the hectic, competitive way of life modernisation had thrust upon them. Soon its people would re-emerge in their natural state: *mañana*-minded workers who, after unwinding on Saturday, were now ready to indulge fully their infinite capacity and appetite for leisure and pleasures. This was, above all, a day for family outings. They would be picnicking in their hordes in Chapultepec Park,

15

crowding onto multi-coloured punts to cruise the Aztec-made waterways of Xochimilco, engaging in good-humoured banter and bargaining at countless flea markets, packing their local *charro* rings, and the deep cauldron of the Plaza México that was the largest bullring in the world, and generally nourishing their senses on a day enlivened by itinerant musicians, by ubiquitous food sellers, and an abundance of colourful activities. All this, to Kemal's mind, made up a unique carnival of life.

He joined his wife at the breakfast table. "You know, Dolores, it occurs to me that if every day could be Sunday, this would be one of the most enchanting cities on Earth."

"Yes dear," she replied without giving the notion a moment's thought. She folded her copy of *Excelsior* into a fat square and slid it across the table. "This might interest you. They have done you proud again, though it's a bit too jokey in my opinion. Do you want me to read it for you?"

Kemal politely declined the offer. He was not interested. After six months of unremitting attention from the world's press he had become completely indifferent to publicity, good or bad. Moreover, he had long since reached the conclusion that to read constantly about oneself was to invite unhealthy introspection. He merely glanced at the headline and smiled. It boldly proclaimed: *Adiós Fantasma Grande*. He could guess the rest.

"One thing I shall miss about the Mexican press is their keen sense of humour. They are never too reverent."

"Hmm! But they can be guilty of downright bad taste."

"You're absolutely right, dear." He was remembering how he had felt rather guilty about being amused by an item in the city's English-language *The News*. It reported the grisly details of a mugging near the Zócalo in which a man had been robbed not only of his wrist watch and pesos, but also of his four gold teeth. The writer then asked. "Was this perhaps the work of the same criminal who last week broke into the home of a Las Lomas dentist?"

"Yes," said Dolores. "This *El Fantasma* business has become tedious. You'd think they would be a little more serious and respectful - especially today."

She picked up the paper again. "Just listen to this: 'Tomorrow, we bid farewell to the most distinguished diplomat in Mexico City: senor Kemal Tunaman, the

16

ambassador of Turkey. He has served here for less than three years and yet, within that time, he has risen from obscurity to world renown, winning the Nobel Peace Prize for his successful efforts as a mediator in the crisis which briefly threatened war between Turkey and Greece.

" 'We wish senor Tunaman every success in his new appointment as Turkish ambassador to the United Nations in New York. But, in truth, we cannot say that we will miss him. For all his undoubted skills as a peacemaker, the fact remains that, in the past six months, he had spent only three full weeks in Mexico City. Not without reason is he known as The Great Phantom...' "

Kemal laughed. "That's fair comment. It's absolutely true, what they say. There is no reason why your country should miss me."

He poured himself a cup of coffee, then slowly directed his gaze around the rooftop garden as though trying to memorise every detail of its multi-coloured brilliance. "But I shall miss Mexico."

They made an odd pair, the Tunamans. In public, they conveyed an image of a reasonably contented and devoted couple. In private, they were worlds apart, resigned, after only two and a half years of marriage, to the fact that they were complete opposites with no interests and scarcely any opinions in common.

Physically they presented such absurdly contrasting figures that Doña Tunaman would never willingly consent to their being photographed together. He was tall, thin and gaunt; she was short, dumpy and round-faced. In temperament, too, they were diametrically opposed. He was calm, good-humoured and patience personified; she was high-strung, moody, possessive and impatient.

From a strictly practical viewpoint, it could be argued that Dolores was a considerable asset to her husband, and especially now that he was under excessive working pressure. By nature, Kemal was a dreamer, an academic prone to absent-mindedness and disregard of formalities. Yet his new lifestyle— crowded with high-level engagements and travel abroad— demanded organisation and attention to detail.

Dolores was nothing if not an organiser and a stickler for detail. Supplementing the work of Mehmet Haybat, the ambassador's PA, she organised her husband's personal appearance, dictating the clothes he wore, the aftershave he

17

used, and how and when his hair was cut. The crescent-moon beard, too middle-eastern for her tastes, had long since had to go.

Having polished her English while reading sociology for three years at Georgetown University, Washington, D.C., she was able to give valuable service as an interpreter. Kemal was fluent in three foreign languages: English, Greek and German, but had only a rudimentary knowledge of Spanish. In addition, and by no means least, she organised— though largely to suit to her own emotional needs— his social life.

Kemal bowed to almost all her demands, not because he lacked strength of character, but because he usually saw them as too trivial to be worthy of argument. Also, he was glad to make concessions that made her a more contented person. His only real complaint was that she sometimes added unnecessarily to his burden of social engagements, and too often involved him with certain relatives and friends he found tiresome.

The bonding together of these opposite poles was further evidence of Dolores' forceful personality and organising skills. Following their very first meeting— at a presidential reception— she had decided he was a suitable catch, and subsequently she had contrived, through her relatives in government circles, to be invited to every state function he attended.

There was no physical attraction. Dolores, at that time a forty-two-year-old spinster, had simply resolved to acquire a husband. Her three sisters and two brothers were all married and raising families of their own. And more and more she felt handicapped socially by her lack of a permanent male partner and, to a lesser degree, by her lack of children. But not any man would do. Over the years she had dismissed several Mexican suitors whom she recognised intuitively as fortune hunters. Also, she observed how so many of her friends tolerated unfaithful husbands. That was not her way. She sought a man she could respect and trust completely, and romance entered into her calculations not at all.

Kemal, as she realistically assessed, qualified perfectly to meet her needs. He was a gentleman in the truest sense of the word, a man of quiet dignity and transparent integrity. He had status and, as a fifty-nine-year-old widower, he had a ready-made family to give her a matriarchal role. Astutely, too, she recognised that he was emotionally vulnerable, a man

18

alone in a foreign environment and without the support of a woman for the first time in thirty years.

Indirectly, it was the loss of his beloved first wife that had brought Kemal Tunaman to Mexico City. Her sudden death from cancer had left him so devastated that friends feared for his sanity. He no longer felt able to fulfil his duties as a professor of philosophy and classical studies at Istanbul University. A few weeks of compassionate leave dragged into months, as everywhere he turned, he seemed to encounter sights and sounds that reminded him of his blissful years with Raife. Though he himself could not recognise it, he was in the grip of a nervous breakdown.

It was an old friend from his student days - Erkan Gursoy, President of Turkey, no less - who came to the rescue. Kemal, he suggested, needed a complete break from his haunting past; some new challenge that would absorb him in the present. "I have just the thing for you," he said. "We are now in the process of establishing an embassy in Mexico, and you would be a perfect choice as our first ambassador there."

Tunaman laughed, then politely pointed out that he was totally unqualified for such a position. And anyway, he could not speak a word of Spanish.

"Nonsense," said Gursoy. "At that level, you can get by with English. Also, you would always have access to interpreters, though, knowing you, I expect you would pick up the language quickly enough.

"As for qualifications, our trade and tourism with Mexico are minimal. Any junior official can deal with the day-to-day business. On the other hand, the North American trade pact with the U.S. and Canada has made Mexico a far more important player in world affairs. Mexico City has become a major focal point for international conferences. We need someone there to represent Turkey in a favourable light— not some smart-ass career diplomat, but someone with a touch of class. Someone like you, Kemal. Why not give it a try? And if it doesn't work out, well, dear *kardesim,* you can be immediately relieved."

As it happened, the escape was unnecessary. By the time Kemal arrived in Mexico City his melancholic depression had run its natural course, fading into acceptance of reality. One week later, when he was first introduced to Dolores at a reception, he was already thinking about an early return to university life, though only on a part-time basis, so allowing

19

himself more time to spend with his two married daughters and his three grandchildren.

Shortly afterwards, he found himself seated next to Dolores at a state banquet held to mark the opening of the World Trade Exhibition in Mexico City. Now, after preliminary small talk, she explained that her father, who had recently retired to Cuernavaca, was holding a weekend house party in one month's time. Her family would be honoured if he could attend.

Kemal graciously declined, explaining that he could make no plans so far in advance because he might soon be returning to Istanbul. By subsequent probing, Dolores learnt of Kemal's background, and of his conclusion that he had rushed too hastily into accepting the ambassadorship. She responded artfully.

"How awful for you. Of course, you are quite right to go home. But really, before you leave, you ought to see something of our wonderful city and culture. Why not treat it as a holiday? There are so many wonderful things to see, and it would be a shame to waste the opportunity. I am completely free and would love to show you around."

Kemal prevaricated uneasily. There were official duties to fulfil, rearrangements to be made. But Dolores had persisted, and soon she had pinned him down to one small commitment. He could at least find time to visit the finest of all monuments to Mexico's past: The National Museum of Anthropology in Chapultepec Park. It would be unthinkable to miss it.

After that initial outing, Dolores had her prey neatly baited. Tunaman found himself totally enthralled by the wondrous range of the National Museum. All at once, he was returned to his natural element, and instinctively he wanted to learn more of the development of ancient Mexico, with its extraordinary succession of pre-Columbian cultures: Olmec, Mixtec, Zapotec, Mayan, Toltec and Aztec.

One outing led to another, and increasingly Tunaman came to look forward to their little weekend trips as a welcome diversion from the embassy routine. Dolores seemed so knowledgeable, with a gift for bringing Mexican history vividly to life. She was so original in her approach, taking him far beyond the well-worn tourist track of the Aztec pyramids of Teotihuacán and the city's numerous archaeological sites and museums.

He remembered especially their visit to the 16th-century church of the Hospital de Jesús, a badly-neglected structure three blocks south of the Zócalo, and standing roughly on the spot where Hernan Cortés had had his first fateful meeting with Moctezuma, Emperor of all the Aztecs. The church was deserted, except for an elderly caretaker, who directed them to a simple plaque on the north wall of the sacristy. It recorded that here were buried the mortal remains of Cortés, the greatest of all *conquistadores* who, landing with some five hundred fifty fighting men, had conquered an empire of more than five million people, and had so brought Christianity and the Spanish language to Mexico.

"It's incredible," Dolores explained. "No single person has played such an important part in our history. Yet not more than one Mexican in a hundred knows he is buried here. The truth is they don't want to know. All over the city, you will see hundreds of statues... of Aztec leaders and Mexican revolutionaries. But you will not find one monument to Cortés."

She was right. At various functions Kemal took pleasure in asking prominent Mexicans where Cortés was buried. Not one of them knew. And nor, if truth be told, did Dolores - at least not before she had begun boning up on Mexican history as part of her husband-seeking campaign.

The weeks now rushed by for Tunaman. In his spare time, he became so immersed in his reading of pre-Columbian history that he rarely gave an introspective thought to his roots in Istanbul. He had no real appetite for his ambassadorial duties, which were largely confined to a never-ending round of social engagements. But nor did he feel any urgent need to resign. There was plenty of time. Six months or perhaps a year at the most, and then he would go home.

His only regret was not seeing his family, and especially the grandchildren he adored. He confided as much to Dolores, and immediately her organising mind went to work. "Of course. You must bring them over for a visit. After all, they may never have such an opportunity again."

By the time they next met, she was already armed with airline schedules and suggestions for the most suitable dates. "Perhaps they would like to split their holiday - a week in Mexico City and a weekend at one of my father's hotels, in Cancún perhaps, or Acapulco. You will need to check on school holidays, of course."

Such was Dolores' persistence that a suggested holiday almost at once became an inevitability. One by one, obstacles were removed until eventually a grand family reunion had been arranged.

From Istanbul came Kemal's younger daughter, Nilufer, together with her husband, Sertac, and their two children, five-year-old Melissa, and Deniz, aged four. Their initial flight to Paris was cost-free since Sertac, an accountant, was an employee of the Turkish Airline, THY. At the same time, Kemal's elder daughter, Yasemin, flew out from Athens via Paris, together with her six-year-old son Georgios. The only absentee was Yasemin's husband, Nicholas, who, as the family lawyer, was involved in a major legal case on behalf of his father, the Greek shipping magnate, Stavros Stephanopoulos.

Largely through Dolores' organising precision, the holiday was a spectacular success, a whirlwind programme of sightseeing, visits to the theatre and sports events, children's parties, and a long seaside weekend culminating in a New Year's Eve barbecue and fireworks display at Cancún. Suddenly, after two action-packed weeks, the visit seemed to be over before it had scarcely begun. After tearful farewells Kemal was left feeling completely flat, as though he had stepped into an emotional void.

The very next day, Dolores delivered her *coup de grace*. As a way of thanking her for all her efforts, Kemal had invited her out to dinner at an exclusive Italian restaurant in the Zona Rosa. When the brandies came, she proposed a toast to their two families, and then, with a disarming smile, she added, "And why don't we really bring our families together? Let's get married, Kemal."

Ambassador Tunaman laughed. He thought she was joking. Then she leant across the table, fixed him with her large dark-brown eyes, and said firmly, "No, don't laugh. I'm serious. Marriage would be good for both of us. We need each other, don't you see?"

Kemal was absolutely stunned. He had never thought of Dolores as more than a good friend. Moreover she was sixteen years his junior. He felt flattered, but also uncomfortable. Not for a moment had he previously contemplated remarriage. Now, at its first suggestion, he felt a sense of guilt - as though it might be an act of betrayal, of disloyalty to the memory of his beloved Raife.

Dolores read his thoughts, immediately reassuring him that she had no wish to take his first wife's place. Marriage would simply cement their companionship, giving themselves a truer sense of belonging, of not being alone in life.

Her timing was perfect. The departure of his daughters and grandchildren had left Kemal with an acute sense of loneliness and emptiness. And now, at a time when Dolores represented his only close personal contact in Mexico, he was reluctant to jeopardise their friendship by flatly rejecting her proposal.

He reached out and rested his hand on hers. "You are very kind, Dolores. And I feel most honoured. But let's think about it a while, shall we?"

Señorita Castillo smiled and gripped his hand firmly. In her heart she knew she had virtually won. She would do the thinking for both of them. Two weeks later, having affected the utmost gentleness and charm, she gained his agreement. They would have a small, strictly unpublicised wedding at her family's private chapel in Cuernavaca, fifty miles south of Mexico City.

Secretly, Dolores favoured a ceremony held with full pomp and ceremony in the monumental Catedral Metropolitana overlooking the Zócalo. But she knew her man too well to suggest it. Kemal had once explained that he rather envied people who gained extraordinary strength from their religious faith. But he himself, though raised as a Muslim, could never adhere to one particular creed formalised by man. All his studies had taught him that such separatism had been, and remained, the greatest cause of human conflict. As a humanist, he took a composite view of all the major religions, regarding their great prophets as historical figures in the same rich tapestry of spiritual life.

Since he chose to remain totally neutral on religious matters, Kemal would not object to a Catholic marriage *per se*. But nor, as Dolores rightly perceived, would he agree to a ceremony conducted with such public ostentation and extravagance that it suggested his recognition of the superior power of her Church.

The forgoing of a full-scale wedding was to be the last major concession Dolores ever made. Once married, she progressively asserted her stronger will. At the same time she firmly established her own identity, using as her power-base the wedding present bestowed by her father: a lavish colonial-style house set amid groves of oranges and mangoes in Cuernavaca. Here she regularly entertained friends and relations. Theoretically the home was only a weekend retreat, but Dolores gradually spent more and more time there, choosing to stay at the embassy only when prestigious social occasions were on the agenda.

The arrangement suited the Tunamans admirably. Both benefited by being supported in their respective social commitments. At the same time, they were rarely together long enough to get alarmingly on each other's nerves. As it was, she found him boring because of his total disinterest in gossip and material possessions, while he was disappointed to find that she had no real interest in history, or indeed any abstract topic of discussion.

Neither of them, however, could have remotely imagined that their well-ordered routine would eventually be shattered by an international crisis on the other side of the world. Yet so it happened. Eighteen months after their marriage, they were to find themselves apart for periods too long even for their disparate tastes... and dangerously so because Kemal, in his new globe-trotting role, was learning by necessity to do without Dolores very well.

But everything was changing now. Tunaman was no longer involved in negotiations between Greece and Turkey. Today, as reported in *Excelsior*, he was spending his last day in Mexico City quietly with his family: Dolores, his visiting daughter Yasemin, and his grandson Georgios, and in the evening, together with his wife and daughter, he would be attending a very exclusive dinner party to be held in his honour at the Presidential Palace.

The next day, January 26, Kemal was leaving Mexico indefinitely. And this time Dolores was going, too. She would have a new social power-base, on New York's Long Island, as the wife of the new Turkish ambassador to the United Nations - and of a super-diplomat who, just one month ago, had been presented with the Nobel Peace Prize for his key role in pulling Greece and Turkey back from the brink of war.

VVRRROOOMM.... VVRRROOOMMM. Looking around the roof garden, Kemal was reflecting on the extraordinary silence of a Sunday morning in the world's third largest city, when suddenly the peace was shattered by a roaring noise. The Tunamans looked round to see a model fighter plane speeding towards them, its underbelly held by a pyjama-clad boy whose dark-brown eyes glared in wide-open simulation of aggression.

Kemal rose from his chair like an old man who had just been injected with some miraculous and instant elixir of life. Bending low from the knees, he spread his arms wide and cried out, "Georgios! Happy Birthday!"

The boy, exactly nine-years-old, promptly ran into the awaiting bear hug, embracing his grandfather so enthusiastically that one of the aircraft's wings scraped the back of the ambassador's neck.

"Look, grandpa. It's an F-22 fighter plane. It can fly by remote control. Isn't it cool?"

Kemal smiled, reflecting once again on the mixed benefits of having a grandson educated at the Kolonaki American School in Athens. "Yes, Georgios. It's really cool."

"Yeah. And my father says it has a range of mote than half a kilometre".

Dolores raised her eyebrows in surprise, then looked towards a tall, slim young woman who was standing in the sliding-glass doorway that led on to the patio.

"Father?" said Dolores.

The woman in the doorway did not reply immediately. First she moved silently and gracefully across the patio and pulled up a chair beside Kemal. She was without make-up and jewellery, and wore only a wraparound silk dressing gown of palest pink with matching bedroom slippers. Yet her poise and beauty were astounding. Shining raven hair framed her finely chiselled features and cascaded over her shoulders at the front. If any one adjective summed up her overall appearance it was regal. With her swarthy looks, dazzling dark eyes and faintly aquiline nose, she could have been taken for a Mayan princess.

"That's right," she said finally, while taking her seat. "Nicholas just telephoned. We arranged that he would ring precisely at eight o'clock, just as Georgios was opening his present. It's 4 p.m. in Athens, a bitterly cold afternoon. Nicholas sends his love to you all."

She then leaned over and kissed Kemal on the cheek. "Good morning, *baba*. And how are you feeling on this very special day?"

"Very good, sweetheart," he replied. And he returned her kiss. "I won't ask how you are. I swear, Yasemin, that you

25

look more beautiful and healthy with every passing day." And they both smiled a knowing smile. He adored his elder daughter, and she positively worshipped him.

Georgios was now kneeling on a chair, preoccupied with bringing his plane in to land on the breakfast table with a gentle whirring sound. "Hey," said Dolores. "Don't you have a kiss for your grandma this morning?"

The boy grinned and, in his usual good-natured way, he immediately climbed down from the chair to give her a kiss. "Happy birthday, Georgios," she said. "You are going to have a wonderful day. You wait and see."

Then, more formally, she spoke to Yasemin. "And how is Nicholas today? As busy as ever, I suppose."

Yasemin nodded. She knew what her stepmother was thinking. Once again, pressure of business had prevented Nicholas from joining them on holiday in Mexico City. It irritated Dolores. She had been eager to meet him, ever since she had seen an article in *Ladies Home Journal* that detailed the luxurious lifestyle of Nicholas's father, Stavros Stephanopoulos. Several times she had mooted the idea of visiting the family in Athens, but always business commitments had got in the way.

Her mind now turned to the order of the day. It was time to take command and get things running smoothly. "Right, now everyone listen. We've got a busy programme ahead and it's imperative we keep on schedule."

Dolores looked at her wrist-watch, more for emphasis than information. "It is now almost 8:30. I want breakfast out of the way by nine o'clock, and everyone ready to leave for the park by 10:30. The first thing, Georgios, is for you to get washed and dressed. Would you like your favourite breakfast with the ham and eggs sunny-side up?"

Georgios nodded and parroted the new words she had taught him, *"Huevos con jamón, por favor."*

"Off you go then, and it will be ready for you in exactly fifteen minutes." She picked up the mobile lying on the table beside her, pressed a button and then gave instructions in Spanish to a maid named María.

Georgios grasped his aeroplane on the table. Then, just before take-off, he cocked his head on one side and looked at Kemal with an irresistibly wistful expression. "Grandpa, will you help me fly it in the park today?"

"Of course, my boy. It will give me the greatest

26

pleasure." And Georgios roared off towards the patio doors with the same noisy vigour with which he had arrived. His mother immediately followed.

Soon after, María arrived with a fresh pot of coffee and newly-warmed croissants. This, plus fruit juice, was all the adults wanted for breakfast, especially today when the prospect of two major meals loomed ahead.

Now that they were alone, Dolores looked sternly at her husband. "I don't think that was very wise of you—promising Georgios you would help fly his plane in the park. It could be rather awkward, you know."

"Awkward?" Kemal looked confused. "What can be awkward about it? I will not be expert, I know. But I should be able to get the plane in the air."

"You know I don't mean that," said Dolores. "It's the principle of the thing. You can't just concentrate on Georgios, and ignore all your other guests."

The conversation that followed left Kemal surprised and, most uncharacteristically, downright angry. He had thought that just the immediate family was going to have a party-cum-picnic in the park. They would give Georgios his presents, and then have a nice quiet afternoon together before facing the formalities of the farewell dinner at the Presidential Palace. Now Dolores was telling him it was going to be a full-scale birthday party with about forty people attending in all.

"Don't you remember? I told you days ago. We are having a truly traditional Mexican-style party. *Piñatas*, organised games with prizes, a clown and a conjurer. The lot. Everything's arranged. I've even had two of the servants go down to the park and mark off the best spot with paper chains and balloons. You wait and see. Georgios will love it. A birthday he will never forget."

Kemal didn't remember, and he cursed the fact that he was without Mehmet Haybat, who had gone on ahead to supervise advance arrangements in New York. Normally, his efficient Personal Assistant would brief him every evening on his programme for the following day, and he always made it his business to check very carefully with Doña Tunaman in case she was making conflicting plans.

This had happened before. Without Mehmet's backing, Kemal was always at the mercy of Dolores's favourite ploy: playing on his alleged tendency to absent-mindedness and failure to listen. But this time he was

27

absolutely positive that he had not forgotten. He might forget little things— like not calling his wife "Dolly" and not wearing the particular cuff-links or tie she had chosen. But he would never forget about plans for his last few hours with Georgios. All week, he had been looking forward to the time they would spend together.

His natural impulse was to scream out in protest. But he suppressed it. Experience had taught him that to challenge his wife head-on could only make matters worse. There was no court of appeal. It was only his word against hers whether he had been told, and in that kind of Mexican stand-off she always prevailed.

"So, who exactly is coming to your party?" he asked.

"Don't take that tone with me, Kemal," Dolores snapped. "It's not *my* party. It's all for Georgios— a proper children's party. He needs to be with boys and girls of his own age. It's selfish to think that you can have him all to yourself on his birthday."

With one masterstroke, she had put Kemal on the defence.

As an international diplomat, Kemal's greatest strength was his reputation for total impartiality, his ability to appreciate everyone's point of view. As the husband of Dolores, it was his greatest weakness... and she knew it. Now, all at once, she had unerringly struck at his Achilles heel. It was true: His motives were rather selfish in wanting to have time of his own with Georgios. He felt guilty.

"Yes, dear," he said in a conciliatory tone. "Perhaps you are right. So who is coming then?"

Dolores reeled off a few names. "I can't remember them all, but altogether there are sixteen children of members of the embassy staff. Then, of course, there are my brothers' and sisters' children. Seven of them are coming, plus children of the American and British ambassadors, and of the Greek consul."

Kemal sighed, but said nothing. He was thinking that it was a mistake to have invited Ricky, the son of U.S. ambassador James Henderson. He was a nice enough boy really, but the fact remained that he was terribly spoilt, and he tended to dominate company of his own age.

Ricky, a year younger than Georgios, was one of those super-bright, computer-orientated kids, who seemed to have a gift for latching onto any information of a sensational and/or

28

sinister nature. If a meteor was reported to be heading towards planet Earth, if a serial killer was on the rampage in America, or Muslim fundamentalists were responsible for a bomb massacre in the Middle East, he could be relied upon to be the first to give his young friends a graphic account.

To be specific, Ricky's name had filled Kemal with misgivings since the previous weekend when Georgios had had terrible nightmares after Ricky's detailed description of an old video-nasty he had seen about some dreamtime child-killer called Freddy Krueger. Protectively, Kemal felt there was enough ugliness in the world without having fictional horrors inflicted on his grandson.

Still, he reflected, Ricky couldn't do much harm today. They would be far too busy with organised entertainment and games to have time for the boy's attention-seeking stories.

"Hmm! Quite a crowd!" he said. "That makes about twenty-eight children. But I thought you said you were expecting nearly forty."

"Not all children, silly," replied Dolores, flashing a friendly smile. It was time for a little finesse. "You've got to have plenty of grown-ups at these affairs. It's traditional. Everything's strictly family and friends. We have to manage the barbecue and organise the games ourselves. No servants to wait on you today, Kemal."

She laughed. He inwardly groaned. "I see. So, who are these helpful friends?"

Her answer confirmed his worst fears. Naturally, she had invited her two closest friends, Isabel and Teresa, even though their children were too old to attend. Plus someone called Carmen whom he had never met, together with her husband who was "something in real estate". Naturally, also, two of her younger sisters— Yolanda and Esperanza— would be coming, as well as her elder brother, Felipe, and his wife Rosa, plus her other sister-in-law, Josefina.

Then, last of all, as if it was a trivial afterthought, Dolores added, "And, of course, Roberto and Guillermo will be there. Roberto, as you know, is a wizard with barbecues."

Kemal took a deep breath. It was news good and bad. He liked Roberto Martínez immensely. Married to Yolanda, the most charming of the four Castillo sisters, Roberto was an exceptional figure in Mexican politics: a man of middle-class background and liberal outlook who had risen through the ranks of the ruling National Action Party (PAN) entirely on his own merits.

A protean scholar, he had graduated with a first-class law degree from Mexico's national university, and had then earned two master degrees and a doctorate in political economy from Harvard University. By the age of thirty-two, he was a deputy attorney general, and now, at thirty-seven, following his success as a PAN candidate in the national elections, this soft-spoken lawyer-turned-economist had been appointed Minister of Finance, the youngest member of President Pérez's new Cabinet.

Guillermo Velázquez, the husband of Esperanza, the youngest of the Castillo sisters, was an entirely different character: a pushy and unscrupulous opportunist whose prominent social position was entirely the product of his dashing good looks and flair for double-dealing. There were few people in whom Kemal could not discern some redeeming quality. Guillermo was one of them. Even Dolores, to her credit, had recognised him from the start as a no-good fortune hunter. But Esperanza, like so many young women before and after, would not hear a bad word spoken about him.

One of five sons of a wealthy industrialist, Guillermo had defied his father's wishes by dropping out at the University of the Americas near Puebla, where he was reading business management studies. He chose, instead, to try to make his mark on the international lawn tennis circuit. Two years later, immediately following his first-round exit in the Monte Carlo Open, he had returned to Mexico, still without a single tournament success to his credit and having incurred a string of fines for ill-mannered behaviour on court.

Off-court, his playboy lifestyle had secured him a regular place in the society gossip columns. There were indeed rumours of his involvement in a major scandal but, without confirmation, these were too legally dangerous to print. Only the U.S. *National Enquirer* was so bold as to ask, cryptically, "Which American teenage tennis champion has recently had an abortion after a love match with a Mexican player?"

But that affair— to his mind, a harmless peccadillo— was not Guillermo's primary concern when he returned to Mexico City to take up a tennis-coaching job at the Chapultepec Sports Club. He was most disturbed by the intransigence of his father. Don Carlos Velázquez was firmly refusing to settle Guillermo's outstanding gambling debts until he had served a six months' managerial apprenticeship in the family's steelworks at Monterrey.

For Guillermo, social exile in Monterrey was unthinkable. Reluctantly, he recognised there was only one practicable solution: he would have to sacrifice himself to a strategic marriage. And Esperanza Castillo, one of several infatuated young ladies on his coaching rota, was the obvious choice. She brought with her a handsome dowry. In addition, her father was to make his new son-in-law assistant manager of his colossal Esmeralda hotel complex in Acapulco, a position that offered Guillermo enormous scope for his philandering.

Though Esperanza very quickly bore him a son, Guillermo remained an outrageous womaniser. But he no longer frequented casinos. In recent years, he had confined his gambling to playing the stock market, and here, for the first time, he began to show a useful profit. His success was largely based on his frequent visits to Mexico City to cultivate valuable social contacts, who, very occasionally, gave him useful pointers to future market moves. In the process, he also picked up information and gossip of purely general interest. This, too, did not go to waste. As a number of prominent citizens were beginning to suspect, he had secretly secured a fat retainer from Mexico's newest, big-selling scandal sheet, *El Informador*.

It was this last activity that aroused Kemal's instant alarm. More than once, he had attended a strictly confidential high-level meeting only to find it reported in *El Informador*. By process of elimination, the source of these leaks had become fairly obvious.

"My goodness," Kemal exclaimed. "You might as well sell tickets. I thought this was going to be a strictly private and informal party."

Dolores smiled. "Oh, don't worry so much, dear. I have told everyone that this must remain our little secret. Why, not even Georgios knows all about it. It's going to be a wonderful surprise."

VVRRROOOMMM... VVRRROOOMMM. At the sound of Georgios' approach, Dolores swiftly played her last card in the sure knowledge that Kemal would have no reply.

"Of course, you do realise, Kemal, that you don't

31

have to go the party. If you don't like the idea, I can easily make an excuse. Everyone will understand, what with the presidential dinner tonight, and the big day tomorrow."

She turned her head and smiled, suddenly all sweetness and light. "Ah! There you are, Georgios, darling. My, you do look smart!"

CHAPTER 3

1000 hours, Sunday, January 25

Manuel Ramírez was sweating. He thought it was too much sun, and so, after mopping his brow, he shifted into the shade. He now sat in the open hatchway near the centre of the tower, his feet resting on the last iron step of the stairwell and his face shielded by the hood-like hatch-casing. It made no difference. He was sweating with fear.

For the first time, he could hear footsteps on the stone pathways of the roof garden below, and then came a confusion of scraping noises and the sound of human voices. From the few words he could discern, he gathered that men were arranging chairs in preparation for a children's play to be performed in one of the nearby marbled galleries.

But it wasn't the chance of discovery that filled Manuel with dread. No one, he had been assured, was going to climb the tower's ninety spiralling steps. The tower was always closed to the general public, and now even museum employees were deterred from venturing inside. The previous evening, at closing time, he had entered the tower by ducking under a chain that was wrapped in dark velvet. Beside the chain a large placard declared in both Spanish and English: *PELIGRO. NO ENTRE. ESCALERAS EN REPARACIÓN.* DANGER. KEEP OUT. STAIRWAY UNDER REPAIR.

No, what frightened Manuel was the looming prospect of coming face-to-face with the real world. His feelings, if he had been able to rationalise them, were akin to those of an actor stricken with terror at the imminent prospect of making his stage debut in a starring role. Earlier, his nervousness had centred on memorising each move in the part he had to play. But now he was lurking in the wings. And the theatre was coming alive.

No longer were people the insignificant ant-like figures perceived from his secure eagle's nest. The sound of footsteps and garbled voices gave them a fully human

33

dimension. And soon the air was vaguely filled with a medley of more distant noises rising from the park: the ting-a-ling of an ice cream vendor's bell, the clang-clang of horse-drawn carriages, the laughter of children, the oompah-pah-pah of a small brass band.

All sense of remoteness and isolation was gone. He was at the centre of a living world, and that world was steadily closing in on him. Seated in an open doorway, he felt somehow exposed, and so he changed his position again. He curled up foetus-like on the floor with his back hard against the tower wall, his knapsack serving as a pillow, and his rifle lying at his side. He was still sweating. But inside he felt cold.

Marginally below him, in the southeastern corner of the castle, was the bowl-like summit of another, much slimmer tower. At its base, he remembered, he had seen a plaque recording that from the turret above, one of six teenage army cadets, Vicente Suárez, had wrapped himself in the Mexican flag and jumped to martyrdom, rather than surrender to the American invaders in 1847. Now, he wryly reflected, he didn't even have that way out. He was atop a tower known as *La Torre del Caballero Alto*. Yet there was no sheer drop onto rocks far below, only a fall of perhaps 20 feet to the protruding walkway around the tower's square, lower section.

Less than two hours remained before he had to begin watching out for the signal to act. It didn't bear thinking about. He had to put it out of his mind, concentrate on other things. He knew only one sure means of escape; a few months earlier he had begun snorting cocaine and each time, within five minutes, all his worries had vanished as he was lifted into a half-hour highflying state of euphoria. How he wished he had some stuff now. Better still would be some crack. He had tried it once, only a week ago. And one puff had made snorting seem so terribly tame. No waiting for it to take effect. Instantly he had been swept off his feet into a different world, as though he were an astronaut floating in space. Afterwards he had felt deeply depressed. But no matter. It was great while it lasted, a high like nothing he had known before. Ever since he had longed to try it again.

Thinking back on it, he realised he should have demanded a supply as part of the contract. How could they have refused? Instead, he had tamely accepted their ruling that there were to be absolutely no drugs of any kind until the job was done. After that it was different: then, they said, he could have all the "rocks"— and anything else— he wanted.

Manuel closed his eyes and made a conscious effort to render his mind a blank, to think of nothingness. It didn't work. Somehow his brain refused to be inactive. It kept ticking over as though it was some independent supercharged computer, which refused to be switched off. It threw up thoughts at random, and perversely every thought was related to the danger ahead.

One titbit dredged deep from its memory bank was a long-forgotten saying that *Papá* had quoted to little Manuelito on his first outing to the *Plaza México*: "To fight a bull when you are *not* afraid is nothing, and to *not* fight a bull when you *are* afraid is nothing. But to fight a bull when you *are* afraid, now that really is something." Perhaps the free-running brain was trying to offer a crumb of comfort. If so, it failed. Reminded of the saying, Manuel had thought of one of his own: *a matador who is afraid is all the more likely to die.*

Since the brain would not rest, it occurred to Manuel that he might at least control its direction by setting it specific tasks. He began by asking it to recall in chronological order all the women he had screwed. Briefly, the exercise provided a welcome diversion, and a much-needed boost to the ego. But then it all turned sour as the brain interrupted the process by raising the question of who had been the very best lay. And all at once he found himself thinking of bloody Consuelo again.

Carajo! How he had loved her. In return the bitch was not content with breaking his heart. She had to scramble his brains as well, driving him out of his mind with the nightmare of that serenade. And to think he had actually paid to be polluted by that shitty tramp; all those pesos wasted on hiring *mariachis* and all because he had loved her.

A thousand times he had told himself to forget Consuelo. What was it Julio used to tell him? *Think positively. Think only of the present. Just live in the now. The past is gone forever, the future has yet to exist.* But shit! That advice wasn't any help. The 'now' had become his living hell. *Papá*, so Manuel was thinking, had more of the right idea. As he used to say, "All life is a joke— a bloody cruel joke— and the only purpose of life is to enjoy it as much as you can."

Without realising it, Manuel had successfully escaped his obsessive fear of the immediate future. He was now remembering— and appreciating more fully— what *papá* had been trying to explain so extravagantly that day he got out the thirteen tequila glasses. They all thought he was a bit loony at the time. But now, as Manuel tried to recall *papá's* argument, step by step, it began to make sense, and it led him onto a chain of thoughts that, for a long while, focussed exclusively on the past.

It had happened four years ago... on February 21; he remembered the date because it was the eve of his eighteenth birthday. They had all gone to a restaurant in the Zona Rosa as the guests of Julio who was throwing a farewell party before leaving for the United States.

Afterwards, they went back to Julio's place, a rented bachelor apartment twice the size of the two rooms in Tepito which had once housed their family of thirteen. *Papá* said it was disgusting, one person occupying so much living space. But he greatly approved the idea of having a bar in one corner, and it had been his suggestion that they should keep drinking till midnight "and see little Manuelito become a man."

As usual, Fernando dominated the family gathering from the start, and Julio, though he was the host, was quite content to take a backseat and observe the proceedings in his quiet, thoughtful way. He knew how it would develop. The old man was always aggressive after a couple of drinks and then, more and more, he became nostalgic and philosophical as the evening wore on. Julio already had a spare bed prepared for when he crashed out.

Manuel could remember clearly what had set the whole thing off. They were all sitting round the central dining table and, after his umpteenth tequila, *Papá* was puffing on another of Julio's cigars, and reflecting expansively that he, too, might have had such a fancy apartment if he hadn't suffered that terrible eye injury in his fight against *El Tanque*.

"You're right, *Papá*," said Ricardo. "When you come down to it, it's all a matter of luck."

"Luck," bellowed Fernando. "That's not the fucking word I would use. I'll tell you what it is. It's bloody fate, that's all. Our bloody destiny. Did I tell you about the dream I had the other day?" He hadn't, but they all knew he soon would.

"It was the strangest dream I ever had. In fact, it was a fucking revelation. I can even re-create it, if you like. Manuelito, get me some more glasses from behind the bar.

And another bottle of tequila."

Fernando then proceeded to demonstrate his dream by lining up two rows of six glasses. Above them, at the centre, he placed a solitary glass. "Now this is how it was. Just as it came to me in the dream."

He poured tequila into the glasses of one row, taking care to give them variable measures. "See this, *muchachos*? That's the genes you were born with. Each glass represents something different, like brains, health, looks and strength." He took a swig from one glass and replaced it. "Not much left in there. Must be your physique, Manuelito."

He guffawed, took a big puff on his cigar, and then became serious again. "The point is you didn't have any fucking choice about any of these measures. Just the cards bloody life dealt you. Am I right?"

Everyone agreed. And Fernando went on to pour tequila into the second row of glasses. "Now these are the same things as in that first row: brains and looks and the rest. But you see the difference, *muchachos*. They no longer have the same levels. Some are higher, some are lower. Why is that?"

Manuel remembered how he had wanted to make some joke about *Papá* being unable to pour with a steady hand. But he knew better than to interrupt the old man when he was in full flow. "I'll tell you why. My dream explained it. This second line represents your upbringing, the circumstances of your youth. It's like this. You're born into money and get a good education and your brain level goes up. You live in a rough neighbourhood and get beaten up and your health ain't so good. Don't have any fucking choice about that either. Just another deal of the cards."

Julio pointed to the one empty glass left standing alone. "And what's this, *Papá*? A joker in the pack?"

"Ah! Smart boy," said Fernando. "In a way, you're kind of right. It is a bloody joke. It's what you would call self-determination. You know... free will." He filled the glass with tequila, swilled it down in one swig, and then held it aloft.

"Now then. See this glass. I have got two choices. I can put it back on the table... or, if you like, I could throw it against the fucking wall. It's my choice. Right?"

Fernando, his eyes dancing wickedly, looked around his audience as if to study their reaction. Then, with a bellowing roar, he hurled the glass against the farthest wall.

"*Chingada madre*," said Ricardo. "What a mess!"

But Julio remained completely calm. "Yes, *Papá*. That's free will, all right."

Fernando grinned. "Ah, but it isn't. That was the whole bloody point of the dream, you see. It was explained to me. You have to see all the glasses like parts of an electric circuit, all wired together, all contributing to the make-up and behaviour of the individual. That glass you call 'free will'; it don't exist on its own. Why d'you think I chose to throw it against the wall? Not many people would do that. But then not many people have had my kind of screwed-up life. And it's changing all the time, you see. The genes, your experiences from day-to-day, they're all having a continuing effect on how you behave and how you make decisions at any given moment."

He leaned back in his chair, puffed deep on his cigar. "Bloody hell, I feel thirsty. I could empty all these glasses."

And he did.

Momentarily, Manuel smiled at the memory of his father who, after talking so much, had slumped into a stupor like some suddenly burnt-out volcano. And then, his eyes still closed, Manuel began to ponder grimly how he himself had been the victim of his environment and genes. Was it true what *papá* said, that he had no real control over his destiny?

Sure, he had had a bad deal of the cards. For as long as he could remember he had felt handicapped by his lack of a powerful physique. *Papá* had told him it didn't matter. "*Mira hijo*, I once knew a flyweight skinnier than you. He became champion of all Mexico. Of course, he had guts and speed. You're going to need that much, kid."

But he didn't have guts and speed in his genes. He had found that out soon after his twelfth birthday, the only time he could remember *Papá* giving him anything more than words of advice. That day he had been told to cup his hands, and into them his father had slowly counted out 60 pesos. Then, with all the solemnity of a priest giving a benediction, he declared, "This, Manuelito, is your passport to fame and fortune. It's the greatest gift my father gave to me, and it's the greatest gift I can make to you."

The gift was, quite simply, a year's subscription to the *Centro Social y Deportivo*, the recreational centre tucked behind the church of San Francisco de Asís. The centre had two main facilities a grassless football pitch so dusty that a man was engaged in re-whitening the sidelines while matches were being played, and a boxing club that was open to any boy who could produce birth and medical certificates, and the necessary joining fee.

But Fernando was hopelessly out-of-date. It was true that in his youth, in the 1950s, the Centro had been the university of Tepito life. There, by fist or by foot, a Tepito boy had his one real hope of acquiring a well-paid professional skill and moving out and up to the world of affluence. For the ambitious, the only real alternative— one commonly taken, but rarely with lasting success— was crime.

It was entirely different, however, when Manuel reached his teens. Much of Tepito had been reconstructed following the earthquake of '85. In the late 1990s, the sports centre was a bright, air-conditioned complex serving seven hundred members, and yet no longer an especially rich source of young sporting talent. The population of Mexico City had risen in forty years from five million to over twenty million, and it was increasing by two thousand a day, as the *campesinos* continued to pour in from the countryside. No longer was the boy from Tepito the hungriest fighter in the gym. Indeed, he was positively pampered compared with the new breed of slum-kids who came in from the city's far-flung suburbs.

Like his father, Manuel made no allowance for this change. *Papá* had given him his chance and he simply wasn't good enough to take it. For this, his genes were entirely to blame. It was the same when he failed to take the chance he had been given by *Mama,* who had queued all night to get him a place at *la Escuela Vocacional* on Melchor Ocampo Street. There, like his brothers Antonio and Ricardo, he could have learnt a technical skill. He had studied carpentry, but had never completed the course. Was it is his fault he had no aptitude for working with his hands; that his natural impulses drove him to persistent truancy and to a life of petty thieving only briefly cut short when the Juvenile Court put him on probation? Wouldn't the same have happened to anyone with exactly the same genes, the same upbringing, the same experiences? It was like *Papá* said, "Your character is your destiny."

Julio, on the other hand, said you make your own luck in this world. But it was easy for him to talk. He had good genes. He had been given a brilliant brain and a fine physique.

Top of his class at school, he could have gone to a university. Moreover, the lucky bugger had played football for the Chrysler Motors team who paid their players 100 U.S. dollars a game, plus a bonus for each goal.

Manuel was thinking he would have given his right arm for half of Julio's talent. But what had the bugger done with his gifts? Incredibly, he had chucked it all in because, so he said, he wanted 'to travel and do something adventurous'.

Yeah, and still Julio had prospered, being good enough with his fists to get himself sponsored by a wealthy cattle-breeder and sent to the United States. Everyone said he was a success because he had used his brains. But, fuck it. It was more than that. The fact was that he was born under a lucky star. He hit the jackpot because he happened to be in the right place at the right time, just like, *Papá* when he got his freakish once-in-a-lifetime shot at the championship.

In the end it all came down to *la suerte*, to fucking luck. Choice had nothing to do it. Did he, for example, have any choice when he fell under Consuelo's spell? Christ, no! Consuelo! Bloody hell, he couldn't even choose what to remember from the past. Bad memories, like the good, were flooding back with a will all of their own.

Manuel was wide-awake now. On opening his eyes, he needed to shield them from the dazzling light. There was a dull ache in his right shoulder that had been bearing much of his weight. And he badly wanted a pee. He was truly back in the present now; once again alert to every sight and sound, and most immediately concerned with the time. He pushed himself up into a sitting position with his back against the wall, and then he looked at his gold watch. To his horror, it was flashing 11:22. He couldn't believe it. But then it was never wrong. He must have dozed off while thinking about the past. Now only eight minutes remained until he was supposed to keep looking out for the starburst of a rocket in the sky - the signal for him to shoot.

Nature dictated his first move. He crawled to the centre of the tower and then, in a kneeling position, unzipped his fly and pissed towards the far wall. That done, he crawled back and sat with his haversack on one side, his rifle on the other. He reached out for the rifle, checked that the safety catch was off, then grasped the pistol-grip while he scanned the sky. This, he reflected, was really "living in the now"... or perhaps dying.

40

Strangely, Manuel was no longer sweating with fear. He was thinking that perhaps he still had a choice. Like *Papá*, with that thirteenth tequila glass, he could put the gun down or use it to make a bloody mess. Either way, of course, it was fated. His character at the given moment would decide... because all life was designed as a joke.

Then he remembered an old Mexican saying: *Tell me how you die and I will tell you who you are*. It made him think briefly of those Military Academy cadets who, at this same castle, had laid down their lives in the last heroic stand against the *yanqui* invaders. More especially it prompted him to recall the classic example of *la muerte grande;* of how, in dying, the ill-fated Emperor Maximilian had showed himself to be a true son of his adopted Mexico.

Manuel had never forgotten the story of that poignant moment: how, on the *Cerro de las Campanas* at Quéretaro, an Austrian - incurably romantic, naively idealistic - had given each soldier in the firing squad an ounce of gold, and had asked them to aim well for the body so that his mother could look once more on his unmarked face. Finally he had called out in Spanish, "*Muero por una causa justa*. I die for a just cause. I forgive everybody. I pray that everyone may also forgive me. And I pray that my blood, which is about to be shed, will flow for the good of the country; *Viva México! Viva la Independencia!*"

Four bullets struck their target: three in the chest, one in the forehead above the left eye. As the Emperor lay on the ground, his body still twitching convulsively, the young squad captain rushed forward and pointed with his sword, directing a soldier to fire a fifth bullet into the heart. In death, as never in life, Maximilian had become a legend. He had died, as they said, *con valor mexicano*.

It was 11.30 a.m. At that moment, for the first time in four hours, Manuel stood upright. In deliberate defiance of fate, he leant against the central flagstaff, his rifle held vertical at his right side with the butt resting on the stone floor.

As he looked up at the clear-blue heaven, his mouth stretched again into a hard, teeth-flashing grin, and one more time he muttered, "*La suerte es como la muerte.*"

His eyes, squinting into the sun, gave no hint of fear. Only of derision and hate. And then he shouted out mutely and long, "Fuuuuck youuuu, Connnsueeelo."

41

CHAPTER 4

1130 hours, Sunday, January 25

At 11.30 a.m. Kemal Tunaman's chauffeur-driven Mercedes-Benz pulled into Chapultepec Park. He was nearly an hour behind Dolores's schedule, having had to remain at the embassy to await an important phone call. But no matter. He knew she would be delighted by his news: they had been invited to spend their first weekend in the United States as the guests of President Carmichael at his country home in Middleburg, Virginia.

In recent months, because of his high profile, the ambassador had never been allowed to appear in public without at least one Turkish security officer at his side. This was at the insistence of Mehmet, who effectively countered Tunaman's protests by arguing, "You may think it is unnecessary, but if you don't care about your own safety, then at least think of me. If anything happened to you, I would be the one left to shoulder the blame."

But Kemal's devoted PA was now far away in New York State. Without him, there was no one to challenge the ambassador's view that he was entirely safe in Mexico, half a world distant from the fading Aegean crisis. As for Dolores, on this occasion she was in full agreement with her husband. Mexicans had scant interest in European politics, and anyway, no one was going to pay attention to a birthday party in the park, so long as it was being conducted in traditional style.

So it was that Kemal arrived at the park accompanied only by his chauffeur and a diminutive Mexican woman named Elvira. Ever well organised, Dolores had arranged that her personal maid should escort her husband, so ensuring that he did not lose his way to the remote picnic spot.

The ambassador's limousine entered the park via the main gate beyond the fountain of Diana the Huntress, slowed to a mandatory 10 km/h, and headed towards six colossal, eagle-topped columns ranged in a spectacular semicircle of marble. There, at the monument to *Los Niños Héroes*, the boy-cadets martyred in the defence of Chapultepec Castle, the Mercedes swung right. Shortly afterwards, it halted beside a bridle path that led across grassland to the picnic area of *el Parque Rosario Castellanos*. The last quarter of a mile had to be covered on foot.

Kemal thanked the chauffeur who had instructions to return in three hours' time, and then he strode out in the company of Elvira. The maid, dressed in an ankle-length frock of bright-patterned cotton and a lightweight *rebozo* of faded gold, looked like a mechanical doll tripping along beside her asthenic companion. She needed to take two steps to Kemal's one, and so he reduced his walking pace to a mere amble. He felt no need to hurry. It was a glorious, comfortably warm afternoon, and all around there were so many sights and sounds to take in: a group of men playing a makeshift game of volleyball, a man and boy flying an eagle-shaped kite, a vendor roped to a rainbow-cluster of gas-filled balloons and weighted down by festoons of rubber balls attached to his waist-belt, and, in the far distance, day-trippers boating on a tree-fringed lake.

Already, Kemal had become less apprehensive about the socialising that lay ahead. As he had found on his two previous visits, the park's atmosphere of carefree relaxation was totally compelling; its aspect, to his mind, near-Utopian. Here were first-class recreational and cultural facilities for people of diverse interests and all ages, and because so many of its attractions were free of charge, it was one of the few places in Mexico City that did not give disturbing evidence of a society divided into haves and have-nots.

"*Ahí!*" cried out Elvira, smiling as she pointed to the right and led the way towards an area occupied by a dozen or more picnicking parties, large and small. The scene of Georgios' party was easily recognised from afar. It had the grandest display of paper-chains and balloons; also, as they approached, Kemal saw Dolores hurrying out to meet them.

"Hello, dear," she called out. "Did you get your telephone call?"

He told her the news, and at once her large, round face beamed with approval. "Wonderful! Wonderful!" Then she grinned mischievously. "I'm afraid I don't have such good news for you, Kemal. You'll be sorry to hear that Guillermo couldn't come. Esperanza says there was some kind of crisis at

43

La Esmeralda." She flashed her eyes knowingly. "Something to do with the catering."

"Really?" asked Kemal. "What a shame!." He, too, was smiling now. But, unlike Dolores and her friends, his first reaction to the news was not to suppose that Guillermo had seized a golden opportunity to "play around" in Acapulco. He was thinking only that he would be spared Guillermo's prying questions, and that, with any luck, there would not be any pressmen on the scene.

As far as he had been able to tell, no one had followed him en route to the park. And now he was relieved to find that the birthday party was, with one exception, entirely confined to friends and relatives. The exception was a tall, crew-cut American named Mark Ballantyne. Kemal had seen him before at a number of official functions, but then, unlike now, he had been dressed in the uniform of a private of the U.S. Marine Corps.

In all capital cities, the American ambassador and his family are guarded on public occasions by men drawn from the pool of marines attached to the U.S. embassy. And in Latin American countries, the security arrangements are especially rigid. It has been so ever since 1968 when left-wing political groups switched from rural to urban guerrilla techniques following the death of Ché Guevara in Bolivia. That year, the American ambassador to Guatemala, plus two U.S. military advisers, were killed in kidnap attempts, and it marked the beginning of a long series of abductions and murders of diplomats.

In recent years, the threat had greatly diminished as terrorists found it more cost-effective to make prominent businessmen their main targets of kidnapping for ransom. But ever since the devastating attacks of September 11, 2001, the U.S. marines world-wide had remained under strict orders to provide round-the-clock protection for their country's diplomatic heads and their families. It was a procedure that the current American ambassador to Mexico sometimes found irksomely intrusive.

On strictly private and informal occasions, ambassador Henderson insisted on having low- profile, plain-clothed bodyguards of his own choosing. And young Ballantyne, a private earmarked for a potential officers' course, was invariably the marine chosen to escort his son, Ricky. The soldier genuinely liked the boy, and maturely he never minded the assignment despite the taunts of fellow marines who referred to his 'baby-sitting duties'.

When Kemal arrived, all the children— twenty-nine in number— were seated cross-legged on the grass, forming a semicircle of two rows. Georgios, the birthday boy, was in the centre of the front row. Above him, on a line strung between trees, were two high-hanging *piñatas* representing the comic strip characters Snoopy and Tweetie-Pie. And directly in front of the children was an improvised stage that merely comprised a large purple backcloth stretched across three poles, with, on one side, a table bearing various props, and on the other, an easel and blackboard, which proclaimed in large white-chalk print: MARCOS EL MAGO.

Mark Ballantyne was seated on a canvas chair, directly behind Ricky at the end of the second row. Immediately on his right was Felipe Castillo, thenYasemin and Roberto. The sisters and women friends of Dolores were seemingly uninterested in the show. Busy in chatter, they were seated further right, about ten yards away, beside large trestle tables bending under the weight of a banquet: a multi-tiered birthday cake, trays of salad, beans, rice, strips of grilled beef, chicken tortas, a bowl of punch, crates of soft drinks and enormous glass jugs of *agua de jamaica*.

For Chapultepec Park, it was not an unusually extravagant scene. Middle-and lower middle-class families commonly celebrated on such a scale. The only difference was that Dolores had hired relatively expensive English-speaking entertainers and had used embassy staff to bear the main burden of work: preparing the cold food, setting out before dawn to reserve the best site, stringing up the *piñatas* and decorations, and setting out the fold-up tables and chairs. Otherwise, as she had said, all was traditional. No servants remained to wait on the guests, and soon the womenfolk, aided by Roberto, would get to work on the barbecue, making tacos by frying tortillas that had been filled with bean paste, shredded meat and red or green tomatoes, flavoured with chilli sauce.

Kemal was impressed. His life of late had been full of surprises, and now he was surprised to find himself enjoying Georgios's party. Dolores had been right, after all. There was nothing to compare with a Mexican-style birthday celebration in the park. As he could see from other parties being held nearby, a pervasive joyfulness was at large, a spirit of well-being that transcended class and material wealth.

Taking a chair, which he purposefully moved to seat himself between Yasemin and Roberto, the ambassador remembered something that Dolores had once told him: that in all her years of visiting Chapultepec Park she had never seen or heard a child crying. It was true. Everywhere, among families rich or poor, children looked wonderfully contented.

At this point, the children on his left were unusually quiet. Marcos the Magician was about to begin his big finale. Dressed in a black top hat and a voluminous black cloak lined in red, the man clapped his hands three times, and from behind the backcloth there emerged a midget wearing a yellow turban and a blouse and baggy trousers of silky blue. At first, only his bare hands and feet were visible, as he carried before him a wicker basket taller and wider than himself. The midget was introduced as Ali Baba. Then, after a preamble about the mysteries of Arabia, Marcos lifted the midget into the basket and made much play of strapping down the lid and covering the container with a white sheet.

"Now, boys and girls, you will see some real Arabian magic with your own eyes. Watch carefully." From inside his cloak he produced a white wand, flourished it with a circling motion above his head, and then, after uttering some incomprehensible mumbo-jumbo, he tapped the basket three times and cried out, "Ali Baba, fly away."

Seconds later he pulled off the sheet, released the straps, and toppled over the basket so that its gaping interior faced the audience. "Hey presto, *amiguitos,* Ali Baba has disappeared."

Everyone clapped and no one louder than Felipe Castillo, the extrovert brother of Dolores. "Bravo," he cried out. "Next time you do that trick, I'll bring my mother-in-law."

Marcos grinned. "Alas, the magic doesn't last." He clapped his hands, again three times, and immediately the midget re-emerged from behind the backcloth. More applause.

"Thank you, boys and girls. Now there will be a short interval. But don't go away. Marcos will soon be coming back on his magic carpet, and then he will bring you his *compadre,* Chico the Clown."

At that point, Georgios noticed for the first time that Kemal had arrived. Hoping that they might soon be able to fly his new fighter plane, he left his place in the front row and

46

ran over to greet his grandfather.

"Hello, grandpa," he cried joyfully.

They were the last words he ever spoke. One second later, precisely at noon, a 7.62-millimetre bullet slammed into the back of Georgios' skull, narrowly missing Kemal on its exit. The boy, instantly killed, fell into the open arms of his grandfather who had prepared to embrace him.

Momentarily, Kemal was unaware of what had happened. Yasemin and Roberto, in contrast, had immediately seen the blood spurting from the boy's head. Yasemin screamed and reached across to hold her son. Roberto jumped to his feet and also moved across to help. Both were hit by successive bullets.

The second bullet— fatally— tore a gaping hole in Yasemin's neck. The third struck Roberto in the back and ripped through his aorta, spleen and liver. With blood swamping his white T-shirt, he automatically clutched his abdomen; then, moaning, he doubled up in agony and slumped to the ground.

Dolores, seated at one of the far tables, looked across just in time to see a fourth bullet strike her husband in the upper forehead. She screamed, and soon afterwards yet another bullet— the fifth and last— ripped into the Snoopy *piñata,* splitting it asunder and sending an assortment of sweets, toys and cracker-size novelties cascading down onto the astonished children.

It had all happened in no more than fortty seconds— a lightning flash of horror that ended with Kemal Tunaman and his grandson physically entwined in death, and Yasemin lying motionless at their feet alongside the still groaning Roberto.

Within those forty seconds, only one person fully grasped the situation. Alerted by Yasemin's scream, Mark Ballantyne reacted instinctively; he threw himself forward and knocked Ricky sideways to the right in order to shield the boy with his body. With Ricky yelling beneath him, he eased over onto his left side so that his back faced the direction from which the first bullets had come; then he drew a .38 special from the shoulder holster under his zip-jacket, and looked around.

The scene was utter chaos and madness. Some children, frightened and confused, were calling out *"Mamá"* and *"Ani"*; others, thinking it was all a game, were gleefully scrambling for candy and toys. Yolanda had rushed to Roberto's side and was weeping as she tried to stem the flow of blood with her scarf. Other women were screaming, and none more hysterically than Dolores, now kneeling beside her husband and grandson.

"Stay still, Ricky. It's all right," said Ballantyne, as the boy continued to yell and squirm beneath him. Then he turned to the man who had just landed beside him, and who was lying face-down with his hands covering the back of his head. "*Señor*," he shouted. "Get up. Get the women and children away from here. As far away as possible. Come on. Get up. Do it now. MOVE."

The command was so authoritative that Felipe Castillo, though trembling with fear, responded at once. He sprang to his feet and, frantically flapping his arms at the children, screamed for everyone to run.

With Ricky still clutched to his side, Ballantyne returned his gun to its holster, then reached down to a slit-pocket in the lower right leg of his jeans. He drew out what looked like a pocket calculator, and pressed a single button with his thumb. The cellular phone put him through directly to the duty officer at the U.S. embassy on Reforma.

He spoke slowly and distinctly. "Control. This is Ballantyne. Chapultepec Park, north side. Code Four. Full red alert. Repeat, full red alert. Four down. Turkish ambassador dead. Subject okay."

His message acknowledged, Ballantyne re-sheathed the phone and, still holding Ricky down, knelt up to survey the area more carefully. Now, for the first time, he saw two heads peering out from behind the stage backcloth. The faces, wide-eyed with fear, were of the hired magician and, surrealistically, of the midget half made-up as a clown.

Only a few yards away, Yolanda was still attending her stricken husband, and Dolores, her head buried in Kemal's lap, was sobbing and crying out, "*Por qué? Por qué? Por qué?*" Otherwise, as far as the U.S. marine could judge, the immediate vicinity was clear. It was time, he decided, to risk making a move.

"Ricky," he said softly. "Everything's all right. I'm going to let you get up now. Remember what I told you to do if there was ever any trouble? You must keep calm and you must do exactly as I say. Do you understand?" The boy nodded earnestly, and Ballantyne eased his grip.

"Right. Stand up now. But don't look around and be ready to move quickly. We're just going over to see the clown." He held the boy by the shoulders so that he was facing away from the carnage, and then steered him at the double towards the improvised stage. There he made Ricky take cover beneath the props-table and, crouching down, called the entertainers to his side.

"Listen," he told them. "I am a security officer and I want you to stay exactly where you are until the police get here. They will arrive very soon. Meanwhile, you are to look after this boy until I get back. Stay down and guard him with your lives. Is that clear? Oh yes, and I shall need this."

Ballantyne ripped the purple backcloth from its supporting poles and trailed it behind him as he raced over to the wounded Roberto. Rapidly, he tore from the cloth a ten-foot-long strip, and doubled it over. Then, with the aid of Yolanda, he tightly wrapped it three times around the Mexican's upper body, and used the remaining cloth to form a rolled-up pillow.

Roberto, laid on his side, whispered his thanks. Ballantyne put a hand to his forehead. "Don't try to talk, *señor*. And keep as still as you can. You've lost a lot of blood. But keep fighting. The ambulance will be here very soon."

He looked at his watch. It was 1204 hours. Incredibly, only four minutes had elapsed since the first shot was fired. And already events were moving rapidly elsewhere, as Ballantyne's call from the epicentre of the disaster sent shock waves spreading far and wide.

CHAPTER 5

1201 hours, Sunday, January 25

As recorded on the duty-log, the U.S. embassy had received Ballantyne's call at 1201 hours. In an emergency, the duty-officer would automatically contact either the ambassador or the Deputy Head of Mission (DHM) who would then decide on appropriate action. But neither man was on the premises. The officer therefore passed on the Code 4 message to the security desk, which was currently manned by Jim Pollard, one of several agents who, though based at the embassy, actually worked for the Central Intelligence Agency, colloquially known as "The Company".

At the time, Pollard had been half-heartedly trying to improve his Spanish by reading Octavio Paz with the aid of a dictionary. He was relatively green to his job, a young college graduate only three months out of the CIA training school at Cape Peary, known as "The Farm", on the York River in Virginia. And already he was bored.

This Sunday, not for the first time, he had reflected on the irony of his situation. When asked by college chums why he aimed to join the CIA, he used to say that he wanted some adventure and to avoid being stuck behind some desk. So far there had been no hint of adventure and, since leaving Cape Peary, every day of his working life had been spent at a desk.

At training school, he remembered, the lectures had included a discussion about lessons to be learnt from past CIA operations. To illustrate the importance of eternal vigilance and attention to detail, the elderly instructor had cited events in Mexico City, way back in the fall of 1963. "At that time we had the Commies under round-the-clock surveillance. The Soviet and Cuban embassies were fully bugged, and we had cameras across the street photographing everyone who went in and out. Nothing was too trivial to be followed up.

"And what came out of it? I'll tell you what: we got

the first evidence that Lee Harvey Oswald, a known defector, was in Mexico City. Think about it. That was seven weeks before the assassination of President Kennedy. If the bungling FBI had followed up our tip-off, and kept a watch on the bastard, who knows how it might have changed history."

But Pollard had read enough to know the reality of those times. In truth, the CIA of the 1960s had been notorious for its inefficiency; an agency overloaded with hot-headed rednecks who promoted a succession of madcap schemes ranging from failed plots to assassinate Fidel Castro to the monumental debacle of the Bay of Pigs when, in open defiance of the President's orders, CIA operatives had joined 1,400 Cuban exiles in a suicidal invasion of Cuba.

At least the Oswald example reflected the scale of operations in the old days, and even as late as the 1980s Mexico City had been a lively enough place, riddled with agents working for the DGI, the Cuban intelligence agency which reported to the KGB. It was there, in 1983, that CIA agent Aldrich Hazen Ames had got hooked up with Maria del Rosario Casas Dupuy, a Colombian cultural attaché. Subsequently, as all agents posted to Mexico were reminded, Ames became head of the CIA's Soviet counter-intelligence... and Russia's super-spy inside the Langley headquarters. Not until 1994 that Ames was exposed as a KGB informer who had received more than 2.5 million dollars for treachery that had cost the lives of at least ten double agents serving the U.S.A.

The Mexican scene was entirely different now. Since the end of the Cold War and the economic breakdown of Castro's Cuba, Mexico City had ceased to be a beehive of espionage and intrigue. Furthermore, CIA activities had been concentrated elsewhere in support of the 'war on terrorism' arising from the 9/11 suicide missions of Al-Queda fanatics. Now, in Latin America, their undercover work had become largely confined to supporting the Drug Enforcement Administration (DEA) and the FBI in the war against drug trafficking.

In this role they had had some success: most notably in helping Mexico's National Institute for Combating Drugs (INCD), then headed by Attorney General Gaston Pérez, to smash the powerful and ruthless drug cartel, which had been based in Juárez, just across the Rio Grande from El Paso in Texas. For his leading part in that operation, Wade Hellman, the CIA station chief in Mexico City, was soon to be transferred to Langley, Virginia, as the new Deputy Director of the Latin American section.

But otherwise there was no longer any real sense of adventure. The number of CIA personnel in the city had been slashed to a bare minimum, and, under new budget restrictions, they had been made accountable for any services provided by the embassy, ranging from the cost of borrowing cars to the use of photocopiers. With paperwork far outweighing fieldwork, the busiest staffers were the computer operators and translators. As agents joked, there was not even hope of being targeted by some *femme fatale* for the classic honey trap.

Thus, in a perverse way, Pollard welcomed Ballantyne's call. A Code 4— assassination situation— was extraordinary. For the first time his adrenalin was positively flooding.

The procedure on receiving such a code, together with a full red alert, was very clearly defined, and he responded with maximum speed and efficiency. The Company had neither the resources nor the authority to deal directly and immediately with such an emergency on foreign soil. Therefore, his first duty was to alert the Mexico City police, advising them that both security and medical units were urgently needed.

His second call— as dictated by circumstances— was to alert Brad McClellan, the veteran CIA man who was assigned to shadowing U.S. ambassador James Henderson.

Pollard held McClellan in positive awe: as an agent who had seen more front line action than anyone he knew. In a career spanning thirty years, "Big Brad"— six-foot, three-inch tall and a burly fifteen-stone— had frequently distinguished himself under fire, a pattern first set when he was in the Honduras jungle, helping Contra rebels to organise cross-border guerrilla raids in their fight to overthrow the Marxist Sandinista government of Nicaragua. Yet he had never sought promotion to a desk job, nor had it been offered. He was strictly an agent's agent, the equivalent of the eternal army sergeant who demands and gains absolute loyalty from his men, and who, in return, will never sacrifice them unnecessarily in blindly following orders from above. Quite simply, McClellan was a maverick. He did not always play it "according to Hoyle", and more than once he had been severely reprimanded for acting— usually to good effect— on his own initiative.

But what McClellan called the great game was virtually over for him now. Six months ago, following a final "front line" mission in Colombia, he had been posted to Mexico City, where he was virtually filling in time until his retirement, now only five weeks away. By his standards, it was a veritable holiday, his duties involving nothing more than maintaining contact with undercover agents recruited by the CIA's anti-drug division.

Meanwhile, ambassador Henderson had taken such a liking to McClellan that, contrary to normal procedure, he had requested his weekend services— in preference to one of the young marines— for informal engagements. As a result 'Big Brad' enjoyed many perks in the company of the Texan rancher-turned-diplomat he called boss, and by now he was treated more like a buddy than a bodyguard.

This day was typical. The ambassador, a keep-fit fanatic, was engaged in his ten-to-one Sunday routine, which involved two hours of hard singles on the tennis court, followed by a midday swim and a light lunch. His opponent, as always, was Dr Sánchez Becerra, Mexico's most distinguished and well-connected obstetric and gynaecological surgeon.

Henderson and Sánchez Becerra had first met eighteen months ago at an exclusive weekend house party arranged by Doña Cholita Pérez, sister-in-law of the new president. Finding themselves perfectly matched on the tennis court, they had arranged a return, and in time, it had become a regular fixture with Dr Sánchez Becerra acting as host at his vast colonial-style residence at San Angel, seven miles directly south of Chapultepec Park. His mansion not only had two finely maintained clay courts and a thirty-metre swimming pool, but also outstanding security.

On these occasions, McClellan doubled as the ambassador's chauffeur and bodyguard, and they used an ordinary embassy staff car so as not to attract undue attention. The grounds of the house, surrounded by a twelve-foot high wall topped with jagged glass, could only be entered by an electronically operated iron gate. More than two hundred acres of open parkland lay between the perimeter and the mansion's amenities, and this area was regularly patrolled by two armed guards accompanied by Doberman pinschers. The threat from outside was absolutely minimal. And so, encouraged by the boss, McClellan had got into the habit of bringing a swimming costume, lounging beside the pool, and

53

taking a dip when he pleased.

When agent Pollard rang, McClellan was pool-side, sipping a *cuba libre*. Since the weather was mild, he was fully dressed, except that his jacket and his gun and holster were lying on the chair beside him. Following Pollard's call, he immediately reverted to type: a man of action, thinking fast on his feet and as alert as a spring deer to any sudden movement or sound. The parkland, he noted, was completely clear. Meanwhile, Henderson and Sánchez Becerra were heading towards him, towels around their necks, both dripping with sweat after three hard-fought sets. He grabbed his gear and went out to meet them.

Henderson's initial reaction to the news was of great relief and thankfulness that his son was unharmed. Then he thought about it more deeply. He decided he would not bother to shower and change. Instead, striding over to a table, he grabbed his tracksuit and hurriedly slipped it on. "Christ, Brad," he said. "We've got to get moving fast."

McClellan shook his head. "I don't think so, boss. If there are terrorists at large, you are as safe here as anywhere. Back on the road, you would be an open target."

"Stay here?" cried Henderson. "Are you crazy?"

McClellan switched to formality. "No, sir. I'm serious. My orders are to keep you out of danger at all times."

"Damn your orders, Brad. It's my boy we're talking about, you hear. He may still be in danger. I've got my own gun in the car and we can get to the park in ten minutes. Are you with me or not?"

McClellan smiled approvingly. "I'm with you, boss."

At the embassy, after contacting the police and McClellan, agent Jim Pollard made two more emergency calls. Normally, his third call would have been to his station chief, Wade Hellman. But Hellman had left Mexico City only twenty-four hours ago on compassionate leave, having received news that his father was critically ill in Stockton, California. With his sudden departure, Pollard realised, McClellan had become the top dog in the local pecking order.

Therefore, still strictly following routine, he moved on to making an internal call to Legal Attaché Robert Carruthers. Here, as in all American embassies, the Legal Attaché (*Legat*) was the representative of the Federal Bureau of Investigation. His purpose: to liaise with the enforcement and intelligence forces of Mexico on matters of common interest, from narcotics to international terrorism.

The call to Carruthers was more a formality than an urgent necessity. Long ago, the Warren Commission on the assassination of President Kennedy had exposed an appalling lack of liaison and coordination of information between the CIA and FBI. More damningly, findings of the 1979 Congress' Assassinations Committee had shown them to be behaving more like deadly rivals than servants of the same government. It had, for example, taken the CIA a full week to notify the FBI of the Mexico City presence of Lee Harvey Oswald, and even then they had bypassed the "Legal Counsellor" who worked in the very same building.

Subsequently, a far greater degree of cooperation was demanded of the Company and the Bureau. But, in reality, little changed. In May 1985, round-the-clock FBI surveillance of the Soviet embassy in Washington had recorded on film a visit by Aldrich Ames. But the Bureau, with primary responsibility for counter-espionage in the U.S., did not pass on the information to the CIA. Conceivably, if the CIA had known that Ames was making unauthorised contacts with the Soviets, they might have averted the nine years of appalling betrayal that followed.

The FBI was held in still greater contempt in 2002 when a former agent, Robert Hansen, was found to have spied for Russia for twenty years, betraying fifty agents and selling key defence secrets for $1.4 million and diamonds. When he was finally uncovered by the FBI he asked the question echoed by the CIA. "What took you so long?"

But the CIA's smugness was short-lived. Two former employees now openly condemned the Company's failure to penetrate terrorist groups, and deplored the falling number of field agents and the expense-account lifestyles of operatives living in the suburbs of Washington. And then— most damning of all— came the inquiry into intelligence operations prior to the suicide attacks of 9/11. It found the CIA and FBI equally guilty of gross inefficiency, of engaging in intense rivalry that had led to a series of missed warnings, which, if shared, might have averted the cataclysmic World Trade Center disaster.

Never again, after 9/11, could the two agencies risk failing to communicate with one another. Ever after, if only superficially, they would take care to be seen to be dutiful in the swift exchange of information of possible mutual interest.

In short, Pollard's call to Carruthers was to cover his ass.

Like all the calls he made this Sunday afternoon, Pollard made sure that it was tape-recorded. He buzzed Carruthers first at his office, then at his private apartment. In both cases, the result was the same. An answering machine told him: "I am not available at the present time, but if you will leave a message after the bleep I will get back to you as soon as I can. "Pollard left a message on both machines, saying no more than that he had important information that might interest him.

Pollard's fourth and final call— one absolutely essential if he wanted to keep his job— was made on a scrambled line to the CIA's headquarters at Langley, some eight miles north-west of downtown Washington. The most senior officials were on weekend leave from their top, seventh floor offices. But there was a rigid standby procedure to deal with any emergency. Within five seconds of his mention of a Code 4, Pollard found himself being transferred directly to the private residence of William J. Stanleigh, the man currently responsible for the entire operational area of the CIA.

Under the overall command of its Director of Central Intelligence (the DCI), usually a political appointee, the CIA has two main arms: the Directorate of Operations, responsible for the clandestine gathering of foreign information and often engaging in covert activities, and the Directorate of Intelligence, responsible for the less glamorous, often tedious, task of collating, interpreting and analysing information from a multitude of sources. Each branch is run by a Deputy Director, known to all Company workers simply as the DDO and the DDI respectively.

Bill Stanleigh, the DDO, was also the President's current nominee to succeed Admiral George Stanton as DCI. Recently, he had moved into the affluent Washington suburb of McLean, occupying a beautiful white colonial-style house in Savile Lane, which directly overlooked the wooded grounds of CIA headquarters.

At the time of Pollard's call, he had just finished poring over foreign news sections mined from a mountain of Sunday papers. There were no stories of particular interest to him - only the usual assortment of reports of bombings, rioting, drug-related violence and failed peace talks. Political unrest was virtually the norm, confirming his cynical view of world affairs: that governments rarely made genuine progress, but mainly sidestepped from one crisis to another. One month it was the Balkans and Afghanistan, then it was the Aegean crisis, and now, yet again, all attention was focussed on the Middle East. *Plus ça change, plus c'est la même chose.*

Moreover, events continued to bear out the prediction that had been made as long ago as 1996 by John Deutch, the Clinton-appointed CIA chief: that there would be a world-wide upsurge in terrorism, and that ideologies and regimes inimical to democracy would continue to flourish as strongly as ever. The world was indeed in perpetual turmoil, and his job of directing the CIA's multifarious operations never got easier.

Stanleigh was the one person who received Pollard's news with a measure of equanimity. He was surprised, but not unduly shocked. "Hmm! Is that all you've got? Not much to go on, is it? Who else knows about this?"

Pollard listed the calls on his log, and warmed at the DDO's response. "Good. You've done right. But listen. From now on, you give me top priority. As soon as you have a detailed report, I want it first... absolutely first. You understand? And you are to keep me informed of any developments. Have you got that? Anything significant and you give me a call."

Stanleigh hung up and then, after a full minute's careful thought, he picked up the phone again. It was time he decided to make his first official call to the newly elected President of the United States.

It was 1207 hours when Pollard had made his final call. Only seven minutes had elapsed since the killing began, and already a major development had occurred. At Chapultepec Castle, the sniper's nest— atop the tower known as *La Torre del Caballero Alto*— had been located.

At the time of the shooting, several thousand day-trippers had been roaming over the castle terraces and courtyards, and through the museum's labyrinth of halls and galleries and staterooms. The majority of those on the ground floor mistook the gunshots for the sound of fireworks or of bursting balloons. However, on the second floor, in the east side Alcázar section, each crack of rifle-fire was much more distinct.

Most especially, it aroused the attention of those people who were standing in a gallery directly in the shadow of the tower. In front of them, some forty children were seated on the floor and in chairs, forming a circle within which harlequin-like figures were performing a simple play.

The children were undistracted as the actors played out a piece of buffoonery with exaggerated gestures and absurdly loud, high-pitched voices. But a number of parents were drawn out of curiosity to the tower base, along with an organised party of tourists who had just completed a guided tour of the nearby bedchambers of Don Porfirio and Doña Carmen Díaz.

At the entrance to the tower they encountered two soldiers dressed in green-and-brown camouflage gear, one helmeted and armed with a lightweight FAL (Fusil Automatico Ligero) 7.62 rifle, the other wearing a peaked cap and carrying a .38 revolver in a holster on his right hip.

Shoulder epaulettes— black with three aquamarine stripes— identified the senior soldier as a *Sargento Segundo* in the *Cuerpo de Guardias Presidenciales*. This élite corps has its barracks on the south side of Chapultepec Park, close by Los Pinos, the official residence of the President of Mexico. From one of its 300-strong companies, fifty men were assigned to guard the Castle by night and day.

The sergeant, who had been the first to arrive on the scene, ordered the gathering crowd to stand well back and to keep quiet. Then, while drawing his revolver from the holster, he addressed his colleague. "I'm going up. You stand guard here and be ready to shoot on sight if anyone else comes down. I'll give you a warning shout if it's only me."

Ducking under the velveted chain, he then side-stepped into the entrance and disappeared up the spiral staircase. Roughly two minutes later, a single shot echoed from inside the tower. Then, after calling out to identify himself, the soldier reappeared.

"All right, everyone," he shouted, "the show's over. Now I want all of you to clear this area completely. There is no danger, nothing to worry about. Just go off and enjoy yourselves."

He then turned to the younger guardsman and grinned. "No problem, Eduardo. We got the sonofabitch."

CHAPTER 6

1214 hours, Sunday, January 25

Half a mile east of Chapultepec Park, just south of Reforma and bounded on the east side by the great north-south artery of Avenida Insurgentes, lies the Zona Rosa, or Pink Zone, a wedge-shaped, cosmopolitan enclave of about one square mile that abounds with gourmet restaurants, pavement cafes and elegant boutiques, and proclaims its international flavour with street names such as Hamburgo, Londres, Liverpool, Tokio, Berlin, Florencia and Havre.

This is Mexico City's most fashionable shopping and dining quarter, primarily the haunt of tourists and wealthier citizens. And here, on Liverpool, at the heart of well-ordered commercialism, the police had their relocated headquarters, formally known as the *Secretaria de Seguridad Pública del Distrito Federal.*

In his office, on the tenth floor of a newly designed tower block, Coronel Salvador Hernández was breathing more easily after the initial shock of confronting a potential crisis on his first Sunday as senior duty officer. Following Pollard's call from the U.S. embassy, he had immediately alerted all available police units in the vicinity of Chapultepec Park. He had then notified the anti-terrorist squad and summoned a full-scale turnout of emergency units at the *Centro Medico Nacional* on Avenida Cuauhtémoc, less than two miles east of the park.

Next— and some would say most importantly— he had telephoned *Molino del Rey*, the presidential guards' barracks, so called because it is sited on the eastern side of the eponymous street that divides the old and new sectors of Chapultepec Park. From this red stone building, close by the president's residence of *Los Pinos*, crack guardsmen would be able to reach the scene of the shooting within three or four minutes.

As it happened, this fourth call proved unnecessary. *El*

Cuerpo de Guardias Presidenciales had already been contacted by guardsmen on duty at the castle. Placed on full alert, the corps had mounted a protective screen around Los Pinos and had ordered other troops to reconnoitre the surrounding area.

Having dealt with emergency procedures, Hernández had then taken the mandatory step of contacting the headquarters of the *Procuraduría General de Justicia del Distrito Federal* (the Federal District Attorney General's Office).

It now only remained for him to call his chief. With luck, he reckoned, he would be able to hand over all responsibility within the next half-hour.

"Thank the saints it happened on a Sunday," he said to a junior officer. And knowingly they both grinned.

Whenever he was absent from headquarters, Mexico City's Chief of Police, General Juan Delgado, normally left with his secretary a telephone number where he could be reached in an emergency. But very occasionally, as now, he neglected to do so; in which case his immediate subordinate could find himself placed in a somewhat delicate position.

If it was a weekday, the deputy had three conflicting options. He could make a discreet call to the *casa chica* in Cuernavaca where Delgado was liable to spend a half day with his senior mistress Leonor Contreras and their two children. On the other hand, if it was after seven o'clock nightfall, a better bet was Delgado's *casa-chiquita*, the apartment near the Zona Rosa that was reserved for his second, much younger paramour, Lupita Linares. Since Delgado did not have a third mistress installed in a *casa-chiquitita*, the final option— only after trying the others— was to ring his *Casa Grande*, the official family home in the south-west district of Coyoacán.

But happily this was a Sunday, and like all good Mexican husbands Delgado strictly reserved Sundays for his legitimate wife and family. His mistresses could be forgotten. He would be at his *Casa Grande*.

On receiving Hernández's call, General Delgado reacted with the commanding authority for which he was both renowned and feared. "Four down and the Turkish ambassador dead," he snapped. "That doesn't tell us a lot, does it? Well, we must presume the worst: that a major terrorist action is in progress. The first priority is the safety of the Head of State. You realise, of course, that *El Presidente* is in residence at *Los*

Pinos this weekend."

"No, *Jefe*," said Hernández. "I wasn't sure." Already he was feeling flustered.

"Never mind. You've already alerted the presidential guards. You can now leave it to me to telephone *El Presidente* personally. Meanwhile, keep in touch with the emergency services. Above all, make doubly sure that officers accompany casualties to the hospital. We must have men standing by to take statements as soon as people are fit to talk. See to it at once. Otherwise you take no further action without my approval. Is that clear? You can reach me on my car radio. I'll be with you in ten minutes."

Hernández looked at his watch. It was 1215 hours. He should be out of the hot seat by 1225. Seconds later, he was on the radio to police cars heading to Chapultepec Park when the duty sergeant buzzed his office. "Coronel, we've got a security guard on the line from *El Castillo*. Says they've got the assassin. Shot dead."

"*Dios mío*! Put him through." On another line he tried to call Delgado. It was busy. There was no alternative; he had to take action on his own.

Approaching westward via Reforma and Avenida Chapultepec and southwest along the Melchor Ocampo highway, three emergency groups— police cars, ambulances, and two armoured vehicles of the paramilitary anti-terrorist squad (*Zorros*)— independently converged on Chapultepec Park. Almost simultaneously, around 1209 hours, they arrived at the downtown corner of the park beyond the Diana Fountain, and when they met, the harsh screaming of their sirens merged into an appalling cacophony that put hordes of feeding pigeons to flight.

As the first police cars, led by motorcycle outriders, rounded *la Fuente de la Diana Cazadora*, they passed a green-and-white VW Beetle taxi heading east on Reforma. Slumped on the back seat of the cab, mopping his brow with a large white handkerchief, was a grey-suited man who looked the perfect candidate for a coronary. He was grossly overweight, and his heart was pounding like a pneumatic drill after the combined exertion of walking briskly for half a mile and humping a three-kilo shoulder pack.

Furthermore, the man was in an acute state of hypertension. He was literally trembling with both fear and exhilaration. The fear would soon fade. But the exhilaration was mounting all the while. His excitement was very much akin to that of a punter who strongly suspected he had won first prize on the National Lottery, but who still needed to double-check the numbers on his ticket.

"*Me lleva la chingada*," said the taxi driver. "Look at all those *pinche* cops. Must be something big." He chuckled. "Maybe they just discovered another great Christmas Eve robbery."

More than two decades after the event, Mexicans still liked to joke about the night that the eight security guards at the park's National Museum of Anthropology were so busy celebrating Christmas that they neglected to make their two-hourly night patrols. When the relief crew took over at 8 a.m., they found showcases shattered and one hundred forty gold, jade and obsidian artefacts missing. It was the biggest ever heist of its kind, a haul of ancient relics whose value could only be vaguely estimated in tens of millions of dollars.

The fat man, glad to release some of his inner tension, bellowed out a forced laugh. "Yeah! You could be right."

In reality, he knew better. He had not only witnessed the killings in the park; he had also videoed the entire bloodbath from start to finish. The unique videotape was still in the antiquated Hi-8 camcorder that was stored, together with a large pair of binoculars, in the knapsack on which he was now resting his right forearm.

Alfredo Gómez worked for *El Informador*. Indeed, some would say he *was El Informador*. His weekly gossip column had become the dominant feature of Mexico's newest and most notorious scandal sheet. Everyone who was anyone turned immediately to his centre spread, and, apart from a few outrageous or publicity-hungry show business personalities, no one welcomed a mention there.

Chance had been a major factor in Gómez's rapid progress from run-of-the-mill reporter to bylined columnist. Two years earlier, by way of a cousin who worked as a barmaid at the Chapultepec Sports Club, he had heard a rumour that the tennis coach Guillermo Velázquez had been threatened by men demanding settlement of his gambling debts. Gómez sought confirmation of the story. At the time, Velázquez was courting Esperanza Castillo and was desperately anxious that her family should not learn of his financial predicament. He could not offer Gómez money for his silence. But he could, and did, promise to feed him information on a regular basis.

Velázquez more than fulfilled his promise. He gave Gómez enough ammunition to gain him a staff job on the new-founded *El Informador*, and he subsequently provided valuable contacts, which led to Gómez's promotion to columnist. But once Velázquez was married, his attitude changed. He wanted money for his services, and *El Informador* readily met his price with an annually renewable contract.

Meanwhile, by the style of his column, Señor Gómez had given a new twist to newspaper work. In Mexico, a number of columnists, and not a few feature writers and reporters, still depended for a good living on *ex gratia* payments from public figures seeking a favourable plug. It was a recognised professional perk, a part of the Mexican way of life. In the case of Gómez, however, it was entirely the opposite; his main income derived from persons who paid *not* to be mentioned in his rag.

His conduct could be seen as bordering on blackmail. But, taking a broader view, many Mexican cynics would say that Gómez was merely conforming with traditional working practice. He was naturally exploiting his position; just as a lowly-paid cop would accept a bribe— universally known as *mordida* (a bite)— for not booking an alleged traffic offender, or a minor bureaucrat would accept payment for not delaying in the issue of some urgently required document.

But again there was a difference. Gómez was not operating from a position of real power or authority. He had neither the backing of a strong organisation nor the machinery of a bureaucracy to support him. Out on his own, he had to be absolutely sure of his facts to avoid a disastrous libel action. And even then his work was fraught with danger. In a sense, he was no more secure than a common blackmailer whose only protection was the information he threatened to release.

Gómez was not actually breaking any law. He never demanded money by menaces, merely accepted 'gifts' from people with something to hide. In some orderly societies, this might be seen as a reasonable risk. In Mexico, however, it was hazardous in the extreme, especially with the mushrooming of so-called *guaruras* in the last three decades.

Originally, the *guaruras*— a word meaning "guardian" in the language of Mexico's Tarahumara Indians— had emerged in the 1970s when a spate of kidnappings prompted leading officials to have themselves accompanied everywhere by personal bodyguards. By the 1980s, political terrorism had markedly declined. But businessmen were still targeted for financial gain and the number of bodyguards had continued to grow apace, especially from 1994 onwards, following the kidnapping of Alfredo Harp Helú, president of Banamex, Mexico's largest bank, and the abduction of Angel Losada Moreno, heir to a billion-dollar supermarket fortune, who was ambushed in his Cadillac by an armed gang.

By now a phalanx of *guaruras* was more than a security necessity. It had become a status symbol, confirming that the person escorted was an *influyente*— someone with influence. In Mexico City alone, there were an estimated thiry thousand *guaruras*.

Following an outcry in the press and among the public, the government had introduced a three-month course to train such private agents in courtesy as well as security. But many were still recruited among barely literate ex-policemen or even unemployed men with a criminal record, and cases of unwarranted violence by *guaruras* continued to occur.

On public highways, it was not extraordinary for a motorist to be jousted off the road by the fast-moving convoy of an *influyente*. Sometimes a driver had been forced to stop, and then beaten up for cursing or waving a fist at road-hogging *guaruras*. On one much-publicised occasion, the heavily guarded son of a politician had spotted a female friend in a car with two men. His bodyguards blocked the car and, while they trained their guns on the two men, the politician's son began slapping the woman. When one of the men, an off-duty marine from the U.S. embassy, tried to defend her, he was pistol-whipped and left unconscious.

With so many prominent men and women having ready access to armed bodyguards, Gómez was all the more conscious of the need for caution. He could never be seen to be threatening an *influyente* for fear of some impulsive or calculated reaction. His muckraking role required, above all, nerves of steel, and in that department Gómez was deplorably lacking. He no longer had the stomach for his work. He desperately wanted a secure, more respectable job. And it was the pursuit of that ambition that had taken him to Chapultepec Park on Sunday, January 25.

On the previous Friday, Velázquez had telephoned Gómez, giving him precise details of the birthday party in the park: the time, the place and the provisional guest list. As a gossip item, the information was worthless. By the following Thursday, when the weekly *El Informador* next hit the streets, the story would be as stale as yesterday's tortillas. Nonetheless, it was useful to Gómez. For many weeks he had been cultivating his contact with Francisco Romero, producer of Channel 13 television news and the thrice-weekly peak-viewing *24 Horas* show. But he felt the need to demonstrate his worth before making a direct approach for a job.

On Saturday he rang Romero with a proposal. "As you know, the Turkish ambassador is dining with *El Presidente* tomorrow before leaving for the States. You'll be covering it, of course. But that'll be little more than shots of his limousine disappearing through the palace gates. How would you like much more, enough to put together an exclusive? We could call it '*El Fantasma's* Last Day in Mexico City.' "

Romero's reaction was cool. He didn't like Gómez and his use of 'we' made him positively cringe. "You know, there's really not much interest in Turkish affairs. At least not any more. The ambassador has promised to give a short press conference at the airport, and that should be enough for us. Of course, if you have some really unusual angle I might be able to send out a television crew. What's the setup?"

Gómez cursed him under his breath and immediately backed off. His information, he said, was confidential. He would get the coverage himself, and then it would be up to Romero to decide if he wanted to use it.

At 1210 hours on Sunday, as the taxi turned off at the *glorieta* Cuauhtémoc and headed north on Insurgentes, Gómez smiled at the memory of that conversation. *If he wanted to use it!* *Puta madre!* The stuck-up, condescending bastard would be begging to use what he had on videotape.

By 1220 hours Coronel Salvador Hernández was the only person who had a composite picture of the drama in Chapultepec Park. He had the report of a security guard claiming to have killed a lone, unidentified assassin in the castle's round tower. He also had the regular bulletins, virtually a running commentary, from the squad cars at the scene of the slaughter. Overall, the picture was of a crisis passed and a situation fully under control.

Most reassuringly, President Pérez was safe. On full alert, the presidential guard at *Los Pinos* was still standing by, guns at the ready, but with no one, except curious day-trippers, in sight. Meanwhile, a handful of armed guardsmen had reached the site of the tragedy. They arrived only seconds ahead of the swarming emergency units.

From far and wide across the park, hordes of holidaymakers were now converging on the picnic area to see what all the excitement was about. Soon, the police and anti-terrorist troops found that their main task was keeping the general public well back while the paramedics went about their gruesome business.

Before the victims were moved, a police photographer recorded the precise position of the bodies. He completed his work in a few minutes, but it seemed much longer as Dolores Castillo de Tunaman, refusing to leave her husband's side, screamed out abuse. She was still crying aloud as they lifted the ambassador onto a stretcher and carried him into an ambulance.

Señora Tunaman could not be consoled. She insisted upon staying with her husband. Meanwhile, the bodies of her step-grandson and daughter-in-law were placed in a second ambulance. Without delay, both vehicles moved off across parkland, their sirens screaming to clear a way through the ring of sightseers.

From the moment of their arrival, the paramedics had given top priority to attending the one surviving victim, Roberto Martinez. The young finance minister was unconscious now, his condition so critical they doubted he could endure the journey to the *Centro Medico Nacional*. The only hope, it seemed, was immediate open-heart surgery, and a massive transfusion of blood. With that aim, they gently lifted him into the special ambulance that was equipped like a miniature operating theatre.

Fortunately, Roberto's two children— Daniel, aged six, and Isabel, five— were shielded from the scene. They were some forty yards away, in a group of women and children gathered together by Felipe Castillo and Carmen's husband. Now their mother, Yolanda, was persuaded by medics to join them. "They are right," Mark Ballantyne gently told her. "There is nothing more we can do and we will only be in their way."

The emergency phoracotany was carried out by Dr Armando Morelos, who had gained experience of the procedure while working in the casualty department at the Los Angeles General Hospital. Inside the stationary ambulance, he cut through the sternum with a saw, prised the patient's ribs apart, and then tried to repair bullet damage to the aorta and blood vessels to stem the flow of blood. Meanwhile, his assistants administered a transfusion of eighteen pints of blood, and soon after, in desperation, the doctor began to massage his heart inside the chest cavity to keep the blood circulating.

They were still fighting for Roberto's life when Coronel Hernández received his last bulletin from the park. At 1213 the police reported the arrival of the U.S. ambassador and bodyguard McClellan. The ambassador had collected his son, who was unharmed, and he had ordered his embassy to send transport for all the other children and womenfolk. The boy's protector, a Señor Ballantyne, had been asked to remain behind as a material witness.

Alfredo Gómez was feeling much more relaxed now. He was breathing normally again, and growing in self-confidence as his taxi, nearing the offices of *El Informador*, turned down a quiet back-street far removed from the crowded chaos of Chapultepec Park. For the moment, only one great worry preyed on his mind: Had the video really captured everything he had seen? What if the tape was faulty, or he had failed to adjust the focus correctly?

As a cameraman, Gómez was strictly a novice. It was only a month since he had begun experimenting with the ancient camcorder he had picked up for a song at La Merced. He still did not understand the technicalities of getting the correct exposure. Moreover, his position in Chapultepec Park had been far from ideal. Lacking a tripod, he had supported his absurdly large camcorder on the low branch of a tree. He had been standing in shade, and he had remained roughly one hundred yards from the scene he was shooting.

Worse still, when the killing began, he had frozen in horror and disbelief. What had followed was like some half-remembered nightmare: all flashing images - of bodies falling, blood gushing, people screaming, people running - but no detailed picture. Memories of his own actions, or rather inaction, were blurred. As a result he was now even beginning to worry that, in the confusion, he might have inadvertently switched off the camcorder by pressing the "record" button a second time.

When Gómez arrived, the modest premises of *El Informador* were deserted, except for a cleaning lady whom he caught using a telephone to make a private call. He curtly told her that the offices were clean enough, and that she should leave immediately. "I'll forget about your telephoning... just this once."

Left alone, his first action was to remove a half bottle of whisky from a filing cabinet. He took a long, hard swig. Then, after pouring a large measure into a tumbler, he unpacked the camcorder, connected it to a television set, and rewound the videotape. It was time to end the suspense, to discover once and for all whether or not he had hit the lottery jackpot.

Fast-forwarding the tape to the moment of Tunaman's arrival, Gómez now sat back, riveted to the screen, as it replayed in colour the full horror of the slaughter in the park. It was all there in bloodstained close-up - Georgios dying in his grandfather's arms, his mother hit by a bullet in the neck, the Mexican Finance Minister felled by a shot in the back, the ambassador killed instantly by a bullet in the forehead.

The framing was just wide enough to take in the shattering of the *piñata*. But Gómez had failed to zoom out to capture the overall scene of chaos and confusion. Until the end, the camcorder had remained focussed on the victims, and anyone who ventured into the frame of the dying and the dead.

There were other faults: the poor lighting conditions, which made it look more like dusk than midday, and incongruous sounds of joyful picnickers close by. But the impact of the pictures remained. For a moment Gómez was left stunned; in close-up the scene seemed even more horrific than before. Then the screen went blank, and slowly his look of awe gave way to a broad self-satisfied smile. He had done it. He had the scoop of a lifetime.

Without careful thought, Gómez grabbed the telephone. He couldn't wait to give the news to Romero and win his respect. "I've got something for you, *amigo*," he said. "But I should tell you that it's going to cost you. Maybe a million pesos."

Romero laughed. "Yeah? How much tequila have you had today?"

Gómez leaned back in his chair and emptied his tumbler of whisky. "You're right. I've had a drink. But then I've got good reason to celebrate. Now listen to this..."

The producer listened carefully, and at the same time waved a reporter into his glass-box office. Shielding the mouthpiece, he rasped, "Get this on tape. Quickly!"

"You mean, they got the Finance Minister as well? Is he dead?"

"I don't know," said Gómez. "But Jesús! Isn't that enough?"

"It sure is. But could you talk us through it again? Not so fast this time. We need to get the facts right for a one o'clock newsflash."

"Okay," said Gómez. "But first let's agree terms. It's all on videotape: the party, the magician, the shooting, the lot. The picture quality is fine. Of course, you'll need to see it before we agree a price. But let's get one thing straight. I want to be on the seven o'clock show. Not just a credit. I want to be interviewed, and I want to talk through the footage. Is it agreed?"

Romero agreed. "If it's all you say it is, then all right. We'll put you on the show. But you understand, we must see what you've got first. Get it over here as soon as you can. Meanwhile, let's have the facts again. Who exactly got hit and when?"

Somehow, by the end of the call, Gómez felt deflated. He had given out so much information— perhaps too much— and he had received precious little in return. Not even a word of praise. He didn't trust Romero. Now, more calculatingly, he decided to do what he felt he should have done in the first place. He would ring Arturo Menéndez.

Gómez had no special relationship with Menéndez; indeed, he disliked his cold, quietly authoritative manner. But in one respect the Bolivian-born lawyer was totally reliable. Given sufficient financial incentive, he always fought his client's corner with ruthless efficiency and skill. On two occasions, he had secured out-of-court settlements that had saved *El Informador* a small fortune in the face of seemingly hopeless libel suits. He was a supremely professional negotiator, and he had the ability of a master poker player to convince the opposition that he held a winning hand.

Menéndez was at his Las Lomas town residence when Gómez called. Like Romero, he said he would need to see the videotape before making a commitment. "But I can tell you one thing now, *señor*. I am not interested in your offer of ten per cent of the proceeds. If the property is everything you say it is, it will need world-wide marketing. And really expert handling. Like the Zapruder film of the Kennedy assassination.

"My fee will be fory percent, and that's not negotiable. If forty percent is not acceptable, say so now and we can save both of us from wasting valuable time."

Gómez swallowed hard. Menéndez had called his bluff. It was no longer just a matter of money. He felt in desperate need of moral support, the reassurance of having a true professional on his side. And so, reluctantly, he agreed. "Okay, but I need your help right away. I just don't want to make any mistakes."

"Very wise, *señor*," said Menéndez, maintaining his usual courteous, but strictly formal style. "Now this is what we do. First, I get over to your place and see the videotape. Then, if it's okay, we go together to the television studios. But one thing you must understand. When we are there I do all the talking. You say absolutely nothing. Right?"

"Right. I'll be here waiting for you."

Menéndez already had a strategy in mind, but he knew better than to show his hand. If he had explained his plans, Gómez might not have so readily agreed. The lawyer recognised that if the full videotape was shown on television, anyone might copy and pirate it. He needed Channel 13 to show only selected shots, and he needed their expertise to produce and market edited versions.

To him, the solution was clear. He would negotiate a deal whereby the television company paid a large sum for exclusive Mexican rights, plus twenty-five percent of the foreign syndication rights.

It would then be in their interest to maximise the property's earning potential.

CHAPTER 7

1225 hours, Sunday, January 25

At 1225 hours, the sound of sirens screaming alerted everyone at police headquarters to the coming of General Juan Delgado. When the occasion warranted it, he could always be relied upon to do things in style. From his local Coyoacán station, he had ordered four motorcycle outriders to carve him a fast, clear lane up Avenida Insurgentes to his downtown office in the Zona Rosa. He arrived in his black Mercedes Benz, invisible behind dark-tinted glass, and he only stepped out after his chauffeur had raced round to open the rear door. As usual, his appearance was immaculate: boots like polished black marble, knife-edge creases in his custom-tailored dark-blue uniform, and eyeshades topped by a cap-peak trimmed with gold braid. In his left hand, he carried gloves of patent leather, in the right, a silver-knobbed swagger stick.

Delgado was not extraordinary in his pomp and ceremony. Neither vanity nor love of the theatrical prompted such ostentatious style. It was pure Mexican machismo that impelled his show of authority and power, the same machismo that impelled *influyente* to parade their phalanxes of *guaruras,* and presidents always to appear in public with an extravagant entourage. If you had power, you flaunted it, and so, superficially at least, commanded respect.

Briskly, the police chief now strode through the front lobby without so much as a glance as he passed by two officers behind the duty desk. On one side, a third officer was manning a switchboard. He tapped him on the shoulder with his stick. "Any reports from Chapultepec Park, and you put them straight through to me."

After taking the manned elevator to the tenth floor, Delgado turned down the long corridor leading to his office at the rear of the building. On the way, he paused only to rap twice with his stick on an open doorway. Responding immediately to the signal, Hernández gathered together his

71

notes and hurried after him into the inner sanctum.

The chief was already seated at his desk when he entered. He was about to say, "*Buenas tardes, Jefe*," but he was forestalled. Delgado set the tone with his crisp command, "Shut the door, *coronel.*"

Hernández was a highly efficient officer; he had to be to achieve, without social connections, the rank of *coronel* by the age of thirty-five. The fact remained— much to his own irritation— that he still found himself strangely unnerved whenever he was left alone with the chief in his plush and spacious office.

As usual, Delgado made no attempt to put him at his ease. Not even an invitation to take a seat. He was left standing before the enormous desk, an expanse of shining mahogany with everything neatly in place: an intercom unit, two telephones, a glass ashtray, a gold box of Havanas, a silver table-lighter, and the chief's inevitable clipboard and rack of ballpoint pens.

Delgado took up a pen. "Right, *Coronel.* Let's get up to date. Any developments since we last spoke?"

"*Si, Jefe.* A lot." Consulting his notepad, Hernández began to reel off all the new information of the past eleven minutes: the killing of the assassin, the identities of the victims in the park, the efforts to save finance minister Roberto Martínez and the arrival of the U.S. ambassador.

"Oh yes, *Jefe.* And we have also just had a call from Channel 13 TV asking for confirmation that four people, including the Turkish ambassador and Secretario Martínez, have been shot. It was taken by Suárez on the duty desk. He simply replied that there had been an incident in the park, but that no details were yet available."

For a few seconds Delgado continued jotting down notes on his clipboard pad. He tore off the top perforated sheet, put it to one side with the pen, and then, with elbows on the desk, placed his hands together as if in prayer. He pressed his nose against the fingertips. More seconds ticked by as he remained deep in thought. Then he took a deep breath and raised his head, fixing the *coronel* with a steely-eyed look that suggested barely contained rage.

Hernández tried to anticipate him. "I'm sorry, *Jefe,* but I just could not get through to your car radio. There simply wasn't time. I had to make a decision on my own. I redirected a police unit to the tower with instructions to seal off the area, and leave everything untouched. It seemed the logical thing to do."

"It was. And you couldn't get me on the radio because I was busy making calls of my own." Then Delgado hammered the desk with his fist and snarled, "But who the hell authorised a junior officer to make any kind of statement to the media? That was your responsibility, Hernández. And did it ever occur to you to ask how the TV people could possibly know about the shooting so soon? Even I didn't know that Martínez had been shot."

At that moment, Delgado's intercom buzzed and he pressed down the receiver switch. *"Sí?"* he snapped impatiently.

The voice came through loud and clear. "Capitán Hidalgo, *Jefe*, reporting from Chapultepec Park. Bad news, I'm afraid. The finance minister died at 1215 hours. Any special orders, *señor?*"

The chief sighed. "I don't think so." He paused for a second, recomposing himself. "No, wait. You can do one thing. If Señora Martínez is still there, pass on to her my deepest condolences. And you can tell her if it's any consolation, we've probably got the killer already."

The news had visibly affected Delgado. Gone was any hint of anger in eyes, and his voice was softer, too. "A sad day, Hernández, a very sad day indeed. An ambassador, a mother and child. And now we have lost perhaps the most brilliant of our young politicians."

"Si, Jefe," said Hernandez, shifting his weight from one leg to the other.

Delgado smiled grimly. "It's also one hell of a challenge. Of course, it's entirely the responsibility of the PGR now. No doubt, they'll grab all the glory. But at this stage, I am treating it as a general emergency. It's our business to maintain law and order, to see things don't get further out of control, and in the process we can show those PGR boys a thing or two."

He took up his clipboard and pen. "There are a still a million-and-one things to be done. Sit down, Salvador. You will need to take notes."

All at once Hernández felt more at ease. The rare use of his first name was an instant comfort. Also, he had a sense of having been taken into his chief's confidence, and he could fully empathise with his attitude. It was true enough that, in this kind of situation, they took on all the donkey-work while the glory and glamour went to the PGR.

Delgado's position was a curious one. He had the formal title of *Secretario de Seguridad Pública del Distrito Federal,* and below him were sixteen *Jefes de Sector,* one for each of the *delegaciones* into which the city was divided. As such, he presided over a fifty-nine thousand strong force, policing some twelve million people within a metropolitan area of 1,794 square kilometres, which had at least one robbery every five minutes and one murder every ninety minutes. His power was immense, his opportunities for self-aggrandisement almost unbounded.

Yet, in one important respect, his authority was severely limited. While his department had total control over policing the city in terms of traffic and combating common crime, it had no responsibility for investigating major criminal acts such as murder, kidnapping and extortion. That role, depending on the circumstances, belonged either to the National Attorney General's Office, *the Procuraduría General de la República* (PGR), or to the Office of the Federal District Attorney General, the *Procuraduría General de Justicia del Distrito Federal.*

Both of these law enforcement bodies had a huge force of plain-clothed detectives called *judiciales* who operated under the charge of a comandante, a subcomandante and various *Jefes de Grupo.* In this instance, one involving national security, it was a safe assumption that the PGR would automatically take command.

In fact, Delgado was already well aware of his subsidiary role. By telephone, President Pérez had advised him that he was putting the National Procurador General, José Rodríguez, in complete charge of the investigation. "He is on his way from Cuernavaca right now. Meanwhile, I am counting on you to give his department the fullest possible support."

In his interpretation of the word "support", Mexico City's police chief now chose to take the broadest possible view.

"Are you ready?" he asked Hernandez. "Right then." And as he spoke, he began to make a shorthand list of his own.

"One. The tower. Keep it sealed off until further notice, ready for the PGR, who will be sending in their forensic team as soon as possible. I want that area guarded with one hundred per cent efficiency.

"Two. The killer. Under no circumstances should his body be moved. Meanwhile, we need to establish his identity as quickly as possible. In this case, we can't wait for the PGR findings. The man may have accomplices who threaten other lives in our city. Make your own arrangements to get fingerprints and photographs, and have them rushed through to 'records' for immediate attention.

"Three. The park. We can advise the presidential guard it's free to stand down at its own discretion. But keep a unit at the killing area. The PGR will want the area sealed off, so that it can be carefully combed for bullets or fragments of shells.

"Four. *El Centro Medico Nacional*. Again, keep a unit there until *judiciales* arrive to gather evidence.

"Five. Witnesses. Get on to our men at the tower and make sure they hold onto anyone who may have seen anything. They will be required to give formal statements. The PGR will also want to interview our security guards who were at the castle. Be sure they don't go off duty. The same goes for the park. Hidalgo is in charge there. Have him detain all useful witnesses, including this man who first reported the crime." He checked his notes. "Ballantyne.

"Six. The media. No one— absolutely no one— is to talk to the Press or TV people. Any inquiries, and they are to be referred to me. Have you got all that?"

"*Sí, señor.*"

"Hmm! So, do you think that covers everything? Nothing, perhaps, that I may have overlooked?"

"No, *Jefe*. That seems really comprehensive."

The chief fixed him with a sardonic smile. "You know, Hernández, you're a very good officer in your way— hardworking, technically correct. But, bloody hell, you have a lot to learn if you're ever going to survive at a higher level."

Delgado leant back in his chair and tossed his clipboard onto the desk. "So much for all that official crap. Now let's get down to serious business. And don't take any more notes.

"What we've got here is a classic no-win situation. Think about it. Think, for example, about what happened after the Colosio assassination. The Tijuana police grabbed the killer of the presidential candidate and he duly confessed. Then the PGR took over, and all at once the local police were the villains. There was talk of negligence, and when the police chief disagreed with the PGR's lone-gunman conclusion, he was promptly bumped off. And even then people were saying he had been killed by corrupt members of his own force. Typical!

"And we are just as vulnerable now. A presidential guardsman got the killer, but what were our own security staff doing at the castle? How could an assassin get into the tower? And why were we not providing special protection for a VIP function in the park? These are the questions that are going to be asked - by the Press and by the PGR investigators. And as far as we're concerned, that's what all this is really about.

"We're talking about survival here, pure and simple. Like we saw at the *Plaza México* last Sunday, it can be fatal to turn your back on *el toro* when it is not totally subdued. We can't take anything for granted. We've got to stay ahead of the game, address these awkward questions *before* they are asked. Then maybe, just maybe, we can come up with some good answers.

"What this means, Hernández, is trying to keep one step ahead of the PGR. Follow your official instructions. But at the same time, get our men to take statements independently from all available witnesses. Also, I want a detailed report from our officers who were on duty at the castle at the time. They have got some explaining to do - most pointedly, just how a man armed with a rifle could have slipped through their security net. Any questions?"

"No, *Jefe.*"

"Right then. Get to it. I will want to see you again." He looked as his wrist-watch. "In twenty minutes. Also, I shall want all available officers to be in the operations room for a special briefing at 1 pm. No exceptions. This case takes precedence over all others. Oh yes, and you can pass on the word - all leave is cancelled indefinitely. Meanwhile, I've got urgent business to attend to."

As soon as Hernández had left, Delgado used his direct private line to the Santos Dumont headquarters of the *Procuraduría General de la República*. It was 1230 hours. He knew that the Procurador General would not yet have arrived from his Cuernavaca weekend retreat. But no matter. José Rodríguez was a *pistachio*-green political appointee. The key contact was the *de facto* chief investigator: Comandante Sebastián Fidel Barraza, the veteran operational chief of the

PGR.

Barraza was not yet in his office, but the call was switched through to his apartment in the exclusive Lomas suburb. It was time for Delgado to play the solicitous comrade-in-arms.

Salvador Hernández had entered the chief's office filled with apprehension. When he left, it was with a certain sense of awe. He could not, but admire Delgado's versatile mind. Undeniably, the man was tyrannical, moody, unpredictable. But whatever they might say about him, he could also be incredibly methodical, quick-thinking and incisive. And, in one important respect, he was predictable: he could always be relied upon to rise to a crisis.

Juan Delgado thrived on crisis. He had first revealed his potential in 1985 when Mexico City was shattered by an earthquake so powerful it set skyscrapers swaying as far north as Houston, Texas, 1,100 miles from its offshore epicentre. As a young officer, he had served with distinction in his leading of one of many small police units made responsible, in conjunction with the army, for the prevention of looting. His leadership qualities had been noted, and within nine years, he had become, at thirty-two, the capital's youngest ever *Jefe de Sector*.

At that time Mexico City faced the threat of terrorist activity in support of the 1994 peasant uprising in the impoverished southern state of Chiapas. The rebellion— by the self-styled Zapatista National Liberation Army— coincided with the formal start of the North American Free Trade Agreement, signed by the United States, Canada and Mexico, and heralded as the dawn of a new age of Mexican prosperity and modernisation. Swift, decisive action was imperative if economic confidence and a booming stock market was to be sustained.

In four days, the Mexican army and air force overwhelmed the ill-equipped insurgents in the hills and forests of Chiapas. Meanwhile, Delgado played a leading part in successfully organising counter-terrorism operations in the capital. With the crisis over, the problem of Mexico's huge rural underclass quickly faded from prominence. The stock market, having briefly plummeted, returned to boom conditions, and once again there was talk of the economy being poised on the brink of a bonanza in the light of Mexico's membership of NAFTA.

Briefly, Delgado had high hopes of promotion. But events conspired against him. Mexico was now thrown into turmoil by the assassination of Luis Donaldo Colosio Murrieta, the presidential candidate of the *Partido Revolucionario Institucional* (PRI), the monolithic party which had maintained a vice-like grip on Mexican government for six-and-a-half decades. Violent demonstrations were staged far and wide, since it was popularly believed that PRI hardliners had conspired to have Colosio killed because he had pledged political reform and the investigation of powerful figures suspected of graft and corruption.

Miraculously, aided perhaps by the mysterious breakdown of vote-tallying computers, a bitterly fought election campaign ended in August 1994, with yet another victory for the seemingly indestructible PRI and its substituted presidential candidate, Ernesto Zedillo Ponce de León. And in December, when a new government was formed, PRI supporters could look back contentedly on a six-year term which had seen free-market reforms bring enormous benefits to many of the middle class, and boost the ranks of the super-rich. Mexico was now fourth in the world in its number of billionaires, among them the outgoing president, Salinas de Gortari, and not least his playboy brother Raul, who had secretly salted away some $100 million in foreign bank accounts.

Subsequently, the free-market policies of Salinas were maintained by President Zedillo, an American-orientated technocrat and economist. By now, the richest ten per cent of Mexicans had boosted their ownership of the nation's wealth to sxty percent. But all the while, the impoverished majority were growing poorer and the crime rate was soaring. Most especially, in the wake of the NAFTA agreement, drug-trafficking was expanding apace as Mexican traders were allowed free access to America's southern borders, with commercial traffic rising so sharply that US customs officials were searching only about one of every ten vehicles crossing the frontier, and just a fraction of cargo containers.

By the late 1990s, the Mexicans had usurped the Colombians as the world's leading narcotics traffickers, a switch largely engineered by drug baron Amado Carrillo Fuentes who had set up the Juarez cartel, a vast distribution network that supplied up to a third of all cocaine consumed in the United States. In 1997, Fuentes died in a Mexico City hospital from an overdose of anaesthesia administered— allegedly on payment by Columbians— during major plastic surgery to alter his appearance. But then, after a bloody turf war with its Tijuana-based rivals, the Juarez cartel re-established its dominant position, aided in no small part by the protection of bribed senior policemen and politicians.

Meanwhile, to his dismay, Delgado had not been rewarded for his services to the establishment. Instead, in the wake of a new wave of kidnappings, killings and drug scandals, President Zedillo chose to allay public anxiety by assigning an army officer, Brigadier General Enrique Salgado Cordero, to take control of Mexico City's demoralised police force. In turn, Salgado Cordero installed military officers in each of the top fifteen commands at police headquarters.

Several years later, after a group of army colonels had been found guilty of involvement in cocaine retailing operations, there was a reversal of policy. Experienced civilian law enforcement officers were put back in command. But still Delgado was denied the highest office, and he feared that his ambitions were doomed to failure when, on July 2, 2000, the opposition National Action Party (PAN) achieved the momentous and hugely popular election victory that ended 71 years of continuous PRI rule.

The new president, PAN leader Vicente Fox Quesada, promised to eradicate corruption and tackle the cross-border drug trade more forcefully. So, in turn, would his successor, Felipe de Jesus Calderon Hinojoa of the PRD (Party of the Democratic Revolution). But, for all their good intentions and determined efforts, drug-running would eventually flourish more strongly and more violently than ever, and there was to be no reduction in Mexico City's crime rate. Finally, in response to public demand, there was a drastic shake-up in police forces, and, at last, to Delgado fell the fattest plum of all: the coveted power-base of Mexico City's Chief of Police, a modestly paid position, but one which, by way of backhanders, automatically assured him millionaire status.

Just as every Mexican president begins his term with promises of a major campaign against graft and corruption, so Delgado took office with the announcement of a relentless war to be waged against crime. Under his vigorous, often ruthless leadership, the city police force moved into overdrive. More patrol cars were put onto the streets and, following the American pattern, he made far greater use of decoy patrols, with officers disguised as soft touches for muggers and bag-snatchers, and as likely customers for drug-pushers.

In his first half-year of office, a record number of arrests were made, and month-by-month statistics showed a steady decline in new offences. There were critics who complained that his dragnet approach trapped only small-time operators and dangerously aggravated the problem of overcrowded prisons. But they were an insignificant minority. The fact remained that he had made Mexico City a safer place to live, and in so doing he had endeared himself to the city's burgeoning middle classes.

All the while, General Delgado— he chose to style himself "General", though he had no military background— was acquiring powerful friends, and not inconspicuous wealth. Ultimately, his lifestyle came to be compared with that of Arturo Durazo Moreno, Mexico City's police chief during the presidency of José López Portillo (1976-82).

Remarkably, Durazo, on an official salary of $65 a week, had contrived to funnel more than $600 million into Swiss bank accounts. Overtly, he also acquired a $2.5 million estate outside Mexico City, complete with heliport, private racetrack, casino, shooting range and artificial lakes, plus a mansion on the Pacific Coast of such columned splendour it was dubbed the Parthenon.

Delgado was not quite in that class; at least not as far as the public could judge, for unlike Moreno he had never invited television cameras into his homes. But he was certainly a multi-millionaire, with prospects of achieving billionaire status if he remained in office throughout the current term of President Enrique Perez.

Now, what most concerned Delgado, was securing his position of power and prestige. The past six months had been severely damaging for his reputation, specifically because his *preventiva* forces had failed dismally to forestall outbreaks of violence during the mass demonstrations in the wake of a severe recession which had thrown more than a million people out of work. Three prominent politicians had been murdered in Mexico City, the scene of the worst riots, and though numerous suspects had been arrested by the PGR, none had been convicted.

It could be argued that the *Procuraduría* was equally,

if not more, responsible for that failure. But this was no consolation for Delgado. The PGR had a lower profile, but far greater political pull. And at any time, he realised, he could be made the scapegoat for their failings. Thus, on Sunday, January 25, all his actions were geared to survival.

When Salvador Hernández was summoned back to Delgado's office, he was not surprised to find a third officer in the room. Seated at one end of the long desk was Coronel Ignacio Torres, a man of only medium height, but with a bulging physique that accurately suggested years of body-building work. His features— a balding head, hollow cheekbones and narrow, darting eyes— seemed misplaced on such a burly frame, and the man's whole appearance contrasted dramatically with the slim and dapper figure of his *Jefe.*

For the past three years, Torres had served as Delgado's trusted aide. Only loyalty to the chief could explain his rank. Unlike his elder brother, Ernesto, now chief of police in Acapulco, he had never rated highly in examinations to evaluate promotion candidates, had never distinguished himself when in charge of an investigation of his own. He was strictly a man of action dependent on the thinking of others, and, though he never knew it, he was known throughout the force as *"El Robot"*

On entering, Hernández acknowledged Torres' presence with a cursory nod. Then, at the invitation of Delgado, he took an upright wooden chair at the opposite end of the desk. Leaning back in his leather-cushioned chair, the chief now proceeded to talk directly to him as though they alone were in the room.

"Before we go ahead, I want to put you straight on a few things. Firstly, as you already know, *El Presidente* has instructed we give the PGR our fullest support in their investigation of today's killings. He wants our maximum effort. Well, we're going give it even more than that. Because this is the biggest, most important case we've ever experienced.

"The killing of a government minister makes it big enough. But the murder of ambassador Tunaman gives it a whole new dimension. Sooner or later, we are going to have the world's press on our doorstep, and it's up to us to show them that we have a police force second to none.

"Unfortunately, it's not our job to investigate this

crime. But we are responsible for maintaining law and order, and so I am putting all our *tránsito* and *preventiva* forces on full alert. The *jefes de sector* have been instructed accordingly. We want no further outrages while the eyes of the world are upon us. Therefore, there will be maximum security at all public buildings. All baggage is to be thoroughly searched, and anyone behaving suspiciously is to be held for questioning. The same applies on the roads. The *tránsito* police will not merely book traffic offenders, but also search their vehicles. In the process, anything might turn up, even something with bearing on the killings in the park.

"Anyway, the procedure is this. Torres will be responsible for interrogating anyone arrested in this process. And he will be working closely with me on analysing and following up information obtained. You, Hernández, will be responsible for coordinating all the units and for assembling any information obtained, ready for our examination. The rest I will be outlining in detail in the operations room. Any questions?"

Hernández had none. It was just as he had expected. As usual, Torres was going to be the chief's right-hand man - and that suited him fine. He preferred a subsidiary role. Unlike Delgado and Torres, he was a contented family man whose love for his wife and children transcended professional ambition. Specifically, he saw the situation as being too high-profile for his tastes. There would be great kudos in a successful conclusion; also a danger of heads rolling in the event of failure. He favoured a back-seat ride.

Delgado looked at the clock on the wall. It was 1259 hours. He stood up, his clipboard clutched to his side. "Okay, then, let's get this show on the road." To Hernández, he seemed positively exuberant, a man galvanised by a new sense of purpose.

When they entered, the Operations Room was crowded with more than sixty men and women, some in uniform, others in assorted civilian gear for undercover duties. Unusually, however, the assembled officers had not all taken their seats in readiness. A large number were standing on one side of the room, huddled in silence around a television set.

Flanked by his two *coronels,* General Delgado strode up to them. "All right then," he said loudly. "What's the big attraction?"

The semicircle parted to let the chief through. A

woman was talking. As he saw on the screen, it was Isabel del Río, seated behind a desk, and, as always, immaculately groomed and looking strikingly elegant in a pink jacket with a deep V-neck framing her pearls. The newsreader had once been voted in a TV magazine poll as "the male viewers' favourite fantasy". On this occasion, however, it was the words, not the body, that commanded attention.

"At this stage," she continued. "The police say that they are unable to confirm these details. However, from our contact within *el Centro Medico Nacional*, we are able to reveal that Finance Minister Martínez died before reaching hospital, the fourth victim of this cold-blooded shooting.

"What exactly happened in Chapultepec Park this afternoon? For a full-length report watch Channel 13's *24 Horas'* show at seven o'clock. At that time, we hope to bring you a complete reconstruction of the crime of the century. An interview with an eyewitness, plus exclusive pictures of all the murders. And now for the rest of the news..."

Delgado hit the off-switch. "Like hell they will," he snapped. "Any pictures are vital to the PGR's inquiry, and anyone who took them is a material witness guilty of suppressing evidence."

He turned to *El Robot*. "Torres, I want you to get over to the TV studios right away. Confiscate all pictures and any copies they may have. And arrest the *cabrón* who took them."

CHAPTER 8

When ordinary Mexican citizens first heard of the killings in Chapultepec Park, their shock could be measured on three distinct levels. Highest on a Richter-style scale was the shock reaction to the death of Finance Minister Roberto Martínez, a young and unusually popular politician who had seemed destined for a long and brilliant career. Secondly, there was horror at the gunning-down of an innocent child and mother while celebrating a birthday in true Mexican style. Lastly, and decidedly least, there was dismay that Mexico City should have been singled out for the assassination of a prominent world figure.

Over the past six months, everyone had been made aware that a highly distinguished diplomat held the position of Turkish ambassador to Mexico. The achievements of Kemal Tunaman as an international peacemaker had rarely been out of the news. The fact remained, however, that European politics were of scant interest to the average Mexican citizen. Also, Señor Tunaman had made no personal impression on their lives. He was indeed *El Fantasma*, a man whose spectacular appearances were only to be made on the other side of the world.

Nonetheless, General Juan Delgado was absolutely right in his assessment. The killing of ambassador Tunaman did give the multiple crime a whole new dimension. Via eight satellites, Cable News Network sprayed the story over every continent, and the shock waves rebounded progressively according to variations in Greenwich Mean Time. Within twenty-four hours, just as Delgado anticipated, it would bring the world's press to his door— a movement which began on Sunday afternoon with the instant dispatch of reporters and television teams from North, Central and South America, and which mounted into a stampede as pressmen scrambled for the first Monday morning flights out of European capitals.

President Enrique Pérez of Mexico was the first to make an official statement to the media. At 1330 hours, shortly after it had been issued for general release by his Press Secretary, he personally delivered the statement to a select group of television crews invited into his study at *Los Pinos*, the yellow-stone presidential residence which stands almost at the edge of Chapultepec Park, on the western side of the *Molino Del Rey* and directly opposite the great statue of Mexico's first twentieth-century president, Francisco Madero.

Seated at his desk, on which he rested his tightly entwined hands, *El Presidente* spoke in slowly measured funereal tones: "Today, with the death of our Minister of Finance, Secretario Roberto Martínez, Mexico has been cruelly deprived of one of her finest sons, a young man of prodigious industry and talent, a public servant of infinite promise, and, above all, a patriot of the highest integrity and honour. On this saddest of days, I mourn not only the loss of an eminent colleague, but also the loss of a greatly valued personal friend. My heart at this time of sorrow goes out to Señora Martínez and her two lovely children.

"Also, I wish to express my deepest and most sincere condolences to Doña Castillo de Tunaman, who has suffered the most grievous tragedy. In the short time I knew him, I came to recognise ambassador Tunaman as a man of extraordinary modesty, charm and intellect. I cannot understand how any human being could have assassinated such a perfect gentleman, who was seeking peace and understanding in a free world. I cannot say any more. I am too filled with emotion."

In the following hour, glowing tributes to Kemal Tunaman were delivered on television in New York by the U.N. Secretary-General, and in Washington by newly elected U.S. President Carmichael. The latter talked of the irony of political assassination: "Lincoln, Gandhi, Kennedy, Martin Luther King, Sadat, Rabin ... so often it claims men of goodness rather than of evil."

In London, on the nine o'clock news, the British Prime Minister declared: "This monstrous act has taken from us a wise and valiant man, and the loss to European stability is incalculable. We can now best honour his memory by striving to preserve the peace he toiled so hard to secure."

Similar sentiments were echoed on radio and television in Paris, Brussels and Berlin. In every case, these tributes were significantly different from that delivered by President Pérez. They focussed almost exclusively on the grievous loss of ambassador Tunaman, with only a passing mention of the death of a fledgling Mexican minister.

In Athens, Istanbul and Ankara, the timing allowed only late-night newsflashes interrupting scheduled programmes. There, the following day, the death of Tunaman would arouse the most emotional expressions of grief and consternation.

A significant measure of that grief came when the Greek Prime Minister, Christos Andriopoulou, called his Turkish counterpart on their hotline to convey his heartfelt condolences. Only six months earlier, the two men had been refusing to speak to one another. Now they were united in their sense of loss. However, although Mr. Andriopoulou meant well, his parting message to Premier Selim Suman of Turkey was not altogether diplomatic. "You will be pleased to know I have issued an order for the Greek flag to be flown at half-mast. It will be the first time a Turkish citizen has been so honoured."

Early in the morning, on Monday, January 26, the blue-and-white flag of Greece was lowered to half-mast above the Parliament building on the east side of Athens' Syntagma (Constitution) Square. But it was not the first. On the other side of the world, a Greek flag had been set at half-mast on Sunday mid-afternoon. This flag hung limply above the *Prometheus*, a sleek sixty-eight-metre, four-hundred-ton mega-yacht that was anchored in the great natural harbour of Charlotte Amalie on the south shore of the U.S. Virgin island of St. Thomas.

Powered by three gas turbine engines and capable of a maximum speed of seventy knots, the *Prometheus* was one of the most sophisticated turbo-diesel yachts in the world, an ocean-going vessel with the aspect of a gigantic powerboat. And complimenting its structural extravagance was a twelve-man crew whose workload was minimised by two onboard computer systems, one for navigation, the other controlling the engines and three water jets.

The *Prometheus* was the floating home of Stavros Stephanopoulos. It had been built on behalf of French and Italian industrialists who had combined to make a corporate challenge for the Blue Riband, the fastest sea crossing of the Atlantic. When their bid failed, the Greek shipping magnate

86

had bought the three-year-old yacht at two-thirds of its original $30 million cost.

Unknown to the shipbrokers, the hard-bargaining Stavros had been prepared to pay much more. Two years ago, a severe heart attack had made him acutely aware of his own mortality. Since then, with 'health before wealth' as his guiding slogan, the sixty-year-old Greek tycoon had ruthlessly redesigned his lifestyle in pursuit of his physical well-being and personal happiness. The *Prometheus* exactly met the requirements of this new design.

Stephanopoulos had long been one of the most respected and influential figures in Athenian society. Following the OPEC oil embargo crisis of 1973, he had diversified his business interests, acquiring a publishing empire composed of two national dailies and four magazines, plus a hi-tech printing complex outside Athens and a large stake in commercial television. His wealth multiplied apace, but his health suffered alarmingly because of his stubborn refusal to delegate operational control of his varied enterprises.

The Greek's lifestyle then changed dramatically after he had been rushed to England's Papworth Hospital for quadruple heart bypass surgery. Subsequently, on leaving hospital for a period of convalescence— cruising in the Mediterranean, the Aegean and then the Caribbean— he took with him one of the two physiotherapists who had been attending him. Jennifer Morrow was a buxom Australian blonde, twenty-five-years-old, and exuding a warmth and vitality that was totally lacking in her frail, prematurely aged employer. Yet three months later, seduced by a new exotic lifestyle, she had become his mistress.

She was by no means the first. Stephanopoulos was a notorious womaniser, and after thirty-six years of storm-wreaked conjugal life, his long-suffering Greek wife had come to bear his infidelities with quiet dignity. "Eventually he always returns to me," Elena would say to her closest friends. Quite rightly, she judged that he had no intention of allowing a casual sexual adventure to destroy his cherished family life. But this time it was different. Stavros, the new-born hypochondriac, had no plans to return to smog-ridden Athens. Henceforth he would conduct his business from warm, invigorating climes.

The *Prometheus* now served as his permanent home and office. It had all the comforts of a private residence. At the same time, it was a high-tech control centre, affording instant communication by satellite-linked phone and telex with employees who were on alert for his call twenty-four hours a day. But, above all, Stephanopoulos was attracted by its speed. He had never ventured onto an aircraft since his father's death in an air crash twenty years ago. Now, at any time, he could comfortably move between the new and old worlds within three days.

Such a journey, however, was far from his mind when the *Prometheus* dropped anchor at Charlotte Amalie. On that day, January 24, the Greek went ashore with his nubile paramour, shopping in the quaint alleyways of the duty-free port and then renting a mini-Moke to explore the island. Like all vehicles in the U.S. Virgins, their jeep-style car had a registration plate bearing the legend "American Paradise", and soon they had come to agree with that claim.

Three miles north, on the opposite side of the island, beyond the dividing range of mountain peaks, they stopped at the exquisite, heart-shaped Magens Bay for Stavros' mandatory daily swim. Except for one family picnicking in the shade of palms, the white-sanded beach was deserted, and all was idyllic tranquility.

For a while they lazed together on a twin-Lilo, and as they floated on the motionless, sapphire waters, watching majestic sea hawks gliding silently overhead, Stavros remarked that not even a financial crisis of the first magnitude could induce him to face another European winter. They would cruise in the Caribbean waters for another three months, and then head back to his beloved Aegean in the spring.

Stephanopoulos was now unrecognisable as the potbellied pasty-faced little man who had left Papworth Hospital seven months before. Slim, bronzed and relaxed, he owed his condition entirely to the influence of his strong-willed companion who had taken control of his diet, and given him the incentive to exercise more and more to increase his physical stamina.

Most importantly, Jennifer had changed his mental attitude. He no longer hyperventilated, and for the first time in his life he did not allow stressful commercial considerations to dominate the mind. In Athens, his newspaper chiefs now had full editorial control, being judged solely on their circulation figures. And in all enterprises requiring his personal presence, he was content to be represented by his only son,

Nicholas.

The woman who had worked this metamorphosis was unlike any the Greek had known before. Miss Morrow, he found, was completely devoid of artifice, or what he called womanly wiles. Nothing was hidden. She was a straight-talking, bullshit-free Aussie, who made no pretence about her feelings or ambitions.

Initially, not realising that such a creature existed, Stavros had followed his standard strategy for luring a desirable woman into his bed. In conversation, he suppressed his natural inclination to talk about himself, about his own interests and views. For days he made her the main focus of attention, encouraged her to talk about herself and listened attentively. Then came the *coup de grace*: the intimate candlelit supper, with food, wine, flowers and music all artfully designed to captivate the senses.

The Greek's final move was invariably the same. He had a little gift to mark the occasion - always an expensive piece of jewellery, and usually a diamond necklace, which he would offer to fasten and so make the first physical contact. Then came his declaration of love, which would be met either with an encouraging or politely discouraging response.

But Jennifer's reaction had been something else. She threw back her head and roared with laughter. "Oh, Stavvy! You are a funny man. You sound just like something out of a Noel Coward play. Come off it now. I know you better than that. If you want to have sex, why don't you say so? It's not really your style, all this pussyfooting around."

Later that night, Stavros ventured to ask if she loved him. Her reply was no less blunt and straight to the point. She did not love anyone, and she possibly never would, in terms of being overwhelmed by romantic illusions, a condition that seemed to her to verge on a kind of temporary sickness. But she did love his lifestyle and his wealth. She also enjoyed his worldly company, and she suspected they could both give each other what they wanted.

"And what is it you want?" Stavros asked.

Jennifer grinned. "Just children, Stavvy. Lots of them. But with the guarantee I can enjoy bringing them up in an atmosphere of total security."

At that moment Stavros could not believe his good fortune. In the beginning, he had been attracted only by her youthful freshness and energy. He valued her as a rejuvenating influence, and he wanted her as a conquest to recharge his flagging ego. But now he adored her and saw her in a new light, as the perfect marriage partner.

It was enough that Jennifer was physically attractive, and had a blazing honesty that, for the first time, made him feel completely relaxed and not remotely threatened in a woman's company. But now there was this huge bonus. It turned out that she wanted exactly what he had always wanted: the emotionally rewarding experience of raising a large brood.

As he well knew, it was not Elena's fault that she had failed him in that respect. She had given him a beautiful daughter and, more importantly, an extraordinary son. The fact remained that their marriage had never been the same after the breech birth of Nicholas. The ordeal had left her frigid, ever conscious of the doctor's warning against having more children.

Stavros could sympathise with her physical condition. He could accept, too, that she no longer loved him. What he could not understand was her stubbornly entrenched position as a matriarch. She did not want him for himself, but she would not release him from his role as a husband and father-figure. It was as though she saw her entire existence in terms of a mother at centre stage in a play that required all other family members to remain firmly in their place.

Even now, when he was offering a multi-million dollar divorce settlement, plus full title to their Athenian home, Elena Stephanopoulos was not surrendering her status without a fight. It offended his shrewd business sense. By delaying the divorce proceedings, she was only further enriching the lawyers in a case where the ultimate outcome was certain. At the very latest, he was assured, the divorce would be finalised by October.

In the circumstances, Jennifer was already wearing an engagement ring, and during their brief call at Charlotte Amalie they had begun to make wedding plans. After a summer cruise in the Aegean, they would head for Australia, meet Jenny's parents in Adelaide and marry sometime around Christmas. If, by that time, the new Mrs Stephanopoulos was pregnant, they would seek a permanent home overlooking Sydney harbour. They would keep the *Prometheus* to sail north during the few colder months of the year, and gradually Stavros would release control of his empire to Nicholas, his only son and heir.

And then, all at once, their dream world fell apart.

On board the *Prometheus*, three crew members shared the duty of manning the communications room, and keeping a round-the-clock check on video-recorded news and business reports, with special attention to events liable to affect stock market moves. On January 25, at 1330 hours local time, the duty-officer recorded CNN's first report of the killings in Mexico City.

A few minutes later, the videotape was replayed. As Stavros listened to the American newscaster, Jennifer looked across, and immediately she was reminded of the pale and drawn old man she had first encountered at Papworth Hospital. It was as though the clock had suddenly been turned back seven months. The face was now bronzed, but the expression was one of overwhelming pain and despair.

At the end of the bulletin, Jennifer switched off the video and cradled his head against her breasts. The Greek was sobbing uncontrollably, like a child. "Oh Georgios! My Georgios!" he cried.

Eventually Stavros regained his composure, and the mind took over from the heart. That mind was now racing as in stress-filled days of old. He was the head of the family. It was his responsibility to take control. But what was he to do? How could he help Nicholas get over the news that he no longer had a wife and son? And what about Elena? Without him, she could never cope with the loss.

He remembered how long it had taken Elena to come to terms with Nicholas' marriage. What was it she used to say - those words of Sophocles about sons being the anchor of a mother's life? She looked upon her only son as a god; no woman was good enough for him, and certainly not a Turk. But then, in time, she had become captivated by Georgios' irresistible innocence and charm. She saw him as a second son, and now that anchor too was lost.

It was, Stavros recognised, a time for responsible action. And he knew automatically where his duty lay. He buzzed the ship's captain on the intercom. "Milo, prepare to get under way as soon as possible. We're going to Piraeus. At maximum speed."

At that moment, no less instinctively, Jennifer realised their dream was ended. The real world of Stephanopoulos had been reactivated, a world to which she could never belong.

That afternoon, as the *Prometheus* powered away from Charlotte Amalie, its computers humming loudly above the whine of its turbines, Miss Morrow gave one last wave from the waterfront. It had been her suggestion that she should remain behind. "This tragedy is strictly a family affair," she had said. "It would only make matters worse if I appeared on the scene." And Stavros had had to agree.

By her own choice, Jennifer had booked into the Gramboko, a homely, inexpensive hotel on the south shore, a mile or so from the town centre. The agreed plan was simple: Stavros would keep regularly in touch by telephone, and return as soon as the family crisis was over. But she knew better than to wait, and already she was thinking about going back to Australia.

Two days later, her plans were resolved. From St Thomas' Harry S. Truman Airport, she flew via San Juan to New York. Then, during a stopover with friends, she booked a flight to Australia. Through influential contacts, she had secured a nursing position at the Royal Children's Hospital in Melbourne.

As for Stavros, Jennifer was no sooner out of sight than out of mind. For the first time since his heart attack, the Greek was not thinking about his own welfare and interests. All his thoughts were about his family in Athens, and about Nicholas, above all else.

His feelings for Nicholas transcended paternal love. He positively idolised him, and to his mind, no man was ever blessed with a finer son. Nicky had wit and charm and maturity far beyond his thirty-one years. More than that, he seemed to be one of life's born winners, succeeding in every field of endeavour: as a scholar, an athlete, a family man, and more lately, as a lawyer-businessman.

But now? Stavros doubted that even Nicholas, for all his strength of character, would be able to adjust to the loss of the two people he valued most in all the world. Certainly, he could not expect his son to continue overseeing his huge commercial interests in Athens. He would have to take complete command again.

All this was racing through his mind as the *Prometheus* sliced across the Atlantic on its direct, computerised course to the Strait of Gibraltar. And one thing made his torment all the greater. He could not make contact with Nicholas on the satellite-linked phone.

Before leaving Charlotte Amalie, Stavros had tried to call Nicholas at his Kolonaki apartment on the southern slope of Mt. Lykabettus. His son was not at home, but as always he had left a message as to when and where he could be reached. The answering machine said, "Gone for run. Back by 2215 hours." This was not unusual. Three times a week, deterred only by snow or ice, Nicholas ran over the spiralling road of Lykabettus, covering three miles in fast and slow intervals.

In the meantime, Stavros rang his own home in Ekali, some thirteen miles north of central Athens. When a maid answered, he asked to speak to his daughter, Christina, rightly judging that she was tough enough to take the news without breaking down. "Oh no," she cried. "Not Georgios, too." Then, after a pause, she remarked, "You realise, *patera*, this could have terrible political consequences."

Stavros sighed. Christina would never change. A left-wing radical since her Athens University days, she lived and breathed politics, and maintained such an irrational anti-Turkish stance that she had even refused to attend her brother's wedding.

"Damn the politics, Christina. Think of Nicholas and your mother for a moment. I want you to tell her as gently as you can. And tell her I'm coming home as fast as possible."

At 2215 hours Athenian time, Stavros telephoned Nicholas' apartment again. The machine's answer was the same as before. He tried again fifteen minutes later. Still only the old recorded message.

Where was he? It was possible that he could have gone for a meal at his favourite restaurant in Kolonaki Square. Especially since he was currently living on his own. But then again, he would have needed first to go home for a shower and change of clothes. Could he have for once forgotten to leave an updated message?

His anxiety mounting, Stavros telephoned the restaurant. No, they had not seen Nicholas all day. At 2245 hours he rang the apartment a fourth time; still the same message: "Back by 2215 hours." Now he was truly alarmed. He called the Kolonaki police station.

The duty sergeant thought it madness to be worrying about a young man who had been missing for no more than half an hour. But he could ill-afford to express his opinion to this particular caller. "Yes, of course, Mr Stephanopoulos. We will immediately send an officer round to your son's apartment."

"Thank you," said Stavros. "I'll check back with you in half an hour." Then, he added an afterthought, "Oh yes, and if necessary your men should force an entry. For all we know, my son may be at home and unable to answer."

This now was the nightmare scenario, as Stavros allowed his imagination to run riot: that his son, having returned home from his run and heard the news on the television, had then collapsed with shock or even chosen to end his own life. He could think of no other explanation to fit the facts.

CHAPTER 9

Within two hours of the multiple murders in Chapultepec Park, it had become clear that, in terms of international interest, the killing of Kemal Tunaman was Mexico City's biggest crime story in six decades. The last comparable crime had occurred in August 1940, when a Stalinist assassin plunged an ice axe into the head of Leon Trotsky at his fortified villa in Coyoacán.

For Comandante Sebastián Fidel Barraza, it could not have come at a more ironic time. At the end of February, he was due to retire after twenty years' distinguished service in the office of the *Procuraduría General de la República*. Now, at the indirect request of President Pérez, he had reluctantly agreed to postpone his departure, if necessary, until the investigation of the so-called crime of the century had been completed.

A decade ago, in his ambition-driven prime, Barraza would have welcomed such a challenge. But now he accepted it with certain misgivings. In this instance, he knew, he would be propping up a young, newly appointed Procurador General who owed his position to powerful family connections, and who had no useful skills to contribute to the investigation. If the case was satisfactorily concluded, he could expect to see the P.G. reap the greater glory. If not, he would be the one held primarily responsible.

Barraza was not accustomed to failure. He had first come to prominence as a *jefe de grupo* leading the deputy attorney general's campaign against drug trafficking. Promotion had followed swiftly, albeit in part by circumstances of chance. One such circumstance came when the 1985 earthquake led to the discovery of tortured bodies amid the ruins of the headquarters of the Procuraduría General de Justicia del Distrito Federal. The federal attorney general was forced to admit that tortures had taken place. Subsequently, two senior officers were prematurely retired and a new law, greeted with much public scepticism, banned the use of torture.

The vacancies led to Barraza's transfer to the PGR, and his advancement was aided again, in 1994, by the failure of his superiors to apprehend the kidnappers who had successfully demanded a multi-million dollar ransom for Alfredo Harp Helú, a billionaire banker and close friend of President Salinas. Subsequently, as Subcomandante and then Comandante, he had figured in a number of spectacular, highly publicised successes - most notably in September, 2005, when three *guaruras* were shot dead after their kidnapping of the eldest son of bank president Miguel Bernal Garcia.

The case typified Barraza's ruthless efficiency. While stalling over the payment of a ransom, he had launched an unprecedented assault on the criminal underworld: a round-up that saw more than a hundred known villains hauled in for questioning. His *judiciales* were renowned for their conduct of gruelling, if not brutal, interrogations, and ultimately they found their informer. As a result, the kidnappers were ambushed in a warehouse on the outskirts of Mexico City. They surrendered their hostage in exchange for their lives. Then, on emerging into the open, they were mowed down by some sixty officers armed with submachine guns.

The following day, Comandante Barraza, standing beside colander-like bodies laid out for the benefit of television cameramen, delivered his message: that this was the inevitable fate of all men who sought to profit by kidnapping and extortion. The deterrent effect was considerable - not one more noteworthy case of kidnapping in the remainder of the year.

That was a rare television appearance by Barraza. Unlike Police Chief Delgado, he normally shunned personal publicity. "Detection— not acting— is my business," he would say. "I ask to be judged only on results."

But there were more specific reasons for Barraza's calculated reserve. For one thing, he was conscious of his physical shortcomings: only five feet, five inches tall in his platform shoes, and so unpleasantly bulbous-eyed he felt the need to wear dark-tinted spectacles at all times.

More significantly, however, he avoided Press interviews because he did not wish to discuss his *modus operandi*. To him the cliché, familiarity breeds contempt, was the truest maxim of all. No self-respecting conjuror explained his methods, and in the case of Barraza, those methods did not always bear close examination.

Nevertheless, the fact remained that he was a truly outstanding investigator. He had a brilliant, analytical mind and enormous powers of concentration, and— most unusually for a Mexican— he lived for work rather than vice versa.

It was at 1235 hours on Sunday, immediately after receiving a call from Police Chief Delgado, that Barraza had been contacted at home by Procurador General José Rodríguez. The new political appointee spoke gushingly about how much he would appreciate his assistance. And he left the Comandante without any option when he added, "Moreover, *El Presidente* has personally requested that I take advantage of your expertise."

By 1300 hours, shortly before the Press and television reporters began to swarm, Barraza was secure in his office on the second floor of the PGR headquarters. Temporarily at least, he could take total command of the investigation while the Procurador General gave priority to his responsibility for public relations. He worked fast to make the most of his freedom.

Within forty-five minutes, courtesy of Delgado's office, the Comandante had on his desk a dog-eared red folder that gave him the vital launch pad for his investigation. The police file was labelled RAMÍREZ, Manuel, No. 932857, and it recorded a history of petty juvenile crime.

Barely ninety minutes after the Chapultepec murders, a computerised fingerprint check at the Criminal Records Office had produced a positive identification of Ramírez as the young man who had been killed in *La Torre del Caballero Alto*. Subsequently, pictures of the man had been matched with the mugshot in the numbered police file.

Photocopies of the file were now distributed in the PGR operations room at a meeting attended by more than forty *judiciales*. Most of those present were familiar with Barraza's introductory pep talk. "Remember my three golden objectives in a major homicide inquiry: *Quién? Cómo? Por qué?*

"Our most immediate task is establishing the *Who*. By the time you have finished, I expect to know absolutely everything about this Ramírez, from the day of his birth to the moment of his death. I want to know about his family, his friends, and criminal associates, about his politics, and— most importantly— about his precise movements in the weeks and

97

days prior to the killings.

"Was he operating alone? To answer that key question we will need to focus on the *How* and the *Why*. How did he get into the tower? How did he know the precise time and place of a private birthday party? And why did he do it? What was his motive?

"One final point. Under no circumstances is anyone to discuss this investigation with people from the media... or with anyone else for that matter. Until this office has released a formal statement, the position remains that we simply have a prime suspect— as yet unnamed— and are seeking out persons who might be able to assist in our inquiries."

Senior officers now fully expected their Comandante to trot out his usual "quality out of quantity" maxim. It was his favourite theme: that the more information obtained, the more likely some telltale fact was likely to be uncovered. No detail was to be considered too trivial for inclusion in reports; for, as proven so often in the past, he had a rare gift for panning through a morass of information and isolating some unsuspected nugget of gold.

But this time there was no such talk. Barraza was in a hurry, recognising the need to advance swiftly while the trail was still clearly marked. The *judiciales* were split into ten separate groups, each with a specific field of investigation, and dispatched immediately.

Meanwhile, in the Comandante's office, the stacks of printed matter were already beginning to mushroom: statements by witnesses and by security guards in the castle; preliminary reports from the forensic laboratory and ballistics department; an inventory of all items recovered from the tower; scene-of-the-crime photographs of the murder victims, of the alleged assassin and of important objects discovered, the prime exhibits being one high-powered rifle with telescopic sights and five spent cartridge cases found by the turret wall on the west side.

An interim report from the ballistics department identified the gun as an American M-21 7.62-calibre self-loading sniper's rifle - a weapon not available in gun shops, but manufactured almost exclusively for the U.S. Army. Its magazine could hold up to twenty rounds of precision-made 190-grain bullets, which were fired at a velocity of 2,800 ft/sec, and the rifle was fitted with a Weaver telescopic sight, which had a variable magnification of four to sixteen, depending on visibility conditions. Though the weapon had a maximum range of two-and-a-half miles, it could only be fired with reasonable accuracy up to a thousand yards. The M-21 found in the tower had its sight set on twelve, suggesting that a highly skilled rifleman had allowed for the hazy conditions.

The identification of this rifle as the murder weapon had been confirmed by a test-shooting which had matched the rifling marks etched into the surface of trial bullets with bullets recovered from the crime scene in the park.

Most importantly, the Criminal Records Office had confirmed that the fingerprints taken from the rifle, and from the alleged assassin, matched those on file under the name of Manuel Ramírez. In addition, there was a transcript of tape-recorded observations made by the PGR pathologist while carrying out an external examination of the body found in the tower.

This preliminary examination was conducted after all of Manuel's clothing had been carefully removed and stored in separate plastic bags for detailed scrutiny. The results were largely negative: no bruises or debris beneath the fingernails to suggest a struggle; no needle marks indicative of drug-taking. However, swabs taken from the nostrils had revealed traces of cocaine.

The cause of death was self-evident: a bullet hole drilled clear through the upper skull. As already established by forensics, there were powder burns around the entrance wound, slightly above and between the eyes. This, together with the huge gaping exit wound at the back of the head, indicated the man had been shot at very close range. More could only be learnt by a full post-mortem dissection.

For one hour now, Procurador General José Rodríguez had observed every step of the investigation being carried out in his name. He found it fascinating. As an attorney, he had appeared in a number of murder trials. But this was a novel experience. For the first time he was witnessing a murder case in embryo, working forwards rather than backwards through the gradually mounting evidence. And so far he was impressed.

Already he was congratulating Barraza on the progress being made, and now he invited him into his office for a little "celebratory drink". He poured himself a straight whisky. Barraza, who never drank spirits, settled for a plain tomato

99

juice.

Up to this point, by necessity, Rodríguez had played a subsidiary role while police procedures took their course. Now, seated behind his own desk, he was ready to assert his authority. He began by announcing that he had decided to hold a full-scale press conference almost immediately, at 1500 hours.

"Is that wise?" asked the Comandante, his large, darkened spectacles shielding his disapproving glare.

"Absolutely. You can leave it all to me. Oh, but there is just one other thing I would like. It would make a better show if we could present to the press this *sargento* of the presidential guard— what's his name?— who so bravely confronted the assassin. Give it a nice human touch. Can he be made available?"

Barraza nodded. "You mean *Sargento Segundo* Jesús Moreno. Yes, he can be made available, if necessary. He's in the building right now, going over his formal statement. But, *Señor Procurador*, may I ask you to reconsider the idea of having a press conference so soon? The problem is the identity of the assassin. Am I right in thinking that you will be giving out the name of Manuel Ramírez?

"Of course. That's essential. It's the first fact they will want to know."

"Quite so. It is certainly the usual procedure. I can remember as far back as the Kennedy killing when those Dallas cowboys immediately released the name of Lee Harvey Oswald. We did the same when Aburto killed Colosio. But in my opinion it's a mistake, especially in this case.

"Consider the consequences if you release the name of Ramírez right now. What will happen? I'll tell you what: one thing's for sure - people closely associated with him will make themselves scarce. Pronto! No one wants to be hauled in for questioning, and in this city, with its huge *ciudades perdidas*, it's all too easy to disappear. At this very minute, our *judiciales* are on their way to round up people who knew Ramírez. All I am asking is that we give them more time. Say just another two hours."

Rodríguez fortified himself with a drink of whisky. "Sorry, Comandante, but that's quite impossible. The press boys will never wait that long. They'll start speculating and inventing all kinds of stories of their own. Won't do us any good at all."

Artfully, Barraza tried a different approach. "Of course, you are absolutely right... up to a point. But there are other advantages in delaying. Think about it. You will have more time to assemble your presentation of the facts. It will also allow more time for the foreign press corps flying in. And then there is this *Sargento* Moreno. He's not a professional TV performer, you know. He could go off at half-cock. We really ought to go over his statement with him.

"One other thing. There's *El Presidente* to consider. Do you want him to get all this information second hand, via TV? Why, he might even have his own views on how all this should be presented to the Press, especially since our prime suspect is a Mexican citizen."

The last shot hit the target. Rodríguez rose from his chair, in a manner indicating the discussion was at an end. "You have a good point there. I think perhaps I should give *El Presidente* a rundown of our progress. In fact, I'll do it now. But as for two hours' delay, that is positively out of the question. I can give you one extra hour at the most. The press conference will be at 1600 hours."

Barraza smiled. He had never expected to get more than one hour. Back in his own office, he put through a call to Police Chief Delgado. "I am just ringing to confirm that the embargo on naming Ramírez has been officially approved."

He then turned his attention to two sheets of foolscap lying on his desk. One was the brief preliminary report from the forensic department, the other an inventory of all items recovered from the tower, including the personal effects of the man identified as Manuel Ramírez.

Once more, he pondered on their significance. It was not what the inventory listed that interested him, but what was missing. His conclusion was that he was tackling a case far more complex than it had first appeared. For the present, however, he was feeling positively smug. The *cabron*, Rodríguez, had completely missed the discrepancy. He would have to tell him, of course. But that could wait until he had the full forensic report - and until after the Procurador General had stampeded into his precious press conference.

By 1520 hours Comandante Barraza was totally absorbed in his work, no longer giving a thought to his impending retirement. In keeping with his title, he thrived on

101

having absolute command, and in this case, following his initial assessment of the Procurador General, he already felt confident that he could direct operations without any serious interference.

But Barraza's confidence was misplaced. As he would very soon discover, the investigation had international implications of such magnitude that no single individual could expect to exercise independent control. Indeed, two men were already combining to influence the way Barraza approached his last major challenge: Presidents Pérez and Carmichael.

It was just five days since the Democrat Sam Carmichael had stood on snow-blanketed Capitol Hill to be inaugurated as the President of the United States. Though his personal popularity was immense, he anticipated hard times ahead. He had only marginal Democratic majorities in both houses of Congress, and these were likely to prove inadequate if, as he expected, a small core of hard-line conservative Democrats chose to join with Republicans in blocking his legislative efforts, especially in respect of welfare reform and stricter gun controls.

More immediate, however, was the need to respond to extreme right-wing groups, which had become more and more vociferous in demanding sterner measures to counter the alarming increase in drug-related crimes at home and in anti-American acts of terrorism abroad. In this respect, the new president was well ahead of the game. Since his election in November, he had paid particular attention to plans for strengthening the leadership of security and intelligence organisations.

A key priority was the appointment of a new Director of Central Iintelligence. Automatically, the chosen DCI would also be head of the CIA, head of the intelligence community, and the primary adviser to the President and the National Security Council on intelligence matters.

Carmichael had already decided on the best man for the job. He wanted a true professional in charge, not some high-ranking brass hat or political strategist being rewarded for his campaign support. His nominee, already cleared by FBI investigators and by the Senate Intelligence Committee, was William J. Stanleigh, Deputy Director, CIA operations, the man who had telephoned the President only fifteen minutes after the assassination in Mexico City.

That afternoon the President had summoned for early

Monday morning an emergency meeting of his closest advisers: Arthur Stephenson, an unusually bright U.S. Vice-President who had been a professor at Yale before his election to Congress; James Hathaway, Secretary of State; Melvin J. Holmes, the Attorney General; Charles Fairbrother, Secretary of Defence; and Bill "Skerry" Butler, his National Security Advisor. All except Holmes were statutory members of the National Security Council.

In the meantime, he bypassed Admiral George Stanton, the outgoing and out-of-favour DCI, and the Deputy DCI., Brigadier Lawrence Holt, who was on indefinite sick leave. Both men were too closely associated with the scandals that had hit the CIA during the previous administration. Instead, he would rely entirely upon Stanleigh to keep him informed of all developments in Mexico City. He authorised his CIA chief-elect to initiate his own discreet investigation into the killing of Tunaman, and he asked him to have a written assessment of the situation ready for the 9 a.m. meeting in the Oval Office of the White House.

Carmichael's next action was as much personal as official. He telephoned the U.S. embassy in Mexico City, and, one hour after the killing, he was speaking to ambassador Henderson on his return from Chapultepec Park. The two men had been friends for more than thirty years, ever since playing on the same football team at the University of Texas at Austin. And only last summer, their two families had got together for a golf-and-riding holiday on the Carmichael ranch near Fort Worth.

"Jimmy, I just heard the terrible news. How is Ricky?"

"Ricky is fine, Mr. President. You know the son of a gun. He's already telling his pals about his great adventure in the park. But I must admit that we were shit-scared at the time."

"Hey, cut the Mr. President crap. Tell me about yourself, Jimmy. Are you okay? And what's the situation down there?"

Henderson explained that he had been well-protected by a CIA man called McClellan, and had never been in danger. "I don't think there was anything anti-American in this business, Sam. But we may know more when they identify the killer. I understand that they've already got the man; someone killed while resisting arrest. Anything special you want me to do?"

"No. But I'll get back to you. Meanwhile, I think I should call President Pérez at this stage."

It wasn't necessary. At that very moment, President Carmichael was buzzed on the intercom by his PA. "Sorry to interrupt you, sir, but we've got President Pérez of Mexico on the line."

From the moment President Pérez heard of the crime, one thought remained uppermost in his mind, and influenced his subsequent actions. At all costs, the tragedy must not be allowed to damage Mexico's finely tuned relationship with the United States, which, since the strengthening of the NAFTA agreement, had become crucial to his country's economic well-being.

He well remembered how, back in the 1990s, the gunning down of presidential candidate Luis Donaldo Colosio in Tijuana had sent Mexican shares and bonds plunging alarmingly. The next day, the United States came to the rescue by extending a six-billion-dollar line of credit in an effort to defend a possible rush on the peso. Temporarily at least, it checked growing uncertainty over an economy which was heavily dependent on the confidence of foreign investors.

This time the assassination fell on a Sunday, giving the advantage of a short breathing space. A similar gesture of extended credit by Mexico's NAFTA partners could stave off a violent downward swing when the markets reopened on Monday, and reduce the threat to the country's policy of a more liberalized economy.

Unlike Carmichael, Pérez was long familiar with the responsibilities of his presidency. It was just over two years since he had donned the green, white and red sash of office on December 1st, Inauguration Day. He was well past the teething stage of his six-year term when it was traditional for Mexican presidents to present a positive, do-gooder image, making every effort to uphold campaign promises to outlaw corruption, and to promote his country's reputation as a fast-modernising bastion of stability.

But now he was moving into new territory. The assassination of Tunaman had prompted him to make his first direct contact with the new U.S. President. After the initial exchange of courtesies, and Sam Carmichael's insistence on their use of first names, Pérez emphasised his fears for the Mexican economy. They were facing what he called "just a passing hiccup", but, to be on the safe side, it might be beneficial to NAFTA if Washington was able to make some expression of confidence in the Mexican economy, before the markets reopened.

Carmichael sympathised, but stressed that he would need to consult first with his economic advisers. "Meanwhile, let's not over-react. I am not at all convinced that this tragedy has financial implications. Let's see how the market goes tomorrow. If there are signs of trouble, I am sure we will be able to do something to help."

He quickly moved on. "It's the political situation that disturbs me most, Enrique. At this point, I can promise to give you our fullest co-operation in the pursuit of whoever is responsible for this dastardly act. All the resources of our intelligence services are at your disposal."

President Pérez judged it expedient to have the United States and Mexico working closely together at whatever level. As he saw it, a shared problem encouraged shared interests. And so he replied that he would welcome any suggestions as to ways and means that their two great countries might co-operate in the pursuit of justice.

One hour later, after conferring with Stanleigh, President Carmichael returned Pérez's call. It was suggested by the CIA, he explained, that they might send to Mexico City their chief expert on terrorism. His name was Arthur Madison, and his specialist knowledge and experience might be useful in a case of such international overtones. "If you wish, he is available to leave for Mexico City at once."

President Pérez agreed. "He will be very welcome. Let us know when he is due to arrive."

"Sure will. Meanwhile, Enrique, I'm advised that the CIA's station chief, Wade Hellman, is on leave from Mexico City at present. Most unfortunate. But at least they have a very good man there. A chap called McClellan. The Agency says that it would be useful if he could observe your investigations in the early stages, and so be able to brief Madison and Hellman when they arrive. Is that okay?"

"Absolutely, Sam."

"Oh! One more thing, Enrique. The FBI would also like to be represented by their man in Mexico City. His name is Carruthers. D'you think he could be kept up-to-date with developments, too?"

President Pérez agreed again. Subsequently he rang

Procurador General Rodríguez, telling him to expect McClellan and Carruthers, and later Madison and Hellman, and to give them his full cooperation. "Let us hope they can find that some foreign terrorist group— not just one demented Mexican— was behind this terrible atrocity."

It was 3 p.m. in Mexico City and, for the first time that afternoon, General Juan Delgado was feeling relaxed. He took an Havana from his gold cigar box, clipped it with a guillotine cutter and lit it with his silver table-lighter. Then, after taking an expansive draw, he at last swivelled round on his chair to face the immaculately suited Bolivian who was seated to his left on the other side of the desk.

He blew a huge cloud of smoke into the air. "Now then, *Señor* Menéndez, what exactly is the point you are trying to make?"

Menéndez smiled. One thing he had learnt from previous dealings with Delgado was not to be too exact in their conversations. It was the unstated, the discreetly implied, that mattered. He had learnt, too, not to be unnerved by the chief's calculatedly offhand manner. They were two of a kind: both adept, in their individual way, at life's poker game.

On this occasion, the Bolivian lawyer recognised that Delgado had the power hand; that he himself was in no position to bluff as he had been when dealing with the nervy Gómez. The best he could hope for was a small share of the pot.

"I am just saying, *Señor Ssecretario*, that a videotape is of such extraordinary international interest should be released for public viewing. I reckon that, taking inflation into account, it could at least match the quarter-of-a-million dollars that *Life* magazine paid for the *Zapruder* film. But every hour it remains confiscated, it decreases in market value.

"Think of it this way, *senor*. A large portion of the profits could be put to good use. For example, you yourself could control a share in order to offer a reward for information about the assassination."

La mordida had been correctly offered. And to the astonishment, and total bewilderment of Menéndez, "the bite" was flatly rejected.

Delgado stared at him coldly. "No. The pictures will

not be released. Not today, not tomorrow, nor at any time in the foreseeable future. This matter is non-negotiable. And that is my final word."

Nonplussed, Menéndez fought hard to mask his feelings. He wanted an explanation, but judged it unwise to seek one. Instead, he switched to a subject which was of no real interest to him, but which was his duty to raise.

"One other thing, *señor*. About my client, Alfredo Gómez. He has been in your custody now for more than an hour. Could you advise me whether any charges are to be brought against him, and if not, when he is likely to be released?"

Delgado exhaled another cloud of smoke. "Alas, *amigo,* I cannot help you there either. We have finished with your client, but the question of his release is no longer my responsibility. At this very moment, he is on his way to the office of the *Procuraduría General.* You will have to deal with them."

He stood up. "And now, Señor Menéndez, you must excuse me. I have a million things to attend to. I wish you good day."

The police chief could read clearly what was on the lawyer's mind. But he still chose to say nothing. He might explain to him later, but for the moment he was not prepared to reveal that he was suppressing the videotape, purely in order to curry favour with the President of Mexico.

El Presidente had personally congratulated him on his prompt action in seizing the tape; he had also expressed his hope that such disturbing pictures would never be shown, out of respect for the families of the deceased. It was tantamount to a command, and Delgado judged that the goodwill of President Pérez was currently far more valuable to him in the long-term than a share of any video sales.

Once Menéndez had left, the police chief pulled out the top right-hand drawer of his desk and pressed the "rewind" switch on his tape-recorder. He wanted to hear a second time exactly what Gómez had said during the preliminary police interview.

"*El Robot*" Torres, as usual, had done his third degree work well. No violence was needed. The mere suggestion of physical action was enough. For half an hour, the columnist had been left to sweat in one of the cells adjoining the interrogation room. Then, seated in the centre of a bare room, Gómez had been petrified as Coronel Torres walked around him, all the while slapping his gloved left hand with a swagger stick held in his right.

He could not get out his answers fast enough. Within five minutes he had told Torres everything he wanted to know: exactly how he had recruited Guillermo Velázquez as an informant and how Velázquez had telephoned him last Thursday, giving full details of the arrangements for the birthday party in the park. No, he had positively not told anyone else about the party. No, he did not know whether Velázquez had told anyone else. And yes, he did now accept that the police were entitled to confiscate his pictures.

By the time the interview was over, Gómez no longer had any interest in his precious videotape. He wished he had never taken the pictures, and he had already resolved to get out of Mexico City as soon as it was possible. He would move to Cancún and work for his cousin on a small circulation magazine catering to the tourist trade.

The tape-recording of Gomez's statement confirmed Delgado's opinion that the man was a *cabron*; a chicken-livered arsehole who was unlikely to give him any trouble. All that interested him was the revelation about Guillermo Velázquez. It raised, he later said, intriguing possibilities.

It was now 2330 hours in Athens, and for the second time that evening the Kolonaki police were receiving a telephone call from the *Prometheus* in mid-Atlantic. Their report only added to Stavros Stephanopoulos' overwhelming sense of foreboding. As instructed, they had forced an entry into his son's apartment, and they had found no sign of Nicholas having returned from his run. They were sending a patrol car up Mt. Lykabettus, and putting out a general call for all police cars to be on the alert.

CHAPTER 10

As Marjorie Featherstone swung her red Nissan
Maxima into one of the vast parking lots of the CIA
Headquarters at Langley, she mused that it was on just such a
peaceful Sunday afternoon that three hundred sixty Japanese
warplanes had launched their surprise attack on the American
Pacific Fleet at Pearl Harbour and plunged the United States
into World War II.

On a weekday, the CIA's five-block complex, set in
partially wooded country on the banks of the Potomac, was a
positive hive of activity. At the main driveway entrance, a
dozen armed police of the U.S. Security Protective Service
were on hand, ready to surround and grill any unauthorised
visitor foolish enough to have turned right off the George
Washington Memorial Parkway where a large, public sign
simply proclaimed CIA, without any warning to keep out.
Beyond the gateway— composed of a ten-foot high electrified
wire fence and a stone arch surmounted by floodlights— the
drive led on to parking lots packed with myriad cars, and
inside the sprawling, glass-and-concrete headquarters building,
down labyrinthine corridors, behind bright-coloured office
doors, thousands of employees were engaged in receiving,
storing, studying and analysing intelligence gathered from
around the world.

But today there was no sense of urgency, no indication
that this was the nerve centre of the federal agency
responsible for U.S. counter-intelligence abroad at a cost to
the taxpayer of $40 billion a year. Only a handful of police
were on duty, and in the parking lots, fewer than a hundred or
so cars were to be seen— evidence that the company was
currently operating with a small skeleton staff, mainly clerical
workers and communication operators. As Featherstone was
thinking, it needed a formal state of emergency before
security interests were allowed to interfere with the great
American weekend.

Even now, her immediate boss, James Chester-Allen,

was stubbornly carrying on with his round at the Washington Golf and Country Club in an exclusive area of Arlington. As the CIA's chief specialist on Turkish affairs, he had been one of the first to be informed of the Tunaman assassination. Yet he was determined to finish his game before being galvanised into action.

As usual, he had been quick to ease his workload. From the sixth tee, on his mobile, he had called his chief assistant at home and asked her to help him out. The DDO required an interim report reassessing the political situation in Turkey and projecting possible developments. Could she perhaps make a start on it? And he would join her at the office later.

Ms Featherstone was happy to comply. But she could not understand Chester-Allen's casual reaction. To her, it was only this kind of intriguing and unexpected development that made a CIA desk job worthwhile.

It was just after 2.30 p.m. when she entered the main lobby of the headquarters building. An armed guard immediately greeted her by name, and then went through the strict routine of checking her magnetised plastic pass on the computerised security system. In this case the formality seemed particularly absurd; Ms. Feathertsone was arguably the most instantly recognised individual in the entire establishment.

At Langley, even on the busiest weekday, the scene is liable to disappoint anyone with a James Bond cloak-and-dagger image of the CIA. The atmosphere is very much that of a research institute, one populated with academics studiously beavering away in their own little cubbyholes and working regular office hours. There is no sense of community. Departments keep very much to themselves, and most employees passing in the corridors are strangers to one another. Ms Featherstone was a notable exception.

Her presence had always aroused interest at Langley; an interest that was primarily focussed on her physical attractions. Though she dressed discreetly— without jewellery and favouring, as now, a plain skirt and tailored blouse— there was no hiding her prime assets: voluminous breasts accentuating a slim waist and complementing large, well-rounded hips. Originally, however, she had stood out among intelligence officers for an entirely different reason. She was black.

In the late 1960s, civil rights activists had made much

propaganda of the fact that the CIA had twelve thousand non-clerical employees, of whom fewer than twenty were blacks. But efforts to improve the ratio brought no significant change. The reality was that the service had little attraction for black persons of the graduate calibre required. After all, a black candidate, with a first-class law degree like Ms Featherstone, could expect to enjoy a far greater income in a professional practice.

Money, however, was not a key factor for Featherstone. Responding to a recruiting drive launched by the CIA in American universities, she had inituially been attracted by the opportunity to rise to a position which would give her a privileged insight into world politics. Unfortunately, as she soon discovered, no such opportunity existed, so dominant was the clubby, old boy network that precluded female advancement.

Then, in 1994, everything had begun to change. Jeanine Brookner, the first woman station chief, had sued the Company after her unfair demotion to a low-level clerical job, and there had followed a massive, largely successful campaign by the CIA's women case officers against sexual discrimination.

For Featherstone and her female colleagues, the most significant change came in 1995 when John Deutch, President Clinton's new Director of Intelligence, initiated a major shake-up, sanctioning numerous promotions for women, most notably that of Nora Slatkin, the first woman to become an executive director. Five years later, Joanne Isham became deputy director for science and technology, the equivalent of the fictional "Q" of James Bond fame. In turn, Featherstone was to set another new standard: as the first black woman to be appointed a deputy national intelligence officer (DNIO).

During the Reagan administration, the analytical side of the CIA had been reorganised on a geographical basis. NIOs henceforth specialised in specific regions: the Middle East, Latin America, Africa, Western Europe, East Asia and the Soviet Union. In addition, NIOs were created to cover new subjects: strategic forces, nuclear proliferation, high technology, drugs and international terrorism.

More drastic reorganisation followed the break-up of the Soviet Union and the end of the Cold War. And then, in 2006, came the biggest shake up of all, with numerous sackings and resignations in the wake of 9/11 and wildly inaccurate intelligence relating to Iraq.

There was a major shift in the strategic centres of power politics, and eventually, Turkey, as the key bridge between Europe and the Middle East, was judged to be of such crucial importance that it was given its own NIO, James Chester-Allen. Featherstone was his newly appointed deputy, and, in the light of recent events, she was expected to climb much higher.

The past year had seen much publicity given to a new scandal at Langley. A black secretary alleged that she had been raped by a senior operative who had asked her to work late in his office. Subsequently, other black employees complained of sexual harassment and of being restricted to menial positions. They chose Featherstone to be their chief spokeswoman, and when appearing on talk shows she had become an instant hit - a bubbling, articulate TV performer, now being dubbed the Oprah Winfrey of the CIA.

This Sunday, on arriving in her office, Featherstone immediately began typing on her PC a preliminary list of international developments that might possibly arise from the killing of ambassador Tunaman. Her own view was an optimistic one: that ironically the tragedy would have a beneficial outcome, bringing Turkey and Greece closer together in their mutual grief, a circumstance last brought about by the earthquakes of 1999. But she did not stress the point. Chester-Allen, as she well knew, was liable to opt for a much grimmer extrapolation.

She was pondering his likely reaction when there was a gentle knock at her door. She called out 'Come in', and the door opened to reveal a senior CIA officer she had not met face-to-face before. He was a middle-aged man of unusually pale complexion; slim, slightly built, with a mop of unruly light-brown hair and a muddled attire— brownish tweed suit, fawn pullover and dark-green woollen tie— that clearly defined him as a bachelor.

Before entering the office, the man bowed slightly and wished her good afternoon. "Please excuse the intrusion, ma'am, but it is a matter of some urgency."

His manner was positively quaint - and totally disarming. He had the style of a true gentleman. He smiled through soft grey eyes, and he spoke quietly with a flat, slow drawl that betrayed his Charlestonian roots. For a moment Featherstone looked at him in wonder. Could this most

112

courteous of men— unlike any she had encountered at Langley before— really be the Company's leading authority on international terrorism?

She did not know Arthur Madison personally, but she knew him well enough by reputation. At Langley, he was regarded as something of an oddity: an extremely reserved, mild-mannered Southerner who was a recognised poet and who, years after the introduction of a no-smoking ban, was still to be seen sucking on an empty pipe. He was also renowned for his encyclopaedic knowledge of terrorist organisations.

Much to the disappointment of his father— a retired four-star U.S. Army general— Madison was strictly a thinker, not a man of action. In keeping with family tradition, he had developed a genuine interest in military history. But only the theory and cliometrics appealed to him. He had firmly resisted pressure upon him to take a place at West Point, and he had justified his stance by winning an academic scholarship to Austin University.

With an honours degree in history, Madison had seemed set for a college teaching career when he was personally approached by a CIA recruiting officer. What he never knew was that the approach— successfully made in June, 1984— had been instigated by his father who had recommended him to the DCI as someone likely to a make a first-class specialist in military intelligence.

The timing of his recruitment was significant. That same month, on the initiative of Prime Minister Margaret Thatcher, the leaders of seven major industrial countries— Britain, the U.S., France, West Germany, Italy, Japan and Canada— had endorsed plans for closer international co-operation against state-sponsored terrorism. At Langley, Madison was soon assigned to a small unit geared exclusively to promoting such co-operation.

The CIA's anti-terrorist role was given higher priority in 1988 after the bombing of Pan Am flight 103 had claimed two hundred seventy lives over the small Scottish town of Lockerbie. But it was another ten years before the need for greater advance intelligence was fully appreciated. That need was emphasised by the bombings of American embassies in Kenya and Tanzania— attacks unanticipated even though CIA undercover agents had infiltrated Afghan camps under the command of the multi-millionaire terrorist impresario, Osama

113

Bin Laden.

Even then, it took the suicidal demolition of the World Trade Center in 2001 to provoke a major staff shake-up at Langley. At that time Madison was among a few CIA operatives who cast doubts on the intelligence regarding the threat from Iraq— doubts which, to his dismay, were ignored in the White House and Pentagon because they did not fit in with their political objectives and preconceptions.

With others, he had tendered his resignation. But, with the promise of improved co-ordination of America's sixteen intelligence agencies, he had been persuaded to stay on, and subsequently he was made head of the CIA's counter-terrorism intelligence section. In this capacity, he was not directly involved with anti-terrorist action. That was strictly a police or military function. His unit's purpose was confined to gathering and analysing information on terrorist organisations, and working closely in an advisory capacity with police and intelligence agencies in other countries.

A colleague of Britain's former MI5 boss Stella Rimington— the first woman ever to head a major security and intelligence organisation— once stated that she had a dramatic ability to read the terrorists' intentions and second-guess them. The same might have been said of Madison. The greatest value of his unit lay in its ability, at times, to warn where terrorists were likely to strike next.

Inevitably, there were times when his unit was totally surprised by an outbreak of fanatical violence. But even when surprised, the CIA— and to an increasing degree, the FBI— was usually able to identify quickly those responsible for an act of terrorism. The killing of Kemal Tunaman in Mexico was different. As Madison now explained to Featherstone, he faced the greatest difficulty in attributing this latest assassination to one particular terrorist group.

"So far no organisation has claimed responsibility. And the trouble is that there are too many suspects. I can think of more than half a dozen groups with a motive for this killing. But before investigating them, I need to eliminate one other remote possibility: that this is not a political act at all, but some personal vendetta."

He smiled almost boyishly. "I wonder if you could help me. I have all our records on Tunaman's involvement in the Greece-Turkey crisis, and there have been plenty of profiles in the Press. But it might to useful have some material of Turkish origin about his earlier background. Thought you might have something."

"Of course," Featherstone replied. "I can make you a CD right away, or if you prefer, I'll do you a computer print-out. It won't take many minutes, though I should warn you it's not likely to help. All very mundane stuff. This man is your original Mr. Clean. No hint of enemies in his personal life."

Madison glanced at his wrist-watch. "Thank you most kindly. But I haven't even a few minutes to spare. In fact, I must leave for Reagan National Airport right away. Could you please send it on the satellite for me to pick up at our embassy in Mexico City?"

He stood up and extended a handshake while saying, "It has been a great pleasure to me to meet you, ma'am. And may I say how much I have admired your appearances on television." He bowed again, then quickly turned and left. Once alone, Featherstone covered her face and burst into uncontrolled laughter.

Utterly captivated by Madison's old-world charm, Featherstone chose to supervise personally the selection of biographical material for dispatch by the first-floor cable secretariat. In any event, so she decided, it would be a useful exercise, re-familiarising herself with Tunaman's background before continuing with the report ordered by the DDO.

On a second computer, she summoned up the pertinent files. As she rightly recalled, one Turkish source stood out above all the rest. Everything known about Tunaman's personal life was to be found in one authoritative profile article published by Istanbul's mass-circulation daily, *Hurriyet*. It had been contributed by a lifelong friend, the Turkish author Selim Atasoy, at the time of Tunaman's intervention in the Aegean crisis.

The filed version, as translated by the CIA's Turkey station, began:

On the surface, it may appear curious and improbable that a university classics professor, currently our ambassador to Mexico, should now be the key negotiator in our greatest international crisis since 1976. Yet, to my mind, it is an entirely logical development. Looking back on the life and times of Kemal Tunaman, it seems as though a series of chance events was moving him inexorably towards this

115

extraordinary challenge.

It was in the 1950s, when living at Bebek, that I first met Kemal Tunaman. We were both five-years-old, new boys attending the local kindergarten school, and the selective trickery of memory makes it seem as though life in those days was one long glorious summer, with every leisure hour revolving in and around the blue, clear waters of the Bosporus. Our lives, like the great intercontinental waterway, were unpolluted then: no human conflicts, no menacing traffic, no television to restrain our physical vigour and confuse the mind with pictures of the post-war world outside. We scootered and hop scotched on Baltalimani Caddesi, and, above all, we swam and boated and fished for istavrit and izmarit that rose to our bait like bubbles in champagne.

This was the joyful child-world I came to share with Kemal Tunaman. We were not immediately close friends, and my first impression was not entirely favourable; he was so quiet, so much less extrovert than other boys, and most vividly I remember him for his curious physique, freakishly tall for his age, angular in face and body. Only one thing gave him a certain individual distinction. He had been born on November 10th, the anniversary of the death of Mustafa Kemal Ataturk. Thus, every year, he had a birthday party on the day when our school held remembrance ceremonies.

Some years before Kemal was born, it had been decreed by Ataturk that every Turkish citizen should adopt a surname. His father, an orthopaedic surgeon, had chosen Tunaman because his ancestors came from the region of Tuna— the Danube— and naturally, when his eldest son was born on such an historic date, he named him Kemal after the maker of modern Turkey.

In retrospect, I think it was the position of Kemal's family home, some ten kilometres north of central Istanbul that initially brought us close together. Sited at Rumelihisari, it was not overshadowed, as it is today, by the great Bosporus bridge named after Sultan Mehmet II - Fatih 'the conqueror'. It commanded a glorious view, with the Asian shore less than one kilometre away, and with its long waterfront patio, it became a favourite gathering-point for our swimming and fishing. Much more importantly, its position was responsible for sparking off Kemal's enduring passion for history.

Then, as now, the Tunaman family home was less than one hundred yards from the great castle of Rumeli Hisar that curves majestically over the European hillside, facing across the narrowest point of the Bosporus to its twin castle of Anadolu Hisar on the Asian shore. Kemal was fascinated by those huge fortifications. And by the age of eleven, when we both moved onto Galatasaray high school, he was beginning to amaze teachers with his knowledge of local history.

He knew every detail of the role of Rumeli Hisar in the fall of Byzantine Constantinople in 1453: how Sultan Mehmet, only twenty-one years old, had the fortifications constructed by thousands of masons and labourers in four-and-a-half months; how he installed on its ramparts three massive cannons that enabled him to blockade the Black Sea approach to the city, and how, with a huge Ottoman fleet commanding the only other approach via the Dardanelles, he successfully prevented reinforcements and food supplies reaching the beleaguered city.

The key thing with Kemal was that when he talked about Rumeli Hisar, it was no longer stuffy history. I remember, especially, a day on the Bosporus when he recalled how a great Hungarian-designed cannon had blasted out of the water a Venetian ship that had tried to defy the blockade.

The survivors, he explained, were duly executed. But he didn't just tell us. He showed us. "Just about here, almost where you are standing, is the spot where the Venetian captain was impaled on a stake. Imagine it: his body, rotting in the sun and crawling with flies, was left here for weeks - a grim warning to any passing ships that they would be well advised to drop anchor and have their cargo inspected."

Everyone knows now of Kemal's extraordinary talent for bringing history vividly to life. The point is that he had it even then. His enthusiasm was infectious, and with his inquiring mind, his subsequent interest in the Greeks was a natural progression. When he knew all about the triumph of the Ottoman Turks, he wanted to know more about the Christian people who for seven long weeks had withstood a siege against impossible odds. And ultimately his study of the defeated led to his passionate interest in the classical world, whose heritage had been preserved by the fallen Byzantine Empire for more than a thousand years.

None of us were in the least surprised when Kemal graduated with honours at Istanbul University and later returned there as Professor of Philosophy and Classical

117

Studies. Soon afterwards, he married his childhood sweetheart, Raife Erbay, and they were the most blissfully contented couple I ever knew. She successfully combined raising two daughters with her work as a medical practitioner. He, devoid of personal ambition, felt privileged to be able to spend his life doing what he loved best: teaching classical history and, at every opportunity, revisiting and exploring the great archaeological sites of ancient Greece.

Featherstone skipped ahead to the seminal moment in Tunaman's life: when, after nearly forty years of academic obscurity, he found himself suddenly projected into the public limelight. As Atasoy explained, it had happened purely by chance after the professor had accepted an invitation to act as consultant on a three-part television series called "In Search of Troy". His duties were to be confined to checking the shooting script for accuracy, and advising on any amendments found necessary when on location.

But then the series presenter was taken seriously ill while they were shooting at the supposed site of ancient Troy: on the hill of Hissarlik in the plain of the Troad that commands the western approaches to the Dardanelles. Two instalments remained to be shot, and the tight budget did not allow a second excursion to Troy. In desperation, the producer persuaded Tunaman to stand in as the presenter.

The result was sensational. Discarding the prepared script, Tunaman combined scholarship with unbounded enthusiasm as he focussed on the duplicity of Heinrich Schliemann, the avaricious German multi-millionaire, who, after discovering the so-called treasure of King Priam, had smuggled the thousands of artefacts to Greece, and had them hidden by his young wife's far-flung relatives in stables, barns and farmyards.

For the final instalment, Tunaman moved on to Athens, and, through the influential support of Stavros Stephanopoulos, his daughter's father-in-law, he gained permission from the Greek government to present the programme from Iliou Melathron, the huge, opulent mansion on Venizelou street, which— modelled on palaces unearthed at Troy and Mycenae— had been designed by Schliemann as his own private monument and temple.

He concluded the series from the cemetery of Athens,

standing in the steps leading up to Schliemann's temple-like tomb. There, in summing up, Kemal described the search for Troy as a classic example of the ruthless cupidity of so many adventures of the nineteenth century and early twentieth century who, "without respect for the sanctity of place, carted off their booty to be displayed in a totally alien setting."

Recalling these events in his article, Atasoy noted there was unsuspected irony in Tunaman's performance. *At the time everyone raved about the refreshing way he put across his unscripted lines. Only much later did we come to realise the true significance of his television debut: that it was what he said— more than how he said it— that led to his emergence as a figure of world-wide renown. The key lay in the content of the concluding part of the series.*

Tunaman had ended by expresssing the hope that one day Turkey might recover King Priam's treasure, which had been donated to a Berlin museum by Schliemann, and then moved to Moscow by the conquering Russians in 1945. He hoped, too, that they might claw back many more antiquities, including the contents of the British Museum's Xanthus room— a shipload of friezes and sculptures taken from the Lycian city of Xanthus in 1842.

Finally, and most significantly, he expressed his dearest wish: that during his lifetime he would see the so-called Elgin Marbles— pediment sculptures removed from the Parthenon in 1801 by the British ambassador to Turkey— at last returned by Britain to their rightful home on the Acropolis.

He recalled the words of the late Melina Mercouri, the Greek actress and arts minister. "Asked why she wanted the Elgin Marbles, she said: 'Because they are the symbol and the blood and soul of the Greek people. Because we have fought and died for the Parthenon and Acropolis. Because this is our cultural history and belongs to this country and this temple.'"

"And that magnificent lady was absolutely right. Such precious relics of one's national heritage should never be allowed to lie in some far-off, foreign museum. Britain has no valid title to the Elgin Marbles, which were acquired without Greek approval. They can make perfect copies, if they wish to display examples of classical Greek sculptures, but the originals should be restored to their place of origin so that history may be viewed in physical perspective."

119

These extracts were fully quoted in the Greek Press, and subsequently Kemal Tunaman was invited onto a succession of television talk shows in Athens. Speaking in perfect Greek, he argued still more passionately for the return of the Elgin Marbles. In addition, he called for the return of the Venus de Milo, which had been sold to the French when Greece was part of the Ottoman Empire. Then, in another interview, he also deplored the fact that Greece had not been awarded the Olympic Games in 1996, the centenary of the staging of the first modern Olympiad in Athens. "But at least that wrong was belatedly righted in the year 2004."

The Atasoy article ended: *As a result of these television appearances, Tunaman became a unique figure on the international stage: a prominent Turkish citizen who was respected in Greece as greatly as he was in his own country. It was the making of his new and fateful destiny. Today, he is quite simply the only man who seems capable of ending the ominous stalemate between Turkey and Greece.*

Featherstone loaded a CD with the profile, plus a few other articles, and sent it down to the cable secretariat for transmission to Mexico City. Then, for her own purposes, she scanned through the remainder of the Tunaman file.

It contained press stories, which focussed primarily on his brief career as an international diplomat. Also, evaluations of his work from the CIA's Athens and Ankara stations, plus earlier reports referring to the chain of events that had brought him to world prominence: the chain initiated five months ago when two European nations - neighbours and nominal allies within NATO - began to move perilously close to war.

The earliest of the CIA reports was from Ankara, dated last August 17. It read:

Today, Greece announced plans to drill for oil in disputed waters east of Greek islands in the north Aegean, close to the Turkish coast. In government circles here this is regarded as tantamount to a declaration of war. WE PREDICT A RAPIDLY ESCALATING CRISIS. More to follow.

Featherstone smiled. Lamentably, the CIA had failed to predict such momentous developments as Pearl Harbour,

120

the Korean War, the fall of the Berlin Wall, the Soviet invasion of Afghanistan, the First Gulf War and the blitz on the World Trade Centre. Yet it could always predict the most patently obvious.

True enough, to the surprise of no one, Turkey had responded by issuing licences for the state-owned Petroleum Corporation (TPAO) to start prospecting on the Aegean seabed in Greek-claimed territorial waters. And one week later, no less predictably, they had sent out six warships to escort their exploration vessel, *Sismik II*.

In turn, the Greek premier, Christos Andriopoulou, had dispatched a naval force to patrol the eastern Aegean. Any invasion of Greek territorial waters, he warned, would be fiercely resisted. Turkey, not he, would be answerable for the consequences, which were "likely to bring earth-shattering changes in the Balkans and in the Western defence system."

Thereafter, as chronicled in the press reports, both countries rapidly moved onto a war footing. Greece had tanks and infantry moved to positions near the border with Turkey; also troops were sent in force to the island of Samotheaki near the mouth of the Dardanelles. Ankara replied by placing its navy and air force on full alert.

These developments, as noted in a CIA analyst's report, were by no means unprecedented. They followed a tit-for-tat pattern that had arisen four times in the recent decades— in 1974, 1976, 1987 and 1996— when Greece and Turkey had threatened to go to war over disputed territory or waters in the Aegean.

Indeed, the latest Aegean oil crisis was almost an action replay of 1987 when war between Greece and Turkey was only narrowly averted after a week of frantic diplomatic mediation by their NATO allies. On that occasion, the crisis was defused by persuading the Greek and Turkish prime ministers, Andreas Papandreou and Turgut Ozal respectively, to attend a conference in the Swiss ski resort of Davos. There, importantly, they agreed to set up a telephone hotline to avoid such a dangerous confrontation developing again.

But this time there was a crucial difference. Relations between Greece and Turkey had become strained to such an alarming degree that even the telephone hotline was obsolete. Following a bitter exchange of views, neither the Greek prime minister nor his Turkish counterpart, Selim Suman, was willing to speak to the other. Meanwhile, repeated overtures from

121

the United Nations and from NATO partners had failed to bring the two countries to the negotiating table.

Featherstone glanced atwo CIA reports dated September 3. The first, from the Athens station chief, summarised the Greeks' many deep-rooted grievances. Most notably, these included resentment of the newly signed defence and economic cooperation agreement under which the Americans were channelling hundreds of millions of dollars in annual aid to Ankara.

As we warned earlier, the Greek government is especially sensitive to any sign that the U.S is giving preferential treatment to Turkey. They now take the view that disproportionate security aid has disastrously disturbed the military balance in the Aegean, and that any delay in action will only favourthe build-up of Turkish forces. Mass semonstrations indicate that public opinion is solidly behind the government. OUR ASSESSEMENT IS THAT WAR IS NOW IMMINENT.

The second report, from the CIA Ankara station, reached the same alarming conclusion. Turkish grievances, it noted, included discrimination against the Turkish-speaking minority in Thrace; illegal militarisation by the Greeks of islands off the Turkish coast, and the major collisions involving Greek- or Greek Cypriot-registered oil tankers, which had seriously polluted the Bosporus. Most especially, there was still bitter resentment of the fact that for many years Greece had systematically blocked Turkey's application for full membership of the European Community.

Oil exploration by the Greeks off the Turkish coast is to be seen as the final straw. There is no hope of reconciliation. Relations are now so fraught with emotion that WE SHOULD BE PREPARED FOR HOSTILITIES TO BREAK OUT WITHIN THE NEXT 48 HOURS.

This time, Featherstone reflected, the CIA could be excused for getting it wrong. No one could have anticipated the eleventh hour miracle worked by an obscure ambassador from far-off Mexico City. Indeed, neither the Press nor the CIA was aware that Kemal Tunaman had arrived in Athens on September 2, with the purpose of approaching Prime Minister Christos Andriopoulou in one last bid to initiate a Greek-Turkish dialogue.

Later, press reconstructions of events revealed that the approach— not formally approved by the Turkish government— was entirely the inspired idea of Turkish President Erkan Gursoy. By scrambled telephone, on August 31, he had contacted his lifelong friend in Mexico City. He told Tunaman, "Everyone here is ready for war. It seems unavoidable unless the stalemate can be broken. I cannot authorise you to speak on Turkey's behalf. Your visit would be strictly unofficial and secret. But frankly there is nothing else left to try. If you cannot bring Greece and Turkey to the negotiation table, then nobody can."

In turn, Tunaman solicited the aid of Stavros Stephanopoulos, who was then cruising in the Mediterranean. As they planned, he flew via Paris to Marseilles, and there boarded the *Prometheus* bound for Piraeus. He arrived to find Athens in an advanced state of preparedness for war. Sandbags were stacked around public buildings and monuments, shop windows were fitted with shutters, and large cellars and basements had been requisitioned for air-raid shelters. Already blackout regulations were in force, and already people had begun hoarding food and petrol in anticipation of rationing.

The crucial meeting of Tunaman and Premier Andriopoulou took the form of a private dinner party held at the luxury Piraeus apartment, which Stavros had acquired since the separation from his wife. It was— as the guests were given to understand— strictly a social occasion.

Tunaman was the one Turkish citizen that Andriopoulou genuinely admired, and they were unlikely to have another opportunity to meet. But, so Stavros artfully figured, that alone was not enough to persuade the Greek Premier to accept his invitation at such a critical time. A tastier, more subtle bait was needed to lure his old friend. And that bait was Jennifer Morrow.

Until the Turkish crisis, all Athens had been feeding voraciously on stories about the romance of the media tycoon and an Australian nurse, thirty-one years his junior. While Stephanopoulos-controlled publications remained discreetly silent on the affair, the gossip columns of rival organs were dominated by sensationalised, circulation-boosting reports.

Off the island of Pathos, *paparazzi* had managed to snatch pictures of Miss Morrow sunbathing topless aboard the *Prometheus*. But so far no one in Athens had met the woman who had reportedly tamed the celebrated Greek womaniser.

Andriopoulou, a widower, was certainly as intrigued as anyone. He, too, was involved with a younger woman, his thorty-five-year-old personal secretary, Mirka Kirillis. In this instance, there was only a twenty-year disparity in their ages, but so far it had been enough to make Miss Kirillis resist the idea of marriage.

The Greek premier was advised by Stavros that, besides Miss Morrow and Kemal Tunaman, the only other guests would be professor Leonidas Kritikos and his wife. This made the invitation still more acceptable. Kritikos was an old and trusted friend of Andriopoulou. He was also the director of the Acropolis Museum, so sharing a primary interest with Tunaman.

No one attending that exclusive dinner party ever disclosed what was said by Tunaman to influence Andriopoulou. But the subsequent events were quite extraordinary. The very next morning Andriopoulou contacted president Gursoy, who passed onto Premier Suman the news that, encouraged by a talk with ambassador Tunaman, the Greek Prime Minister was prepared to convene a summit meeting to explore means of easing tension between the two countries. Moreover, he had suggested that Tunaman should preside over the meeting.

Crucially, it was a situation that allowed both political leaders to announce without any loss of face their willingness to attend talks. Neither had made the first approach. To be sure, a Turk had taken the initiative, albeit unofficially, in requesting a meeting. But, in Turkish eyes, that conciliatory action was offset by the fact that one of their own countrymen would preside over the talks.

One week later, amid massive security, Premier Suman landed at Eleftherios Venizelos Airport. In the capital, anti-Turkish groups— Greeks, Greek Cypriots, Armenians and Kurdish political refugees— were preparing to disrupt the visit with demonstrations. But they massed in Syntagma Square in vain. Contrary to advance publicity, there was no motorcade taking the Turkish delegates into central Athens. Instead, they were driven further south to a heavily guarded government hospitality centre, formerly a beach hotel, outside the holiday resort of Vouliagmeni.

As agreed in advance, the talks were conducted in camera and restricted to two thrity-strong delegations composed of the respective prime ministers and foreign secretaries, plus economic and military advisers. No time limit was set on the meeting, and until it ended, there were to be no

124

press conferences, only occasional releases of statements, which had been jointly approved.

The progress was slow, but encouraging. Most importantly, after three days of haggling, it was agreed that both countries should halt all oil exploration for a six-month period during which joint committees would be set up under the auspices of the United Nations to reconsider such contentious issues as the delimitation of the continental shelf in the Aegean, airspace and territorial waters. In the meantime, oil company representatives would examine the possibility of joint exploration in Aegean waters where Greece and Turkey had rival claims.

Thereafter, as press releases explained, the talks focussed primarily on improving Greek-Turkish relations 'by way of shared economic, cultural and sporting ventures, and more development of broad contacts and mutual interests'. Agreement was reached on greater co-operation in a variety of ways, ranging from efforts to combat the transport of heroin from the poppy fields of Iran, Pakistan and Afghanistan to joint tourist ventures aimed at combining visits to Greek islands in the Aegean with trips to the many Greek-founded cities on Turkish western and southern coasts.

After nine days, the talks ended without any concessions made in respect of age-old grievances in respect of Cyprus and E.E.C. membership. Nevertheless, the summit meeting was hailed world-wide as a triumph for common sense. At the eleventh hour, the time bomb in the Aegean had been defused.

At the end-of-summit press conference, Kemal Tunaman insisted that any success was due entirely to the great statesmanship displayed by Prime Ministers Suman and Andriopoulou. They, in turn, stated that progress could not have been made without Tunaman's wholly constructive and impartial guidance. He was, said Andropoulou, the worthy counterpart of Mikis Theodorakis, the celebrated Greek composer who had presided over the Greek-Turkish Friendship Society in the 1980s.

As Marjorie Featherstone reviewed reports of these events, one unanswered question loomed ever larger in her mind: What exactly had been said at that private dinner party in Stavros' Piraeus apartment? Specifically, what argument could Tunaman have made to succeed where all the combined efforts of U.N. and NATO representatives had failed?

The question intrigued her. As she saw it, the answer could be invaluable now that there was no longer a Tunaman-like figure to intervene if the Greek-Turkish rapprochement fell apart.

She was thinking along these lines when, without knocking, Chester-Allen breezed into her office. "Hiya, Marj! How's it going?"

"Okay," she replied flatly. "And how was the golf?"

"Terrible. Lost fifty dollars to that bastard Jackson. Reckon I was rushing my game too much to get back to the office. Anyway, sweetheart, I'm here now and all ready to go."

Featherstone sighed. *What a contrast with that charming man, Madison. Next thing, this chauvinist pig would be calling her kid.*

Chester-Allen leaned over her shoulder to see what was on her monitor, so close that she could smell the brandy on his breath. "Hey, kid, that's ancient history now. Forget about Tunaman. We're into a whole new ball game."

He turned and paced across the room. "You know, I was thinking about it on the way here. Seems to me, we should be prepared for the worst, and go back to that scenario we drew up before Tunaman came into the play.

"Let's start by digging up that war scenario and going over it again. It could apply just as well now— the suggestion that, if the Turks feel threatened, they will begin by seizing two or three Aegean islands, and very probably destroying the Greek military installations on Lesbos. Certainly, we should recommend moving a few guided-missile destroyers from the Sixth Fleet to patrol the Aegean. What do the latest reports from Athens and Ankara say?"

Featherstone got up and fetched a folder from a filing cabinet. She said nothing, but in her view Chester-Allen's approach was all wrong. There should be no hint of U.S. sabre rattling, no suggestion of lack of confidence in the Greek or Turkish leadership. Recommendations should emphasise the need for constructive policies, and underline the notion that the greatest tribute to the late Tunaman would be keep alive his dreams of Greek-Turkish co-operation.

To her mind, there was no reason to suppose that all the progress towards harmony in Aegean could be destroyed, at a stroke, by the death of the man who had initiated it. All the same, she thought, it would have been useful to know precisely what line Tunaman had taken at that private dinner party, and how the seemingly intractable Andriopoulou had suddenly been swayed.

Only one person in the world knew exactly, word for word, what Tunaman and Andriopoulou had said to one another at that fateful dinner party held in Piraeus on September 3. That person was Stavros Stephanopoulos. Partly to protect his business dealings, and partly because he planned to publish his memoirs after retirement, it was his custom to tape-record surreptitiously all important or interesting conversations. His Piraeus apartment, like his mega-yacht *Prometheus,* was extensively bugged.

On the day of the assassination, as the *Prometheus* ploughed its way across the Atlantic, Stavros refreshed his memory by playing again his recording of the dialogue between Tunaman and Andriopoulou. He fast-forwarded to the point where, after dinner, he and Jennifer Morrow had purposefully left the two men alone on the pretext of showing Mr. and Mrs. Kritikos their floodlit, rooftop garden and the dramatic overview of Piraeus harbour. As he recalled it, their conversation has been fairly innocuous. He listened again.

"Well, Kemal, here's to your very good

health. *Igia!* Or, as you say, *'serafe!'* I fear, dear friend, that this may be the last time we can have a drink together."

"Alas, so, *azizim.* Anyway - *Yiasou."*

"And here's to your family, too. I worry about them, you know. Will Yasemin stay on in Athens? It could be a very difficult time for her. I hate to admit it, but anti-Turkish feeling is not easy to control."

"Oh yes, she will be staying on."

"Hmm! Could be a mistake. But then I guess they knew what they were getting into from the start. Ah, the madness of young love! I suppose we were like that once. All living for the moment with little thought for tomorrow."

"Perhaps."

"Funny, though, how these things happen. Where was it they met? At an English university? A thousand-to-one chance. Must have come to you as a hell of a shock."

"Not really, Christos. You see, our daughters were never fed on old anti-Greek prejudices. It was much more difficult for Nicholas. His family was totally opposed to the marriage, but I guess the fact that Yasemin was already pregnant made all the difference. A matter of honour, you see."

"Yes, of course. I can imagine. I remember the trouble I had in my courting days. No Greek girl, it seemed, was good enough to satisfy my mother. But - *mnistiti mou kirie!* - if I had come home with a Turkish girl, she would have kicked me straight out of the house."

"Ah-ha! Nicholas has told me the same sort of thing. Do you know that he was once keen to marry a Greek girl, that is, before he went to Manchester University and met Yasemin?"

"Really? What happened?"

"Well, as Nicholas tells it, he was very immature at the time and infatuated with the daughter of Kostas Bandanidis. You know, the supermarket tycoon. Anyway, I understand there was a serious breakdown in negotiations over the *proika*. Apparently Bandanidis proposed a dowry, which Stavros regarded as derisory.

"I don't know all the details. But certainly it ended up with the two family heads refusing to speak to one another. Eventually they settled their differences. But by then it was too late. Nicholas had been packed off to a university in England."

"I see."

"I suppose it's all a matter of what you call *philotimo.*"

"That's right, Kemal. *Philotimo.* Love of honour. National honour. Family honour. Personal honour. It's all the same. It's the driving force behind every true-blooded Greek; what we live and die for. If you don't have *philotimo,* you are nothing - just an empty vessel.

"Quite simply, whatever happens in life, it is essential to maintain your *philotimo* - your self-esteem, and the respect of others. And you should never lose face, never be seen as the *koroido.*"

"*Koroido?*"

"Yes. You know, Kemal. What the Americans call 'a sucker.'"

"Huh! So much pride! *Christe mou*! I guess it was what stopped Nicholas marrying that Greek girl. And now, Christos, I suppose. it will stop you averting a war with Turkey."

"You could say exactly the same thing to your Prime Minister Suman. Why should we Greeks be the first to make concessions?"

"That's true. But in this case, you don't have to be seen as the *koroido*. Instead, you could gain enormous kudos by making the first move towards peace talks. It would be an act of superior statesmanship.

"Remember, Christos, that time we dined out at the King George. We all haggled over who was going to have the privilege of paying. But no one saw you as the *koroido* when you picked up the bill. In fact, it greatly boosted your *philotimo*."

"Ah, Kemal, if only all Turks understood us as well as you do. And you could be right about initiating talks. I will have to think about it..."

"Hello, Leonidas, what did you think of the view?"

Stavros snapped down the "off" switch on the tape-recorder. It had reached the point where he and his other guests had entered the room.

"*Bastarthos!*" he muttered audibly. Then he reached out for his *komboloia* and began twisting and clicking the beads impatiently. Suddenly he had realised the truth, the real meaning behind this trite discussion, which had preceded the Greek Premier's surprise emergence as a peacemaker. *O vromeros ipokritris!* The wily old fox was just playing a game.

It was all so clear to him now. He was remembering the curiously smug smile on the face of Andriopoulou when they had parted on that last meeting. He had seen that same self-satisfied smile on television only two weeks ago. At the time, Andriopoulou was telling reporters how he welcomed the fact that the U.S. Senate had formally approved the plan to restore the traditional ratio in granting defence and economic aid. As in the mid-1990s, there would again be seven dollars to Greece for every ten dollars granted to Turkey.

I poniri alepou! thought Stavros. He no longer merely suspected. He now felt that he positively knew: that the old fox had been playing at brinkmanship all along. He had never intended to wage a war with Turkey that he could not possibly hope to win. He had simply been raising the stakes to the limit, to the point where the United States would recognise the need to encourage the peace process with the promise of a multi-million dollar increase in aid.

Ordinarily, Stavros would have admired the cunning of Andriopoulou. Hadn't he himself often played such a bluff hand in the power game of commerce? But this time it was different. This time it had involved Tunaman, a well-meaning novice in the political game, and indirectly, perhaps, it may have led to the death of his beloved Georgios.

Stavros thought of the old saying: *whenever a Greek and Turk strike a deal together, at least one of them has been cheated.* It was true. In this case, the Turk had been cheated. He had come on the scene at precisely the moment when Andriopoulou was looking for a means of avoiding war without any personal loss of face. And from that point on, Tunaman was unwittingly being used as a pawn.

Stavros cursed the Premier for his double-dealing. More harshly, he cursed himself for having ever agreed to bring Tunaman and Andriopoulou together.

And soon his self-torment was to become greater still. At midnight, Athens time, he put through his third call to the Kolonaki police station. They reported that his son, Nicholas Stephanopoulos, had just been located by a patrol car making a second run up Mt Lykabettus.

This time, driving more slowly, they had caught Nicholas in the full beam of their headlights as they rounded a bend. He was lying, foetus-like and unconscious, on a grassy bank; the body partly covered in leaves scattered by the bitterly cold north-east wind. His tracksuit was frozen stiff, and around his neck hung a set of headphones linked to a Sony MP3 Player clipped onto his trousers at the waist.

At this very moment— seemingly more dead than alive— he was being rushed by the patrol car to Evanghelismos Hospital.

CHAPTER 11

At 1530 hours— only three-and-a-half hours after the killings in Chapultepec Park— the scene at the Mexico City headquarters of the *Procuraduría General de la República* was fast becoming one of organised chaos. Two circumstances were largely responsible for the mounting bedlam: firstly, the unprecedented, ever-rising number of press, radio and television people on the premises, secondly, and more seriously, the breakdown of *La Jaula*, the so-called cage which transported prisoners and interviewees directly from the drive-in basement to the fourth floor interrogation centre.

One hour earlier, the ground floor Press Reception Room had proved hopelessly inadequate. Therefore, all media representatives had been transferred to a nearby conference room. Outside, a large improvised cardboard sign bore the legend: *CENTRO DE INFORMACIÓN DE PRENSA.* For its occupants, this was an object of much derision. The centre provided seating, television, hot and cold drinks from two automats, and snacks delivered on a trolley from the canteen. But one thing it had not provided was information.

And something else was lacking: toilet facilities. Without such, media men and women could not be confined to the press centre. They needed access to the toilets at the end of the outside corridor, and on the pretext of needing relief, they were able to roam about at will, attempting to buttonhole any senior official they might encounter along the way.

Only half an hour now remained until the full-scale press conference when, they were promised, all would be revealed. In the meantime, however, their impatience was fuelled by the rumour that some news hounds, with valuable police contacts and big *mordida* to offer, had already learnt the identity of the assassin and were out and about digging up background material.

To Comandante Sebastián Barraza, the disorder and distraction caused by the media's presence was outrageous. Unlike the Procurador General, he had no interest in the well-being of press and television people. Indeed, if he had his way, not a single reporter would be permitted inside PGR headquarters.

But what distressed him still more this morning was the breakdown of *La Jaula*. He himself had recommended its installation when the PGR building was extended as part of the *Programa de Desarrollo du Milenio*. Via the cage-like basement lift, adjacent to the underground police garage, his men could maintain total security and secrecy in hauling in citizens they wanted to question.

It was not so simple now. Without *La Jaula*, detainees and witnesses had to be led up the basement stairs to enter one of the main elevators on the ground floor. The elevator nearest to these stairs was in the west wing of the building, halfway down the corridor that led from the press information centre to the toilets.

Already, reporters had spotted a number of nondescript men and women being escorted to the fourth floor. They remained unidentified – with one exception. A reporter recognised a fat, grey-suited Mexican, who emerged puffing from the basement stairs. He attempted to interview the man, only to be pushed back by one of the escorting officers. Meanwhile, Alfredo Gómez was quickly bundled into a vacant elevator.

In the circumstances, Barraza ordered extra security measures. Whenever citizens were being taken up to the fourth floor interview rooms, the ground floor corridor was to be completely closed off between the basement steps and the elevators.

Initially, Procurador General Rodríguez questioned the procedure. It would, he said, be rather inconvenient for the Press. Barraza glared invisibly behind his dark-tinted glasses. "*Señor*, we may be bringing in some major suspects. Did you ever hear of Jack Ruby and what happened to suspect Lee Harvey Oswald when he was in police custody in Dallas? Of course, I cannot imagine that kind of fiasco happening here. But do you want to take the risk - just to ensure that some damned reporter can quickly take a leak?"

Rodríguez acknowledged that he had a point.

At 1535 hours five Mexicans were gathered in the Procurador General's first-floor office for an exclusive, top-level briefing by José Rodríguez prior to his press conference. All but one were dressed in civilian suits. The exception, seated cross-legged to support his clipboard, was a man in a dark-blue uniform, immaculately pressed and with bright, gleaming buttons of silver.

Police Chief General Delgado was present largely as a matter of courtesy. He had no authority in the investigation, and he would not be attending the press conference. On the other hand, he needed to be kept informed of all developments, and to understand the strict limits on information to be released to the media.

Never missing an opportunity for self-publicity, Delgado had already arranged to make a personal appearance on Channel 13's *24 Horas* show at 7 p.m. Protocol demanded that he should make no comment on the PGR's investigation. But he could - and would - have plenty to say about police vigilance in general, and his determination to tighten up security in Mexico City.

The others present at the meeting were Comandante Barraza, Subcomandante José Ibarra, Deputy Attorney General Arturo Contreras, and Emilio Ortega, a fresh-faced young advertising executive whose effeminate manner and surprising selection as personal assistant to Rodríguez had given rise to malicious rumour. All had already been informed of the procedure for the press conference.

The Procurador General would be identifying the assassin, releasing details of his police record, and summarising the wealth of evidence against him. For the benefit of photographers, the two main exhibits - an M-21 sniper's rifle and five spent cartridges - would be put on display. Finally, he would be presenting to the conference the hero of the hour, *Sargento Segundo* Jesús Moreno of the Presidential Guard, who would read out a formal statement, explaining how he had confronted and, in self-defence, had shot and killed the armed assassin.

Although he never acknowledged the fact, Rodríguez was thankful that he had followed the Comandante's advice by postponing the press conference for one hour. Even now, with twenty-five minutes to go, there were still several important loose ends to tie up.

"As you know," he began. "We are very shortly to be joined by two Americans - a Señor McClellan of the CIA and Señor Carruthers representing the FBI. These agencies have generously promised to give us their support, and in turn I have promised *El Presidente* that we will give them our full

133

co-operation. They will, of course, be attending the press conference.

"Before they arrive, however, I want to stress that one aspect of our investigation must remain strictly confidential. That is the statement which we have obtained from this *hombre*, Gómez."

He glanced towards General Delgado. "It has rightly been pointed out to me that it would be most indelicate to reveal that a member of the Castillo family had sold information about the birthday party in the park. Moreover, I have spoken to *El Presidente* about it, and he agrees. He feels that the family has suffered enough grief without this added embarrassment.

"Of course, this matter must still be pursued. We will want to know whether Señor Velázquez or Gómez gave out this information to anyone else. And we cannot dismiss other possibilities. After all, dozens of people must have known about the party well in advance.

"But I cannot emphasise too strongly: this is a matter to be pursued with the utmost discretion. And certainly Señor Velázquez will not be brought in for questioning. Comandante Barraza and I have already agreed that a *judicial* should be sent down to Acapulco to interview him privately.

"Meanwhile, there is to be absolutely no mention of Velázquez in connection with this investigation."

Ortega forced a cough.

"You want to say something, Emilio?"

"If I may, Señor Procurador, there is just one small problem. A reporter recognised Gómez when he was brought in for questioning. He asked me about him, and I simply said he was helping us with our inquiries. Nothing more. But what if there are more questions?"

Rodríguez grimaced and thought about it for several seconds. "Hmm! That's the right line to take - *just helping us with our inquiries.* And you cannot say any more. At the same time, don't forget that the Channel 13 people already know about his video of the killings. If and when that issue comes up, we will have to explain that the video may reveal valuable evidence and cannot be released at this stage."

"And what about Gómez?" asked Barraza. "Is he to be released?"

"Of course not. Officially, he is still helping us with our inquiries. He should be held in protective custody overnight and we will review the situation tomorrow.

"Now, for one other important matter. As you can see, the case against this Manuel Ramírez is already overwhelming. The fingerprints and palmprints on the rifle, and his presence in the tower are enough to condemn him. Indeed, if he could be put on trial tomorrow and I was the prosecuting counsel, I would be totally confident of gaining a conviction.

"The fact remains that there is just one small discrepancy in the evidence. As you will see in the report from the *Departamento Forense*, they made tests which failed to reveal gunpowder residue traces on Ramirez's hands. Such traces would have indicated that he had recently handled a firearm."

Barraza smiled. Without his help the Procurador General had belatedly picked up the point that he had failed to observe in the preliminary forensic report. Rodriguez went on.

"There is one obvious explanation: that the assassin wore gloves for the shooting. But unfortunately no gloves are listed on the inventory of items recovered from the tower.

"It is a minor detail, but just the kind of thing the Press are likely to seize upon in trying to promote sensational conspiracy theories. So we will not be releasing the forensic report at this stage.

"But let me make this absolutely clear. We are not seeking to cover anything up. Our aim is to arrive at the truth. At the same time, we do not wish to complicate this case unnecessarily with a detail which could prove totally irrelevant.

"At this very moment, Comandante Barraza has men not only making a second search of the tower, but also combing the surrounding area. It is entirely possible that they may yet find the missing gloves. So until this search has been completed, no mention is to be made of the tests for gunpowder traces."

Ortega audibly cleared this throat. "*Señor,* what if some bright reporter should ask if such tests were carried out?"

"Most unlikely. But that brings me to one final point. After I have spoken to the Press, only a few minutes will be allowed for direct questions from the floor. I shall be emphasising that it is only a few hours since the killings, that it is much too early to speculate about motives or other persons behind the shooting, and that we cannot afford any more time for questions while there is urgent investigative work to be carried out.

"If, Emilio, you are personally approached with difficult questions, you should follow my example at the press conference. There are two standard answers. One. We cannot release information which might jeopardise our current inquiries. Or else you can say the question must be referred to Comandante Barraza.

"Incidentally, our Comandante, by his own request, will not be present at the conference. He has more urgent work to attend to.

"Oh yes, and there is just one other thing. The Comandante has brought to my attention that there is evidence that one or more officers may have already leaked information about the identity of the assassin. This is inexcusable. I have issued a memo to all departments that any officer found communicating with the Press will not only be summarily dismissed from the force, but may also be charged with obstructing justice. Perhaps, *Jefe*, you will do the same."

Delgado smiled. "Señor Procurador, it has already been done."

"Excellent. Now just to sum up. I want this press conference to strike a positive note. So far we have everything well under control...."

The Procurador General paused to press a switch in answer to a buzz on his intercom. It was his private secretary. "Excuse me, *señor*. You wanted to be told the minute the American gentlemen arrived. They are with me now."

The uproar in the PGR headquarters could not have come at a more embarrassing time - at 1559 hours, just as the Procurador General and his deputy were escorting the American observers to the Press Information Centre. On the ground floor they were approaching the west wing, close by the main toilets, when an appalling noise was to be heard from the corridor around the corner.

There was a loud thumping sound, then a bellowing voice. "You are all a lousy bunch of fucking crooks. Lackeys of the capitalist system and corrupt politicians. I tell you, my boy couldn't kill nobody. Come on then, you chicken bellies. Who will take me on? Put 'em up. Let's see how you can fucking fight."

The Procurador General rounded the corner to see three officers wrestling a fat, grey-haired man to the floor.

136

While two of them held him down, the other sought with difficulty to apply a pair of handcuffs. And all the while the man kept struggling and shouting. *"Cabrones!* Fucking cowards! I could beat any one of you motherfuckers!"

By now the disturbance had brought inquisitive reporters down the corridor beyond. Their way was blocked by police officers who were under orders to seal off the main elevator area on the ground floor. But they pushed several yards forward and one photographer held his cameras aloft, taking pictures over the guards' heads.

At this point, the fat man, securely handcuffed, was being hustled by officers towards the elevator. When the first flashbulb popped, he cried out, "That's it, *muchachos.* Get your pictures right. See, there ain't a fucking mark on me. I'm a hundred per cent fit. Make sure I look the same when I come out of this fucking joint." The camera flashed again.

A few seconds later he was out of sight, as the elevator carried him up to the cells adjoining the fourth floor interrogation centre.

"Hey, that was Quasimodo," cried an elderly reporter. He turned to the photographer accompanying him. "You've got to get those pictures back to the office. Pronto!"

Both men, along with other reporters, were now pushed back down the corridor. Meanwhile, behind the advancing guards, Ortega was shouting in his high-pitched voice, *"Señores, por favor, por favor,* return to the press centre and the Procurador General will be with you immediately."

Retreating beyond the press room door, the elderly reporter drew the photographer aside. "Listen. Forget about the conference. Any pictures there can be picked up from the agencies. It's more important you get back to the office."

"Okay. But just tell me. Who the fuck is Quasimodo?"

The reporter put his right index finger to his lips. "Shush, not so loud. You're too young to remember, kid. But that *hombre* fought the most sensational boxing match I ever saw. He was no good, just bloody brave and cunning. Modelled himself on an old *yanqui* fighter called Archie Moore. Some called him *El Cangrejo* because he was always shuffling sideways like a crab. But we called him Quasimodo because he was so hunched up and disfigured.

"Look. There's no time to talk now. I want you to give this note to Cabañas." Then, resting his notepad against the wall, he scribbled a message to his editor. It read: "*GRANDE*. Suggest dig out files on Fernando Ramírez, light-heavyweight boxer of some forty years ago, and have profile prepared. Lead to follow. Ortiz."

For José Rodríguez, his first press conference as Procurador General was a veritable nightmare. It lasted forty-five minutes, far longer than he had intended, and entirely because he lacked sufficient steel-like maturity to keep the voracious news hounds at bay.

Initially all went well. He had a wealth of meaty scraps to feed them: the identity of the assassin, his age, last known address and criminal record, the murder weapon, which he held aloft for all to see, pictures of matching fingerprints and palmprints taken from the rifle. Then came the high point: his presentation of the hero of the hour, *Sargento* Jesús Moreno.

The guardsman made an imposing figure: ramrod straight in his bearing, with a moustache and close-cropped hair slightly tinged with grey. He wore a green-and-brown camouflage uniform and carried a .38 revolver in a leather holster on his right hip. And like so many men recruited to the *Cuerpo de Guardias Presidenciales*, he was six feet tall.

Reading into a microphone from a carefully scripted statement, the sergeant recounted how the sound of gunfire had drawn him to the tower. "My main concern was for the public, especially with so many women and children gathering around. If there was going to be a shoot-out, I thought it best to confront the intruder as far away as possible.

"Because the stairs are so narrow, I decided it was safest to go up alone, leaving another soldier on guard at the entrance. I tried to creep up quietly, but unfortunately the stairs are made of metal. That was my big worry, that my heavy boots would give me away. The light was also a problem. Several windows provide beams of natural light, but there are only a few light fixtures on the walls. For most of the time I was in semi-darkness.

"But I had one big advantage. I knew that spiral staircase very well. In the past I had even counted the steps. I remembered that there were two circular resting platforms within the tower - one after 35 steps, another after 27 steps. When I reached the second platform I could hear the footsteps of someone moving above.

"There were another 28 steps to the top. I counted

138

them on the way. Then, when I came to the final curve, I sprang round the corner with my revolver extended ready to fire. I immediately saw a man silhouetted against the sky - a man standing with a rifle held in his right hand. I shouted, '*Sueltela*!' But he didn't drop it. Instead he raised his gun as if to shoot.

"I was lucky. Though the sudden light was dazzling, my shot hit him square in the forehead. And that was it."

The statement, delivered in a quiet, deadpan manner, brought spontaneous applause from a section of the Mexican press. As the clapping died away, Rodríguez stood up and beamed his approval. "Thank you all very much. And may I join with you in expressing our thanks to *Sargento* Moreno for giving us such a precise account of what happened.

"And now, if you will excuse him, the sergeant must return at once to barracks." He smiled. "I understand that the *Cuerpo* is planning a little celebration in his honour."

It was the last time the Procurador General smiled that day.

Several reporters protested at the sudden departure of Sergeant Moreno. They had a few questions they would like to put him. In reply, Rodríguez reassured them that they would be given ample opportunity to do so at the next press conference. "Give the man a break, *señores*. After all, he's had a pretty stressful day."

From that point on, the mood of the conference palpably changed. Questions became more aggressive, the tone being set by an Argentine reporter who called out, "Why wasn't the assassin spotted before he got in the tower? I understand it's always hept closed to the general public."

"That is true," replied Rodríguez. "You need a special permit to enter the tower. Also, I am told that there is always a chain across the entrance. The castle authorities say that until now they did not see any need to have a guard permanently stationed there."

In the face of more probing questions about security, the Procurador General said that he had no more time to spare. He would hold another conference tomorrow morning when he hoped to have much more information. But his last point was never heard amid the howls of protest, primarily from the foreign press corps. Inhibited by the presence of television cameras, he then made the fatal error of compromising with his audience.

More questions were allowed. At first he dealt with them deftly:

No, the origin of the rifle had not yet been established, but they were working on it. Unfortunately, the serial number on the breech had been filed down. However, the last time the police in Mexico City had seized an M-21 sniper's rifle, it was found to have been part of a consignment reported stolen from a U.S. Army base in Houston, Texas.

No, it was too early to speculate about the possible motive for the killing. No, as far they knew, Manuel Ramírez did not have any record of mental illness. And yes, they would be considering the possibility that Ramírez had been hired by some terrorist organisation. At this juncture he took the opportunity to introduce his two American guests as 'representatives of the CIA and FBI who, at the request of *El Presidente*, will be assisting us in our investigation in any way that they can'.

Then he began to stumble as other questions came in quick-fire succession. Who was the man who had caused a disturbance in the outside corridor? Why was Alfred Gómez of *El Informador* in the building under escort? Was he involved in the crime? What special police protection had been provided for ambassador Tunaman's appearance in the park?

More and more, Rodríguez was forced to fall back tamely on his standard reply: that to give an answer might jeopardise ongoing inquiries. Finally, and belatedly, the flustered Procurador General snapped, " *Señores*, this conference is now at an end," and he walked briskly out of the room. It had not been an auspicious start to his new Cabinet appointment.

For Comandante Barraza, in contrast, the beginning of the press conference brought a period of welcome relief. At last, at 1600 hours, he was able to concentrate on the task in hand without, for the time being, having to explain every move that he made to a Procurador General who lacked first-hand experience of police procedure.

While the conference was in progress, he took the opportunity to have a private interview with the one person who could give him a detailed account of events in Chapultepec Park prior, during, and immediately after the shooting. In the case of this witness, there was no unnerving wait outside the fourth-floor interrogation centre. U.S. marine Mark Ballantyne was shown directly into the Comandante's

140

office and extended every courtesy.

The interview was conducted with the aid of a female interpreter for whom it came as a considerable revelation. She had never before seen Barraza exude so much personal charm and patience. It was, she presumed, purely a diplomatic concession because the Comandante was dealing with someone from the U.S. embassy. But she was wrong.

Barraza's charm was genuine - prompted by the rare pleasure of dealing with a man who came up to his own exacting standards. Ballantyne, it soon emerged, had a near-photographic memory and an extraordinary matter-of-fact eye for detail. There were no wishy-washy answers, no emotional impressions: only precise information - about who was present, who was sitting where, how they were entertained, and the time and number of shots heard.

Most of this ground had already been covered in Ballantyne's formal statement to the police. Under Barraza's patient probing, however, the American's account of events took on more the aspect of a slow motion action replay; one that brought out such minutiae as the time of ambassador Tunaman's late arrival and his moving of a chair to seat himself between his daughter Yasemin and Finance Minister Martínez. The only thing Ballantyne could not be sure about was the order in which the victims were hit by bullets. For part of the time, while shielding the U.S. ambassador's son, he had had his head to the ground.

Barraza did not tell him that he had all the killings recorded on the Gómez videotape, and that the pictures clearly showed that, in turn, the boy Georgios, his mother, and then Martínez, were all shot as they moved into the line of fire, directly in front of the ambassador. What mattered was that Ballantyne's recollections were consistent with everything on the video. They confirmed him as a most reliable witness.

"*Gracias, gracias,*" repeated Barraza as he shook the marine's hand on parting. Then, through the interpreter, he told him, "You have been most helpful, *señor*. I only wish I had more like you under my command."

Shortly afterwards, Subcomandante José Ibarra arrived to give his boss an account of how the press conference had gone. It brought an unseen glint to Barraza's bulbous eyes. Ibarra, however, did not share his chief's *schadenfreude*. Unlike Barraza, he was a long way short of retirement. He

141

wanted a satisfied Procurador General, especially to safeguard his expected promotion.

"But there is some good news, Comandante. *La Jaula* has been fixed. It was working when I passed by."

"Huh! All too fucking late. The damage has been done."

By 1700 hours the ground floor of the PGR headquarters had been restored to orderly normality. In the press information room, only a dozen or so junior reporters remained behind on stand-by duty in case any new information was released. Some played cards, others watched TV. Meanwhile, their more senior colleagues had stampeded out of the building. They called their offices on mobiles, then frantically competed to hail taxis. The great majority of them were heading for Tepito - to scramble for background material on Manuel Ramírez.

A few reporters, with the advantage of purchased inside information, were well ahead of the game. But like those who came after them, they had found the pickings were thin: plenty of spicy tittle-tattle, but precious little of substance.

Welcoming attention, or else hungry for pesos, Tepito residents were all too willing to talk. Indeed, more than 300 people could claim to be neighbours of Manuel Ramírez since they shared the same *vecindad,* a large one-storey tenement, enclosed by high cement walls and shops, and comprising three separate concrete-paved courtyards onto which opened some seventy windowless apartments of either one or two rooms.

The Cuauhtémoc *vecindad,* named after the last Aztec emperor, was one of the few *vecindades* remaining in redeveloped Tepito: a self-contained community so intimately designed that everyone knew everyone else's business. Within its rectangle, families - many of them related by marriages or bound by ties of *compadrazgo* - came together in celebrating religious festivals. Women shared communal washing lines and outdoor water taps. Their children played and partied in the same courtyards, attended the same schools and joined the same gangs. And the men, mainly local tradesmen, artisans and labourers, joined in regular card schools and drank at the same nearby *pulquería.* Here inter-family gossip was an integral part of life.

Oh sí, our Pedro played football with Manuel at the

Centro Social Deportivo. Never liked him, even then. Too much of a loner. Always thought he would come to no good.

Manuel? An assassin, you say? That skinny little kid? I don't believe it. Are you sure you don't mean his papá? Now that Fernando, he's a real wild one. Did you hear what happened to him last New Year's Eve? Got arrested and fined for pissing against the side of a car. Silly bugger was so pissed, he didn't realise it was a police car.

Dios mio! Thank Our Lady his mother is no longer alive to suffer this news. It would have broken the poor woman's heart. I never knew anyone who worked so hard to give her children a better life. A living saint she was.

Hey! You want to talk to Consuelo Gutiérrez. If Manuel was going to kill somebody he should have killed her. What a bitch! Fuck me! You wouldn't believe what she did to him. Treated him worse than a dog. We all laughed at the time but it wasn't really funny.

Literally every adult in the Cuauhtémoc had heard the tragicomedy of Manuel's passionate pursuit of Consuelo Gutiérrez. It was the story most repeated to reporters.

Beyond the *vecindad*, the prime source of information was the headmaster of the Vocational School on Melchor Ocampo Street.

Sure, I remember Manuel Ramírez well. Always playing truant, that boy. Would you like to see his miserable report cards? I still have them on file, you know.

I'm not surprised he turned out bad. Why, even in his schooldays, he was working the bus racket. Trouble was he fell in with another boy called Ignacio Galván, the biggest villain in the school. It was Galván who got him into thieving - snatching purses in the market and then moving onto the buses. Landed them both in the Juvenile Court.

So the great scavenge hunt went on, producing sufficient jigsaw pieces to enable reporters to build up a composite picture of the life and times of Manuel Ramírez - until, that is, early August of the previous year. No one, it seemed, had seen or heard of him since then. The last five months of his life remained a blank.

Much more galling to the news hounds, however, was the fact that they could not track down one major character in the Manuel Ramírez story. There was no Consuelo Gutiérrez. No Iganacio Galván. Worse, they could not make contact with a single member of the huge extended Ramírez

143

family that had its roots in the Cuauhtémoc *vecindad.*

There was no mystery about this. Everywhere they went, reporters learnt Barraza's *judiciales* had been there before.

It was 1430 hours when four Shadows, two burgundy and two white, had pulled up at the entrance to the Cuauhtémoc *vecindad.* Immediately the cars attracted inquisitive onlookers. Their doors were boldly labelled with the sign: *Procuraduría General De La República.* And from them stepped a uniformed police officer and six plain-clothed *judiciales,* each carrying a .38 revolver in a shoulder-holster beneath his casual jacket.

Guided by the officer from the local police station, the detectives proceeded halfway down the first courtyard to the two-room apartment that was the last known address of Manuel Ramírez. The onlookers, who had now snowballed into scores, were duly ordered to stand back. Then the *judiciales* drew their revolvers, and standing to either side, hammered on the red door, which had been left half-open to admit fresh air and natural light.

An aproned woman wearing a helmet of blue curlers appeared in the doorway. Before she had a chance to speak, a detective grabbed her arm and pulled her outside. "Is there anyone else inside?" he snapped.

"Only my sister Ester."

"Call her outside. Tell her she is needed at once."

The man's voice was so authoritative that she automatically complied without protest. From within someone testily called out, *"Qué pasa?"* Seconds later, another woman came to the door, and was also promptly pulled out into the open. Then, with guns held double-handed at arm's length, two *judiciales* rushed into the apartment.

At the same time, another *judicial* climbed the wooden ladder which was resting against the outside front wall. It led up to a low flat roof which was crowded with a line of washing, a stack of chicken coops, various pots of flowers and herbs, and a large TV antenna. *"Nada aquí,"* he shouted down.

Once the apartment had been checked-out, the women were escorted back inside, and seated at a gleaming rosewood dining table in the centre of a room that was crammed to near bursting-point with furniture and appliances.

It seemed incredible that this had once been home for a family of thirteen. On either side of the doorway, a narrow single bed and a wardrobe occupied the interior front wall, and ranged along the right-hand wall were a washing machine, a wicker laundry basket, a refrigerator and a work-table with a manual sewing machine.

The far wall was largely taken up by a long dresser draped with a purple cloth and bearing a display of white-wedding photographs and individual family portraits. A gap alongside the dresser indicated the usual position of a convertible settee, which had been drawn out to be positioned only a few feet in front of a large colour television set, and a radio cassette player that stood at an angle in the left-hand corner.

In this main room, the only real open space was in front of the left-hand wall, which had a wooden crucifix at its centre. Below it, on a shelf illuminated by a red electric light, stood a glass-framed image of the dusky Virgin of Guadalupe borne aloft on clouds stitched in a needlework frill, and on either side an array of holy pictures and unlit votive candles.

In the far right-hand corner, an archway opened onto a small vestibule, which contained a wash-basin and a curtained-off flush toilet. From there, a narrow kitchen area formed a passageway to a bedroom at the rear. This second room was so small that almost the entire floor space was occupied by a single bed, a wardrobe, a reed chair, and a TV set and video recorder. Its walls were bare, except for a shelf piled untidily with books and videotapes. And unlike the main room, redolent of furniture polish, it stank of stale tobacco.

There was a time when this apartment would have qualified as a slum dwelling. But over the years, occupants had died or moved away, and progressively the released living space had been taken up with the trappings of an acquisitive consumer society. And for the few family members who remained, a low fixed rental was sufficient inducement to live on in relatively cramped conditions.

When the PGR men entered, the front-room TV was showing an old Debbie Reynolds movie with Spanish subtitles. Without apology, a burly, moustached *judicial* - self-evidently the senior detective - switched off the set and took a seat facing the two women. Two of his men stood by in front of the image of the Virgin. The others began searching the apartment.

Timidly, Ester asked what they wanted. The detective ignored her. "Don't you have an ashtray in this bloody place?"

As he lit a *Baronet,* Ester moved quickly to the dresser and brought out a glass ashtray from the top drawer, together with a lace doily to protect the table from being scratched.

The detective signalled for her to sit down again. "All you need to know is that we are conducting a murder inquiry, and that you are required to answer certain questions." He drew a notebook and ballpoint pen from his inside jacket pocket. "Firstly, what are your names?"

From his initial questions, the *judicial* established that the apartment was occupied by Fernando Ramírez, a 65-year-old widower, and his two unmarried daughters, Ester, 28, and Marta, 27. Fernando's youngest son, Manuel, 22, had lived with them until five months ago. Then he had moved out. He had not told them where he was going, and they had not had any contact with him since. Not even a postcard.

"And where is your father now?"

Ester could not be certain. "But usually at this time on a Sunday, he is at the *pulquería* on Tenochtitlán Street."

The detective turned and whispered something to the two officers standing behind him. They immediately left. Meanwhile, another *judicial* had begun removing family snapshots from their picture frames.

Ester cried out in protest.

"*Silencio,*" shouted the senior detective. "It is necessary. Give me any trouble and I will have you arrested for obstructing our inquiries." He was handed the snapshots. "Now, look at these carefully. I want you to identify everyone in these pictures. I want their names and their addresses."

In a trembling voice, Ester began. And to her horror, the detective marked the pictures accordingly, writing a number above each head and a corresponding name and address on the back of each photo.

Meanwhile, the other *judiciales* were completing their search of the apartment. The result of their work appeared in the shape of a supermarket cardboard box which had been emptied of vegetables, then refilled with letters and documents taken from the drawers of the dresser, and with books from a shelf in the rear bedroom.

The detective announced that he had finished. But he would require the women to accompany him back to headquarters where they would need to sign formal statements.

146

The Ramírez sisters looked horrified. Marta protested that she had to get ready for the evening *vecindad* dance. Ester said she had to rest because she was on the night shift, working as a cleaner at the Majestic Hotel close by the Zócalo.

The detective looked at them coldly. "*Señoritas*, the sooner you get ready to go, the sooner you are going to get back."

And then he had an afterthought. "Just one more question. Why did your brother Manuel leave home so suddenly?"

"He was upset," Marta replied. "He had just had a bust-up with his *novia*, Consuelo Gutiérrez."

The detective called out to the Tepito police officer who, all the while, had been standing guard at the front door. "Hey, González, you know a *señorita* called Consuelo Gutiérrez?"

The officer grinned. "Ah *sí, señor*. Everyone round here knows Consuelo. She lives down the other end of the *vecindad*."

The detective got up from his chair. "*Bueno*. With luck we can pick her up on our way back."

At 1715 hours Comandante Barraza was seated at his desk, still in the company of Subcomandante Ibarra. But now they had been joined by a third officer: Luis Enrique Montaño, the *judicial* who had led the raid on the Ramírez home in Tepito. On the desk were the family photographs removed from the Cuauhtémoc apartment.

Barraza picked up his TV remote control and pressed a button. Immediately a panel of six television screens lit up on the opposite side of the office. One screen gave an overview of a rectangular room furnished only with benches along the walls; another showed merely a blank wall and an empty bench in close-up. Three of the monitors gave different angled shots of six women and five men sitting in a row. The sixth screen portrayed a burly, crew cut man, shabbily dressed in faded-blue denims and, seated incongruously beside him, a young woman of flashy good looks.

It was Barraza's favourite toy, a device he had found of incalculable value over the years. By closed circuit television, he was able to monitor any detainees sitting in the main waiting-room of his interrogation centre on the fourth floor. People could see the overhead cameras and realise they were on view, just as they might be at a supermarket. None, however, could see the sound microphones that were well concealed beneath the wall benches.

The Comandante turned up the volume, and by pressing another button, he was able to isolate the sound on a selected screen. The crew-cut man was asking the young woman whether she had ever been to the *El Ratón Loco* nightclub in Eje Central. She shook her head.

"Ah, you should try it," he said. "It's real crazy..."

Barraza switched off the sound. "I think you will agree, *señores*, that we've seen and heard enough of this lot. What's the latest position with the father?"

"Last time I looked," said Montaño. "He was snoring like a pig in his cell. We could always give him the cold shower treatment."

"I think not. It could be a disadvantage to have him cold sober and alert. We'll let him sleep a little longer. Then put him in the waiting- room before we interrogate him properly. It could be interesting see how he reacts to that odd pair."

Montaño gave a toothy grin. "Ha! I like it, Comandante. The bull in the arena with the beauty and the beast."

All their eyes were now on the beauty as she stood up to move away from the beast. Consuelo Gutiérrez was dressed provocatively in a red knee-length skirt and a white, lace-trimmed off-the-shoulder blouse. When she rose from the bench, her stretch-blouse slipped sufficiently low to reveal a glimpse of her black areolae, and to confirm that she was not wearing a bra.

On standing erect, Consuelo ran her hands down her hips in order to straighten her tight skirt. Then, while swelling her ample, half-exposed breasts, she hitched up her flimsy blouse. Montaño licked his lips. Seconds later, the girl had vanished from the screen.

When she reappeared it was on a different monitor, and she was seated alone. Meanwhile, the man who had been cast as the beast was making a crude gesture: shaking a clenched right fist with his left fist tapping the inner crotch of his tattooed right arm. It did not need a lip reader to discern what he was saying.

Of all the detainees now in the interrogation waiting-room, Ignacio Galván had been the easiest to trace. He had been brought in because his name appeared on Manuel Ramírez's record sheet. And the computer at criminal records had immediately given his exact location. He was in *La Penitenciaría del Distrito Federal* in Iztapalapa, serving five years for armed robbery.

The other men and women in the waiting- room were seated close together. All were relatives of Manuel Ramírez: one brother, Ricardo; Ester and Marta; and four married sisters with their husbands. As already revealed by their tape-recorded conversations, and by their videoed actions, they detested Gutiérrez and Galván, and chose to sit as far away from them as possible.

Their conversations had also clearly established Ricardo as the dominant member of the family. He was the one who had kept talking about a possible abuse of human rights, and about their entitlement to legal representation. He had told his married sisters that the *judiciales* had had no right to invade their home without a search warrant. And he had advised everyone to keep a careful note of how long they were detained and, if necessary, to seek compensation for any loss of earnings.

Barraza switched off all the screens. "Let's get on. If we're going to get anything useful from this, I would have expected it by now. All we have got from them are more questions: *How could he do such a thing? Why would he do it? When are we going to get out of here?* And a lot of family crap.

"It's time to start questioning them one by one. Luis, I want you to take charge of the interrogations. The sisters look pretty useless to me. If you are satisfied with their answers, you can release them. The husbands, too. But we'll hang on to that smart-arse brother, and of course we'll detain Gutiérrez and Galván. And be sure they all sign the usual statements."

Detective Montaño smiled. He was feeling pleased with himself. The Comandante's use of "Luis" was confirmation in itself that he had done his job well. Indeed, he could not think of any detail he might have overlooked.

Within two hours of his arrival at the Cuauhtémoc apartment, the PGR had rounded up every available member of the Ramírez family, plus Manuel's former girl friend. He himself had brought in Ester, Marta and Consuelo, and, on the strength of information he had sent over the car radio, teams

149

of *judiciales* had tracked down other relatives in their Mexico City suburban homes.

Ruthlessly, the *judiciales* had insisted on the married sisters being accompanied to headquarters by their husbands. In each case it had been necessary to ask neighbours to take care of their younger children. And one sister, Señora Anita Herrera, had been hauled in for questioning even though she was seven months pregnant.

The only error in Operation Round-up had been made by the men delegated to seek out Fernando Ramírez in the local *pulquería*. But that was no reflection on Montaño. He had already pointed out that, if he had been in charge of the mission, he would have handcuffed the old man from the start.

As the meeting broke up, Montaño turned to his chief. "One last point, Comandante. Is there any news of the other brothers?"

"That's all under control," Barraza replied. "Our men in Guadalajara are already on their way to the home of Antonio Ramírez. If necessary, we'll be having him flown down here. As you know, the other brother, Julio Ramírez, moved to the U.S. four years ago. Our FBI friends are tracking him down."

CHAPTER 12

At 1900 hours, as always, the cloak of darkness spread itself swiftly over the Valley of Mexico. For the Azteca, five centuries before, it had been a sorrowful hour, a time to pray that their warrior-god Huitzilopochtli, the Blue Hummingbird, would successfully put the night gods to flight lest they vanquish the sun. And just to improve the odds, they made mass sacrifices to the sun god Tonatiuh, who needed a constant diet of human hearts and blood to keep up his strength for the eternal struggle.

For the inhabitants of modern Mexico City, however, there was no disturbingly sudden transition from day into night. The coming of darkness was anticipated by the twilight glow of myriad illuminants— the floodlighting of monuments and *glorietas*, the flashing of neon advertisements, the beam of car headlamps in their countless tens of thousands, and far and wide the soft candescence of street lights set in traditional five-bulb clusters.

Gazing out of his office window, Comandante Sebastian Fidel Barraza was very much aware of the closing-in of night. It reflected his mood: a sense of bleak foreboding born out of the realisation that his investigation was becoming more complex and contorted by the hour. For the most part, the evidence seemed clear enough. But it was all too superficial, and now bathed in a wholly artificial light.

The coming of night reminded him of the time; a few minutes late, he switched on to catch Channel 13's *24 Horas*. Isabel del Rio, glamorous as ever, was on screen and in the midst of expressing regret that they would not, after all, be able to show viewers exclusive pictures of the killings in Chapultepec Park.

"We did have extraordinary pictures to show you— pictures of the killings as they happened. These were taken by chance when the birthday party in the park was being videoed on our behalf. Unfortunately, the police have now seen fit to confiscate our film as an aid to their investigations.

151

"Nevertheless, in the next hour, we will be bringing you a detailed reconstruction of this appalling crime. You will see where and how it was committed, meet the man who heroically tackled the armed killer, and hear first-hand interviews with friends and neighbours of the assassin, who has now been identified as Manuel Ramírez, a twenty-two-year-old, unemployed carpenter from Tepito. But first, to put you in the picture, we go over to the headquarters of the *Procuraduria General de la República* for a dramatic press conference."

Having observed that already no one was referring to an "alleged" killer, Barraza followed the press conference with cynical interest. It was a bigger cock-up than he had imagined. From there, the cameras moved on to the Cuauhtémoc *vecindad* where residents with trivial recollections of Manuel Ramírez eagerly seized their few minutes of TV immortality.

Here, the coverage was marred by the conspicuous lack of interviews with a single person who was either related to the named assassin, or had known him intimately. Nevertheless it had impact in two respects.

Firstly, there were colourful accounts of Manuel's disastrous courtship of Consuelo Gutiérrez. These were effectively brought to life by way of interviews with Consuelo's mother, who proudly held up to the camera a family album opened to show a bikini-clad teenager receiving second prize in a local beauty competition.

(The TV crew did not record the event that immediately followed this interview. Consuelo's father, a stallholder in *el Mercado de la Merced*, proceeded to auction all pictures of his daughter, one by one, to the assembled representatives of the press. The bikini shot alone fetched 1,000 pesos, more than Señor Gutiérrez earned in a month)

Secondly, and visually more important, there was the discovery that Manuel's father was none other than Fernando Ramírez, a boxer who had been a one-fight wonder over forty years ago. There were no up-to-date pictures of Fernando. But Channel 13 was able to dig up from the archives some black-and-white footage of the sensational Alvarez-Ramírez light-heavyweight championship bout. (Subsequently, following a flood of telephone calls from viewers, they promised to screen a recording of the entire fight on Monday evening.)

For balance, Channel 13 needed at this stage some weighty and live in-studio discussion of events. Both the

Turkish embassy and the PGR's office had declined an invitation to send a representative. But the gap was adequately filled. Centre stage now was General Juan Delgado, immaculate as ever in his dark-blue uniform, his moustache newly trimmed, his black hair sleeked back and parted down the middle.

Channel 13 had not needed to request his appearance. He himself had insisted upon it. This procedure was quite normal. Such was the power of a Mexico City chief of police that he could demand television time at will. In the same way— as had happened in this case— he could command a national newspaper to give him a half page or more to publish an official statement of his own design.

Delgado was now in his element. Not only was he being interviewed by Señorita Isabel del Río, a personal friend, but to his advantage, he was appearing soon after the inept press conference performance of the Procurador General.

Barraza knew exactly what was coming: the police department's equivalent of a party political broadcast. Yet he kept watching, fascinated by the style of a consummate self-publicist who could make even a tragic failure seem like a personal triumph.

Del Rio, to her credit, did not pull her punches. After the mandatory exchange of courtesies, she went straight to the point. "Señor Secretario, about today's terrible events. Could not this dreadful tragedy have been averted with proper police vigilance? To be specific, where were your police when a great international diplomat and a government minister were so vulnerable in Chapultepec Park?"

Like a skilled politician, Delgado did not address the question until he had delivered his well-rehearsed spiel. Putting on a suitably grave face, he replied, "Firstly, Isabel, let me say how appalled we all are at this senseless slaughter. My heart goes out to the families of ambassador Tunaman and our Finance Minster, Roberto Martínez. All our thoughts and prayers should be with them at this time. They have suffered the most grievous loss."

He paused. "But to return to your question. Yes, I believe this tragedy could have been averted, and that makes it even more sad."

Turning to look directly into the red-lit camera, he continued, "In this great city of ours we have a police force second to none, I am truly proud of the brave, conscientious

153

men under my command. But the truth is that we cannot always be effective without a measure of civilian co-operation. Sadly, in this particular case, such co-operation was lacking. We were *not* informed that distinguished persons were attending a party in the park. Otherwise, according to strict procedure, we would automatically have provided special protection. And these security measures would have included screening all high vantage points overlooking the location."

Del Rio persisted. "That is indeed unfortunate. But, Señor Secretario, the fact remains that an armed assassin was able to gain access to a tower at the heart of *El Castillo* – and this despite the presence of numerous guards. In the end, it was the military who dealt with the situation. Should not the police have done more?"

Delgado was smiling sardonically now. "You are absolutely right, Isabel. There are serious lessons to be learnt from today's tragedy. Not least, it reinforces what I have been saying for a long time: that all my men on duty at Chapultepec Castle – and at other major tourist attractions – should be properly armed.

"At present, we have the *preventiva* police in *El Castillo*. They wear navy blue uniforms, but they carry no guns. Then there are private security personnel. They are equipped with walkie-talkies, but again they are without guns. The only armed guards are the 50 or so troops drawn from *El Cuerpo de Guardias Presidenciales* and assigned to watch *El Castillo* 24 hours a day.

"I appreciate that *El Castillo* has a great military tradition. The fact remains that law enforcement is best left primarily to the police, and it is my earnest hope that this tragedy will result in a review of castle security, especially regarding the restriction on having armed police there."

Predictably, they had reached the point where the interview turned into a monologue. As was his wont, Delgado had taken full control. Now in full flight, he was speaking directly to the on-vision camera. "I want to take this opportunity of reassuring viewers— and especially foreign tourists— that we are not on the verge of a major outbreak of terrorism in our great city. I am satisfied that we have the situation under firm control. Maximum security operations are already under way. At this very moment we are..."

Barraza hit the off-switch. Delgado was saying nothing of substance. But he had to admire the man's style. Unlike the

Procurador General at his press conference, the police chief had not once been thrown on the defensive. He was a master of media control.

The Comandante returned to the work he did best: panning through a mass of statements and reports to sift out tell-tale golden nuggets that others might have missed. Reminded by the TV recording of the press conference, he went directly to the statement delivered by Sargento Segundo Moreno. It was as he thought: there were blatant discrepancies in the man's recollection of events. But then, so it seemed to him, this investigation was riddled with discrepancies and contradictions.

Not least, there was the absence of powder traces on the hands of the alleged assassin. Within thirty minutes of the shooting, forensic experts had taped the hands, wrists, and shirt cuffs of Manuel Ramírez. Subsequently, those tapes had been placed under a scanning electron microscope (SEM), which bombarded with electrons any particles present. In the process, individual particles gave off X-rays, which could be viewed in a spectrum on a TV screen. Then, by careful scrutiny, it was possible to analyse elements within each spherical particle.

Given the short time that had elapsed since the shooting, the scientists had fully expected to find traces of metal elements – lead, barium or antimony, which were concomitant with particles found in condensed gun smoke. But there were none. There was absolutely nothing to indicate that Ramírez had recently fired a gun.

By now, as the shadows lengthened around Chapultepec Castle, Barraza had called off the search for a pair of gloves. All the possible ground had been covered twice over. But the Comandante was not disappointed; from the beginning he had never believed in the existence of gloves. Why, he reasoned, should Ramírez protect his hands when he had already left fingerprints and palmprints all over the rifle?

Earlier, he had put that question to the Procurador General. But Rodríguez had dismissed it, saying that he no longer attached any importance to the lack of gunpowder traces. It was, as he had put it, "one negative molehill on a mountain of positive evidence." Moreover, he had spoken to some legal friends, and they had suggested that it was entirely possible that the assassin's hands were sweaty after the shooting, and that he had therefore wiped them thoroughly.

155

The police had, after all, found a yellow rag in the turret.

The Comandante had smiled at the time. This possibility, in fact, had occurred to him several hours before. Consequently, he had instructed the forensic department to check for gunpowder traces on the yellow rag. Again the tests had proved negative.

Barraza chose not to mention it. Rodríguez could have his little moment of self-satisfaction. It was hardly worth arguing about since the absence of powder traces, taken on its own, was not critical to the investigation. Nevertheless, he found this detail disturbing when viewed in conjunction with other emerging inconsistencies.

The most obvious of these was the conflicting evidence of professionalism and amateurism, of careful planning and reckless, almost kamikaze-like execution. The time and place had been expertly predetermined, and someone had taken the precaution of filing down the registration number on the rifle so that the gun's origin could not be traced. Yet the assassin had used a high-velocity rifle which could not be fitted with a silencer to muffle the sound of gunfire. There had been no apparent effort to avoid leaving fingerprints and palmprints, and there was no evidence of a feasible escape plan.

Methodically, Barraza now took out a notepad from his desk and began to draw up a list of the pluses and minuses in the case against Manuel Ramírez. In terms of hard facts, the pluses easily won the day. But on the minus side, he assembled a wealth of intangible evidence largely based on his personal impressions. And those impressions, too weighty to ignore, were reinforced as he analysed the statements sent down from the fourth floor.

The interrogation centre of PGR headquarters took up almost the entire fourth floor. It comprised two waiting-rooms, one large and one small, which were flanked on one side by a corridor leading onto a block of cells, and on the other by a corridor lined with doors to small interview rooms, each furnished only with one table and three chairs. In addition, there were offices for on-duty *judiciales*, and a restroom for guards who worked twelve-hour shifts.

Here, between 1730 and 1900 hours, relatives and acquaintances of Manuel Ramírez were individually questioned by a team of *judiciales* who worked in pairs under the direction of Luis Montaño. All interviews were recorded on audiotape, and at the end every interviewee was required to sign a formal statement.

At the Comandante's instruction, they began with the one brother available, Ricardo Ramírez. But not before they had subjected him to an unnerving experience. He was chosen to make the formal identification of the alleged assassin, whose naked body lay on an operating table in the basement laboratory of the PGR forensic pathologist.

Ricardo was escorted to the laboratory by a *judicial* who, on their arrival, pulled away the white dust sheet to reveal, deliberately, the entire cadaver. "Is that your brother, Manuel?" he coldly asked.

Ricardo clasped a hand to his mouth and quickly turned away. He felt sick. Following a full autopsy, which included the removal of the whole stomach for analysis, little Manuelito had been padded out with old newspapers and then zipped up like a body bag, with crude stitching that ran straight from the pubis to the neck, except for one small detour around the tough tissue of the navel.

But it was the head that shocked the brother most. Between the eyes was a gaping hole that ran clear through the skull. The huge exit wound at the rear was not visible to him, but he could clearly see the circle of stitching to repair the external damage caused by sawing off the top of the head to remove the brain. The overall effect was of a Frankenstein-style monster.

Ricardo moved quickly to a wall fixed basin, and vomited. "Well," said the *judicial*, as he handed him a length of thick tissue torn from a dispenser. "Is that him?"

The brother nodded, and vomited again. Ten minutes later he was seated in a cell-like interview room, facing his inquisitor across a table that was bare except for a tin ashtray and a portable tape recorder.

The identification procedure, it seemed, had had the required effect. Ricardo was no longer the barrack-room lawyer. Looking pale and drawn, he timidly asked if he might have a cigarette. His inquisitor smiled and tossed a pack of *Fiesta* and a box of matches onto the table. "Of course, *amigo*. Help yourself. How about you, Ramos?

A second *judicial* emerged from the shadows and stepped into the hooded beam of the central overhead light. He said nothing as he reached for a *Fiesta,* and then leaned over the table to share Ricardo's trembling match, all the while fixing the detainee with an icy stare.

From experience, Barraza had judged Ricardo to be the most promising subject for interrogation. He was more intelligent than the rest, but also more vain and garrulous: a man ever eager to command the conversation and impress others with his superior knowledge.

More importantly, Ricardo had long since acquired middle-class respectability. The Tepito streetwise kid was now a balding businessman, very comfortably off with his own record and video/TV store strategically well-sighted on Lázaro Cárdenas, a broad avenue north of Calle Tacuba. In this downtown area, close by movie theatres, colourful bars and burlesque clubs, he also operated as a part-time agent for budding entertainers.

At 37, Ricardo was the second oldest of the four Ramírez brothers, three years younger than Antonio, and ten years and fifteen years older than Julio and Manuel respectively. The key to his relative success was a flair for electronics, a talent developed at *la Escuela Vocacional* on Melchor Ocampo Street. From working on stolen TV sets and videos, he had graduated to starting a legitimate business in Tepito.

It was only three years ago that he had opened his store on Lázaro Cárdenas. Since then, he had prospered dramatically. Business was booming. He drove a flashy Jaguar XJ6, and he had a steady turnover of mistresses in his bachelor apartment above the store. He was a man with a lot to lose.

How did he explain the sudden advance in his fortunes? More precisely, how had he found the capital to transfer his business to such a prosperous area? Those were questions that his inquisitors most pointedly asked, and his reddened face told that they had struck a sensitive nerve. At the very least, he thought, they would get him for tax evasion.

For fifteen years, Ricardo explained, he had been carefully building up his savings from his TV repair shop in Tepito. But no, he did not have any trading records to account for his income in detail. Then, under pressure, he admitted that he had had important financial assistance.

"It came from my brother, Julio. After his first year of fighting in the States he sent me 50,000 dollars to get started. We were to be partners. The idea was that he would come into the business when his boxing days were over. It was

158

his insurance for the future, see."

"Oh yeah? So where is Julio now?"

Ricardo shifted awkwardly on his chair. "I don't know. That's the odd thing. A year ago he sent me a postcard from Chicago. Said he had some kind of eye trouble, and was planning to retire, and would see me soon. And I haven't heard from him since. Nor has anyone else. We're all worried about him."

"So how do we know that the money came from him? Have you got any proof? Any bank records or written agreement?"

Ricardo shook his head. "Nothing. The money came in a parcel. All in $50 bills. There was a letter about our business plans, but I didn't keep it. I wish I had now."

The questioning went on for another hour – questions about his politics, about his relationship with Manuel, about his precise movements and contacts over the past week. Then, after he had signed a detailed statement, he was sent back to the main waiting-room with the parting words, "We may want to talk to you again later."

By 1900 hours, after all thirteen detainees had been interviewed, only three remained in the waiting-room: Ricardo Ramírez, Consuelo Gutiérrez, and the convict, Ignacio Galván. All the others had been released on the proviso that they did not leave the city until further notice.

In addition, the eldest of the Ramírez brothers had been eliminated from inquiries following receipt of his statement faxed from Guadalajara. There the local *judiciales* were satisfied that Antonio Ramírez, a forty-year-old metalworker, had long since broken off contact with his Mexico City relations. Currently he was immobile, recuperating from hepatitis.

In Barraza's estimation, the interviewing had been a largely worthless exercise. The testimony of the Ramírez sisters fully supported Ricardo's accounting for his sudden wealth. And in their separately made statements, all the relatives adamantly agreed on key points. They had not seen or heard from Manuel in the past five months, nor from Julio in the past year. They were all totally amazed that Manuel could have become involved in any kind of killing, and they could offer no explanation as to his motive.

Of all the interviewees, none was more eagerly co-operative than Ignacio Galván. In the hope of improving his chances of parole, he talked freely and in great detail about his teenage days of petty thieving with Manuel; how, from shoplifting and pickpocketing in the markets, they had moved on to "working the buses".

But his statement, too, contributed nothing of value. Bitterly, he recalled the last time they had worked together. It was on a packed city bus in the rush-hour. While Galvan 'accidentally' blocked the path of any would-be pursuer, Manuel had snatched a lady's handbag and ducked out the automatic rear doors as they were closing.

"It was a simple operation. All the *cabrón* had to do was walk away without attracting attention. But then a police patrol car passed by, and he panicked. Just dropped the bag and ran. *Chingado*! How that chicken Manuelito could run! It was all he was good for.

"I tell you, that kid was a real *cobarde*; had a yellow streak as long as a *verga de burro*. If he killed someone, as you say, he must have been high on some fucking powerful pot."

Looking through all the statements, Barraza read only one that lent any credence to Manuel in the role of an assassin. Consuelo Gutiérrez said she wasn't entirely surprised. "I always thought he was a little bit loco. He lived in a dream world, that one. Again and again, I told him I wasn't serious about him. But he wouldn't listen. Just kept on pestering me.

"The last time I saw him was back in August. For once he had plenty of money. Told me he had won a 1,000-peso prize on the *lotería*. But he soon squandered all that, and then he disappeared.

"I reckon he was looking for a way to get rich quick, and that he was so desperate he might try anything. He thought he could buy me, you see. But while he kept promising me the moon, he could only come up with peanuts.

"No, he never talked to me about politics. What he talked about most was memories of his *mamá*. He absolutely adored her. I don't think he really wanted a *novia*. He wanted a *mamá* substitute."

It was now shortly after 1930 hours, and the Comandante decided to play one last card before calling it a day. By phone, he gave Montaño the go-ahead to have Fernando Ramírez woken up and escorted into the waitingroom. Then he switched on his video screens to look and listen.

160

Barraza knew it was a long shot: putting the bull in with the beauty and the beast. But even he was not prepared for the fiasco that followed.

When Fernando entered the room under armed escort, he was visibly still the worse for drink. While two guards remained in the doorway, he lurched forward into the welcoming arms of Ricardo. Then, over his son's shoulder, he glimpsed Galván seated in a corner. "What's that bum doing here?" he bellowed.

Pushing Ricardo aside, he advanced on the convict, who promptly rose from the bench. Fernando prodded him in the chest and growled, "You fucking *cabrón*. What you done to my little Manuelito?"

Immediately, Galván jerked his head forward to butt Fernando just above the eyes. Then his right fist sank deep into the old man's flabby midriff. Fernando crumbled to the floor.

It was all over in a few seconds. The guards rushed forward to put Galván in handcuffs. Fernando, with blood oozing from his forehead, was carried back to his cell to await examination by the PGR's resident doctor.

Barraza had seen enough. After ordering Montaño to have Ricardo and Consuelo driven home, he abandoned work for the day. He would get an early night and make a fresh start at the crack of dawn.

CHAPTER 13

On Sunday evening, after being driven home by PGR *judiciales,* Marta Ramírez did not go to the Tepito dance, and her sister Ester did not report for her working nightshift at the Majestic Hotel. Instead, they were virtually prisoners in their Cuauhtémoc apartment where two policemen were posted outside to keep the hordes of reporters and photographers at bay.

Long after dark, reporters and television crews remained in the *vecindad* in the hope of waylaying Consuelo Gutiérrez or Fernando Ramírez on their return. They waited in vain. Fernando was held in police custody overnight, and Consuelo, on her release, was not to be seen until eight days later.

As prearranged, Consuelo was met at PGR headquarters by her father. To her astonishment, he picked her up in a chauffeur-driven BMW. "It's okay, *querida,*" he told her. "Your troubles are over. From now on, you'll get paid for answering questions. Then we're going on a holiday to Zihuatanejo."

Without consulting her, Señor Gutiérrez had made a deal with *Alarma!* Mexico City's most lurid news rag was paying 75,000 pesos for Consuelo's exclusive first person story with pictures. Included in the deal was a one-week, all-expenses-paid holiday, on condition that Consuelo posed for beach shots in a topless tanga.

After four hours in the PGR building, Consuelo felt tired and dirty, and she was so sweaty that her nipples showed large and black through her flimsy white blouse. But the promise of a small fortune for one evening's work now brought fresh sparkle to her dark, expressive eyes. As her self-appointed agent explained, they were staying overnight at the *Alarma!* offices and flying out early next morning. He had a bag packed with her favourite dresses and accessories.

162

That evening, with stretch blouse positioned revealingly low, Consuelo posed for the picture which was to take up the entire front page of *Alarma!*, together with the bold caption: *MI VIDA SEXUAL CON EL ASESINO DE CHAPULTEPEC.*

Then, over a takeaway meal of *enchiladas con guacamole*, plus liberal measures of *Ron Rico* rum and coke, she talked for almost an hour, recalling for a reporter everything and anything she could remember about Manuel Ramírez. The spice of her ghost-massaged words emerged as follows:

...I have heard what people are saying: that I screwed up his life, that it was my fault that he turned into a killer. Well, it wasn't really like that. The boy was pure loco from the start. Never listened to anything you said, but seemed to live in a dream world of his own. It was a funny thing. We had grown up in the same vecindad, but he never really noticed me until last Easter when I came second in a local beauty contest. Mind you, he was five years older than me, and for a long time I was so skinny that they used to call me la campamocha.

I guess I was a late developer. Because suddenly, when I was seventeen, my bust ballooned up like it is today. And that was when Manuel started pestering me for a date. Other girls had warned me about him, that he was just a fast-working stud with no money and no prospects. So I kept saying, 'no.' But that only seemed to turn him on more.

In the end, I agreed to go with him to the movies. But it was more like going to lucha libre. Straight away, he was groping inside my blouse. No finesse. It was obvious he wanted only one thing. Why, he even took my hand and placed it between his legs just to show me how big his one-eyed snake was. It was big, all right. But who cares? He wasn't going to get inside my knickers for the price of a movie ticket.

After that, we went to the movies a couple more times, and then on to a meal at a nearby fonda. But I didn't like it. So much groping, and only eating in cheap dumps. Also, I found him impossibly boring. His only idea of fun was a lot of love talk, kissing and trying to get physical. I told him to get lost.

The trouble really started several weeks later when he

163

bumped into me at the Prostitutes' Ball in the dance-hall on Niño Perdido Street. He immediately got the wrong idea. Like so many newcomers, he jumped to the conclusion that all the girls at the nightly dance were on the game. But that isn't quite true. You don't have to go bed with the customers.

To me, it is just an easy way of making money, and having some fun on the side. To get in, we have to pay a 50-peso cloakroom fee. After that, we get paid 10 pesos a dance and a small percentage of the price of any drinks we can hustle from the men.

All the girls wear off-the-shoulder cotton dresses or satin blouses that slip teasingly lower and lower as each dance progresses. This way your partner is encouraged to ask for a second dance or more, and since each dance lasts only three minutes, the money can add up fast.

Sure, most of the girls are available for a longer, more intimate duet. Some charge 500 pesos or more to go off to the nearby bordello. And if you leave with a customer before 1 p.m. closing time, you have to pay another 50-peso fee to the club. But that wasn't my way. I'm fussy who I sleep with. Especially with so much Aids about.

Anyway, one night Manuel turns up, and right away he makes a grab for me. Wants to know what the hell I am doing there, and didn't I have any shame. What a cheek, coming from him!

Then he sees one of the staff glaring at him, and he gets the message. He has to dance or buy me a drink. So he pulls me over to a table and orders an overpriced bottle of cheap brandy. I didn't mind. I was glad to rest my feet.

He is still looking angry, and straight away he asks me how long I have been coming here. I tell him it's none of his fucking business, but if he must know this is my first time. It was a lie, but it did the trick. All at once, his attitude changed. He got all soft and protective. Began to sound almost like my mamá.

He told me I should get out of this place before it was too late, that I was too young and talented to be throwing my life away. With my looks, he said, I ought to be in the movies or at least be trying to get work as a professional model.

I told him that it took money to get the gear and portfolio for modelling. Why else did he think I was here? Then he flashed his wallet and asked how much it would take to make me leave right away. I just smiled. He suggested 500 *pesos, and I nodded.*

What a hypocrite! He didn't want me to lose my virginity at the Prostitutes' Ball. But once we were outside he got all physical again, and for 500 pesos I didn't put up much resistance.

That night we made it at the bordello. I didn't mind because he was clean-shaven and had a nice firm body - not like so many of the slobs you meet at that dance-hall. And at least it was quick and easy. He was in and out like a rattlesnake.

Afterwards he was grinning from ear to ear. "Wasn't that great?" he asked. I felt like telling him that it was the length of the fuck, not the length of el pene that counted. But I didn't. After all, it worked out that I was getting paid about 150 pesos per minute. Not a bad night's work.

Manuel had got what he wanted, and so I thought that was the end of it. But I was wrong. Quite the reverse. As we walked back to the vecindad, he came on real serious, and declared his undying love for me. From now on I was his novia. I need never get so desperate for money again because he would do his best to support me.

I should have told him there and then I didn't fancy him, and that, anyway, I had already met someone who could satisfy all my needs. But it was late, and I was tired, and I didn't feel like getting into an argument. Also, to tell the truth, I felt a bit sorry for him. I couldn't understand how someone his age could be so naive.

It was my big mistake. Two nights later came the crazy scene that people are saying sent Manuel clear out of his mind. I couldn't believe it. The time was well after midnight, into Sunday morning. And because my parents and sister were visiting relations in Toluca, I had brought home my real novio, Armando.

Then, just when we were in the middle of making love, I heard guitars gently strumming outside the door. Suddenly a trumpet sounded and a loud, tenor voice began singing, Despierta, dulce amor de mi vida. Despierta!"

Despierta! Jesús! It was enough noise to have awakened the dead. The music rose to a beautiful crescendo, and all the while, through two more choruses, Armando kept thrusting inside me, deeper and deeper, faster and faster.

It was pure ecstasy. But then, as we lay back exhausted, I grasped what was happening. Outside I could

165

hear someone saying, *"Are you sure she's sleeping in there? Let's try one more song."* And the guitars started playing "Paloma querida."

The serenade was for me!

I gave Armando a big kiss and hug. *"Oh, querido,"* I cried. *"How wonderfully romantic! How clever of you to arrange a serenade with such perfect timing."*

He laughed and replied, *"Not me, mi amor. You must have some other admirer."*

Then he got off the bed, collected omething from the top of the dresser, and said, *"Whoever he is, he deserves some reward."*

He was a devil, that Armando! He went to the door and opened it. Then, after standing there stark naked and pretending to jerk himself off, he tossed a small package into the crowded courtyard below.

"Here you are, Romeo," he called out. *"A present from the señorita."*

I didn't see what happened outside, but I guess one of the mariachis must have picked up the gift. Because I heard someone say loudly, *"Caramba! It's a packet of condoms!"*

Armando shut the door, but long afterwards we could still hear the shrieks of laughter outside. And someone shouted out, *'Viva La Trevi!'* You know, recalling how the singer used to throw condoms into the crowd at her concerts.

At the time I couldn't help giggling. But really it was more sad than funny. And next morning I heard the full story. Everyone was talking about it.

Apparently, Manuel had spent 600 pesos— all that remained of his lotería winning— on hiring an eight-man mariachi group from the Plaza Garibaldi. Not just any old group, but a class act called Los Galleros de Mexico.

What a waste! I had always dreamed of being serenaded in traditional style— you know, stepping out onto a verandah and throwing down a rose to my one true love. But this!

Manuel had to be loco. Coming here to make his great declaration of love; here in his own seedy backyard with all our neighbours looking on.

No wonder he was shattered when Armando appeared naked in my doorway and threw out those rubbers.

A girl friend of mine was out there, and later she told me that Manuel just stood there for a while, gaping in silent

166

horror and disbelief. Then, with laughter echoing all around
him, he clapped his hands over his ears, gave out a piercing
scream. and ran out of the vecindad.

I guess he must have crept back later to collect his
things. Anyway, as far I know, no one has seen him since.

All very sad. But really he had only himself to blame.
I certainly didn't encourage him. It was a fantasy all of his
own making.

Why did he become a killer? I never heard him talk
about politics. My own belief is that someone was paying him
big money, and that whatever he was doing, he thought he
was doing it all for me.

The Consuelo Gutiérrez story was sure-fire spice for
the lascivious readership of *Alarma*! But for mass appeal, it
could not compete with the comprehensive coverage of
Excelsior. At 2100 hours, the first copy of Monday's issue
was delivered to Vicente Cabañas, editor of Mexico City's
most prestigious daily. He called in two of his staff men for a
congratulatory drink.

For veteran crime reporter Félix Ortiz and
photographer Juan Serra, it was a day they would never forget.
They rightly anticipated fat bonuses from TV and agency
pick-up fees. But more importantly, they enjoyed the
exquisite pleasure of seeing an edition of *Excelsior* that was
dominated with their by-lined work.

Like all the main dailies, *Excelsior* had the full story
of Manuel's disastrous wooing of Consuelo, albeit cobbled
together from the much-coloured accounts of witnesses and
gossiping neighbours. In this case, however, the layout had
been greatly enhanced by the successful bid for the family's
picture of Consuelo in a micro-bikini. And *Excelsior* had very
much more.

Accompanying Ortiz's front page story of the
slaughter in the park was Serra's exclusive picture of Fernando
Ramírez pinned down to the floor by two PGR officers. The
caption read: *POLICIA NOQUEA BOXEADOR EN
INVESTIGACIÓN DE HOMICIDIO (Pg. 12).*

The centre pages were taken up entirely by the
Consuelo story on one side and by a profile of Fernando
Ramírez, with more pictures, on the other. Essentially, it was
Ortiz's triumph. He alone had recognised the one-time boxer
at PGR headquarters, and as a veteran reporter, he had the

advantage of having been ringside at Ramírez's famous fight over forty years ago.

Now, under the headline *QUASIMODO AGUANTA HASTA EL CAMAPANA FINAL*, he was able to give a graphic account of Fernando's one night of fame.

Mexico City, Domingo,

This afternoon, at the headquarters of the Procuraduría General de la República, I had the privilege of witnessing the comeback fight of a one-night wonder of Mexican boxing: Fernando "Quasimodo" Ramírez.

Some forty years ago, Ramírez made his swan song as a professional fighter in the most sensational light-heavyweight fight ever seen in Mexico City: a thrill-packed 10-round contest against an ex-policeman named Ramón "El Tanque" Alvarez.

Today, in a corridor of the PGR building, the sixty-five-year-old, Tepito-born scrapper took on an even sterner challenge: fighting single-handed against three armed policemen.

His audience included Procurador General José Rodríguez and his deputy, Arturo Contreras. And the fight— conducted without regard for the Marquess of Queensbury rules— resulted in Ramírez being wrestled to the floor and led away in handcuffs.

Subsequently, the ex-boxer was detained for interrogation as the father of Manuel Ramírez, the twenty-two-year-old, unemployed carpenter who has been named as the multiple assassin in Chapultepec Park.

In today's uneven contest, Fernando looked hopelessly out of condition: grey-haired, obese, a pale shadow of the young man who once tackled Alvarez El Tanque. Yet I recognised him instantly. The same wild, defiant glare was still in his hooded eyes, and it was unmistakable.

It was way back in the 1960s, at the Arena Coliseo, that I had last seen that look of raw, stubborn courage. The occasion was billed by the promoters as a fight for the vacant light-heavyweight championship of Mexico. But, in fact, it was never officially recognised as such. The Mexican Boxing Board judged Ramírez to be too inexperienced to qualify as a titlecontender.

Both the Press and the bookmakers agreed. The fight

was labelled "the mismatch of the century", and only its duration was open to betting. The odds ranged from evens for Alvarez to win by a first-round knockout to 25-1 against Ramírez staying the distance.

All the evidence justified those odds. Durango-born Alvarez was undefeated, having won six light-heavyweight fights in Texas, all by knock-outs. Ramírez was a failed middleweight who had fattened himself up to move into the higher division for the first time.

At the weigh-in, Fernando only just made the minimum weight, then one hundred fifty-five pounds. In tackling Alvarez, he was conceding sixteen pounds. to a man who was also three inches taller and possessed of a far longer reach.

Even so, the promoters were not entirely unjustified in calling this a fight for the vacant light-heavyweight championship of Mexico. After all, there were no other Mexican light-heavyweights around.

This was a boom time for Mexican boxing, a sport then on a par with bullfighting. But the fact remains that we don't breed our men big and strong. In the 1960s, more than half of all our professional boxers were either featherweights or bantamweights.

We also had a fair number of lightweights and flyweights. But only half a dozen worthwhile middleweights, two light-heavyweights, and just one heavyweight, the national champion Alfredo Zuany.

All boxers above the welterweight limit of one hundred forty-two pounds were compelled to cross the Rio Grande if they wanted to make a regular living. And there, facing the bigger yanqui breed, few of them survived for long.

Like so many middleweights, Fernando Ramírez had had his ambition fired by the long and glittering career of our own Kid Azteca. For eighteen months he based himself in Florida, picking up bouts in Tampa and Miami Beach. But he was fighting in the golden age of middleweights... in the wake of such giants as Sugar Ray Robinson, Carmen Basilio, Gene Fullmer and Paul Pender.

When he returned to Mexico City his record read: eleven fights, ten defeats— six by kayoes— and one win on points. Back inTepito, he took a job as a bricklayer.

Such was the background to Fernando's one venture into the light-heavyweight division. Essentially, he was a

169

failed middleweight lured out of retirement by one last chance to collect a fat purse to support his newly started family.

While we all predicted an easy Alvarez victory, the smart money— including mine— was on Ramírez to last more than three rounds at the rewarding odds of 5-1 against.

The reasoning behind this was simple. Alvarez's ambition was to start taking on leading American light-heavyweights and win recognition as a contender for the world title held by the Nigerian Dick Tiger. But so far he had won all his fights in four rounds or less. He badly needed a more prolonged workout.

Sure enough, the early rounds followed a predictable pattern. Alvarez made no attempt to score a quick knockout. Instead, he was content to throw long jabs and let his opponent run. The crowd booed and slow-handclapped through three tame rounds. Then, under orders from his corner, El Tanque stepped up the pace and began to move relentlessly forward.

To everyone it seemed the end was now imminent. Everyone, that is, except Fernando Ramírez. As we later discovered, he had staked half his 25,000-pesos purse at the 25-1 odds for going the full distance. And he had advised his Tepito compadres to do the same. His sole aim was survival at any cost.

For the next three rounds, undeterred by the jeering of the crowd, he continued to back-pedal without throwing a single punch in anger. He danced, ducked, sidestepped and weaved to such effect that Alvarez looked positively flat-footed. And on the rare occasions that Alvarez did corner his opponent, Ramírez dived inside his long arms, grabbed his would-be destroyer in a bearhug, and hung on for dear life.

By the seventh round, however, Ramírez had danced himself to a standstill. His legs felt like lead weights. And now Alvarez was grinning as, roared on by six thousand fans thirsting for blood, he moved in for the kill.

It was time, as Fernando later explained, to adopt part two of his preconceived strategy. No longer able to run, he merely shuffled crab-like from side to side, his back hugely hunched, his forearms and elbows tucked in to block blows to the body, and his face covered by his gloves with one eye peeping over a thumb.

From that moment on, Ramírez was a human punch bag, almost stationary, and only in the intermittent clinches was there any let-up in the torrent of blows that pounded into both sides of his head and into his visibly bruised forearms.

Every cry of "break" from the referee ignalled a fresh onslaught. Ramírez effectively protected his body and chin, but he could no longer shield his face. Again and again, by sheer brute force, Alvarez smashed through his upper guard, landing hammer blows to the head.

Four times in the eighth round, Fernando was clubbed to the canvas. Three times, he rested on one knee before rising on the count of nine to face another savage attack. The fourth time he was only saved by the bell.

By midway through the ninth round, Fernando's left eye was completely closed; blood oozed from an ever-widening cut above the other. Miraculously, he stayed on his feet, but at the bell he had to be guided back to his corner.

Briefly, as a medical officer examined the cut, it seemed the fight would be stopped. But the crimson-faced Ramírez begged to be allowed to fight on and, perhaps more tellingly, Six thousand hysterical fans were screaming for more.

And so, beyond belief, it came to the tenth and final round. As Fernando, half-blind, shuffled out towards the centre of the ring, his back was so hunched, his face so grotesquely swollen and disfigured, that the TV commentator aptly described him as "Quasimodo responding one last time to the peal of the bell."

Fernando never reached the centre of the ring. He was barely three feet out of his corner when Alvarez was upon him, frantically unleashing a non-stop barrage of swinging lefts and rights to the head. His gumshield was sent flying.

Fernando was now stooped so low that Alvarez could not punch to the body. Instead, El Tanque successfully smashed through the hunchback's guard to open up a fresh cut above the hooded left eye, and then he delivered an uppercut that sank into an already flattened nose.

At this point it needed a miracle to save Ramírez from oblivion. And providentially the miracle came. As he slumped back, only supported by the ropes, the referee called a halt because the bandages on his right hand hadworked loose and were hanging out of the glove like the drop of a toilet roll.

Astutely, Fernando's corner men used up a full minute to make the necessary repairs. At the same time they gave their man a whiff of smelling salts, doused his head with

171

cold water, and slapped his face until they saw his eyes clear. They also took the opportunity to put a styptic solution over the cuts to both brows and to block off the bleeding from the nose.

When action was resumed, a full minute-and-a-half remained for El Tanque to complete the kill. It should have been enough. But he failed for two reasons.

Firstly, there was the almost superhuman courage and stubbornness of a Tepito-bred jungle-fighter who, through blind instinct, stayed on his feet while a fusillade of savage blows pounded into his head.

Secondly, there was the fact that Ramírez remained almost doubled up in his own corner while Alvarez towered over him. Quite simply, the referee could not get a clear view of the damage being inflicted. If he had, he would have stopped the fight immediately.

When the final bell sounded, Ramírez slumped to the floor, his face a raw mask of red. The rate of bleeding was appalling: blood cascading down his face, splattering onto his shoulders, chest and white shorts.

But no matter. The instant verdict was a win for the unmarked Alvarez on points. And, by virtue of those 25-1 odds, a win for no-hoper Fernando Ramírez of 312,500 pesos - in those days worth about $25,000.

Oblivious to the deafening roar of the crowd, Fernando was carried semi-conscious to his dressing room where a doctor attended his injuries, bit by bit cutting out pieces of gashed flesh with surgical shears, and then sealing up the cuts with more than thirty stitches.

Subsequently, in interviews, Ramírez said he had no recollection of the final round, and that he was still suffering from blurred vision.

What happened afterwards? Alvarez had no option but to return to boxing in the United States. The record books show that he won only one more fight after stepping up in class. He retired two years later.

As for Fernando, he never fought in the ring again. But then that had always been his plan. He celebrated his bonanza victory with a marathon drinking binge in the company of his Tepito compadres. Then, after a reckless spending and poker-playing spree, and undergoing a costly operation for a detached retina of the left eye, he faded into obscurity, a soon-to-be-forgotten freak of Mexican boxing

172

history.
  Forgotten, that is, until now.

  "If every day could be Sunday," Kemal Tunaman had said, "Mexico City would be one of the most enchanting cities on Earth."On this Sunday, however, its carnival of life had turned into a nightmare of carnage and confusion. The day of the dark Virgin of Guadalupe had been usurped by *la Santísima Muerte*, the goddess whose skull and skeleton image is ubiquitous every November 2, the Mexican Day of the Dead.
  Meanwhile, as this deranged Sunday drew to a close, a new day had just dawned in another far-off metropolis... in a capital which, much like Mexico City, had been transformed into an environmental Armageddon by over-population and over-industrialisation, and which only at weekends cast off its mantle of smog and reappeared with a measure of its ancient glory and splendour.
  In Athens it was 8 a.m., the peak of the morning rush-hour. Private cars could enter the city only on alternate weekdays, depending on their licence numbers. But still, on this Monday morning, the downtown streets were choked with traffic contributing noxious gases to the *nefos* pollution cloud that blotted out the once-brilliant crystalline Attic light.
  At this hour, a dark-green Porsche threaded through the narrow back streets of Kolonaki. As it passed by the American School, the driver glanced at the *komboloia* swinging on the rear view mirror and, remembering little Georgios, she muttered a private prayer. Then, gritting her teeth, she swung the wheel hard right, and with a squealing of hot rubber on concrete, entered the forecourt of Evanghelismos Hospital.
  Emotionally, not for the first time, 25-year-old Christina Stephanopoulos was in a state of confusion, her feelings a mishmash of profound sorrow and relief and irrational anger. She mourned the loss of her nephew Georgios, and thanked the saints for the survival of her brother Nicholas. But she also cursed the circumstances that had led to such tragedy. In her mind, still, the marriage of a Greek to a Turk had been a sure way to invite the wrath of the gods.
  In the emergency ward, Nicholas quickly changed into the pinstripe suit that Christina had collected from his apartment. She asked him how he was feeling. He replied that

173

he was feeling fine, and that he had no memory of his treatment for hypothermia, being put on a heart bypass machine and having a warm saline solution pumped into his body.

Beyond that exchange, not a single word was said. Christina rightly judged that he was in no mood to talk. Indeed, he was never to speak about his ordeal: how, while jogging, he had been listening to a concert of classical music when the broadcast was interrupted by a newsflash regarding the killing in Chapultepec Park; how, overwhelmed with grief, he had collapsed on the side of the road, curling up in a ball and sobbing uncontrollably while his whole body shivered in the ever-increasing grip of cold; how that night he had completely lost the will to live.

To avoid several reporters and photographers waiting in the main hallway, Nicholas and Christina left by a staff exit leading directly onto the car park. On the way, they encountered the doctor who had attended Nicholas on his admission and who was now going off duty from the night shift.

Smiling, the doctor paused to congratulate Nicholas on his speedy recovery. "You know, when you were brought in your body temperature had dropped ten degrees below normal to 26 centigrade. A few degrees lower— or without having such a remarkably strong heart— you would almost certainly have been beyond our help.

"You are a very lucky young man."

CHAPTER 14

At 0730 hours on Monday morning, long before Procurador General Rodríguez put in an appearance, Comandante Sebastián Miguel Barraza was at his desk, eager to forge ahead with investigating a case, which, by some mysterious subconscious thought process, had become clearer in his mind overnight.

On arrival, he found only one item in his in-tray: an envelope containing a cassette tape and a written report from *judicial* Alvaro Reyes on his trip to Acapulco to interview Guillermo Velázquez. According to orders, Reyes had conducted the interview with the utmost discretion. Not even Velázquez's secretary had been informed of his purpose. Through her, he had made an appointment on the pretext that he wished to organise a private party at the Esmeralda Hotel.

Interviewed in his office, assistant manager Velázquez had confirmed that on Thursday he had indeed notified Gómez of plans for a birthday party in Chapultepec Park. At the time he had thought it was a harmless social titbit. Now he conceded that it may have been an error of judgment on his part, and he had resolved never to deal with Gómez again.

No, he had positively not discussed the forthcoming party with anyone else outside the immediate family. But then it was never supposed to be a secret, except as a surprise for Georgios, so he didn't see that he had really done anything wrong.

"All the same," he had said. "I would appreciate it if the family was not told about my contact with Gómez. They have enough troubles. In fact, my wife is in Cuernavaca right now, comforting her sister, Doña Dolores Castillo de Tunaman. She has had a nervous breakdown, you know."

Barraza played the tape-recorded interview, quickly judging it to be worthless. Then he turned to more pressing matters. Firstly, he contacted the ballistics department, asking them to carry out specific tests with a standard .38 revolver.

Next, he called in his chief *judicial* Luis Montaño. It was time, he said, to get one long overdue piece of business out of the way: the interrogation of Fernando Ramírez.

Montaño had anticipated the order, making sure the guards had stirred and showered Fernando before dawn. But he was not expecting Barraza's next pronouncement. The Comandante explained that, as this was almost certainly his last investigation, he had decided to take charge personally of the interview. Montaño would accompany him, plus two guards to ensure proper security this time.

They entered the interview room at 0810 hours. Fernando was already there, seated at a table on which he had spread a copy of *Excelsior,* opened at the centre pages. Responding to a disapproving look from Montaño, one of the guards removed the newspaper. The *judicial* then set down a tape recorder, notepad and pen, and stood aside for Barraza to take the chair directly opposite the interviewee.

All the while, Fernando wore a sardonic grin, which spread even wider when he looked across at Barraza in his dark-tinted spectacles. He was tempted to ask his inquisitor whether he was covering up a black eye that he might have given him the previous day. But something about the Comandante's superior demeanour made him think better of it.

Barraza began with the gentle approach. "So, Señor Ramírez, how you are feeling this morning?"

"Not too bad," said Fernando. Then, grinning afresh, he tapped the plaster on his forehead. "Considering."

"Ah, *sí*... A most unfortunate accident. We were as surprised as you were."

Fernando gazed back in wonder. "Accident! Accident! You call three policemen beating me up an accident!"

From subsequent talk, it soon emerged that Fernando had no memory of his encounter with the head-butting Ignacio Galván, or indeed of any events from the time of his Sunday drinking session in the Tepito *pulquería.* All his knowledge of the intervening period had been gleaned from his reading of *Excelsior.*

For years this had always been his way— getting drunk and awakening next day, completely oblivious to the trail of confusion he invariably left in his wake. Then— until two or three drinks had begun to release his deep-rooted hang-ups. He was usually contrite, reasonably behaved, and even quite

176

likeable.

This morning the old toper was feeling remarkably clear-headed, and, unusually, almost elated. He had slept well and, following his mandatory shower, he had enjoyed a light breakfast delivered by a guard who not only gave him a copy of *Excelsior,* but also asked for his autograph. Three times already he had read Ortiz's account of the Alvarez fight. It made him feel good; he was somebody again.

Barraza made the obvious observation. "You don't seem too distressed by the death of your youngest son, Manuel."

Fernando's hint of a smile changed to a positive glare. "*Mierda!* Of course, I am upset. But it's no good brooding about it. Nothin's going to fucking change. It's like the boy's *mamá* always used to say, *La suerte es como la muerte.* Luck and death. They can come at any time. Trouble was that luck never came to little Manuelito. Fate was always against him. He was a born loser."

"Then you are not surprised that he turned into a killer?"

"Who says he was a killer? So it's in the papers. Well, I don't believe all I read in the fucking papers. Most of it is a load of capitalist crap. One thing I know for sure: my boy couldn't kill nobody. Ask anyone. He never had the stomach for fightin', let alone killin.' "

"But he was there. In the tower - with his fingerprints all over the gun."

"Okay, so he was there. Lee Harvey Oswald was there. Mario Aburto Martínez was there at the shooting of Colosio. Don't necessarily mean they killed anyone."

Barraza tried a different tack. Reaching into his briefcase, he pulled out five books and laid them out on the table. "Do you recognise these, Señor Ramírez?"

Fernando protested. "Hey! What the fucking hell you doing with my property? Who gave you permission to touch my books?"

Barraza ignored the question. "You have an interesting taste in reading, *señor*. Let's see." He tapped them one at a time with a stubby forefinger. "C.S. Forester's *El Cañon, Memorias de Don Adolfo de Huerta,* and biographies of Juárez, Zapata, and Trotsky."

He picked up the book on Benito Juárez, opened it at a page marked with a paper clip, and showed it to Fernando.

177

"Are these your pencil marks in the margin?"

"*Sí.*"

"So here, for example, you have marked Juárez saying: *I should like to see Protestantism become naturalised in México, conquering the Indians; these need a religion that would oblige them to read, and not oblige them to waste their savings on candles for the saints.* Do you agree with that view?"

Fernando smiled. He could happily spend all day— given enough liquor— pontificating on his crystallised beliefs.

"Not exactly. I'm against *all* kinds of formalised religion. D'you know, more wars have been fought in the name of religion than anything else? Look what those bloody bible-thumping *conquistadores* did to the Aztecs and the Incas. And what those Christian Crusaders did to the Muslims. Slaughtered them in millions. And so it goes on today. Only the weapons have changed."

"But from what I hear, your family are very good Catholics?"

"True. But that ain't no fault of mine. It was their mother's doing. She was a dear, wonderful lady, but she didn't understand she was making a big, big mistake. D'you want me to explain why?"

Barraza nodded. He was not really interested. But he wanted to encourage Fernando to loosen up and talk spontaneously. So he let him go on. Unwittingly, he had pressed the 'play' button on a speech the old man had parroted in modified forms a hundred times before.

Fernando spread his elbows on the table, his hands joined with fingers interlocked. "It's like this. I remember an *hombre* on TV explaining how a computer virus worked, how you inserted a disc loaded with junk and carrying the instruction 'duplicate me'. And so the computer duplicated the junk over and over again until it was useless for anything else.

"Well, religion works like that. Before you've got the power of reason, you have a 'duplicate me' disc stuck up your arse, and, depending on who your parents are, that disc will programme you to be a Catholic, Protestant, Jew, Muslim, Hindu or whatever. You have no choice at all about the beliefs you are taught; no more than you have any choice about whether you are circumcised or not.

"And so we are stuck forever with this mad, divisive

178

and dangerous system of different religions, each founded on fucking fairy tales dressed up as historical truth, and each believing it is superior to all the others."

Fernando was gesticulating with his hands now. "But, *chingada madre*! We were all born human beings— not Catholics, Protestants, Muslims, Jews and the rest. And we should all develop faith in ourselves, not in man-made gods and religious mumbo jumbo.

"Juárez was right about not wasting precious pesos on candles. Like I used to tell my wife: shuffling on bleeding knees to the shrine of the Virgin ain't gonna protect you from an earthquake, and it certainly ain't gonna save you from exploitation by the capitalists."

"I see. So that's why you have marked this other Juárez quotation: *I know the rich and powerful do not feel or try to alleviate the miseries of the poor. Instead of complaining Mexicans must free themselves from their tyrants?*"

To press home his point, Barraza leaned across the table and spoke in a more aggressive and steadily louder tone. "In short, Señor Ramírez, you are against both Church and State. You are an atheist, a revolutionary, and perhaps even an anarchist."

Fernando laughed aloud. "I'm not that fucking stupid. I admire the Zapatistas down in Chiapas. But they aren't going to achieve a *golpe de Estado* against all the military might of this government." He pointed to the copy of *El Cañon*. "They haven't got a super-gun like those Spanish guerrillas. To get a true and just socialist order we gotta kill the right-wing parties through the ballot box, and that means fucking hard campaigning in the elections, and getting in more foreign observers to stop all the vote-rigging!"

He looked across to one of the guards. "Hey, Luis, all this talking is making me thirsty. Can you get me a drink?" He turned his face towards Barraza and grinned. "Anything will do— tequila, *cerveza, pulque,* mezcal, *ron, aguardiente...*"

Barraza remained impassive. "The drinks will have to wait a little longer. First of all I want to know about this socialist order of yours. Am I right in thinking that you want a redistribution of wealth, and that you are opposed to anyone possessing a vast fortune far beyond his basic needs?"

"That's it. You've got it exactly. And a redistribution

179

of *bebidas* would be pretty good, too."

"And what did Manuel think of your views? Did he share your hatred of the capitalist system?"

"Absolutely. I taught him good— all about the injustices and inequalities in Mexican life."

"I see. And did you also talk about politics abroad? For example, did you ever hear Manuel talk about the conflict between Greece and Turkey?"

Fernando blew a soft raspberry. "You gotta be kidding. We got enough troubles in México without thinking about faraway fucking foreigners. Anyway, Manuel wasn't really interested in politics. *Señoritas*, that's what occupied his wishy-washy mind."

"Quite so. But then how do you explain your son's presence in the park when the Turkish ambassador was murdered?"

"That's easy. How do you explain anything like that? Bloody capitalists, politicians, people in power. Only two things could have got Manuel in that tower. Force. Or money. Either way, he was a fall guy, just being fucking used— like all ordinary Mexicans are used in the end."

"But you aren't interested in that. You're part of the same bloody system."

To Montaño's surprise, Barraza did not react to the barb. In fact, he was smiling. "Señor Ramírez," he said. "You have been most helpful. My men will require you to sign a formal statement, and then you will be free to go."

As he moved towards the door, the Comandante tapped Ramírez on the shoulder. "By the way, *señor*, they are showing your fight on TV tonight. I hope it turns out better for you this time."

Montaño gaped. He had never heard his *Jefe* attempt a joke before.

"*Se permite fumar, señor.*"

"*Gracias,*" replied the American. "*Muchas gracias.*" But he continued to suck on an empty pipe while browsing through his handwritten notes.

Procurador General José Rodríguez immediately apologised in English. "Oh, do excuse me, *señor*. I forgot that you probably do not speak our language. I was saying that it was okay for you to smoke."

Arthur Madison grinned. Then, in his slow Southern drawl, he explained that he had fully understood. It was simply

180

that, after years of being disciplined by the CIA, he could not break the habit of never smoking indoors.

Rodríguez laughed loudly. "Ah, we are much more liberal down here. I myself love Havana cigars."

The Procurador General was in good spirits this morning, and, like Barraza, he had arrived at his office in more confident mood. On Sunday, he had had an uncomfortable sense of playing second fiddle to his Comandante who had perforce dictated the course of the investigation. But it was different now. Today, with the basic preliminaries completed, the investigation was moving into a new, much broader phase.

As far as Rodríguez was concerned, the case against Manuel Ramírez was resolved. Now it was time to concentrate all their energies on establishing who— if anyone— had aided, abetted, and possibly motivated the assassin.

The terms of reference extended far beyond the range of the Comandante's resources. The anti-terrorist expertise of the CIA and FBI had to be brought into play. They also needed to consult with MIT (the Turkish CIA), with Europol and North American intelligence organisations; to check the records of the Mexican immigration authorities and utilise the far-reaching resources of Delgado's *Tránsito* and *Preventiva* police forces to seek out suspicious foreigners.

All these forces and more needed to be coordinated, and, having responsibility for marshalling them, Rodríguez was able to reassert his overall command.

Accordingly, the Procurador General had called a meeting for 0900 hours. Now, in the conference room adjoining his office, he had taken his seat at the head of a rectangular table, around which were gathered his deputy Arturo Contreras, his PA, Emilio Ortega, Comandante Barraza, General Delgado, Madison and Brad McClellan of the CIA, "Legal Counsellor" Robert Carruthers representing the FBI, and Rufino Cordero, *Director General de Servicios Migratorios*.

Only Madison was informally dressed. Incongruous in a greenish tweed jacket, tieless red shirt and light brown corduroys, he was seated immediately to the right of the Rodríguez. And much to his discomfort, he found himself being made the focus of the Procurador General's introductory preamble.

"... and today, on the express recommendation of U.S.

181

President Carmichael, we are privileged to have the assistance of Señor Madison, the foremost authority on international terrorist organisations. With his guidance, it is to be hoped that we can gain some indication of who might have been behind the assassination of ambassador Tunaman..."

Invited to speak, Madison began by apologising for his limited command of Spanish, saying, "Where necessary, my colleague Señor McClellan will help me out." He thanked the Procurador General for his kind remarks, but stressed that he was unworthy of such a high rating. In fact, he rather doubted that he had anything useful to contribute. However, he would try to help in any way that he could.

He had been expressly asked by the Procurador General to advise on persons and/or organisations that might conceivably have a motive for killing Turkey's U.N. ambassador-elect. To save time, he had had a preliminary report prepared in Spanish. If and when judged necessary, CIA dossiers on individual terrorists could be made available later.

He nodded to Brad McClellan, who proceeded to remove a sheaf of papers from his briefcase. The papers— photocopies of Madison's four-page report— were then distributed round the table.

The report was headed SUMMARY OF TERRORIST GROUPS, and read as follows:

1) ISLAMIC FUNDAMENTALISTS. *Ever since September 11 2001, our war on terrorism has been focused primarily on al-Qaeda and other Islamic fundamentalist groups around the world. Arguably, such extremists might be opposed to any rapprochement between Turkey and Greece. It is conceivable, perhaps, that some might wish to promote a Muslim-Christian conflict that could broaden into a jihad, or holy struggle. Some religious traditionalists— for example, the Dev Sol guerilla group in Turkey— might have seen Señor Tunaman as a threat because he was promoting closer relations with the West.*

But this is spreading the net very wide indeed, and let me say at once that we have absolutely no reason for relating this assassination to the great assault launched against the United States by the followers of Osama Bin Laden. There are, of course, individual Muslim fanatics residing in this hemisphere, and in that respect the FBI will be much better equipped to advise you. Meanwhile, three other categories of terrorists may be considered.

2) ARMENIANS. *In the 1970s and early 1980s, a wave of terrorist attaks were carried out by Armenian underground organisations, most notably ASALA (the Armenian Secret Army for the Liberation of Armenia). Here we have positive precedents for the killing of a Turkish diplomat in the Americas.*

ASALA's first terrorist act was the killing of the Turkish Consul General in Los Angeles in 1973. Two years later, Armenian terrorists attacked the Turkish embassy in Ottawa, seeking to kill the ambassador who escaped by jumping from a window. A guard was killed and the terrorists – all Armenians resident in Canada— took twelve hostages before later surrendering.

Over the next ten years Armenian terrorists, operating in Asia, Europe and America, killed forty-five Turks, mostly diplomats or state officials. These assassinations were by bombs, grenades and guns.

The declared primary aim of ASALA was to force Turkey to admit its guilt for the first holocaust of modern times - i.e. the so-called genocide of 1915 when, it is alleged, Turks slaughtered an estimated 1.5 million Armenians, and forced hundreds of thousands more to flee the country. In addition, unrealistically, ASALA hoped to free its ancient homeland in Anatolia, and to establish a second independent Armenian republic.

Twenty years ago, Armenian fanatics would automatically have been prime suspects following the killing of a Turkish ambassador in Mexico City, or anywhere else for that matter. The fact remains, however, that ASALA— founded by young radicals— has been relatively inactive for many years. Also, in the past, Armenian terrorists have always been quick to proclaim their responsibility for killings. In this case, I understand, no organisation has so farclaimed responsibility.

It should be noted, too, that the situation has changed radically following the break-up of the Soviet Union, and the emergence in 1991 of Armenia as an independent state. Since then, the energies of Armenian radicals have beenlargely directed towards a different aim: unification with Nagorno-Karabakh, the Stalin-created Armenian enclave in the oil-rich, neighbouring state of Azerbaijan.

Not that this has totally changed the Armenians'

attitude towards Turkey. There remains some resentment that, during hostilities between Nagorno-Karabakh and Azerbaijan, Turkish opinion supported the Azeris, their ethnic cousins. More seriously, anti-Turkish feeling was intensified for a time by extreme hardship in Armenia arising from the fuel blockade imposed by Azerbaijan and Turkey. Also, of course, the age-old grievance over Turkey' s responsibility for events in 1915 remains unresolved.

In 1987, the European Parliament in Strasbourg voted by a narrow majority to recognise as genocide the slaughter of Armenians living in the Ottoman Empire during World War 1. But the MEPs also voted to absolve the current Turkish government of responsibility, and Armenian bitterness was further fuelled a few years ago when the U.S. Senate threw out a motion for America to recognise the alleged genocide of 1915.

Meanwhile, successive Turkish governments have continued to deny that 1.5 million Armenians were massacred or forced into a death march in 1915. The most they have conceded is that perhaps some three hundred thousand Armenians died as a result of conditions of war and deportations Their position on this remains so firm that in the year 2001, they immediately recalled their ambassador to France, when a vote by the French parliament recognised that genocide had been carried out.

This burning issue was further fuelled in 2005, when French Foreign Minister Michel Barnier insisted that Turkey must officially recognise the 1915 genocide before it joins the European Union.

Arguably, this continued use of the word "genocide" - meaning the deliberate extrermination of a people or nation – is much too strong. A more balanced view is that, as in so many wartime situations, there were indeed atrocities and massacres executed by military groups led by extremists. But that does not exactly equate to an all-out holocaust.

In 2008, before his election, Preident Obama declared that he would recognise the events of 1915 as genocide, but he avoided using the word when he visited Turkey the following year. Instead, he urged Armenia and Turkey to "deal with a difficulty and tragic history".

Encouragingly, Armenia and Turkey then signed historic accords described as "normalising relations"and ending a century of hostility by re-establishing diplomatic ties

184

and reopening their common border.

But really nothing had greatly changed. That move towards reconilliation aroused fierce opposition among the 5.7 million Armenians living abroad. Demonstrations were staged in many countries, including the United States where members of the Armenian National Committee of America (ANCA) paraded banners declaring "Don't betray us". In the Lebanon the placards read: "We will struggle" and "We will not forget". Even in their homeland, one political party, the Armenian Revolutionary Federation, organised a hunger strike in protest.

All this underlines how such an ancient grievance is being kept alive. The problem was well expressed by Haig Deranian, grand master of the Knights of Vartan, an Armenian-American fraternial organisation that does charitable work. While supporting moves to bury the past, he explained that, as a first generation Armenian-Ameican, he had "lived the genocide since childhood, hearing the gruesome stories from my parents and grandparents about what happened."

Clearly, in the light of so much extreme bitterness, one cannot rule out the possibility of an Armenian fanatic, or a group of fanatics, having masterminded the killing in Chapultepec Park.

France, with some four hundred thousand Armenian residents, has been the main breeding ground of extremists in the past. But we should perhaps note that— outside of Armenia itself— our continent has the largest Armenian population. More than half-a-million Armenians now live in North America, and a number of them are extremely rich and powerful.

At the same time, it seems to me highly improbable— not to say pointless— that any such killing would be engineered without those responsible proclaiming their purpose. Furthermore, the style of this killing - i.e. a single sniper who is not an Armenian— does not fit in with the past MO of ASALA and kindred groups.

If required, we can provide profiles of a few Armenian radicals known to have been active members of ASALA. However, your best source of information in that regard is DST (Direction de la Surveillance du Territoire), the Frenchcounter-espionage agency.

In 1982, an ASALA booby-trapped suitcase exploded

185

near the Turkish national airline counter at Orly Airport, killing seven people and injuring 65. The Paris police then searched the homes of hundreds of Armenians known to be hostile to Turkey. From those raids and subsequent undercover operations, DST has built up the most extensive files on Armenian extremists.

3) GREEK RADICALS. In view of ambassador Tunaman's diplomatic activities, no one would seem to have a stronger and more obvious motive for killing him than Greek extremists favouring a tougher line - perhaps even war – with Turkey.

Various Greek terrorist factions have surfaced over the past quarter century under names such as Revolutionary People's Socialism, May 1st and Popular Rage. Most noteworthy, in terms of assassination, has been the urban guerrilla organisation known as November 17, so named after the day in 1973 when Greece's military regime used tanks to crush a student uprising at the Athens Polytechnic and killed some 20 anti-junta demonstrators.

November 17 became active in late 1975, one year after democracy had been restored. Its first victim was Richard Welch, our own CIA station chief in Athens. Subsequently, in more than 20 attacks, it killed Greek politicians, magistrates, politicians, industrialists and police officers; also various U.S. diplomatic and military personnel. Often— even as late as 2000, when the British defence attaché was shot dead in broad daylight— the victims were found to have been shot with the same 1911 model Colt .45 pistol used to kill Mr. Welch.

It was back in 1988 that it first struck against Turkey, with an unsuccessful attempt to kill four Turkish diplomats in a booby-trapped car. The following year, it wounded the Turkish chargé d'affaires in Athens, and in 1991 it was responsible for the murder of the Turkish press attaché, shot five times at close range. Its targets seemed to vary according to the current political situation. In 1999, for example, a rocket-propelled grenade exploded in the German embassy in Athens, in the room next to that of the ambassador. that attack, a week after a similar one on the Dutch ambassador, came at the start of NATO's bombing of Yugoslavia over Kosovo.

November 17 stated in its communiqués that it was anti-capitalist, anti-Turkish, anti-American, anti-NATO and *anti-Greek membership of the European Community. Certainly it would have had every reason to favour hostilities between NATO allies Greece and Turkey, and that would provide reason enough for wishing to eliminate ambassador Tunaman, the chief promoter of peace.*

We, at the CIA, came to regard November 17 as one of the most proficient and lethal terrorist groups in Europe. For years, all efforts by our undercover agents to penetrate the organisation failed, and even our offer of a $1million reward for information failed to bring results.

However, I think we can now safely eliminate November 17 as a suspect since— most unexpectedly— its leading protagonists were finally identified and captured by the Greek police as Athens prepared to stage the 2004 Olympics. Hopefully, this urban guerrilla group has been permanently destroyed. In any case, it has never been active overseas, limiting its attacks almost entirely to Athens. Also, following an act of terrorism, it was always its custom to proclaim responsibility or leave behind its calling card: a written communiqué bearing its insignia, a five-pointed star enclosing the name "17 N."

4) KURDISH TERRORISTS. *Here we are looking at a veritable army of so-called freedom fighters: the Kurdish Workers' Party (PKK), a radical left-wing organisation that has waged a full-scale guerrilla war in its campaign for an independent state in south-east Turkey.*

The PKK's standing as a major terrorist force dates from 1984 when it came under the charismatic leadership of Abdullah "Apo" Ocalan, an Anatolian peasant who established his base in Damascus under Syrian protection, and had his fanatical followers sent to a military training camp in eastern Lebanon.

Subsequently, the PKK— armed with Soviet-made AK47 Kalashnikov rockets and mortars— extended its anti-Turkish operations throughout the world. Its far-reaching organisation was best demonstrated in 1993 when it struck simultaneously in twenty-eight cities, launching firebomb attacks on Turkish embassies and offices in Germany, Switzerland, Sweden, France and Denmark.

The PKK's most concentrated attacks were on Turkish travel agencies in Germany, and in an effort to deprive Turkey of valuable tourist evenue, it even targeted German tourists abroad, being responsible for murders in Florida,

Guatemala, the Philippines and Thailand. So Mexico City is certainly not out of its operational range.

In 1999, following Turkey's capture of Ocalan, demonstrations showed that the PKK had supporters in major cities all over Europe. The most violent of these were in Germany, and it is German intelligence that now has by far the most extensive files on PKK activists who may number as many as five thousand of the four hundred thousand Kurds living in Germany.

CONCLUSION. *Again, I must stress the point that no political purpose is served by this assassination if responsibility is not claimed by some organisation or interested party. Therefore, until such a claim is made, I must seriously doubt that this crime is politically motivated.*

Here, of course, I have referred only to terrorist groups with political or ideological aims. Quite separately, perhaps, we might consider the possibility of individuals or big business interests, or even governments, that might have something to gain financially from sabotaging current moves towards joint Greek-Turkish economic ventures, especially in respect of exploration of the oil-rich Aegean.

Procurador General Rodríguez had no more than scanned through the pages before putting them to one side and declaring, "I am sure we are all very grateful to Señor Madison for providing this report at such short notice."

Madison smiled. "Thank you kindly, *señor*. But I am afraid that this summary is not really very helpful."

"Nonsense, *mi amigo*. At least it gives us a starting point." The Procurador General then went on to discuss ways and means of checking on non-residents— especially Armenians, Greeks and Turks— who had been in Mexico at the time of the assassination.

Delgado announced that he already had his men checking on all hotel registers in the city. Cordero, in turn, promised to initiate a thorough examination of his department's records: visa applications and the mountain of tourist cards— giving name, age, place of birth, profession, permanent address, passport number and main destination in Mexico— which every foreigner on arrival was required to fill in.

At this juncture, Comandante Barraza stressed that the seeking out of foreigners with a possible motive for killing

188

ambassador Tunaman served no useful purpose without evidence connecting them directly to the crime.

"The key to this investigation lies in tracing the whereabouts of Manuel Ramírez in the months, and especially weeks, immediately prior to the assassination. It would be more useful if the vast resources of *la policía del Distrito Federal* could be geared to that purpose."

General Delgado concurred. He would see to it that officers of the *Preventiva* force were issued with photographs of Manuel Ramírez, and that they made appropriate inquiries during the general course of their duties.

As the discussion broadened, Robert Carruthers remained conspicuously silent... to such a degree that Rodriguez interjected, "Before we end this meeting, I am sure we would all like to hear the views of our *amigo importante* from the FBI."

Carruthers forced a wry smile, then explained that he liked to deal in hard facts, rather than so much speculation. He would prefer to speak when he had something positive to report. However, now that he had been asked...

He went on to express his surprise that Madison had omitted the Russians from his report. "It would be very much in their interests to see two members of the NATO alliance at each other's throats." However, he shared Madison's view that there was so far no evidence to suggest a political assassination.

"It may well be that we are looking too deeply for some kind of subtle motive. In countries far and wide, we have seen cases of a lone, psychopathic gunman going berserk. Only last year, thirty-two people were gunned down in a Chicago shopping mall for no good reason at all. Then again, this killing might be like the case of Charles Whitman, who shot dead fourteen people from a twenty-seven-storey clock tower at the University of Texas, Austin. He told a psychiatrist that he had fantasies about going up a tower and killing people. Maybe..."

At that point, with obvious impatience, Comandante Barraza interrupted. "*Señor,* while we are dealing with facts— and not mere conjecture— could you please advise us whether the FBI has made any progress in tracking down the missing brother, Julio Ramírez?"

Carruthers visibly reddened. "Well, no. But it's still early days. Until a year ago he was living in a boarding house in Chicago. But no one seems to have seen him since."

"Our agents have been remarkably busy, you know. They have spoken to the medical officer who treated the boxer after his last fight. He told them that Ramírez had suffered very bad cuts around the eyes, and that he had advised the boxer to allow at least six months for them to heal properly."

"Just a moment, please." He flipped through the pages of a notepad and then continued. "Ah yes, the doctor also showed our men a copy of his routine report to the Illinois State Athletic Commission. This stated that there was no sign of permanent damage, but he strongly recommended that Ramírez should be subjected to a strict medical examination before being allowed to fight again.

"Moreover, we have already interviewed various Chicago friends of Julio Ramírez. All of them said they had had no idea he was leaving town. His landlady is the last person known to have seen him. She said he checked out with only a few hours' notice. She remembered asking him where he was going because of his vague reply. He told her, "I am not too sure. But it's got to be somewhere sunny and warm.""

"Who knows? Maybe he came back to Mexico..."

"May I make a suggestion?" asked Delgado. "Why not try Florida, the so-called Sunshine State? Florida is always sunny and warm. Also, I note from the article in today's *Excelsior* that the father, Fernando Ramírez, used to live and fight in Miami. Maybe he had family connections down there."

Carruthers smiled for the first time. "Thank you, *Señor Secretario*. But our men had already worked that one out. In fact, our agents in Miami are making inquiries right now, as we speak."

Rodríguez cut the discussion short. "Very good. But it is, as Señor Carruthers says, 'Early days.' For the moment we all have considerable work to do. Let us hope we have more information when we meet again. Meanwhile, *señores*, thank you for your co-operation."

Back in his office, Comandante Barraza scanned through the few notes he had taken during the meeting. He heavily underlined one short sentence, then entered it into the small black notebook in which he recorded all key points relating to the investigation. As he reviewed these points, his round face creased and puffed out into a tight-lipped frown.

Very clearly, he could see a most disturbing pattern emerging.

At 1025 hours, only a few minutes after the Procurador General's conference, Barraza received a call on his intercom. It was José Ibarra. The Subcomandante wanted to see him at once, because some valuable new evidence had come to light while his chief was at the meeting.

When Ibarra duly entered from the adjoining office, he was holding aloft a small package which, judging by his triumphant expression, could have contained the Jules Rimet Trophy. "I think we may have got it, Comandante," he said. "The one missing piece in the puzzle."

Barraza raised his dark glasses to his forehead, and peered down at the package that had been laid on the desk directly in front of him. There, wrapped in a labelled polythene bag, was a pair of dark-brown patent leather gloves.

"An officer of the *Cuerpo de Guardias Presidenciales* brought them in just half an hour ago," explained Ibarra. "He says that one of his men found them while on duty at *El Castillo.*

"I have told the officer that we will need to see the guardsman to get a formal statement. Meanwhile, from what he says, it seems that this soldier was making a routine inspection of the tower when he slipped on the stairs, somewhere near the upper level. It was too dark for him to see clearly, but when he reached out to secure a grip his hand landed on these gloves beneath one of the iron steps."

Barraza smiled sardonically. "How very fortuitous, José! One man accidentally succeeds where all our men failed with two major searches."

"*Sí, señor.* It is a remarkable piece of luck. But then it is very dark up there. Maybe the gloves got kicked into a corner when our men first went up the tower. On the other hand, of course, it remains to be proved that they actually belonged to the assassin."

"Ah, you are right about that," said Barraza. He pushed the package towards his Subcomandante. "Well, you know what to do. Get to it."

Some forty minutes later Ibarra returned with the gloves, together with the findings of the *Departmento Forense.* Yes, they had found gunpowder residue traces on the right-hand glove, evidence of it having been worn when firing a gun. But no, they had failed to obtain any fingerprints. The gloves were clean on the outside and the insides were lined with wool, material too absorbent to allow prints.

The gloves were of a very common design, with no label or markings to indicate their source. They were also virtually brand-new, with no sign of wear and tear.

"Well! Well," said Barraza. "Surprise, surprise! The Procurador General will be pleased! Fingerprints all over the rifle, and now evidence suggesting that Ramírez troubled to put on gloves for the actual shooting."

Ibarra remained silent. He understood his chief's scepticism, but he was certainly not going to support it. One thought remained uppermost in his mind: the more watertight the evidence presented to the Procurador General, the more favourable would be his prospects of promotion on Barraza's retirement.

CHAPTER 15

As Sebastián Miguel Barraza would later recall in his
sensational memoirs, the day after the Chapultepec Park
murders was the most absurd and frustrating day that he had
known in more than twenty years' service with the PGR. It
was the day when suddenly he no longer had any regrets about
the prospect of imminent retirement, the day when the
conduct of top-level police work, ever prone to interference
by the *influyente,* plummeted to new depths of chicanery that
bordered on pure farce.

The pattern had been set by the so convenient
discovery of the gloves, allegedly used by the assassin. This in
itself had not greatly surprised the Comandante. His review of
the evidence had prepared him for some high-level finessing.
But not even his deep-rooted cynicism had braced him
sufficiently for the developments that followed. They came in
swift succession, like the combination of a solar plexus punch
and an uppercut that all at once crushed his spirit and left him
with the realisation that he was fighting a hopeless battle.

The first crushing blow came in the early afternoon
when Barraza had just finished a working lunch in his office. It
was an unusual lunch, indeed unprecedented, since for the first
time he had invited his Subcomandante to join him for a light
snack sent down from the PGR canteen. They had reached the
stage, he explained, where they might usefully pause to go
over all the evidence and determine how next to proceed.

José Ibarra took this invitation as a clear sign that his
chief was feeling more relaxed now that the investigation was
so far advanced. He was further encouraged by Barraza's
unusually informal manner as they lunched on guacamole and
huevos rancheros washed down with a bottle of freshly chilled
Chablis from the Comandante's rarely opened drinks cabinet.

Barraza asked him about the health of his family,
about the progress of his eldest son at the *Universidad
Nacional Autónoma de México,* about his plans for a summer
holiday. At least ten minutes passed by without a single

193

mention of the business in hand.

"How are you finding the wine?" Barraza asked as he poured his deputy a second glass without replenishing his own. "I seldom drink, as you probably know. But this is my favourite: smooth as silk and, most importantly, leaving you clear-headed."

"It's absolutely great, *Jefe,*" replied Ibarra, who, as a lover of hard liquor, had already judged this vintage bottle fit only for old ladies.

But he was not thinking about the wine now. His mind was focussed on trying to second-guess Barraza's purpose. He had a feeling that all this uncharacteristic *bonhomie* was leading up to something. Quite possibly, in view of his impending retirement, the Comandante was going to ask him to handle most of the routine paperwork that remained.

Looking over his glass as he took another swig of wine, the Subcomandante sensed that some such request— equivalent to an order— was now imminent. His expectation was heightened by a pregnant pause in the conversation, and what he took to be the trace of a grin on his chief's fat pudding face.

Ibarra, however, misread the signals completely. Behind dark shades, the bulbous eyes of his chief gleamed only with contempt. At that precise moment Barraza was thinking what a sycophantic shit he had for a deputy: a jumped-up bureaucrat whose freakish promotion had come for so-called special services to the previous Procurador General, then serving on the *Comisión de Celebraciones del Milenio.*

But that millennium madness, all of the gush about giving youth a greater stake in the future, had long since passed. The reality was that a man like Ibarra was fit only for carrying out orders. Sure, he did that with supreme efficiency. The fact remained that he was an obsequious automaton, incapable of original thought.

Probably, at this very moment, the deputy was imagining himself sitting at the Comandante's desk. If so, he was deluding himself. Even Rodríguez, as Barraza knew well, was not stupid enough to risk his own position by having a yes-man as his Comandante. Why, this pen-pushing philistine didn't even know how to sip a glass of *grand cru....*

"Do you play chess, José?"

"Not for years, *Jefe,*"Ibarra replied. "Used to dabble at it, but I found it too slow and time-consuming."

194

"Um! Pity. It's a very good discipline for our job, you know. For example, take the current position in our investigation. Very much like stage two in a game of chess. We have made our routine opening gambits. All fairly harmless so far. But now the key pieces are in position and poised for a confrontation.

"Right then. Let's consider the state of play. We are ready to launch a strategic attack, though remembering all the while that we don't want to over-expose our defence. So what, *mi amigo*, do you think should be our next move?"

Ibarra stuttered. "I don't quite understand the question, *Jefe*. It seems to me the game is nearly over. From now on, it should be straightforward reaching checkmate."

"Nearly over!" exclaimed Barraza. "What happened to those three main objectives— *Quién? Cómo? Por qué?* We certainly don't know why four people were killed in the park. We don't know exactly how it was achieved. And I am not even certain about the *who.*"

"But, *señor*, the evidence against Manuel Ramírez is overwhelming." Ibarra was no longer lounging back in his easy chair, but sitting upright, all alertness and caution.

"You think so. What exactly is this overwhelming evidence?"

"Well, *Jefe*, for a start there is the rifle with his fingerprints and palmprints. That alone is enough to condemn him."

"Really? Let me tell you a true story, José. When I was a kid, a gang of us used to play in the *Parque Hundido*, and we regularly used to run into trouble with the park keeper. He was a miserable *ojete*, very strict. Anyway, one day this official grabbed a small boy and prepared to beat him with his stick.

" 'What have I done wrong?' the boy cried. The keeper then dragged him by one ear over to a wooden park bench on which some kids had carved their names. 'See that?' he said. 'That's your name, is it not?'

"The boy admitted that it was indeed his name. "But look," he said. "There's another carved name: *Papa* Pío X11. Don't mean *El Papa* put it there.'

"Then the boy got his beating."

The deputy forced a laugh. "That's a good one, *Jefe*."

Barraza sighed. *"Sí.* But was the boy guilty?"

Ibarra pursed his lips and gave an exaggerated shrug of

his shoulders. "Who knows?"

"Exactly, José. It is not proven. Except that in this case, I happen to know that the boy was innocent. You see, that kid who took a beating was *me*.

"Mind you, I am not complaining about it now. Because that injustice taught me an invaluable lesson, one that has served me well ever since. That is never to accept the obvious purely on trust, and never to jump to conclusions based on circumstantial evidence.

"Your name carved on a bench doesn't necessarily mean you put it there. And by the same token, your fingerprints on a gun doesn't prove that you willingly put them there."

The Subcomandante grinned. "That's true enough, *Jefe*. But this is a very different case. Here we don't just have circumstantial evidence. Fortunately we have a first-hand witness: the guardsman who caught Ramírez in the tower— *flagrante delicto*, with the murder weapon still in his hands."

"Ah *sí*, the guardsman. I'm glad you mentioned him." Barraza removed a small black notebook from his inside breast pocket, and began to flip through the pages. "Let's have a look at this so reliable witness of yours. This Sargento Segundo Jesús Moreno of the *Cuerpo de Guardias Presidenciales*.

"Here we have his formal statement as presented at the Procurador General's press conference. He certainly has a remarkable eye for detail, this witness— even knows the exact number of steps up the tower at *El Castillo*. In the circumstances, we might safely expect him to have a reliable memory of events.

"Now then. He begins by telling us that the sound of gunfire drew him to the tower, and that he went up alone, having left another soldier on guard at the entrance. For most of the time he was in semi-darkness.

"In his own words: 'When I came to the final curve, I sprang round the corner with my revolver extended ready to fire. I immediately saw a man silhouetted against the sky, a man standing with a rifle held in his right hand. I shouted '*Sueltela!*' But he didn't drop it. Instead, he raised his gun as if to shoot. I was lucky. Though the sudden light was dazzling, my shot hit him square in the forehead.'

"Mark that, José. Square in the forehead. He is very precise. So how is it that the autopsy on Ramírez records a bullet wound extending horizontally clear through the upper skull?

"I have had our ballistics experts simulate the shooting, as described by Moreno. A bullet fired from his position must have a trajectory of at least 50 degrees if it is to hit the head of a man who is five feet, nine inches tall and standing at the top of the spiral stairs. And a bullet fired at such an angle could not possibly strike the target and exit from the back of the head."

Ibarra thought for a moment. "Ah, but *Jefe*, Ramírez would probably have been bending his head over to see who was coming up the stairs. That might explain it."

"Oh yeah?" Barraza sneered. "That would be a mighty big bend of his head. Next, you will be suggesting that perhaps he was down on his hands and knees, searching for those mysterious, missing gloves.

"And even if he was, that would not explain the fatal bullet wound. You see, there is another, even more significant factor.

"This morning, on my orders, ballistics carried out tests on two unidentified male cadavers taken from the morgue. They found they could only simulate Ramírez's wounds - a relatively small entrance wound, but a massive exit wound - by firing a .38 revolver at virtually point-blank range. The distance from the final corner of the stairs to the top is eight feet. And you can add on at least another five feet to the head of a man standing up there.

"Manuel Ramírez, they tell me, must have been shot at almost point-blank range. And their finding is further supported by the powder burns found around the entrance wound."

Ibarra felt aggrieved that his Comandante had not shared this information with him sooner. But he could not say as much. He merely gritted his teeth and muttered, "I see."

"That's good," said Barraza. "In that case, I need hardly tell you what our first attacking move in the game of chess must be."

Ibarra jumped to the bait. "Of course, *Jefe*. It is time to bring in this *sargento* to face some hard questions."

The Comandante smiled. "Wrong again, José. You should remember that it is wise to weaken *el toro* as much as possible before moving in close with *la muleta*. In this case, I think we should let our prey run a little, give him some freedom, see who he contacts, see perhaps if he suddenly comes into some unexplained wealth.

"As a matter of fact, I have already given the order. Moreno is being put under round-the-clock surveillance, but with maximum discretion so as not to alert him.

"Now how about some coffee...?"

For a few minutes more Barraza was feeling smugly in control. And then it came: the solar plexus punch.

His secretary rang to say that she had chief *judicial* Luis Montaño on an internal line, and that he wanted to speak to the Comandante as soon as possible. Barraza told her to put the call through on the open intercom.

"Sorry to disturb you, *Jefe,*" the *judicial* began. "But did you see the one o'clock news on Channel 13?"

"No."

"It's bad news, *Jefe.* Early this morning, the *tránsito* police located a wrecked car that had plunged off the Toluca highway; you know, at one of those treacherous curves at the highest point. One body was recovered, and according to the TV report it has now been identified as that of Sargento Segundo Jesús Moreno.

"It must be accurate because they had an interview with General Delgado who paid a personal tribute to the guardsman. It seems that Moreno was on his way to Valle del Bravo for a fishing holiday. No one witnessed the crash, but the inference is that he was the worse for drink because he had last been seen at a late-night celebration party that was held in his honour at *El Molino de Rey* barracks.

"I am afraid, *Jefe,* that we were unable to put a tail on him before the tragedy happened."

At 1530 hours the scene at PGA headquarters was almost as chaotic as it had been on the previous afternoon. Once again the so-called *Centro de Información de Prensa* was packed almost to bursting-point, a circumstance brought about by the announcement one hour earlier that the Procurador General would shortly be holding a second press conference at which he hoped to have a major announcement concerning the progress of the investigation.

By now, an epidemic of wild rumour and supposition had taken firm hold. Most popularly, it was being said that a foreign terrorist group had claimed responsibility for the assassination of Kemal Tunaman. More sensationally, there were stories that had been fuelled by the death of Sargento Moreno: unsubstantiated stories of a major conspiracy involving corrupt security guards and, so some whispered, a high-ranking Mexican government official who had served as the go-between on behalf of a foreign power.

As they had done twenty-four hours before, reporters persisted in roaming the ground floor in the hopes of spotting someone whose presence might give a useful clue to developments. But this time there was a difference. *La Jaula* was operational, enabling any key arrivals to bypass the ground floor via the securely manned drive-in basement.

During the afternoon, press photographers and TV cameramen loitered outside the PGR building on the chance of capturing significant arrivals on film. But no one of interest was seen using the main entrance, and, with only two exceptions, all the cars admitted to the side driveway leading down to the basement had dark-frosted windows concealing their back-seat occupants.

One exception, predictably, was a chauffeur-driven Mercedes-Benz, all gleaming black and bearing the insignia of the *Secretario de Seguridad Pública*. As was his custom, the Mexico City Chief of Police, General Juan Delgado, had arrived in conspicuous style.

The other was a racing-green, open-top Cabriolet 911 Porsche driven by a grey-suited male Caucasian of about forty years of age. When the car turned into the driveway, its driver made no attempt to conceal his identity. Indeed, grinningly, he turned his head directly towards the cameras as he passed by.

Still more conveniently, he removed his reflector-glasses when stopping at the security booth sited at the head of the incline. There, he reached out to hand over a special pass together with his business card. An armed PGR officer checked the credentials against a list on his clipboard, then raised the barrier and waved the car on.

Photographers got excellent shots of this arrival and recognised him as the FBI representative who had attended the first press conference. But the driver's business card - insufficient to raise a salute from the security officer - read simply: Robert Carruthers, Legal Attaché, United States embassy, Paseo de la Reforma 305, tel: 2110042.

As it happened, Carruthers was the key figure

attending a top-level meeting called by the attorney general prior to his second press conference. His formal masquerade as legal attaché was over.

Seven men had been summoned at short notice to the Procurador General's office: the same seven who had attended the early-morning meeting. But this time, the seating arrangements in the conference room were significantly changed. Pride of place was given to Carruthers, seated immediately to the right of Procurador General Rodríguez. Arthur Madison and Brad McClellan, representing the CIA, were relegated to the far end of the rectangular table.

Rodríguez came directly to the point. "I have called this meeting, *señores,* because in the few hours since we last met, vital new information has come to hand - information that greatly advances our investigation.

"For this we must thank our *amigos americanos* of the FBI. And when you have heard a report on their work from Señor Carruthers, I think you will agree they have made extraordinary progress in a very short time..."

As he spoke, Carruthers removed a sheaf of papers from his zip-round attaché case, then aligned the sheets by holding them upright and tapping them on the table. He was relishing the moment, and in presenting his report, he fully intended to milk the FBI's success for all it was worth.

He began obliquely by recalling the position at their last meeting. "As you know, our agents in Chicago had failed to find any trace of the brother, Julio Ramírez. We only knew that he had probably moved to 'somewhere sunny and warm.' Therefore we extended the search to Florida on the chance that he had family connections there."

He feigned grimness. "Well, *señores,* it is my sad duty to report that our agents in Miami have also failed to find any trace of this Julio."

Then he smiled smugly. "But the good news is that our investigations in Miami have led to a discovery of the first magnitude. Indeed, we have uncovered the one great missing link in this case: the motive for the killings in Chapultepec Park.

"It happened like this..."

Comandante Barraza took a deep breath and closed his invisible eyes. All his instincts told him that he was not going to like what he was about to hear.

CHAPTER 16

Ordinarily, special agent Lou Klein would have welcomed the task ahead: a vague "Missing Person" assignment that involved swanning around Miami with all expenses paid. It allowed him just the kind of independence and freedom he had sought five years ago when leaving the New York PD for a less frenetic life with the FBI. The subsequent transfer to the Sunshine State had been an unexpected bonus.

But Klein was far from content on this Monday morning when he pulled up in his Volkswagen Golf at the corner of Calle Ocho and Memorial Boulevard. Everything felt wrong: the ease with which he had found a parking space, the sound of birds singing, the foul taste of his first cigar, the hangover-throbbing in his head.

Basically, though, only one thing was wrong: the time of day. It was 7.30 a.m.— in the estimation of this bachelor night owl, a time fit only for road-sweepers and garbagemen. After a second puff and a cough, he gently stubbed out his reusable cigar, adjusted the driver's seat, and leaned back and waited.

Through half-closed eyes, he could see across the way an eternal flame burning atop a simple stone monument. The words on the obelisk he knew by heart: "*A los Mártires de la Brigada de Asalto, Abril 17 de 1961.*" Here, for all time, was a heart-warming reminder of the CIA's bungling ineptitude in planning the disastrous Bay of Pigs invasion of Cuba.

For Klein it was also a reminder of why he was on duty at such an ungodly hour. The word had come down from the Washington office of the FBI's Assistant Director (Investigations): top priority was to be given to tracing one Julio Ramírez, wanted for questioning in relation to a Mexico City investigation involving both the Bureau and the T-Bars, "Those Bastards Across the River," as the FBI called the CIA.

It went without saying that the primary aim was to demonstrate the superior efficiency of the FBI whose motto -

201

Fidelity, Bravery, Integrity - was currently said by comedians to stand for Fumbling, Bumbling Idiots. And at this time it was much more than traditional rivalry between the two security agencies. They were now locked into a head-on battle for supremacy in the face of the Carmichael Administration's promise of a major reorganisation of U.S. intelligence services.

On the one hand, senators had drafted a controversial bill to abolish the Company altogether and put the Bureau in charge of counter-intelligence abroad. Most damningly, they recalled how the tragedy of 9/11 might have been prevented, if the CIA had given the FBI access to their intelligence concerning two Osama bin Laden operatives who had sneaked into the country. Now, at the very least, they wanted a doubling of the number of FBI overseas field agents in order to counter the sharp increase in international terrorism, organised crime and drug smuggling.

On other hand, CIA supporters pointed out that the Company had warned U.S. Secretary of State, Condoleeza Rice, of unspecified al-Qaeda plots two months before the attacks of 9/11. They also stressed that the FBI had a track record of headstrong heavy-handedness, which had been maintained ever since their 1993 disastrous assault on the cult compound in Waco, Texas, and they argued that the FBI's increasing role overseas was duplicating CIA activities, and allowing foreign governments to play off one U.S. agency against another.

Klein now reflected cynically on his absurd role in this age-old political duel: looking for some obscure boxer in a greater Miami area bulging with a multi-ethnic, half-Hispanic population of more than two million. He liked a challenge, but this was madness, starting a search while the city was barely awake.

He was almost nodding off when he was alerted by heavily ringed fingers rapping on his near-side window. He looked up to see the familiar smile of a swarthy young woman. He flipped up the catch on the off-side door, and she slid into the seat beside him.

"Mornin', Lou," she chirped. "My God, you do look awful! And no wonder. Could we open some windows, and let out this dreadful stench of cigars?"

Klein forced a grin. "Whatever you want, Anj."

The woman at his side had youthful good looks, but

without any hint of chic: a neat fawn cotton dress ill-matched by a cheap red cardigan, and finely chiselled features marred by over-stated make-up. Long, tousled black hair and two large, golden ear hoops contributed to an almost gypsy-like appearance.

But that appearance changed dramatically as they drove east from Little Havana, and then headed north through the grand canyon of Brickell Avenue. Taking a hand mirror and Kleenex from her shoulder bag, she wiped her face clean. Then she removed her earrings and swept back her hair to form an elegant plait.

The transformation was completed by the addition of a pair of lightly framed spectacles. Looking at least five years older and infinitely more respectable, she smiled at Klein as though seeking approval. He said nothing.

"Staying up too late again, Lou?"

Klein pouted. "No, getting up too bloody early."

"Okay," said the woman. "Be a grouch. But you aren't going to spoil my day."

Inwardly, Klein was starting to feel better already. Angela Cruz invariably had that effect upon him. She was one of those freaks of nature: a woman of extraordinary effervescence and 24-carat charm who could melt the frostiest of spirits. As he recognised, those gifts, combined with high intelligence, made her one of the most effective undercover agents in the business.

For the past three weeks, to establish a new cover, Miss Cruz had been staying at a boarding house off Calle Ocho, in a predominantly Cuban neighbourhood. There she was known as Angelica da Silva, a Nicaraguan, who was taking casual, unskilled work— waitress, barmaid, dishwasher— wherever she could find it. Her story was that she had moved from Fort Lauderdale into downtown Miami to escape her stepfather, a hard-drinking, sometimes violent, American trucker.

Angela's mother was indeed Nicaraguan-born, and living in Fort Lauderdale, but she was very happily married to an architect from Georgia. They had three children, the youngest being Angela who, after graduating in arts at the Florida International University, had qualified for the rigorous, make-or-break sixteen-week training programme at the FBI Academy at Quantico, Virginia.

Every day, while undercover, Miss Cruz had to make a

check-in call from a public phone booth. On Sunday evening, the Miami FBI field office— one of fifty-six in the United States— had told her to report at 1730 hours for an "MP" assignment that might require her fluent Spanish. No more details were given. As always, the rendezvous was the Bay of Pigs Memorial, in walking distance from her lodging.

"Mind telling me where we are going?" Cruz asked as they crossed north over the Miami River.

"Anywhere that does a decent cup of coffee," Klein replied.

A few minutes later they stopped at an open-air cafe near Bicentennial Park. Angela went to the trunk and exchanged her red cardigan for a well-cut beige jacket. Then, over coffee and croissants, Klein briefed her on their purpose.

He handed her a publicity photo of Julio Ramírez in boxing pose. "We got this picture from Chicago."

"Hmm! Nice-looking boy..."

"Not now, he ain't. Got himself cut up badly in his last fight."

"Oh dear," said Angela. "Anyway, it's not much to go on. Where do we start? Making the rounds of plastic surgeons?"

Klein grinned. "Wish it was that simple. Truth is I know only one place to start, and if that fails we could be at a dead end."

Via the Dolphin Expressway, they cut across the park and got onto the MacArthur Causeway linking downtown Miami to the playground city of Miami Beach spread over seventeen islands offshore in Biscayne Bay. The causeway led directly onto 5th Street and to their destination at the corner of Washington Avenue, on the south side of the Art Deco district.

This corner had once been the site of the original 5th Street Gym, famed for workouts by boxing immortals, ranging from Joe Louis to Muhammad Ali. But the gym had always been a dump, losing money even in the '50s when it was run by the tight-fisted Chris Dundee who charged for admission to watch big-name fighters in training. In the '70s it was briefly revitalised by the Latin promoter, Tuto Zabala, then demolished to make way for a car park.

More recently, however, as part of the long-term New Millennium Development Program, a replica of the old gym had been constructed on the site and pretentiously renamed

204

The Muhammad Ali Champion of Champions Center. The ground floor was occupied by a museum-cum-souvenir shop. Above, the old gym had been artfully recreated. with peeling, grey-green walls and faded fight posters, looking much the same as it had been when the loud-mouthing of Cassius "The Louisville Lip" Clay was packing them in.

On entering, Klein and Cruz saw that the gym comprised nothing more than one large, drab room with bare floorboards and strip lighting, and furnished with the usual essentials: boxing ring, two heavy bags, two suspended light bags, three rub-down tables, some mechanical exercise equipment and a full-length mirror for shadow work. In the ring, two black lightweights were sparring vigorously under the supervision of a grizzled white man with a towel draped around his neck. Elsewhere, dumbbells and exercise machines were being used by four middle-aged men who were clearly more concerned with paunches than punches.

While Cruz took a back seat, Klein went round with his picture of Julio Ramírez. He found that the four men working out individually were health club members with no real interest in boxing. They couldn't help.

The sparring session ended, and Klein approached the boxers. Both were young Cubans with limited English, so he signalled Angela to come over. They, too, had never seen or heard of Julio Ramírez. Nor had their elderly American trainer, a Mr. Tony Morelli.

Then Miss Cruz chanced to mention that Julio was the son of Fernando Ramírez, a Mexican who had fought in Miami in the 1960s. Immediately the name registered with Mr. Morelli. No, he had never met Fernando, but years ago he had worked with a cornerman who was always talking about a boxer of that name.

"This guy was a Mexican, too. Diego Anaya. The best cuts-man I ever saw... excepting, of course, the great Angelo Dundee.

"What a tragic waste! He had two big problems, you see: gambling and booze. The gambling wasn't always bad. I remember him making a bomb when he backed Cassius Clay to beat Sonny Liston at 7 to 1. But the booze was something else. Ever see a cuts-man trying to work with shaking hands? Not a pretty sight. Got him thrown out of boxing in the end."

"When was that?" Cruz asked.

"Oh, twenty-five, maybe thirty years ago."

205

"Christ!" said Klein. "So I guess you don't know where we can find this Anaya now."

Morelli grinned. "Oh, that's easy. Everyone knows 'Sparky' Anaya. Most evenings he hangs around the Flagler Dog Track. But there ain't no racing on just now. So your best bet is Ocean Drive. That's his regular beat. He tours the bars and cafés there, giving tourists electric shocks at a dollar a time."

It was almost noon before they came across Diego Anaya: a white-haired little man, at least seventy-years-old, but youthfully dressed in grey flannels, white trainers and a pleated, intricately embroidered *guayabera*. In the alfresco section of the Café Solo, he was going around the tables, inviting customers to test their powers of resistance by gripping the copper leads from his multi-coloured electric box.

Klein and Cruz took a table and almost immediately Anaya zeroed in on them. "*Buenos días!* Ooh, *señor*, you look very strong. Wanna show the *señorita* what you can do? Ten pesos a shock. If you can take eighty volts you are *muy macho.*"

Klein declined, but said they would be pleased if he would join them for a drink. Anaya readily agreed, at the same time hustling them into ordering a *palomilla* beefsteak to go with his *cerveza.*

The Mexican was a garrulous character, who needed no prompting to talk about himself. Long ago, so he said, he had been a top boxing trainer. He had known all the greats - Basilio, Dupas, Rodríguez, Sugar Ramos, Muhammad Ali. But then he had gone broke because of the expense of paying for a hernia operation.

"I opened a shoeshine stand under the 5th Street Gym, but business got so bad I converted my shoeshine box to electricity." He grinned. "This is it. You grip the copper leads and hang on for as long as you can. The voltameter keeps the score. Most people throw in the towel around eighty. The all-time record is one hundred ninety. You sure you don't wanna try?"

Klein decided it was time to be direct. He showed his ID and the picture of Julio Ramírez. "You know a lot of boxers; have you ever seen this one before?"

Squinting, Anaya held up the picture within an inch of his face. "What you want this guy for?"

"Never mind that," snapped Klein. "Do you recognise

him?"

The old Mexican stared thoughtfully into his empty glass. Miss Cruz got the message and called a waiter to bring another *cerveza.* Anaya studied the picture all over again.

"*Sí,* I can positively say that I have never seen this boxer before. He can't be much good. What's his name?"

Klein told him and Anaya shook his head. "No, never heard of him."

"Ah," said Klein. "But I think you know his father. A Mexican middleweight called Fernando Ramírez. Fought in Miami more than forty years ago."

Anaya reacted at once. "*Dios mío!* You mean to say this is Fernando's kid. I can't believe it. Don't look much like the old bugger. Are you sure?"

Reassured, he went on to explain that Fernando had been his *compadre...* 'back in the good old days'.

He went on, "Jesús! We had some great times together. What a boozer! You know, I haven't seen him since the Clay-Siler fight. Soon after that he pissed off to Mexico City. I read somewhere that he got a hiding in a title fight. But I never heard from him again, not even a bloody postcard. Where is he now? What's he doing?"

It now emerged that Anaya knew nothing about the shooting in Mexico City, because he rarely watched TV and only read the sports pages. He could talk endlessly about his long-ago escapades with Fernando. "Remember those times like it was yesterday." But regarding the whereabouts of Julio Ramírez, he had nothing to offer.

Klein decided they were wasting valuable time. He called for the cheque. Meanwhile, in Spanish, Cruz engaged the Mexican in small talk. How was his health? How was business? Did he perhaps have a family to support?

Anaya remarked that, unlike his *compadre* Fernando, he had never married. And then, out of the blue, came the question that gave them an entirely new lead. "*A propósito, como está Hera Maryam?*"

Angela reverted to English. "I don't know. Whoever is Hera Maryam?"

The Mexican looked surprised. "Why, Fernando's wife, of course. I was the best man at their wedding, you know. Don't tell me it didn't last. Wait a minute, maybe you know her as María. That's what Fernando always used to call her. But I always knew her as Maryam. Hera Maryam Kamber. We

207

grew up together, you see. In fact, it was me that introduced her to Fernando. What a lovely sweet girl! Mind you, the family didn't approve of her marriage. Especially old man Seto.

"Liked to keep to themselves, those Armenians."

Nine senior executives, heading respectively Criminal Investigations, Intelligence, Training, Laboratory, Liaison and International Affairs, Identification, AdministrItive Services, Records Management and Technical Services, serve as a virtual board of directors under the Director of the FBI in Washington. On Monday, at 1255 local time, William Prentice, assistant director (Investigations), was personally advised of the interim report phoned through from Miami. He ordered immediate action.

Within ninety minutes, researchers in the Records Department had supplied his investigators with four preliminary profiles. These were based on information taken from the files of the U.S. Immigration and Naturalisation Service in Washington and from birth, death and marriage certificates faxed from the Florida State Archives .The profiles read:

> *HERA MARYAM KAMBER b. Miami, September 29, 1943, daughter of Setrak Kamber, jeweller, and Zabel Kamber, née Anbaroglu. Married St. Kieran's Church, Miami, April 9, 1960, to Fernando Luis Ramírez of Mexico City.*
> *SETRAK KAMBER b. Miami, March 21, 1910, son of Bedros Kamber and Hasmig Kamber, née Margosyan. Married St. Kieran's Church, Miami, July 30, 1938, to Zabel Anbaroglu. Died (heart failure) Miami, January 5, 1992.*
> *ZABEL ANBAROGLU KAMBER b. Angora (Ankara), May 6, 1913, daughter of Avedis Anbaroglu, textile merchant, and Mannik Anbaroglu, née Vartanyan. Arrived U.S. June 21, 1923, sponsored by Hagop Vartanyan of New York City under auspices of American Near East Relief (NER), formerly the American Committee for Armenian and Syrian Relief. Naturalised U.S. citizen, 1926. Married Setrak Kamber, Miami, 1938. Died (cancer) Miami, April 10, 1958.*
> *HAGOP VARTANYAN b. Angora (Ankara), 1883. Emigrated to U.S. 1904. Naturalised citizen, 1908. Died (stroke) Miami, February 4,1965.*

All the names were fed into the 2000 computer system of the National Crime Information Center (NCIC), the FBI's criminal records database which even includes millions of minor traffic violations. All came out clean.

The four profiles were duly faxed to Miami, then relayed to Lou Klein on his mobile phone. By that time, however, Klein and Cruz were already well ahead in the game. With the simple aid of the Miami telephone directory, they had traced one of the two Kambers listed.

The first entry, a Mr. W.A. Kamber, took them to an apartment block on North East 2nd Street. There was no one at home. The second entry, a Mr. A. S. Kamber, was located on Flagler Street in the heart of downtown Miami's commercial area. The address was a three-storey building, sandwiched between an electronics shop and a clothing store. Above the entrance hung a large sign proclaiming *The Ararat Jewellery Company.*

The discount jewellery shop, they discovered, was owned by a Mr. Arto Kamber, aged sixty-seven, in partnership with a Mr. Garo Tingiryan. The former, who lived above the shop with his wife Sofi, was the son of a Mr. Garbis Kamber— now deceased— the elder brother of Setrak "Seto" Kamber. On the third floor— a loft converted into a large one-roomed apartment— lived Arto's sister, a seventy-year-old spinster named Rita.

Arto, an extremely affable and courteous gentleman, shook his head when shown the picture of Julio Ramírez. He had never seen the man and knew no one of that name. But, yes, he did know a Hera Maryam Ramírez. She was his cousin, though he understood she had died in Mexico years ago.

"Look," he said. "I am due to take my lunch break while my son William runs the store. Why don't you join me? Then you can tell me what this is all about."

Upstairs, Klein and Cruz were ushered into a rectangular lounge that, excluding a TV set and video, seemed almost wholly antique: a velvet-covered chaise longue; six high-backed armchairs, a tall, mahogany longcase clock, a sideboard crowded with framed sepia photographs that included women in high-collared, ankle-length dresses and men with walrus moustaches and watch-chains. In the centre, large overhanging chandeliers dazzled in the sunlight filtering through lace curtains.

Arto introduced the agents to his wife Sofi, who automatically asked them if they would like some coffee and homemade shortbread cookies. She smiled warmly. "It's no trouble. It's all ready." Then she gestured towards the easy chairs. "Meanwhile, do make yourselves comfortable."

In one of the chairs, seated beneath a large framed print of Arshile Gorky's *The Artist and His Mother*, an elderly lady was engaged in intricate guipure needlework. Sofi was about to introduce her when she pulled down her spectacles, looked disapprovingly at the visitors, and said snappily, *"Asonk ov yen?"*

Arto answered at length, in words equally incomprehensible to Klein and Cruz. Then he hastened to explain. "This is my sister Rita. Please excuse the language, but among members of the family she insists on speaking only Armenian. She was asking who you are."

Rita, as it turned out, spoke perfectly good English. But for a long time she remained silent, studiously listening while Klein explained the nature of their inquiries.

Both Arto and Sofi expressed their horror that a distant relative was involved in the killing of a Turkish ambassador. They had seen the crime reported on TV, but they had never dreamed that there might a connection with their family. "I don't see how we can possibly help you," said Arto.

Angela Cruz smiled at Mrs Kamber and pointed towards the sideboard. "That's a lovely collection of family pictures you have over there. Do you think we could have a look at some of them?"

"Of course," Sofi replied. And she began by bringing over a large framed photograph of some forty people grouped outside a church for a wedding picture. "This one might interest you. It's the only picture we have of Maryam. It was taken at her wedding."

In the centre, standing next to the burly bridegroom, Angela recognised the unmistakable little figure of a young Diego Anaya, grinning from ear to ear. Meanwhile, Sofi was pointing to two young people on the far right. "Believe it or not, that's me and Arto."

"Oh yes," Angela responded, "I can see the likeness. You look really elegant. And who are all these other people? Mostly Armenian friends, I expect."

"Not really. Many of them are Latin-American

210

friends of Maryam. She was a very active member of the church, you know. I am afraid we know hardly anyone in the picture. We are Orthodox - not Catholics, you see."

"Maryam was a Catholic?"

"Oh yes, her family came from Angora, what is now Ankara in Turkey. Most Armenians in Angora were Catholics, that is until the killings and mass deportations of 1915.

"Now there's an interesting gentleman. See that old man in the wheelchair. That's Hagop Vartanyan. He came from Angora, but long before the massacres. A brilliant man; made his fortune as a financier in New York. In fact, he was responsible for bringing Maryam's mother to the United States back in the '20s.

"It really is a remarkable story. My uncle Seto often used to tell it. According to him, Maryam's family - the Anbaroglus - escaped the Angora massacre purely by chance because they happened to be visiting relatives in Smyrna at the time. They were safe in Smyrna because the Turks didn't persecute Armenians in cities with a big European community.

"But things changed when the Turkish Nationalists came to power. In 1922 their army attacked Smyrna and killed or drove out all Greeks and Armenians. More than a hundred thousand people were slaughtered. Among them were all the Anbaroglus, except for Maryam's mother, Zabel. She was only ten-years-old then.

"Anyway, it seems that Hagop— Zabel's uncle— had been negotiating to get the family to the U.S. through an American relief organisation. By a million-to-one chance, a relief worker recognised Zabel in a huge refugee camp, and so her emigration was arranged. Uncle Seto said it was all down to Fate."

"Do go on," said Angela. "What happened after that?"

"There's not much else to tell. All I know is that old man Hagob lost most of his fortune in the Wall Street crash. Then he moved to Miami and went into the jewellery business with Arto's great uncle, Bedros Kamber. Some years later Zabel married Bedros' son, Setrak, and they had a daughter, Maryam. The rest you know.

"Quite a romantic family history, isn't it?"

At that juncture, speaking fluently in English, Rita Kamber positively exploded. "Romantic! Romantic, my foot! Why don't you ever tell it the way it really was?"

211

"Tell them about what happened in Smyrna. How the Turks set fire to the city and drove Greeks and Armenians into the sea, and how that poor child saw her mother raped and her father put up against a wall and shot. And tell them about how Zabel's brother jumped into the harbour and tried to swim out to the fleet of foreign ships."

She glared at Angela. "Do you know what happened? That boy, only twelve-years-old, got as far as a British warship. And when he tried to get aboard, the sailors turned hosepipes on him. Would you believe it? Then, as he swam back to the shore, his mother jumped in to help him. Both of them were killed by Turkish machine gun fire.

"And that poor little girl saw it all. Seto used to say that she only survived because she had never learnt to swim."

"Of course, all this will mean nothing to you. It's just like Hitler said in 1939 when he talked about exterminating without mercy all men and women and children of the Polish race: 'After all, who remembers today the extermination of the Armenians?'"

"My God," said Klein. "How your family must have hated the Turks! And I suppose Maryam must have heard all these terrible stories from her mother."

"Oh sure," said Rita, now suddenly subdued. "Maybe not from her mother. But certainly from her father. Mind you, I never heard Maryam talk about it. She was a funny one, that girl. Didn't seem much interested in our family history. Why, she didn't even learn to speak Armenian. But she learnt Spanish quickly enough.

"Frankly, I couldn't understand her. Always going to Mass and never having a bad word to say about anyone. I remember mentioning the Turks to her once. She told me it was best to forgive and forget, and she emphasised that the few Turkish people she had met were wonderfully kind, charming and hospitable. She just didn't want to know about the past.

"She was genuinely religious. I'll give her that. But a fat lot of good it did her, all that praying at the Lady of Charity Shrine. Didn't stop her getting pregnant by that Mexican oaf. Wouldn't take precautions, you see.

"I suppose it might have been different if her mother had still been alive. But that poor woman had passed on two years before. And, of course, Maryam refused to even think about an abortion.

212

"Her father never forgave her, you know. He wanted her to marry the son of his Armenian business partner. It would have been a very good match. In the end, Seto refused to attend the wedding.

"And so did I."

It was almost 2 p.m. when the FBI agents left the Flagler Street jewellery store. As they walked back to the car, Klein asked, "So did you get all that?"

Angela Cruz stopped in her tracks. "Oh, thanks for reminding me, Lou. You know, I got so involved that I completely forgot."

She reached down into her shoulder bag and depressed the switch on her tape recorder to "off".

CHAPTER 17

At the Procurador General's meeting in Mexico City Robert Carruthers recounted the events in Miami very much as they had happened... with one significant omission. As instructed, he made no mention of Rita Kamber's comments on Maryam (Maria) Ramírez's forgiving nature, her admiration of the Turks she had met and her total disinterest in Armenian history.

On reaching the end of his report, he looked triumphantly around the table as though anticipating an ovation, or at least some expression of wonder and surprise. But the only spontaneous reaction came from Emilio Ortega, the Procurador General's obsequious PA.

"*Magnífico,*" he exclaimed. "Now we have a real motive for the crime."

The Procurador General promptly concurred. "Exactly. This disturbing family history explains a great deal. Remember that several witnesses have already remarked on Manuel Ramírez's devotion to his mother. Also we have the testimony of Señorita Gutiérrez who says that he talked endlessly about memories of his *mamá.*"

"All the evidence suggests that here we are dealing with an assassination perpetrated by a demented individual. Of course, we cannot tell how far Manuel Ramírez was motivated by his mother's Armenian past. It may be that he was feeling suicidal after his rejection by Gutiérrez; perhaps he merely latched on to the old family grievance as a means of ending his own life with some purpose and style. We shall probably never know what went on in his twisted mind."

Carruthers was fully prepared at this point to see his FBI report strongly challenged, especially by Madison or McClellan on behalf of the CIA. To his astonishment, no challenge was forthcoming. Not one word of criticism of the flimsy evidence presented, nor of the extremely tenuous conclusion that had been drawn.

For a few seconds there was silence. Then General

Delgado added his voice of approval. He was most impressed by what the FBI had achieved. Though he did have two reservations. "Given this background, there remains the possibility that Manuel Ramírez was recruited by Armenian terrorists. Also, until we have traced and questioned him, we cannot rule out the possibility that Julio Ramírez was a collaborator in this diabolical crime."

By now Carruthers was positively confounded by the lack of opposition. Madison was doodling on a notebook, seemingly disinterested in the proceedings. Brad McClellan, his CIA colleague, also remained silent, though his grim, tight-lipped expression suggested that he might explode at any time.

The fact was that, inadvertently, the FBI man had not been fully briefed by his superiors in Washington. If he had been, he would have understood the non-critical reaction; he would have realised that he was merely a messenger delivering news that had already been evaluated by all the key decision makers.

Carruthers had begun his report in the Procurador General's conference room at 1530 hours. By that time, the meeting had already become a mere formality, its outcome a foregone conclusion. Precisely, the reaction to the FBI findings had been resolved one hour earlier, following a chain of telephone calls at the highest level.

Shortly after 1430 hours— 1330 In Mexico City— Klein and Cruz had delivered to their Miami office the tape-recording of their interview with the Kambers. Immediately it had been transmitted to the Investigations Department at the monumental Bureau headquarters at 935 Pennsylvania Avenue in Washington, D.C.

William Prentice, the assistant director (Investigations), judged the contents sufficiently important to inform Henry Strachan, the Director of the FBI, who in turn made direct contact with President Sam Carmichael. Strachan's call to the White House was timely. A few hours earlier, the possible threat of a new Aegean crisis had been discussed in detail at an emergency meeting attended by members of the National Security Council, plus U.S. Attorney General Melvin J. Holmes.

At this meeting they had considered a reassessment of the situation presented by CIA Chief-elect William Stanleigh. It had been prepared by James Chester-Allen, NIO Turkish

215

Affairs, and in response to its recommendation NSC members had agreed that ships of the U.S. Sixth Fleet should be dispatched at once to the Aegean.

The expressed hope was that a strong U.S. military presence would serve as an effective deterrent to Greek-Turkish hostilities. Unresolved was the question of how American forces should react in the event of open conflict between two NATO allies. The President insisted that this could only be decided in the light of more advanced developments.

With luck, as he pointed out, the need for action would never arise. After all, as stated in the CIA analysis, the defused Aegean crisis was only likely to be reactivated "if it were discovered that the assassination of ambassador Tunaman had been engineered by Greek right-wing extremists."

Those words returned vividly to the President's mind when he learnt from Strachan of new evidence pointing to the possibility of an Armenian-inspired vendetta. He congratulated the FBI Director and instructed him that this information from Miami should be conveyed immediately to the Mexican authorities.

What the Bureau did not know, however, was that President Carmichael subsequently made two telephone calls to pass on the news from Miami. One call was to President Pérez who duly contacted Procurador General Rodríguez; the other was to Bill Stanleigh who promptly contacted Arthur Madison in Mexico City and Wade Hellman, who was returning to his duties as the CIA station chief.

Madison was at the U.S. embassy, about to leave for PGR headquarters, when he received Stanleigh's call on a scrambled line. His immediate reaction was sceptical. He explained that he and McClellan had worked very closely with Comandante Barraza, and they had been given access to all tape-recorded interviews with relatives and friends of the Ramírez family. No one had ever mentioned an Armenian connection.

"Quite frankly, sir, I don't believe it. My impression is that María Ramírez was an extremely devout Catholic, far too busy raising an enormous family to have been dwelling on some distant Armenian past. And are we supposed to believe that this simple Mexican kid went to such lengths to avenge wrongs to a grandmother he had never even met?

216

"Certainly, he could not have done it on his own. And if Armenian terrorists had used him, I feel sure they would have claimed responsibility by now.

"No, it is still my considered judgement— as stated in my interim report— that we should accept McClellan's theory that the killings were planned to counter our secret operations in Mexico City."

"Listen, Arthur," Stanleigh replied. "Let me make one thing absolutely clear: this is not a matter for debate. We are simply not interested in alternative explanations... and certainly not one that will lead to exposing our *modus operandi*.

"You need to understand that there's much more at stake here than one man's guilt or innocence. We could be talking about the lives of tens of thousands in the event of a Greek-Turkish war. Then there is the importance of our air base at Incirlik— so critical for our Middle East operations— to be considered.

"At present, the Armenian connection provides the least damaging solution to a crime that could otherwise stir up a major international crisis very much in conflict with American interests.

"Let me put it more simply. I have spoken personally to the President about this. And I will say to you exactly what he said to me: *When you are thrown a pass with no one between you and a touchdown, you don't pause to ponder the next course of action. You gratefully catch the ball and you run with it like a fucking fox out of a chicken coop.*"

Via William Prentice at FBI headquarters, Carruthers had received the same presidential directive. In his case, however, there was the additional order that under no circumstances should he dilute or confuse his report with reference to the ramblings of the old lady, Rita Kamber.

Spurred on by the imagined threat of being tackled by CIA opposition, Carruthers ran with the ball very hard indeed— at the Procurador General's meeting, and again, more importantly, at the ensuing press conference.

In striking contrast to his previous performance, José Rodríguez, too, was wholly effective in addressing the gathering of the world's Press. He had marshalled his facts well, albeit one-sidedly; also, to his great advantage, he had an audience of news hounds that was still digesting the meaty human interest story that had been fed to them by Carruthers.

After a brief review of the evidence, the Procurador General moved into overdrive as though he was back in the courtroom, summing up for the prosecution. "We can only conjecture at the impact made on this impressionable young man by stories of the horrors inflicted on his mother's parents.

"Perhaps he was tormented for years, driven by an Oedipus complex; perhaps he longed to strike a blow for the sake of his family's honour; or perhaps he merely wished to end his life spectacularly after losing all self-esteem through his humiliating serenade of the woman he loved. Who can say what went on in his mind? Who knows what it takes to finally tip the scales against rationality and turn a man into a psychopathic killer?"

Most of the media representatives were now eager to get away and file a story with all the ingredients of a heart-rending family saga. There were few probing questions in the short time allowed, and in answer to the one suggestion of a conspiracy cover-up, Rodríguez stressed that the PGR would "leave no stone unturned in the search for any person or persons who may have aided and abetted the assassin Manuel Ramírez."

The press conference ended with the Procurador General's reply to a question from the representative of *The Washington Post*. "Yes, in the light of overwhelming evidence, I can say that I am completely satisfied that Manuel Ramírez was the lone assassin, and that that will be the official conclusion of this investigation.

"It only remains for me to thank everyone who has assisted me so efficiently in my task. Essentially, this had been a magnificent team effort, a tribute to the outstanding professionalism of the combined police and intelligence services of Mexico and the United States."

The man who had contributed most diligently to the assassination investigation was not present to hear the Procurador General's expression of thanks. Comandante Barraza had asked to be excused from the press conference on the grounds that he was feeling exhausted after making such an early start to the day. Subcomandante Ibarra, he had said, was fully equipped to stand in for him. And Rodríguez had readily agreed.

In reality, Barraza absented himself because he could not stomach the prospect of sitting through a repeat performance by Carruthers and the Procurador General. He had already achieved an extraordinary feat of self-control by maintaining a discreet silence throughout the preliminary meeting. He very much doubted that he could do so again.

From years of experience, Barraza had recognised the futility of expressing dissent when a higher official was clearly resolved on a different course. Inwardly, however, all his sense of reason and justice had screamed out in rage at the Procurador General's distortion of the hard facts and, above all, at his simplistic solution to a case still riddled with unanswered questions.

His greatest outrage had been felt when Rodríguez stressed how Consuelo Gutiérrez had observed that Manuel Ramírez was forever talking about his mother. Totally ignored was the fact that, in the same testimony, the girl had remarked that he never spoke about politics.

Also he thought back to his interview with Fernando Ramírez. Most significantly, the old man, so politically minded, had ranted on about historic massacres without once mentioning the horrors suffered by his wife's Armenian ancestors.

By the end of the preliminary meeting, Barraza had already decided to abandon his Sisyphean task of searching for the truth. On returning to his office, however, he had found that one more piece of business required his attention. A message stated that a *guardia,* Eduardo Jiménez, was now in the fourth floor interrogation centre, ready for questioning.

Stunned and sickened by the facile acceptance of the Miami report, Barraza had completely forgotten that three hours earlier, following news of the death of Sargento Segundo Moreno, he had ordered *judicial* Montaño to bring in for questioning the junior guardsman who had been on duty with Moreno at *El Castillo.*

Now, though regarding his investigation as ended, the Comandante decided that he might as well hear what the guardsman had to say. He instructed Montaño to invite the man down to his office.

When *Guardia* Jiménez arrived, Barraza immediately put the nervous young soldier at ease, explaining that this was strictly a routine interview to tie up a few loose ends. Specifically, he would like him to recount events at the time of the shooting at *El Castillo.*

Jiménez duly explained that he had been on duty at

the Doña Carmen Díaz bedchamber when he heard what sounded like gunfire coming from somewhere above. Going to investigate, he had noticed that people were crowding around the base of *La Torre del Caballero Alto.*

"At the entrance to the tower, I met Sargento Moreno. He said that he thought that someone had been shooting from up in the tower. He told me to keep people well back while he went up to investigate."

Barraza found that the guardsman's recollection of subsequent events fully supported Moreno's own official statement. But Jiménez added one small detail that had never been previously mentioned: to enter the tower Moreno had not only ducked under a velvet-covered chain, but had also passed a large placard which stated: *PELIGRO. NO ENTRE. ESCALERAS EN REPARACIÓN."*

"*Sí, señor,"* Jiménez replied to Barraza's supplementary question. "I am absolutely sure about the sign because I remember thinking about whether it was safe for the *sargento* to climb up the tower."

No one, until now, had ever said anything about the tower undergoing repairs.

Following this last interview, Barraza checked with *El Castillo's* maintenance office. They confirmed that the tower was permanently closed to the public since there was inadequate space to have tourists going up and down at the same time.

But otherwise the tower was perfectly safe. They could state categorically that no repair work had been authorised. And they certainly had no knowledge of a danger sign being displayed.

Barraza checked further with PGR *judiciales* who had arrived on the scene some fifteen minutes after the shooting was reported. They, too, were certain that they had not seen any *"Peligro, No entre"* sign at the entrance to the tower.

The Comandante added the discrepancy to many others recorded in his black notebook. He was entirely satisfied that the soldier had not invented the repair sign. Equally, he regarded it as certain that someone had removed the sign very shortly after the killings.

But he did not trouble to report this detail to the Procurador General. He knew when he was beaten. It was time to concentrate on plans for his imminent retirement and the writing of his memoirs.

That same day brought immediate retirement for another man who shared Barraza's disgust. With the return from compassionate leave of Wade Hellman, the CIA's station chief, the services of Brad McClellan were no longer required.

Before emptying his desk, McClellan explained to Hellman all his reasons for doubting the validity of the so-called Armenian connection. His chief heartily agreed. "But I'm afraid, dear boy, we are not in the business of seeking justice. All that matters is political expediency, what is in the best interests of the U.S.A. So what are your plans for retirement, Brad?"

McClellan looked at him tight lipped. "I haven't exactly decided. But I think I'll get in some hunting and fishing."

"Lucky fellow," said Hellman, who was soon to return to Langley as the CIA's newly promoted Deputy Director of the Latin American section. "I can't wait for retirement myself."

To all intents and purposes, the PGR investigation into the Chapultepec Park killings ended with the delivery of the FBI report on that Monday afternoon. Remarkably, the Procurador General had reached a conclusion barely 28 hours after the so-called "crime of the century" had been committed.

To be sure, the case was not officially closed for two months more. During that time, in separate television interviews, both Procurador General Rodríguez and Police Chief Delgado referred to continuing efforts to seek out possible accomplices. But there were no further developments of any consequence.

Within one week of the assassination of ambassador Tunaman, references to the crime had completely disappeared from the media in all countries excepting Mexico, Turkey and Greece. A series of kamikaze bombings by Muslim fundamentalists in the Middle East took over the headlines, and soon there was no further talk of an Aegean crisis as relations between Greece and Turkey returned to their normal ice-cool condition based on mutual mistrust and suspicion.

For the Mexican Press, the last major event emanating from the killings was the funeral of the young Finance Minister, Roberto Martínez. Restricted to close friends and relatives, plus members of the government and

221

selected representatives of the media, it was conducted amid great security at the *Panteón de Dolores*, the huge cemetery on the west side of Chapultepec Park.

Martínez, killed before his considerable potential could be realised, was not sufficiently distinguished to merit a place in *the Rotonda de los Hombres Ilustres*, the monumental circle of statuary that encompasses an eternal flame and memorialises some ninety illustrious Mexicans. But he was buried in a prime plot very close by; also, he was accorded the rare honour of a tribute by the Head of State. There, with the black-veiled Yolanda Martínez at his side, President Pérez delivered a funeral oration that was transmitted live on nation-wide television.

Irreverently, the popular Mexican Press focussed their coverage not so much on the ceremony itself, but on the one notable absentee: Doña Maria Dolores Castillo de Tunaman, the sister-in-law of the deceased. But for her absence, as one tabloid gruesomely observed, there would have been a complete reunion of the adult party guests who had survived the slaughter in nearby Chapultepec Park.

An official statement, issued by the family, explained, "Doña Castillo de Tunaman deeply regrets that, owing to ill-health, she is unable to attend the funeral of her much-loved brother-in-law. Since her ordeal, she has been stricken with insomnia and nervous exhaustion. Her doctors have ordered complete rest. Meanwhile, she wishes to express her thanks to all the many well-wishers who have sent to her their condolences."

Investigative reporters, however, told a much less cosy story. They revealed that Doña Dolores Tunaman had suffered a serious mental breakdown, and that her family was alarmed at her increasingly irrational behaviour. In the eight days since the family tragedy, the distraught woman had become an almost total recluse, refusing even to see her own relatives.

On the fateful Sunday, when ambulance men had literally needed to drag her away from her husband's corpse, Dolores had refused to return to the Turkish embassy. Instead she was driven in the ambassador's Mercedes-Benz directly to her Cuernavaca retreat. There she was comforted by her personal maid Elvira, and by her younger sister, Esperanza Velázquez, who stayed at the mansion overnight rather than return to Acapulco.

That evening, Dolores was inconsolable, her plaintive sobbing being silenced only by a strong sedative administered by the family doctor. The following day, however, her demeanour was radically changed: overwhelming grief had given way to aggressive hysteria and paranoia. On emerging from the master bedroom, she ordered that it should be kept locked and never entered again. Then, irrationally, she screamed at a maid who had taken the liberty of beginning to unpack bags that had been made ready for the move to New York.

The maid was summarily dismissed and so, during the course of that Monday, were three other servants of long standing. The surviving staff now comprised only two gardeners, plus Elvira, who remained constantly at her mistress' side.

In vain, Esperanza argued that they would at least need to replace the kitchen staff, and when she raised the issue a second time, Dolores responded by ordering her sister to leave her house at once. Then she summoned the gardeners and instructed them to padlock the main gates. They were to take turns to stand guard on the gates, by day and by night, and under no circumstances were they to admit anyone without her permission.

On the day of the Martínez funeral, all this was reported in the popular Press, plus the fact that Doña Dolores Tunaman, dressed in her widow's weeds, was still entrenched in her Cuernavaca home, still refusing to see friends, relatives and doctors alike. With one exception, their reports were based on interviews with dismissed servants, and with the gardeners on guard duty at the main gates.

The exception, significantly, was a story in *El Informador*. By now Alfredo Gómez was in Cancún, writing trivial, part-advertising articles for a magazine geared to the tourist trade. But the weekly scandal sheet was still running a remarkably well-informed gossip column, albeit under the anonymous by-line of "Moctezuma."

On this occasion, there was a special issue of *El Informador*, with the new Moctezuma column promoted to the front page. It led with a story so sensational and so outrageously distasteful that no newspaper picked up its contents for fear of an extremely costly libel action.

"Today," wrote Moctezuma. "I can reveal exclusively that Doña Maria Dolores Castillo de Tunaman, the grief-stricken widow of the assassinated Turkish ambassador, has begun to seek solace in twice daily sessions with an Indian medium, who is endeavouring to put her into direct contact with her deceased husband.

"This is the real reason why she has declined to attend the funeral today of her brother-in-law, Roberto Martínez. She is determined not to miss one of these psychical sessions because she has been led to believe that her husband is liable to make a reappearance very soon.

"There are, of course, excellent precedents for such faith in supernaturalism. President Francisco Madero was himself a practising medium who guided his life and the country with the help of spirit advisers. In the 1940s, President Miguel Alemán regularly consulted a medium to seek guidance from the spirits of great statesmen long since passed away. U.S. President George Bush Snr., after a string of illnesses, paid for a Mexican shaman, Salvador Lunes Collazo, to be flown to Washington to conduct a special ceremony, which included killing chickens and burning candles in front of a shrine.

"More recently, however, prominent personages in Mexico City have preferred to be guided by astrologers and Tarot readers. It is well known, for example, that Señora Theresa 'Pepita' de Terreros, the TV astrologer, gives private readings to politicians and leading industrialists, and to a large female clientele that includes the first lady, Doña Evangelina Arantes de Pérez.

"Until two weeks ago, 'Pepita' gave weekly consultations to Doña Dolores Tunaman. But she failed completely to warn her of the impending tragedy in Chapultepec Park, and now, with her nervous system shattered, the ambassador's widow had turned in desperation to spiritualism.

"Members of the Castillo family are deeply alarmed by this development. Their fears for the lady's mental state are all the greater because her spiritual adviser - a *sacerdotisa* said to specialise in ectoplasmic materialisations - is not recognised in spiritualist circles, and not even known to Mexico's *Instituto de Estudios Parapsichologicals*.

"Who is this mysterious medium? I have learnt exclusively that she goes only by the name of Conchita, and that she comes from a remote village high in the mountains of Oaxaca. She was summoned to Cuernavaca on the

224

recommendation of Elvira Mendoza, personal maid to Doña Dolores Tunaman.

"Señorita Mendoza also hails from Oaxaca, and very possibly the two women are related. What is known, is that Conchita is a woman at least in her seventies, and has a crippled right leg. And, disturbingly, she is reputed to belong to the Chontales, a tribe of Indians who worship many minor gods of nature, and believe in a definitive devil who is responsible for all our misfortunes.

"According to Chontal teaching, this devil is also wholly responsible for our sexual practice. It is accepted by these Indians that one omnipotent God created the first man and woman on Earth. But it seems that He was dilatory in providing them with equipment for reproduction. Seeing his chance to make mischief, the Devil promptly cut off his lips and fashioned them into a vagina, and then uniquely added a clitoris as a spicy and tempting bonus.

"Experimentally, so their legend goes, the Devil tried fixing this vagina to various parts of the female body. But it kept falling off. Finally, in disgust, he threw it at the first woman, and it landed between her legs. This, in turn, guided him in seeking a place for the male genitalia.

"Next, the Devil taught the first man and woman how to have sexual intercourse. This so shocked God that he expelled them from the paradise he had created. He had planned for his Adam and Eve to reproduce in a less elaborate way. But it was too late now; the damage had been done. Humans had developed a taste for the devil's pleasurable style of copulation.

"Such teachings, however, are the least subject of concern for relatives of Doña Dolores Tunaman. One major fear is that the mysterious Conchita may introduce her client to illegal drugs. She comes from a village not far from Huautla, which half a century ago gained notoriety as the centre for hallucinogenic mushrooms. Above all, they fear that such intensive exposure to occultism may lead the widow to irreversible mental derangement.

"In the light of these circumstances, I understand that members of the Castillo family are now planning to obtain a court order to have Conchita forcibly evicted from the Cuernavaca mansion, and to ensure that Doña Dolores Tunaman is given proper psychiatric care.

"Meanwhile, one thing about the future of this tragic

lady can be stated with certainty. She will not be attending the funeral of her husband, which is due to be held next Friday in Istanbul. She has already told relatives, 'They only have Kemal's body. It is his spirit that matters now, and that is with me, here in our Cuernavaca home.' "

To everyone in the Castillo family, the source of so much privileged information was patently obvious. But this time Guillermo Velázquez no longer cared. He had been handsomely paid. More importantly, on the strength of news recently received from the United States, he was planning to leave his wife, and get out of the family hotel business altogether.

For the Turkish branch of Kemal Tunaman's family, the news that Dolores would not be attending his funeral came as welcome relief. She had bitterly opposed the removal of her husband's body from Mexico, but the late ambassador's PA, Mehmet Haybat, had returned from New York to produce certified evidence that it was Kemal's wish to be buried alongside his beloved first wife, Raife, in the family plot in the wooded *Asiyan Mezaligi*, overlooking the Bosporus at Rumelihisari. After Haybat's consultation with the Stephanopoulos family, it was agreed that Kemal's eldest daughter, Yasemin, should also be buried there.

The ceremonial arrangements were complicated by the fact that— in accordance with the revolutionary changes introduced by Kemal Ataturk— affairs of Church and State were strictly separated. To allow tributes by political leaders, the funeral itself needed to be preceded by a secular ceremony, and this was held at Istanbul University, where Tunaman had spent most of his working life.

It was an occasion unprecedented in Turkish history, and one demanding maximum security since it was attended by the Greek Prime Minister, Christos Andriopoulou. At Ataturk Airport, he was met by the Turkish President, Erkan Gursoy, and together they drove in a motorcade to the university. In a unique and highly controversial gesture of goodwill, the presidential limousine flew twin flags: on one wing Turkey's red flag with white crescent and star; on the other, the blue-and-white stripes of Greece.

There was only one blot on this brief armistice: the absence of Premier Selim Suman of Turkey. Officially, he was prevented from attending the funeral by a bout of influenza. His political opponents, on the other hand, alleged that he was shrewdly avoiding the risk of alienating his right-wing supporters on the eve of national elections.

Both Greek and Turkish television covered the memorial ceremony held in the great hall of Istanbul University. There, before a massed assembly of foreign dignitaries, the faculty and students, Tunaman lay in state, his coffin draped in the Turkish flag. In his eulogy, President Gursoy described his lifelong friend as "an internationalist and humanitarian of the first magnitude", words that were echoed in the tribute delivered by Premier Andriopoulou.

In contrast, remarkably, respect for Islamic custom allowed the funeral itself to be conducted publicly with a minimum of media intrusion. From the university, Tunaman's coffin was conveyed to the small, ninety-year-old mosque sited beside the Bosporus in the bay of Bebek. There it was placed on one of two stone tables permanently set into the marble-flagged, open courtyard.

Meanwhile, the coffin of Kemal's daughter, Yasemin— draped in a green shroud embroidered with Koran verses— was brought to the waterfront by motor launch from the mega-yacht *Prometheus*, which had left Piraeus the previous day, and was now anchored off Bebek. Once the launch had been moored, the coffin— accompanied by Yasemin's husband, Nicholas— had to be carried no more than twenty yards to the other table outside the mosque.

Incongruously, only an alleyway leading to the waterfront separated this elegant mosque from the McDonald's restaurant that was now so hugely popular with Bebek's cosmopolitan young set. On this day, however, it was arranged that the restaurant should close shortly before Muslim worshippers— all shoeless and freshly washed— gathered for their regular noonday *namaz*, one of five prayer meetings held each day.

Whenever a coffin has been laid outside the mosque, it is the custom— after their prayer meeting— for the departing worshippers to gather around it and, led by their imam, join in special prayers for the deceased, whoever he or she may be. Thus, complete strangers assembled, together with old friends and relatives.

Outside, the imam stood beside Kemal Tunaman's coffin and began with a short pronouncement about death and Allah. This was followed by a funeral *namaz*, the only prayers at which Muslim worshippers remain standing. Also, according

227

to tradition, everyone stood facing towards qibla, the direction of the sacred Kaaba at Mecca.

Mutely and briefly, the imam mouthed some Koran verses, concluding aloud with the words, *Allahu-Akbar* ("Allah is the Greatest"), to which the worshippers responded by placing their hands over their ears. The procedure was repeated; then, after a third and final *Allahu-Akbar*, all Muslims placed their hands across their stomach.

After more muted verses, the imam finally called upon the congregation to salute the angels: first the good angels by turning their heads to the right; then the evil one, the devil, by turning their heads to the left. In Islam, the right hand is the instrument of good, the left hand of all evil.

The combined funeral *namaz* for Tunaman and his daughter lasted no more than three minutes.

From the Bebek mosque, it is barely a five-minute drive to the *Asiyan Mezaligi* cemetery where an extraordinary assortment of sepulchral monuments, great and small, ranges over the wooded hillside adjacent to the majestic ruins of Rumeli Hisar.

On this day, the entire route was lined, at thirty-metre intervals, by armed soldiers, and the cemetery was closed to all except official mourners. Kemal Tunaman and his daughter were laid to rest at the highest point, their names engraved on a huge white marble tombstone facing towards the Bosporus and the castle of Anadolu Hisar on the Asian shore.

The burial was witnessed only by close friends of the family, and a handful of relatives: Nicholas, plus Kemal's younger daughter, Nilufer, with her husband Sertac and their children, Melissa and Deniz. Afterwards the relatives were driven to Tarabya where they joined state representatives attending a strictly private reception at the President's residence beside the Bosphorus.

But Nicholas Stephanopoulos was not among them. From the cemetery, he headed back to Bebek where the crew of the *Prometheus* was standing by, ready to leave immediately for Piraeus.

On board, in a cabin sumptuously bestrewn with flowers, was a lead-lined coffin, only five-foot long. Nicholas was on his way from one funeral to another. Next morning, in a secretly held ceremony restricted to immediate members of the family, nine-year-old Georgios was to be buried at the Kerameikos Cemetery, in the shadow of the Acropolis, and within earshot of Sunday morning noise from the flea market west of Monastiraki Square.

At the graveside, Stavros Stephanopoulos— too weak to attend the Istanbul ceremonies— was unrecognisable as the aged Lothario who, two weeks before, had been cavorting with his mistress in Magens Bay. Now, in black Homburg and heavy overcoat, he presented a stooped figure leaning on a walking cane. Clinging to his left arm was his wife Elena, totally masked by a black veil.

Beside them, raising an umbrella to protect her parents as the rain began to fall, was Christina, who had flatly refused to accompany her brother to the funeral in Turkey. Nicholas, the mourning father, stood a few yards apart, the rain gently cascading down his forehead and mingling with his tears.

At the close of the Greek Orthodox ceremony, after the bearded priest had given his blessing and made a cross with his censer, they joined in chanting three times, *Eonia e mnimi tou* ("To his eternal memory"). Then, while the others moved away, Nicholas knelt alone to make his own private prayer.

In the bleak wintry days that followed the two funerals, Nicholas was so consumed by grief that he became unapproachable, even by closest friends and relatives. He declined his father's suggestion that he take a cruise on the *Prometheus*. Instead, he chose to isolate himself in his Kolonaki apartment, venturing out only after dark for long, lone walks on Mt. Lykabettus.

For weeks thereafter, throughout the daylight hours, and even when asleep, Nicholas would be haunted by nightmarish images of his beloved wife and child lying in pools of blood in a faraway, alien land. *Why, oh why,* he endlessly asked himself, *should two such innocents have to die?*

He longed to empty his mind of the horrific pictures of the slaughter. Yet he seemed powerless to control his thoughts, and at the same time, irrationally, he sustained his mental torment by poring again and again over press reports from Mexico City. It was as though he was seeking some acceptable explanation, some scrap of logic that might help him to come to terms with his loss. But there was no explanation... nothing except increasing intakes of whisky to marginally deaden his pain.

There was no magic moment when Nicholas somehow

exorcised those ugly visions. It was a gradual process, a drawing-back from the brink of total despair that occurred more as the result of mental exhaustion than anything else. Quite simply, there came a point when his distorted mind no longer had the energy to fuel the hatred and frustration that raged in his soul.

When, finally, he began to receive anxious relatives and friends, they encountered a very different Nicholas: a man who seemed totally devoid of emotion, ice-cold and deliberate. Thoughtfully they eschewed any reference to his tragic loss. But to no purpose. This Nicholas, they soon found, was fully prepared to discuss the post-assassination developments in a strangely detached and analytical manner.

It was not the Nicholas of old. This was a driven man, a man obsessed with just one accepted thought: that the *philotimo* of his family demanded to be served.

On the day Georgios was buried in Athens, yet another funeral arising from the Chapultepec killings was being held on the opposite side of the world. In a remote corner of Mexico City's *Panteón de Dolores*, some twenty men, women and children— mostly relatives of the deceased— gathered around a grave marked with a small, granite tombstone dedicated to *Manuel Gustavo Ramírez*.

The only non-relatives present were three elderly men, all casually dressed, whom Fernando had invited along on impulse while stopping en route at his Tepito *pulquería*. The old toper was reasonably subdued throughout the ceremony, but predictably he became increasingly vociferous at the private family gathering that was held afterwards at Ricardo's apartment, and finally he collapsed into a drunken stupor.

Meanwhile, some twenty minutes after the ceremony, a lone mourner had visited the new grave. Observed only by a tall, crew cut man, peering through binoculars from afar, he laid a large wreath against the tombstone and stood there for a few minutes with his head bowed. The card accompanying the wreath read: *Adios, mi querido hermano - Julio.*

PART 2
La Suerte

CHAPTER 18

The distinctive snub-nose of the Air France Airbus A380 sliced through the clouds beyond the brim of the surrounding mountains, and all at once a dazzling panorama came into view. Seconds before, all was darkness. Now passengers looked down on a kaleidoscope of gleaming lights— not just whites but brilliant emeralds, yellows, reds, purples and blues— as though all the gems from a Spanish treasure chest had been scattered far and wide over the ground below.

For a few magical minutes, prior to a landing at almost a mile and half above sea level, there was no hint that they were descending on one of the largest and most polluted cities on Earth. In this one isolated respect, by enhancing the night approach, the unbridled growth of a megalopolis across the Valley of Mexico could be seen as positively rewarding.

As the 555-seater double-decker circled over Mexico City, passengers craned across for a glimpse through the windows of the myriad lights. *"Mesdames et messieurs, attachéz vos ceintures de securité, s'il vous plaît,"* said stewardess, Louise Fontaine. Then she retired to buckle-up in her own seat at the rear.

The mammoth Olympus jet engines of the Airbus were eerily silent now, muted as the super-jumbo glided gracefully round and down like a giant paper dart. Meanwhile, in the stillness of the descent, Mlle Fontaine's thoughts focussed— not for the first time— on the man occupying the penultimate window seat on the starboard side.

Something about him fascinated her. To be sure, he was strikingly handsome. But it was much more than that. His whole demeanour was strangely magnetic, the key ingredient being a kind of courteous remoteness. Throughout the flight from Paris to Mexico City, he had been the model passenger, undemanding, dividing his time wholly between sleeping and perusing a book which, as she had nosily observed, was entitled *Advanced Spanish*.

The passenger manifest identified him as Nicholas Stephanopoulos, of Greek nationality. The name seemed vaguely familiar, though she could not recall where she had seen or heard it before. But clearly he was man of means. The unoccupied first-class seat beside him was also reserved in his name.

It was 8 p.m. on a Saturday when Nicholas Stephanopoulos passed through customs and emerged in the main concourse of Benito Juárez International Airport. Immediately, he was greeted by a dapper young man who warmly shook his hand and insisted upon taking charge of his luggage trolley. Then, conversing in Greek, they made their way to the car park and a chauffeured Mercedes, which had a grey-numbered licence plate with the legend "SRE DIPL MEX", indicating diplomatic status.

As they headed west on Boulevard Aeropuerto, Nicholas asked his companion if they could abandon their native tongue and speak only in Spanish. "I have taken a crash course," he explained. "But I still need all the practice I can get. So if you don't mind..."

Viktor Gondicas grinned. *"Christos*! You haven't changed. Just like in our college days. You always were a thorough bastard."

Then he fixed his friend with a serious, almost stern, expression. "I admire your determination, Nicholas. But this is different. You should know that I totally disapprove of your plans. And that's not just my view. It goes all the way to the top. Frankly, it's madness, and, but for your father's influence, it would never be allowed.

"Is my Spanish too fast for you?"

Nicholas had missed out on a couple of words. But he had got the general drift. It was what he had expected from Viktor, so professionally correct in playing his role as cultural attaché.

"No, I understand what you are saying. But it changes nothing. I'm going ahead exactly as planned. Assuming, of course, that all my requests have been carried out. Have they?"

Gondicas nodded. *"Sí.* Everything has been arranged. But let me again make one thing absolutely clear. You are on your own from the moment you go public. We cannot be seen

234

to support your activities in any way."

The Mercedes turned into the illuminated canyon of the Paseo de la Reforma, and a few minutes later crossed over the intersection with Avenida Insurgentes. Dominating the *glorieta* was the floodlit figure of an Indian poised to throw a spear.

For the first time, Nicholas registered an interest in his new surroundings. "Is that Cuauhtémoc?"

"Absolutely right. Are you sure you haven't been to Mexico before?"

Nicholas did not answer. He was thinking back some two-and-a-half months to what he had read in an old *National Geographic* guide to Mexico City: about how Cuauhtémoc, the last Aztec emperor, had been treated by the Spanish *conquistadores;* how the young warrior had begged Cortés to kill him with a dagger, but instead had been subjected to prolonged torture by fire. Finally, having refused to reveal the hiding place of his uncle Moctezuma's treasure, he was sentenced to death by hanging, so becoming the first Mexican martyr.

At the time, so soon after the death of his wife and child, Nicholas' reaction to that story had reflected his mental state. Immediately it had struck a savage chord. In his distorted mind's eye, he had pictured himself— like the torturers of Cuauhtémoc— putting a torch to the feet of whoever was responsible for the senseless killings. He relished the moment: torture to the limits of human endurance, inflicting a slow, agonising death.

Even now, his mind was set on similar lines. He thought back to stories about the practices of the Greek security police during the military dictatorship of the late 1960s, how they would torture suspects by *falanga,* the victim being strapped down and beaten on the soles of his feet with an iron bar. After a dozen blows, his father had told him, the victim would think he was being hit on the top of the head, and after twenty blows, he would lose consciousness, only to be revived with cold water so that the beating could start up all over again.

"NICHOLAS!"

It took shouting to drag him from his dark thoughts. "What?"

"You don't seem to be listening," said Gondicas. "I was saying that we will soon be there." At that point, the

235

Mercedes swung left around another major *glorieta*. "This is Florencia street. We are close to the Zona Rosa now."

Nicholas turned to look back at a floodlit column, 130-ft high and surmounted by a huge winged figure in gold. Unseen, beneath its terraced base, lay a crypt containing the remains of revolutionary heroes, plus the severed head of Miguel Hildago, the priest who had initiated Mexico's fight for independence.

"Impressive, eh?" remarked Gondicas. "That's *El Angel*. She came down in the '57 earthquake. Must have made one hell of a mess."

Nicholas had only a fleeting look because almost immediately they turned right into Hamburgo, and pulled up outside a four-storey building. At the pillared entrance, a large bronze wall plate bore the name: *Apartamentos Orleáns*.

"Well, Nick, here's your new home. No swimming pool or room service. But it's got all you asked for."

It was the persistent ringing of a doorbell that stirred the jet-lagged Nicholas from his sleep, and when he got up to draw back the heavy brocade curtains, he had to shield his eyes against the brilliant glare of a noonday sun.

"All right, I'm coming," he called out, instinctively speaking in Greek. Then, after donning a green silk dressing gown, he opened the door to his new apartment.

Standing before him was a diminutive, mestizo woman, perhaps forty years of age. She wore a bright, flower-patterned cotton dress, with a belt drawn so tight around the waist that it accentuated the large swellings both above and below. On the floor beside her was a wicker shopping basket filled with groceries.

"*Señor* Stefan?" she asked, unable to grasp his full name. He nodded.

She smiled warmly. "*Buenos días*. I am Juanita."

"Juanita?" Nicholas paused for a few seconds, then remembered. As arranged, Gondicas had hired a maid from the agency that served the Greek embassy.

"Ah yes. Do come in. And let me help with you that." He picked up her shopping basket, having wrongly concluded that the figure-of-eight woman was in an advanced stage of pregnancy. Then, after placing the basket on the hatch shelf between the main room and the kitchen, he took her on a

236

tour of his quarters.

Nicholas had rented not one, but two apartments, so occupying the entire first floor. Each apartment, identically designed, comprised two bedrooms, a combined bathroom-toilet, a narrow kitchen, and a large open-plan living-room, all with highly polished parquet flooring, except for a dining area that was carpeted in midnight blue, matching the curtains of one large window overlooking the street. Both were sparsely furnished with a three-piece suite, a drinks cabinet, a television set with video, and a small table with a telephone and answering machine.

The adjoining apartment, however, was equipped more like an office. Two computers and two printers had been set up on the dining table. And nearby, lying on the floor, was a fax machine and two more telephones sited on answering machines.

Twice Nicholas expressed to Juanita his concern that she would find her duties far too exacting - keeping both apartments clean and preparing meals as and when required. The second time she noted the direction of his eyes and then roared with laughter. "Oh no, *señor!*" she exclaimed, patting her ample stomach. "Just too many chocolates."

Juanita, according to Gondicas, was a conscientious worker, without the usual *mañana*-complex, and always good-humoured and reliable. On this day, however, her merits were not put to the test. He told her that she was not needed until tomorrow morning. This evening he would be eating out in the Zona Rosa.

By 1 p.m. on his first Sunday in Mexico City, Nicholas was setting out on a painful pilgrimage: walking to Chapultepec Park to visit the spot where his son, wife and father-in-law had died. As he had been told, it was marked by a miniature shrine provided by the Castillo family. Beside it, he laid a large bunch of roses and carnations, which he had purchased at the flower market by the park entrance on Avenida de los Constituyentes.

Nearby, ironically, he saw a children's birthday party in progress, a scene of blissful jollity; much the same, he presumed, as it had been on that fateful afternoon in January. Fighting back the tears that welled up behind his shades, he turned his back on the revellers and began the long walk to the hill path leading up to Chapultepec Castle.

Eventually, with the aid of a guidebook, he made his

237

way to the base of the *Caballero Alto* tower. No guards were in sight, and so, after waiting until several tourists had passed by, he ducked under the velvet-wrapped chain that stretched across the entrance, and climbed the stairs to the turret. For ten minutes he stayed at the summit, deep in thought as he surveyed the thousand-acre pleasure land below. Then, still unseen, he left the tower and headed back to his *Orleáns* apartment in the Zona Rosa.

At 7.30 p.m., after a shower and brief siesta, Nicholas needed to walk only a few hundred yards to keep his appointment at *Il Pirata*, an Italian restaurant, mock-Tudor in style, sited halfway down a pedestrian passageway lined with miniature trees and potted plants. Outside, customers dining alfresco were being confusingly entertained by an accordionist who was competing with an *organillero* cranking a portable organ.

Inside, Nicholas was escorted to a table set on its own in an alcove and reserved in the name of Viktor Gondicas. His Greek friend raised a glass of Chianti in welcome. "*Yiasou!* Excuse me for having started without you."

Nicholas smiled and immediately poured himself a drink. "*Yiasou! compadre.* See, I'm into the lingo already."

"So, have you recovered from jet lag?" asked Viktor, first speaking in Greek and then apologising for having not kept up the Spanish.

Nicholas answered that he had never felt fitter. Indeed, on his long walk in Chapultepec Park he had wished he had worn a tracksuit and trainers for jogging.

"Hmm! Better take it easy, old friend. You need to get used to the altitude. Also, it affects your digestion. I advise you to keep to these restaurants with foreign cuisine. You can find almost every kind in the Zona Rosa. And stick to bottled mineral water and go easy on the booze. When I first arrived here, I had two months of Moctezuma's Revenge. It's not funny."

Nicholas looked around the dining room. "So where is this wonder woman of yours? I need to check her out, you know."

"Don't worry. She'll be here soon. Trust me. Have I ever let you down? By the way, what did you think of Juanita?"

"She'll do fine. But this other job is something else."

"I know, Nick. But trust me. This girl meets all your demands. You'll see." At that moment, he waved across the room to an auburn-haired woman smartly dressed in a matching pale-green skirt and jacket. She waved back and threaded through tables to join them. Both men stood up.

"Nicholas, allow me to introduce Miss Regina Marke."

"How do you do, Señor Stephanopoulos?" she asked, firmly gripping his extended hand. "Nice to meet you."

At once Nicholas was arrested by her sapphire blue eyes. She was not a beauty in the conventional sense, being sturdily built and with a strong, square jaw. But the eyes were magnetic, they positively dazzled, exuding warmth and humour.

He smiled. "Good evening. But please, do call me Nicholas. And may I call you Regina?"

"Of course, as long as you never slip into Reggie. I hate that name."

Having read her curriculum vitae, he soon concluded that this young woman had inherited both Irish charm and wit from her father, an American immigrant from County Down, Ulster. But she spoke Spanish without a trace of a foreign accent, perhaps only to be expected for a graduate from Mexico City's *Instituto Superior de Interpretes y Traductores.*

What surprised him most was her mature manner, well belying her known age of twenty-five.

From the beginning it was Regina, with her light-hearted conversation, who created a more relaxed atmosphere over dinner. Then, unwittingly, after the minestrone starter, she was responsible for steering the small talk towards the more serious business in hand.

"So what is your first impression of Mexico City?" she asked Nicholas

"Well. so far I have been pleasantly surprised. I like the climate and, really, I can't quite see why it is called the smog capital of the world."

"Ah, yes! That's the magic of Sunday. If every day was Sunday, it would be a heavenly place. Unfortunately... well wait till you see it tomorrow."

"How extraordinary," said Nicholas. "I remember my father-in-law saying exactly the same thing."

Regina looked serious for the first time. "Really? How all the more sad that he should have been killed on a

Sunday. He was a truly wonderful man."

"You knew ambassador Tunaman?"

"Not really. But I did meet him once... at an international trade exhibition when I was recruited as an extra interpreter. He made a big impression."

Nicholas frowned at Gondicas. "I didn't know that."

Deliberately, he now switched the conversation and concentrated on probing Regina about her diverse background. She proceeded to explain— as he already knew— that her early childhood had been spent in Seattle where her father worked as chauffeur to William Force, the founder of Force Computer, Inc.

"Some years later, as you probably know, Mr. Force went into politics and moved to Washington after being elected to Congress." She smiled. "I loved the move. The senator had a lovely ranch-style house in Maryland. He let me ride out his hunters, and I have been hooked on riding ever since.

"Unfortunately, it didn't last. Following a stroke, my father had to take early retirement. Force was very good about it: helped my parents to buy a modest house near Rockville and paid for me to take a training course in computer analysis. But, frankly, I was too restless in those days; didn't want to get stuck in an office job.

"Anyway, one day an old school friend told me about the Interpreters' School in Mexico City. She knew my Spanish was pretty good - got it from my mother who is Argentinian - and she suggested that if I came here we could share an apartment at little cost. That was four years ago.

"It was pretty tough at first, taking on translation work and other evening jobs to help pay the school fees. But it has paid off. In three months' time, I start work as an interpreter with the International Monetary Fund in Washington. The work will involve plenty of travel. The pay is good, and what's more, it's tax-free. And that's it. Not much else I can tell you."

Nicholas took a sip of mineral water and looked at her thoughtfully. "Very good. You have done well. So why on earth should this P.A. job interest you?"

Regina smiled. "Frankly, it's not the job, but the excellent money. You see, back in Maryland, I shall be living with my parents. Their house is perfect for commuting to Washington, not far from Shady Grove station at the end of the Metro Red Line. More importantly, it has ten acres of land, and my dream is to save up for a thoroughbred mare and possibly breed from her. So you see, the extra dollars will be a big help."

"Hmm! Are you sure it has nothing to do with having known and liked my father-in-law?"

"Absolutely not. That doesn't mean I don't care about his death and what you are trying to do. But really, this is strictly business."

"You know it will mean working any hours - and with no guarantee of any time off?"

"I understand. Señor Gondicas has made the conditions very clear."

Nicholas nodded. "Very well, Regina, we'll give it a try. But if it doesn't work out, the arrangement can be ended at a moment's notice with your salary being paid until the end of the respective month. Okay?"

"Okay."

"There is no telling how busy we will be. Maybe it will all lead to nothing. On the other hand, if the workload does get too much, I will get someone in to help you. Any questions?"

"Not at this stage. But, in fairness, I should again make it clear that three months is my absolute limit. I don't want to let you down. But what if your work is not finished in that time?"

"That's my problem," said Nicholas. "But I appreciate your concern."

He wiped his mouth with a napkin and signalled to the waiter that he could remove his unfinished main course of *escalope Marsala*. Then he switched the conversation completely. "How are your parents, Viktor? Is your mother still pressing you to find a good Greek wife?"

Viktor slightly reddened. Though he had still to make a first approach, he was secretly rather smitten by Regina. He forced a grin. "Oh, she means well."

Regina sensed his discomfort. "I've heard about Greek mothers. But really, they're not so very different. You ought to hear my flatmate's mother going on. Every week she is on the phone, and she never fails to tell Martha it is time she was getting married to a nice Jewish boy."

Her eyes were laughing. "Now I ask you: How many nice Jewish boys is she going to find in Mexico City?"

They were into the cassata dessert by now, and Nicholas looked at his watch, parading his impatience. "It's getting late and we have a big day tomorrow. If you don't mind, I suggest we forego the coffee and have some back at my place. I want Regina to look over her new home and workplace."

It was shortly after 10 p.m. when they arrived back at *Apartamentos Orleáns*. Thoughtfully, Viktor offered to prepare the coffee while Nicholas showed Regina around his first-floor quarters.

From his own apartment Nicholas led the way to the second apartment, which had its own entrance a few yards down the outside corridor. "Not very homely, I am afraid. But I think it will cater for all your basic needs. There's a bedroom, shower room and a small kitchen."

He pointed to a corner of the main livingroom. "You've got a TV and video recorder over there. The rest, of course, is our office.

"What do you think? Will you be comfortable enough?"

Regina smiled. "Sure. This is positively spacious compared with our apartment on Río Rhin Street."

Nicholas directed her towards the two computers, each wired to a printer and to the telephone answering machines on the floor. "Are you familiar with this model? Any problem with them?"

Regina looked them over and nodded. "Hey, these are great! Haven't actually worked with this model. But I know all about them. They make analysis easy. But why are they connected to the telephones?"

"Ah, that's going to save us a lot of work." He pointed to the phones and answering machines on the floor. "These are USB phones that integrate directly into the software on the PCs. This way we can listen to messages or read them from a print-out."

"That's brilliant. You chose well."

He didn't react to her compliment. "As you can see, we have three outside lines. When they are not being manned, you need to press these keys to switch them onto the answering machine. If you need to make a call of your own, you can use the phone in my apartment."

"Very thorough."

"I hope so, but we won't really know until the method is tested. Anyway, that's enough. We can go over the procedure tomorrow morning. Can you move in by ten o'clock?"

"Certainly."

"Right then, Let's have our coffee and I'll get Viktor to drive you home."

At 10.45 p.m., Nicholas escorted them down to the main entrance. Viktor shook his hand and wished him luck. "Give me a call at the embassy if you have any strictly personal problems. But nothing to do with this business. As you know, we cannot get involved. I've told you all the problems, and my advice remains the same: abandon the scheme and go home. I don't think you know what you are getting into."

Nicholas thanked him, then turned to shake Regina's hand. "See you tomorrow at ten o'clock. And try to get a good night's sleep, because hopefully, by tomorrow afternoon, we will be very busy indeed."

"*Buenas nachas.*"

Regina laughed. "You want to watch your pronunciation. *Buenas nachas* means `nice arse.'"

"*Buenas noches.*"

Regina was on duty alone when the lines began buzzing the following afternoon. Ten minutes earlier, just before 1.30 p.m. on Monday, Nicholas had dropped his bombshell. In a brief nation-wide television interview, he had announced that he was offering a reward to anyone providing information that led to a positive identification of the person or persons responsible for directing the four killings in Chapultepec Park.

He gave out three telephone numbers that informants could ring, plus a fax number and an e-mail address, and he added that full details of his offer would also be advertised the next day in all the national newspapers.

The reward on offer was TEN MILLION U.S. DOLLARS.

CHAPTER 19

At the Channel 13 *Televisa* studios near Avenida Toluca, shortly after fronting the one o'clock news, Isabel del Río was removing her extra make-up when she was called urgently to the telephone. The voice at the other end didn't identify itself, but she recognised it instantly, though never before had she heard her ex-lover sound so stridently aggressive.

"What the hell do you think you are doing? Letting that lunatic Greek on to your programme? More to the point, why the fuck didn't you tell me about this in advance? Don't you realise what a major security problem this can create?

"I can't believe you could do such a thing. After all the co-operation I have given you! What happened to our agreement always to share information of mutual interest? What happened to loyalty and..."

As the speaker ranted on, Isabel held the earpiece away from her head and, looking towards her producer, raised her big, brown eyes to the heavens in an expression of contemptuous despair.

Del Río— alone among media personnel— was one not to be intimidated by General Juan Delgado. She knew him too well. They went back so far - to his *Jefe de Sector* days when their brief affair was ended by her refusal to be tied down as the mistress of his *casa chica*.

The eruption subsided. "Have you quite finished?" snapped Del Rio. "Good. Now let me tell you this: I was as surprised as you when the Greek announced his offer of a $10 million reward. If I had known about it in advance, of course, I would have told you.

"The fact is— and you would know this if you had troubled to watch the programme— he was only brought on to support our last news item. It was fixed up by the Greek embassy. He was supposed to be talking about his plans to commission a permanent memorial to the victims of the shootings in Chapultepec Park.

244

"Well, I asked him about it, and he explained that he was inviting Mexican sculptors to submit designs. Then, suddenly, he switched. Maybe he saw the producer signalling with three fingers that it was time for me to start winding up the programme. I don't know. But whatever. Out of the blue it came: this sensational announcement about the reward.

"It must have been planned. He was so well rehearsed - giving out three telephone numbers to call and then repeating them so precisely. It was like he was taking over my show. And I didn't even have time to put in a supplementary question.

"I don't know why I am telling you all this. You don't deserve it."

Delgado went all contrite. "You are right, *mi querida*. I am afraid I over-reacted. Please, forgive me. I should never have doubted you.

"Could you just tell me one thing. Will you be interviewing this Stephanopoulos again?"

"Very probably. Our producer is keen to do a follow-up. But nothing has been arranged. The Greek said he was too busy at present to make a commitment."

"So you have lost contact with him?"

"Not quite. He left his business card and said to contact him again in a few days' time."

"Do you have the card there?"

"Not in front of me. But I can remember his address. It is very near to my mother's place... at *Apartamentos Orleáns* on Hamburgo."

"Thank you very much, Isabel. You are a sweetheart. Let's have dinner some time."

"We'll see. I've got to go now."

Delgado replaced the phone, took a deep breath, and then reached out to his gold box of Havanas. The muscular officer who was sitting opposite him promptly stood up, picked up the table-lighter and extended a flame to his chief.

The General spoke through a wall of smoke. "No need to trace those telephone numbers, Torres. We have his address." He ripped off the top sheet of a notepad on which he had scribbled *Apartamentos Orleáns*, Hamburgo, then slid it across the desk.

Colleagues of Coronel Ignacio Torres had observed that it seemed somewhat odd that Delgado rarely addressed his long-time aide by either his first name or his rank. But it never occurred to Torres to interpret it as a sign of disrespect. From their earliest days, he had accepted a role of total subservience. *El Jefe* was his sole master and benefactor, a superior never to be questioned or doubted.

Torres picked up the sheet and glanced at the scrawl. "Convenient, *Jefe*. Only a few blocks away."

Delgado puffed impatiently on his Cohiba. "Yeah, with luck we can pick him up before he does any further damage. See to it at once."

El Robot was moving to leave when a red light began flashing on the direct-line telephone reserved for a privileged few. "Hang on," Delgado called out. Torres waited by the door.

For the next minute the conversation was almost entirely one way. All that Torres heard was the voice of his chief speaking most deferentially:

"No, *Señor Presidente.*"

"*Sí, señor.*"

"I understand, *señor.*"

"You can rely on me. Thank you, *Señor Presidente.*"

Delgado replaced the phone. "Sit down, Torres. We need to revise our plans."

El Robot sat upright, patiently awaiting instructions while his chief scribbled some notes, and then puffed on his cigar, deep in thought.

When General Delgado finally spoke, it was softly and deliberately, without any reference to his omnipotent caller. "We've got to handle this carefully, Torres. Bring the Greek bastard in. But no rough stuff; understand?

"You just tell the *pendejo* that I urgently need to talk to him... right away. Be courteous at all times. You are requesting a favour, not issuing a command."

"And what if he still won't come, *Jefe*?"

"He has to come. Stress the urgency. If necessary, say that I have some important information for him. But you don't know any details. That should do it. Right?"

Torres nodded, then had an afterthought, "But if he still refuses, *Jefe?*"

Delgado looked at him sternly. "Then you insist, Torres. *Insist.* You can tell him the truth: that you have your orders and that they must be obeyed. Be apologetic but firm. And whatever happens, you don't lay a hand on him. We don't want this blowing up into an international incident.

"If the worst comes to the worst, you can say that it is a matter of life and death." He grinned, menacingly. "His life, his death."

"At the same time, there is some other business I want you to handle…"

At 1.20 p.m., just as Delgado was calling Del Río, Regina Marke received the first call in response to the offer of a $10 million reward.

Following the procedure rehearsed with Nicholas in the morning, she picked up the receiver, pressed the record key, then parroted, "Thank you for calling. Any information you can give will be treated in the strictest confidence. But first, could you please give us your name, address and telephone number so that we can contact you, if necessary."

The voice on the line came back fast and ungrammatical, "My name is Jesús Suárez and you can send me the ten million dollars to Calle Canarias, *número* 28, Colonia Portales. No telephone there. I ring from street."

"I see. So what information do you have for us, Señor Suárez?"

"I know who did it."

"You do?"

"*Sí.* On the news they say it was a man shooting from a tower. But it wasn't like that. Nothing like that. Two men hiding in the bushes did it."

"How do you know this?"

"Jesús sees it all."

"You were there… in the park?"

"Sort of."

"What do you mean 'sort of'? Either you were there, or you were not."

"I see it in a dream, *señorita*— the park, the gunmen, the bodies— all in colour. The gunmen were disguised as priests, and the bodies were dripping with bright red blood."

"Thank you for calling, Señor Suárez. We'll get back to you if this leads to anything." Regina hung up.

The next caller was even more outrageous. He gave his name as José Santiago and said he could positively identify the real killer. "I know who did it because it was *YO*! José! I did it, and so I want you to put the reward in a shopping bag and leave it in Alameda Park, by the Benito Juárez

247

monument."

Subsequent calls sustained the dismal pattern: a well-spoken lady who said she was a professional clairvoyant and would make no charge for her services until she had identified the killers, a joker who said his mother-in-law was responsible ("The bitch snipes at everyone"), a young man— it emerged that he was only fourteen— who said his history teacher was a member of a gun club and was absent from school on the day of the shooting.

Meanwhile, the two other outside lines were busy, the callers being linked to answering machines which told them: *Thank you for calling. We can only record your message at the moment, but any information you have to give will be treated in the strictest confidence. After the bleep, please speak slowly and clearly, leaving your name, full address, and a telephone number on which you can be reached. Then please state as concisely as possible the information that you wish to provide, and if this interests us, we will call you back in due course.*

"How is it going?"

Regina's heart missed a beat, and she looked up to see Nicholas standing in the outer doorway. She had not heard him open the door with his duplicate key.

She put her left hand over the mouthpiece of the telephone. "Dreadful. This city seems to be full of crackpots. Here's another one."

She removed her left hand. "*Sí.* Very sad. You have our sympathy. *señor.* But I am afraid we cannot help. But thank you for calling." She hung up.

"No good?"

"No. But at least that one was honest. The caller simply asked if we could spare some money for his father to have an emergency prostate operation."

Nicholas flopped into an easy chair. "It's only to be expected. At least we won't have many messages to print out. Put the phone on automatic and take a break for a while."

Regina got up and moved towards the kitchen. "I'm going to make some coffee. Would you like some?"

"Thanks. I'd love one."

"No milk and two sugars, if I remember right."

"Yes please."

Regina talked through the serving hatch. "I watched you on TV. It went rather well, don't you think?"

"I suppose so. But really we needed captions for those telephone numbers. Things should be much better tomorrow when they are printed in the newspapers."

"Better or busier?"

"Both, I hope."

Regina laughed. "Any busier, and we will be up all night listening to the tapes."

Nicholas looked towards the answering machines, all of them recording.

"On the other hand," she said brightly. "It may not be too bad, not if we fast-forward through all the frivolous calls and print out the promising ones."

They had just finished their coffee when three firm knocks were rapped on the outside door. Nicholas opened it to confront the burly figure of Ignacio Torres. The *coronel* was flanked by two much younger police officers. All were uniformed, all armed with .38 specials.

It took them only three minutes by police car to reach the *Seguridad* tower block on Liverpool, less than the time then taken from the headquarters' main entrance to the tenth floor office of Mexico City's Chief of Police.

Totally out of character, Torres had been most courteous and gently persuasive. More so, in fact, than was necessary. The bait of *important information* was enough, automatically, to gain Nicholas' co-operation.

Nevertheless, Stephanopoulos was feeling aggrieved when they were ushered into Delgado's main office. What had disturbed him was Torres' insistence that Regina Marke should accompany them to police headquarters.

He had protested in vain, arguing that she had to attend to urgent office work. Torres countered that they were only a short distance away, and she should be back within half an hour.

Nicholas had argued the point. "But why is it necessary for her to go? Tell me that."

But Torres would not be moved. "I don't know, *señor*. Only that my chief says that his information concerns her, too. I'm sorry, but I have my orders and they must be obeyed."

Within seconds of entering Delgado's office, Nicholas felt still more aggrieved. After being greeted with a two-handed handshake— accompanied by a gushing, "Señor Stephanopoulos, what a great pleasure to meet you! How good

249

of you to come,"— he was told, "We need to talk privately, *señor*. If you don't mind, perhaps the young lady could wait outside. My secretary will take good care of her."

Before Nicholas could frame his reply, Torres— who had been holding the door open— was escorting Regina out.

"Please, *señor*," said Delgado, all smiles. "Do make yourself comfortable." He waved towards a black leather settee fronted by a predominantly white onyx coffee table. "May I get you a drink? Some coffee, or perhaps you prefer something stronger? I have an excellent Napoleon brandy."

"No, thanks," said Nicholas coldly.

Delgado was already opening his drinks cabinet. "Pity." He smiled again. "Please excuse me if I have one. It's been a busy day. Let me know if you change your mind."

He quarter-filled a large brandy glass, placed it on the onyx table, then went over to his enormous desk to fetch his box of Havanas and table-lighter. Nicholas observed him, thoughtfully. *Why*, he wondered was the chief choosing not to sit at his desk? Instead, Delgado pushed up a high-backed easy chair, one matching the settee, except that it was marginally higher.

"Won't you have a cigar, Señor Stephanopoulos? Very best Cohibas."He grinned broadly. "Don't ask how I got them. You'll get me into trouble."

"No thank you. I don't smoke." For a second Nicholas thought of an adapted saying: *beware of Mexicans bearing gifts*. Then his impatience took over. "I understand that you have important information for me, General."

"Ah, I like that. Straight down to business. I can see you are a man after my own heart." The chief helped himself to a Cohiba, carefully peeled off the yellow and-black-and-white check band, guillotined the cap with his cutter, then began heating the cigar's underside.

Nicholas felt that he was deliberately trying his patience. "Well?"

Delgado tipped back his head and slowly exhaled the first cloud of smoke with an air of deep satisfaction. Then he took a sip of brandy. "I have great news for you, *mi amigo*. *El Presidente* has personally asked me to pass on to you his good wishes, and extend to you his deepest sympathy for your tragic loss.

"As you may know, President Pérez is leaving this evening for the Summit of the Americas in Cancún. He will be returning one week later. However, if you should still be in Mexico City at that time, he says that he would be most pleased if you could join him for dinner at his *Los Pinos* residence."

He raised his finely trimmed eyebrows. "A very great honour, *señor*, I am sure you will agree."

Nicholas received the news coldly. "That's very kind of him. I appreciate the gesture. But what is the information you have for me?"

Delgado feigned wide-eyed astonishment. "*Dios mío!* Isn't that news enough? It is most unusual for an unofficial foreign visitor to be invited to *Los Pinos.*"

"I was hoping, *señor*, that you might have news of fresh developments in the investigation into the Chapultepec Park killings."

The chief smiled. "Ah, I am afraid you are talking to the wrong man. Unfortunately this office is not directly involved in the investigations. That is strictly a matter for *El Procurador General.*"

"So perhaps I should make an appointment to see him."

"Perhaps. But he won't be available at the moment. You see, he has been included in the President's entourage flying to Cancún."

"Hmm! Then really there is no way you can help me." Nicholas leaned forward and pressed down on the settee, preparing to rise.

Delgado raised a hand. "One moment, *señor.* I think there is a great deal we can do to help you. But first of all, I want to talk about your reckless offer of a $10 million reward. That's a very large sum of money. Don't you realise, many Mexicans would do anything— even kill— for just a fraction of that sum?"

"You don't approve of the reward?"

"On the contrary. We normally welcome the offer of a reward - but then normally such an offer is announced via the proper authorities, the people in charge of the investigation. Anyone with information is told to contact the police or the Procurador General's office. It is not normal— or correct— for a private citizen to be gathering information."

"But I understand the official investigation has recently been closed."

"True. But it can always be reopened if new information turns up.

"Let me ask you one key question: Just supposing that by some remote chance you should receive valuable new information about the killings, what would you propose to do with it?"

Nicholas paused, and decided against an honest reply. "I don't exactly know," he replied. "I suppose it would depend on the circumstances. Obviously I would pass the information on to your Procurador General if I was sure he would act upon it. Then again, I understand from my lawyers that I could always bring a private prosecution."

Delgado glared at him. "Before you say any more, *señor*, I should advise you that in our country it is a criminal offence to withhold evidence relating to an official inquiry."

"Of course. It is the same in my country. But in this instance, as you have said, the official investigation has been closed. Anyway, General, you were saying earlier that there are ways you could help me. How is that?"

"Ah, yes. Well, first— and most importantly, *señor*— we can provide you with protection."

"Protection? I don't want protection. I just want information. And to get it, I have to make myself accessible. I believe a police presence would only frighten off would-be informants."

"Huh! Sitting on top of a volcano is making yourself accessible. But you wouldn't last there very long."

Delgado paused to take a sip of brandy. "Tell me, *señor*, do you like old movies? I myself love those old black-and-white Warner Brothers productions. You know what I mean - the sort of thing that has Humphrey Bogart playing a private eye."

"Not particularly."

"But you've seen them. Right? Well, let me tell you: real life is nothing like those old movies.

"Take, for example, this cockeyed business of a $10 million reward. Might be all right in a Hollywood movie. In real life, it could get you killed in the first reel. Then again, getting killed in Mexico is not always quick and simple. I have seen some terrible mutilations."

Nicholas was about to protest, but the unwanted lecture went on, "You are a long way from home, young man, and I don't think you understand our country. Life here is

252

very cheap. Do you know how many murders we have in Mexico City alone? At least one every ninety minutes of the day. And that is mostly people getting themselves killed for trivial reasons: like screwing another man's wife or simply honking a horn too loudly in a traffic jam.

"Now you... you offer far more compelling reasons for murder."

"Why is that, *señor*?"

"Well, let us suppose that there was some unknown person or persons behind the killings in Chapultepec Park. If they wanted to kill members of your family, it is entirely possible that they would also want to kill you. Furthermore, your offer of a reward would give them a very good reason for trying to silence you. Don't you agree?"

"Maybe. That's a risk I'm prepared to take."

"Huh!"

"But then again, there is another, far greater risk. Having told everyone that you have ten million dollars to spare, you are a natural target for kidnapping. Do you know how many kidnappings we had in Mexico last year? I'll tell you. Just over eight hundred fifty. And those were only reported kidnappings. Who knows how many ransoms were secretly paid.

"And I'll tell you something else. No private citizen with your kind of wealth survives in México without having his own *guaruras*. Just how many bodyguards do you have, *Señor* Stephanopoulos?"

"None."

"You see. You have not thought this business through. Obviously you are going to need our protection."

Nicholas felt like telling Delgado that he had indeed thought it through. Again and again, Gondicas had stressed to him the need for *guaruras:* 'with your money you could hire your own private army'. Yet stubbornly he had dismissed the idea, arguing that he had to remain approachable, without anything that might discourage informants.

Instead, Nicholas simply repeated that he did not want protection.

Delgado glared again. "You still don't understand, *señor*. It's not a question of what *you* want. It is what we judge to be necessary. *El Presidente* has told me direct that he will hold me personally responsible for your safety while you are visiting this country. So, whether you like it or not, you *will*

253

have police protection."

Nicholas shrugged. Then, for the first time, Delgado made a point that disturbed him. "If you don't want this protection for yourself, then you might think about the young lady who is working with you. You are also putting her at great risk by your reckless action."

Delgado stood up, indicating that the interview was over.

As he opened the door to show Nicholas out, he paused with his right hand on the handle, then spoke *sotto voce*, "My advice to you, *señor*, is to give up this hare-brained scheme of yours. It is both irresponsible and dangerous. Like you have some kind of death wish. Obviously you have been under a great strain and probably need a rest. I suggest you use your visit to our country to take a short holiday, relax and then go home.

"Do understand: our *Presidente* is anxious that we should show you every hospitality, especially after your family has suffered so much. But there are limits. Quite frankly, I regard you as an extremely high security risk, and if your activities should lead to trouble - any disturbance at all - then I will not hesitate to recommend your immediate deportation.

He smiled once again. "I know you mean well, *señor*. And by all means leave open your offer of a $10 million reward. Just close down your telephone lines and announce that anyone with information should contact the police or the Procurador General's office. The rest is best left to the professionals."

Nicholas wanted to counter that the professionals had had their chance and had failed miserably. Instead he replied, "I'll think about it." Then, tight lipped, he accepted Delgado's extended handshake and left to join Regina in the ante-room.

"Thank you but we would prefer to walk," said Nicholas when they were escorted to a police car outside the *Seguridad* headquarters. The driver shrugged and went back into the building to report.

"Hope you don't mind walking, Regina. But I need some fresh air after breathing that man's cigar smoke. Also, I don't want to talk with that driver listening."

Regina laughed. "You call this fresh air! No, of course, I don't mind. I need the exercise after being stuck in that

254

secretary's office. What a waste of time! Anyway, did you get some useful information?"

"No," said Nicholas. "They were wasting my time, too."

Then, as they passed by a fashionable boutique on Liverpool, he shocked her by saying, "You know, Regina, I've been thinking. Perhaps we should abandon this business - or at least your part in it. I did rather rush into it, didn't realise how many stupid calls you would be getting."

For a few seconds Regina walked on in silence, then said quietly, "Why don't you say what you mean: that you don't really think I can handle the work?"

What Nicholas really thought was that he had made a mistake in involving anyone else in his enterprise. He himself didn't care a damn about possible dangers; obsessively, since the loss of his wife and child, he had seen the pursuit of vengeance as his only purpose in life. But that didn't justify putting innocent people in danger.

"No, no. It's not that, Regina. I am sure you will make a very capable P.A. It's just that there are complications I didn't foresee."

The truth of that remark became immediately apparent as they rounded the corner of Florencia and Hamburgo. Down the street they could see a crowd gathered outside *Apartamentos Orleáns*. Close up, they saw that two police cars and two television satellite trucks were parked in front of the building, and that the crowd was composed of newspaper reporters and an assortment of curious passers-by.

Nicholas was surprised. He had not realised how easily, and how soon, the media would trace his address by way of the telephone numbers he had given out on television. All at once he found himself surrounded on the pavement by reporters holding out tape recorders and bombarding him with a confusion of questions:

Señor, has anyone yet claimed your $10 million reward? Have you received any new information about the killings?... Are you dissatisfied with the official investigation?... Who is your lady friend, Señor Stephanopoulos?... Time magazine, señor: do you believe the assassination of ambassador Tunaman was part of a political conspiracy to sabotage the Greece-Turkey peace initiative? ... Will you be working with the Mexican police in your inquiry?

"*Atrás! Abran paso!*" Four police officers, stylishly

dressed in light-blue uniforms with white turtleneck sweaters, were now pressing back the crowd with batons held horizontally in both hands. Working in pairs, and in opposite directions, they gradually created a funnel to the main entrance.

Nicholas and Regina had just reached the doorway when a middle-aged man, tall, powerfully built and with crew-cut fair hair, pushed through and handed Nicholas a business card. "*Agencia Central de Prensa,*" he called out. "If you can give me an interview, please give me a call."

A savage baton blow to the kidneys sent the big man staggering backwards. His assailant looked at Nicholas and snapped, "Get inside if you don't want to start a riot." Nicholas took Regina's arm and retreated into the building. Behind them, policemen blocked the entrance, and two television cameras kept on recording the scene.

With Regina safely inside, Nicholas decided to go back outside and make a statement, reiterating his appeal for information. But a police officer promptly barred his way.

"I am sorry, *señor*, but you must stay inside until this crowd has dispersed. It is for your own safety."

Nicholas protested in vain. Half an hour later, when he looked down from his apartment, he saw that a small group of reporters remained, together with one television van and a few onlookers. Also, the police cars were still parked across the street.

It was now 5.30 p.m. Nicholas was alarmed to hear a key turning in the lock to his apartment. For a second he thought that the police were coming in. Instead, the door opened to reveal the large figure-of-eight presence of Juanita. She was carrying her shopping basket, and there were tears in her eyes.

"Oh, Señor Stefan," she said as she stepped inside. "It is horrible down there: so many police. They wouldn't let me in at first. I had to give my name and address, and then they searched my basket... and my body."

Nicholas took the basket and led her to an easy chair. "I am so sorry, Juanita. Sit down and rest and I'll get you a drink."

Juanita shook her head. "No, I must go home. I just came to bring the fresh *filetes* you wanted." Then she turned

256

to Regina. "It was awful. The man felt all over my stomach and asked what I was hiding in there. He thought it was funny. But I hated it."

Regina put an arm round her shoulder. "You poor dear. Are you sure you don't want to rest?"

She shook her head again and moved towards the door. "Juanita is very sorry, Señor Stefan. But I cannot work here no more. I hate the police and having them touch my body."

"Wait," said Nicholas. "You are not going down there alone. I am going to phone for a taxi to take you home." Ten minutes later he escorted her down to a green-and-white Beetle cab. He paid the driver in advance. Then, as she slid onto the backseat, he handed her an envelope containing 1,000 pesos, the equivalent of a month's salary for a maid.

"A little something for you. Goodbye, Juanita. And good luck."

Only a handful of reporters were on the pavement now. Nicholas ignored their questions, glared at the two police officers on duty, and hurried back inside.

It was Regina, rather than the large Scotch-on- the-rocks, that lifted Nicholas out of his dark, despairing mood. Within half an hour, he found himself filled with wonder at the steadfast character of this bright-eyed young colleen who never wavered in her calmness and cheerful optimism. Above all, he was impressed by her quicksilver mind; her gift for practical and logical reasoning as— one by one— she demolished his negative thoughts and arguments.

The loss of Juanita was easily dismissed. As Regina explained, such a luxury was unnecessary. There were plenty of nearby restaurants and takeaways that would deliver meals to order, and there were home help services in the Yellow Pages that would send round cleaning ladies as and when required.

Nicholas had conceded the point, but had persisted in his argument that things were not working out as he had planned, and that it was probably best if she did not remain involved. "It's all getting out of hand. We are now virtually prisoners in our own apartments, and if this much media attention follows my brief appearance on TV, think what it will be like tomorrow when the reward offer is in all the newspapers. It's not right to subject you to so much danger."

Regina had immediately reversed his argument. Massive media attention, she reasoned, not only helped to publicise his appeal for information, but also provided greater security. "I feel perfectly safe with all those press and TV people outside."

When Nicholas suggested that, like Juanita, she should take a taxi home, Regina countered that she would only be followed and pestered by reporters. Again he had to agree; that it was probably best for her to remain overnight as originally planned. "But hopefully you can get away first thing in the morning, before they come back *en masse*. I suggest that you then leave for the States, and enjoy a holiday before taking up your appointment with the IMF. Don't worry about the cost. I'll take care of that."

Regina bristled at that suggestion, but only her eyes expressed her disgust. "Why don't we see if any useful messages have been left? Then I'll get us something to eat. You'll be surprised what I can do with some best steaks and my own special taco sauce."

Without waiting for his answer, Regina left for her neighbouring apartment. Nicholas did not follow at once. Momentarily he was caught off-balance. He was not used to a woman taking the lead. Then, as so often happened, he found himself thinking of Yasemin, how much he missed her, how she had always been so gentle and totally supportive in her ways.

But this American woman was something else: good-humoured like Yasemin but also assertive and independent. To a degree, she irritated him - not because she had a mind of her own, but because so often her counter-arguments were undeniably right.

Before joining her in the office-apartment, Nicholas remembered that he had an answering machine on his own private line. He pressed the button and found that two messages had been left.

One was from a Señora Alvarez, personal assistant to Isabel del Río. She wanted him to call her back so that they could arrange a second appearance on TV. "We have a great idea for a special discussion, putting you on with Fernando Ramírez, the father of the assassin. He still insists that his son was innocent, so it could make for a very interesting programme."

The second caller was also a woman. "Niki, this is your mother. I have bad news: your father has been having bad angina pains again, and they've flown him back to Papworth

Hospital for further surgery. Please, please, ring me as soon as possible."

Nicholas delayed returning her call. First, he looked up the number of the Cambridgeshire hospital in his Filofax. On ringing, he was put straight through to his father's private room. A nurse answered. "Nicholas who?" And in the background, he could hear his father barking, "Pass me that goddamn phone."

Stavros Stephanopoulos came across as clearly as if he was in the room next door. "Niki, my boy. I was just thinking about you. How are you? How are things going?"

"Never mind me, *patera*. How are you? What's happening there?"

"Me? I feel absolutely great, and nothing is happening - not with this damn boring nurse they've given me." As he spoke, he was grinning meaningfully at a young woman of stunning good looks.

"Seriously, *patera*. How are you?"

"It's true. I feel fine. Just the odd angina pains. But these so-called experts insist that my latest angiogram shows a new blockage. They say a heart attack is certain if I don't have another bypass. It's scheduled for tomorrow. But don't worry about it. I've beaten this thing once and I can do it again."

"I ought to be there, *patera*. I'll book the earliest flight I can get."

Stavros' tone of voice hardened. "You'll do nothing of the sort, Niki. You-know-who has told me all about what you are doing. Excellent so far, but it will all be wasted if you leave now.

"Please, Niki, please. Promise me that you won't give up. There's nothing you can achieve by being here. But if you can nail the fucking killers of Georgios it will be just the tonic I need. It's your duty, Niki; our *philotimo* is at stake."

"I promise, *patera*."

"You are a good boy. I could not wish for a finer son. Remember, you have complete access to my bank account in Mexico City. I don't care what it costs. Get the bastards. But do be careful. And don't trust anyone."

CHAPTER 20

Flanked by two officers of the *Cuerpo de Guardias Presidenciales*, both bearing a gleaming ceremonial sword at the upright, President Enrique Pérez walked briskly past the guard of honour drawn up for inspection on the tarmac of Benito Juárez International Airport. Then, as he mounted the steps to his presidential airliner *Quetzalcoatl IV*, he turned briefly to face the battery of television crews and radio and newspaper reporters.

There was no official statement, just a cursory wave and a smile before he disappeared into the converted Boeing 747, subsequently to be followed by an enormous entourage of government ministers, private secretaries, interpreters and favoured members of the Mexican press corps. Then the TV picture cut back to the newsroom where an economist talked briefly to Isabel del Río about hopes for the summit meeting in Cancún.

"Typical machismo," said Regina, reaching out to her glass of Chablis. "The President can't even catch a plane without having a military parade. How are you finding your six-minute steaks? Not too much chilli and garlic, I hope?"

"Very good," said Nicholas. "You were right, saying we didn't need Juanita."

A few minutes later he picked up the remote control and turned down the volume on the television, which now had an interview with the victim of a gang-rape. Then, while Regina went to get the coffee, he read for the third time the print-out of a message left on one of the answering machines.

During their absence, a dozen messages had been recorded. Most of them, said Regina, were totally absurd - just Mexicans begging for handouts. She hadn't told him that one was positively obscene, suggesting that Nicholas himself had masterminded the killings "to make way for a new wife."

There was, however, one message of real promise. It was from a man who identified himself as Jaime Muzquiz, a taxi driver. On the day of the killings, he said, he had picked up a passenger near the main entrance to Chapultepec Park. He guessed it must have been soon after the crime because he had passed by police cars with their sirens screaming.

This man who got into my cab was fat and middle-aged. I remember him well because he was sweating a lot, and seemed very nervous. Also he was carrying a backpack, which looked rather odd for a man wearing a business suit. I remember him hugging that bag like it was real valuable. Now I wonder: could he have had a gun inside it?

I can't tell you any more about him. But I could take you to where I dropped him off. If you are interested, call the Radiotaxi Reforma on 565-6565, and say you want me personally for a drive.

"You might care to listen to the tape," said Regina as she set down the coffee pot. "He certainly sounds genuine."

"I'll take your word for it. Your Spanish is so much better than mine."

"So what do you think? Are you going to give him a call?"

"Definitely. But not now. I'd sooner go in daylight and see exactly where he is taking me."

Regina glanced at the television. "Good heavens! Look, Nicholas. We're on the box."

True enough, the seven o'clock news was showing pictures of the earlier crowd scene outside *Apartamentos Orleáns*. Most sensationally, the camera captured the moment when a burly newspaperman reeled backwards from a baton blow to his kidneys. Nicholas turned up the sound.

The next TV frame showed Del Río sitting at the news desk. "Well, *Señor Secretario*," she said. "Was that violence really necessary?"

Now the screen revealed that sitting to one side of the news desk was Police Chief Juan Delgado, as ever, immaculate in full-dress uniform with his black hair sleeked back from a central parting.

He smiled. "I am afraid so, Isabel. You see, we cannot afford to take any chances in protecting this unfortunate young man. His family has already suffered terribly. Now we must regard him as a high security risk."

"Ah! So then you are not entirely satisfied that the Chapultepec Park killings were the work of a lone assassin? You think perhaps that someone may be out to kill the entire family?"

261

"I didn't say that. All the evidence clearly shows that Manuel Ramírez was solely responsible for the shootings. Now, whether he was hired by someone else - perhaps by some Armenian militants, for example - that is another question altogether. Either way, we prefer to err on the side of caution and give Señor Stephanopoulos maximum protection."

Isabel Del Río persisted, "But what is your own opinion, *Señor Secretario*? Was someone else behind the killings? And in view of the reward now being offered, do you think that the investigation should be reopened?"

Delgado gave her a gently reproving look. "It is not for me to make such judgements. As you must know, that's entirely a matter for the Procurador General." Then he turned to face the camera square on.

"But I would say this for the benefit of all viewers: If anyone out there has information relating to the Chapultepec Park murders, it is his or her duty to inform the proper authorities— either the Procurador General's office or the police. Failure to do so could lead to their prosecution.

"At the same time, of course, if such information should prove to be useful, then we will be pleased to notify Señor Stephanpoulos so that any reward can be claimed. But this foreigner should not get directly involved."

"Thank you very much, *Señor Secretario*, for giving us your time."

"My pleasure, dear lady."

"And now for the weather..."

"What a creep!" said Regina as Nicholas switched off.

"I agree. But you must admit he is a pretty smooth TV performer. Wasn't the least bit disturbed by that shot of police violence."

"True. But I wonder who that guy was— the one who got beaten up."

"No idea," replied Nicholas. "Said he was from some press agency. Wait! I completely forgot. I've got his business card somewhere." He fished into a pocket of his fawn safari-style jacket draped over the back of his chair. "Ah, here it is."

"What is it?" asked Regina, as he frowned while studying the card.

Nicholas passed it over to her. "See for yourself. There's no printed name or address. Just a scrawled message... in English."

Regina read it aloud: *I don't want any reward, but I*

262

*can help you. Meet me at the Obregón Monument at 9 p.m.
But come alone. And don't tell the police. A friend.*

"Christ, Nicholas! This is pretty vague. Could be anything. Might even be some kind of trap."

"A trap?"

"It's possible. You may not be aware of it, but we have had a lot of kidnappings in Mexico City lately— mostly bankers and industrialists."

"So I understand. But this is interesting: the first person to say he is not after the reward. And, you know, he took quite a chance pushing passed the police like he did." Nicholas looked at his watch. "How far away is this Obregón Monument?"

"Oh, maybe fifteen or twenty minutes, straight down Insurgentes. You are not thinking of going?"

"It's only 7.30. Plenty of time." Nicholas got up and went over to the window looking down onto the street. He drew back the curtain no more than half an inch. "A police car's still there. But I can't see any reporters."

"Yes, I'm going."

Regina stood up. "Then I'm going with you. You don't know this city like I do."

Nicholas looked at her coldly. "You are *not* going. The man said 'come alone', and that's how it's going to be." He put on his jacket, then went into his bedroom and pulled open the bottom section of a chest of drawers. From beneath some clothing he drew out a handgun, and slipped it into his deep right-hand pocket.

"My God! Where the hell did you get that?"

Nicholas' heart missed a beat. He had not heard Regina get up and cross over to the bedroom door. He spun round, his eyes at first registering shock, and then blazing, icy rage. "None of your damned business," he snapped.

Seconds later, his usual quiet demeanour returned, and he sought to restore calm. "It's just a precaution, Regina. The note is probably a hoax, but you can't be too careful."

"Hmm," said Regina disbelievingly, then turning away. For the first time she had seen Nicholas in his true colours: as a man under intense nervous strain, a sleeping volcano that could unexpectedly erupt at any moment. It occurred to her that he was not merely seeking justice, but was fully prepared to dispense it.

Nicholas sensed her hostility. "Sorry if I spoke rather

harshly. But now, maybe, you can see this is not just a game. There are *real* dangers - and that's why I want you out of this. Get a good night's rest, and tomorrow you can get back to a normal life."

As he spoke, he put a comforting hand on her shoulder. She could detect a genuine tenderness in his voice. But also something else: a kind of finality, as though he himself did not care whether he lived or died.

She concealed her thoughts in action. "What a mess! I must clear these things away." She fetched a tray, and began to gather up the plates and coffee cups.

Meanwhile Nicholas picked up the print-out, checked the number of the *Radiotaxi Reforma,* then went over to the telephone.

"What are you doing?" asked Regina.

"Booking a taxi."

"Wait a minute. What do you propose to do about those police across the way? They are sure to follow you."

"I'll have to take a chance. Maybe the driver can lose them along the way."

"Fat chance of that." Regina set down the tray. "Listen, Nicholas, if you must go, I can help you."

He ignored her and picked up the telephone.

"No, listen. I don't need to come with you - at least not all the way. But I can show you how to lose the police."

Nicholas put down the telephone and listened. And yet again he wondered at her quick, logical thinking, and begrudgingly he recognised that she was right.

The taxi was booked for eight o'clock. As they climbed in, Nicholas leaned forward and checked the driver's identity card beside the dashboard. There was a coloured photograph and a name: Alfonso Puentes.

As they drove off, Nicholas asked, "Do you know Jaime Muzquiz?"

"Ah *si*," replied the driver. "Very fine *hombre*. Hey, how you know my *compadre's* name?"

"Oh, he drove me somewhere a few months ago. Just wondered if you knew him". As he spoke, Nicholas turned his head to look out the back window. To his surprise, the police car had not moved.

They turned into Florencia, then rounded *El Angel*

and headed north along the great boulevard of Reforma. Amid the blaze of headlights, it was impossible to tell whether or not they were being followed. But there was no one immediately behind them when they turned off at the *glorieta* Simón Bolívar.

A few blocks east, they pulled up in a large cobblestone square with an illuminated fountain in its centre. All around, people were gathered in separate clusters beside performing groups of *mariachis,* and when Nicholas opened the cab door his ears were bombarded by an extraordinary cacophony of sound created by countless guitars, violins, trombones and, most stridently, by trumpets that dominated with their soaring, high-pitched tones.

This, as Regina had pre-advised him, was Plaza Garibaldi, the touristy haven of the *mariachi* trade. In the small hours, the area could become positively seedy, with prostitution, drunkenness and squalor invading its adjacent back streets. But in the early evening, as now, it was a harmless and diverting delight.

Beside the fountain Nicholas spotted three uniformed policeman, but— seemingly off-duty— they were totally absorbed in listening to *mariachis* whom they themselves had paid for songs to be played.

According to plan, Regina herself took care of the taxi driver. "You know the street at the back of the *Mercado San Camilito?*"

"*Sí.*"

"Well, I want you to wait for us there... maybe fifteen minutes. There will be double this if you do. Okay?

Puentes glanced at the wad of pesos she handed him, and grinned from ear to ear. "*Muchas gracias, señorita. Sí,* I will be there. Take as long as you like."

As they crossed the square, they were briefly stalked by two guitarists in traditional Jalisco cowboy outfits: short black velvet jacket, frilled white shirt with long bow tie, tight pants studded with two rows of silver buttons, high leather boots and broad sombrero.

The *mariachis* strummed a few bars of a dulcet, sentimental ballad that Regina recognised as *Las Mañanitas,* then turned away after Nicholas had raised a hand with a negative shake of his head.

Ahead of them, Nicholas now saw the largest of several cantinas facing onto the square: the popular Tenampa

Saloon, evoking western-movie shaped images with its wooden swing doors leading directly onto a long bar. From within he could hear the haunting sound of a trumpet solo.

Regina took his arm. "You should try that place sometime. It's fun. But we're going this way. And prepare yourself for a shock."

She steered him down an alleyway, and through an open doorway that led onto the largest public dining-hall that Nicholas had ever seen: an instant food market as large as a football field, and teeming with Mexicans who snacked at myriad stalls offering the most bewildering array of cooked foods imaginable.

"All the locals eat here," said Regina. "They like the communal atmosphere. Also, it's much cheaper, and they can find everything they fancy."

"I can believe it," said Nicholas. As they threaded their way between stalls, he looked around and concluded that this must be a vegetarian's concept of Dante's Inferno. All around them were displays of steaming hunks of animal flesh and entrails, plus dishes composed of unidentified insects, some of them squirming and still very much alive.

Regina picked the simplest of stalls, one that offered only beef or chicken tacos with a wide choice of added fillings and toppings. Drawing up a stool, she ordered two beef tacos with chopped onion and peppers, and a topping of sliced avocado and taco sauce.

They both studied other customers in their vicinity. If any policemen were trailing them. they were in plain clothes and indistinguishable.

Regina pointed down their aisle. "Now's the time. If you go to the far end, you'll find an exit beyond the toilets. Good luck, and do be careful. See you later, back at the apartments."

Nicholas moved briskly down the hangar-like dining-hall, brushing past men and women who were idly hovering between stalls. Looking back, he could see no one trying to keep pace with him.

Then, rounding a high wooden screen, he arrived at the men's toilets, and was both astonished and horrified to see that the *excusados*— like the food stalls— were entirely open-plan. Here, in long rows, scores of Mexicans were seated, cheek by jowl, with their pants down, straining, farting, dumping, and some even conversing. Their love of a communal atmosphere, he reflected, seemed to extend to the output, as well as the input, of food.

Deliberately not looking to either side, he hurried on through the shithouse, rounded another wooden wall, and suddenly found himself in a narrow street. Nearby, under a streetlight, was the parked taxi of Alfonso Puentes.

Ten minutes later, having barely touched her taco, Regina left the dining-hall by the main entrance, and in Plaza Garibaldi grabbed a taxi that was unloading four American tourists.

In 1928, a garden banquet in honour of President-elect Alvaro Obregón was held at the Bombilla restaurant in Mexico City's lush southern district of San Angel. While the dignitaries were dining, a young caricaturist called José de León Toral approached the head table to show the drawings he had just sketched. Then, as Obregón began to inspect his work, the artist pulled out a pistol and fired five shots into the President-elect's head.

What was the assassin's motive? Were others involved? Torture by the police failed to gain answers. But when they threatened to inflict torture on his family, Toral promptly talked. He was a fanatical *Cristero*, a supporter of the militant Catholics who, in pursuit of the restoration of Church power, had turned to guerrilla warfare.

Toral confessed that he had begun target practice two weeks earlier... with a handgun provided by one of several militants who met regularly at the house of a nun, Sister Concepción Acevedo de la Llata. A number of zealots were arrested, and in the subsequent show trial, Toral was sentenced to death and Sister Concepción to twenty years' imprisonment.

Politically, the killing marked a watershed in Mexican history. In the wake of Obregón's death came a new mechanism for stability: the formation in 1929 of a widely-based political party, subsequently renamed the *Partido Revolucionario Institucional* (PRI), which clung to power for the next seven decades, providing a succession of presidents who ruled like Aztec emperors.

Today, the Obregón Monument stands on the site of the assassination: a rectilinear, two-storey structure of concrete and marble set in a small attractive park, the *Jardin*

267

de Bonilla, just off Insurgentes. For years it had nothing to commend it beyond a few stylish sculptures and, in an illuminated recess, a glass jar containing the right hand and wrist that General Obregón had lost in battle during the Mexican Revolution.

But now even its principal attraction was gone. In 1993 its grotesque exhibit— a half-clenched fist that was a sickly shade of white with the nerves and ganglia drifting beneath it in formaldehyde— had been returned to the Obregón family and cremated.

Thus, Puentes expressed surprise when Nicholas asked to be driven to the monument. "Long time, *señor*, since I took anyone there. And I can tell you now that it will be closed this late in the day." True enough, the single door to the Obregón Monument was locked when they arrived only a few minutes before nine o'clock, and no one was standing near the entrance.

Having paid off the driver, Nicholas felt uneasy as he waited alone for his anonymous friend. There were plenty of occasional passers-by: people on their way to or from nearby restaurants, couples out for a stroll in the park. What concerned him more were the strangers *not* on the move.

In the half-light provided by five-cluster street lamps, he could discern two men in dark suits standing near a tree some 30 or 40 yards to his right. He also observed that, by a disturbing coincidence, two more men were standing a similar distance away, to his left. He kept a hand in the deep right-front pocket of his jacket, tightening his hold on the pistol-grip of his .38 snub-nosed Smith and Wesson.

For fifteen minutes he waited. Still the men on either side had not moved. Two Indian women, apparently street-sellers, approached, both shouldering a heap of striped woollen *sarapes*. As they passed by, they giggled, and the younger one gave Nicholas a fetching look. It was time, he decided, to leave.

At that moment, he was suddenly confronted by a mestizo boy, perhaps no more than eleven-years-old. He seemed to have come out of nowhere. Under his arm was a battered shoeshine box.

"No thanks," said Nicholas. "I've already had a shine today."

The boy grinned, then fished inside his zip jacket and pulled out a rolled-up copy of *Time* magazine. "Man pay me to give you this, *señor*."

"Hey, wait a minute," said Nicholas, as the boy started to walk off. "What man? Who gave you this?"

"Don't know, *señor*. Just a man, a big gringo. Outside the café over there." He pointed across to Avenida Miguel Angel de Quevedo. And then he was gone.

Nicholas looked at the magazine, saw it was the current issue, and then noticed a piece of paper sticking out between the pages. It was a restaurant menu, and on the back there was a message handwritten in English. After reading it, he hurried across to Quevedo and hailed a taxi. No one, he felt certain, was following him.

At *Apartamentos Orleáns*, Regina poured herself a large vodka and tonic, and flopped on to the settee in front of the TV. An old Hitchcock movie called *Spellbound* was showing, but having missed the first hour, she could not follow the plot. Briefly she surfed the other channels, then switched off.

She was in no mood to concentrate on any programme. One side of her was high on excitement as she impatiently and anxiously awaited Nicholas' return. The other, burgeoning side was low on disappointment as she dwelt on the fact that tomorrow it would be back to her relatively mundane existence.

Meanwhile there was nothing more to be done. She had checked the answering machines, and not a single new message had been left. Closing her eyes, she tried to envisage her future: commuting every day on the Washington Metro Red Line, a thiry-five-minute journey to the IMF building on 19th Street. Hopefully, by the summer, she would have saved enough to buy a useful mare, and pay a stud fee.

Normally, this day-dream led into her favourite fantasy: the breeding and training of the winner of the Maryland Hunt Cup. But her mind was too attuned to current events. Inexorably, her thoughts reverted to Nicholas. She found him incredibly attractive: a strong, virile personality and yet, paradoxically, so vulnerable - like some wounded lion bravely, but perilously stalking shadows in an unfamiliar jungle.

Half-asleep now, her mind began to wander, imagining a nightmare scenario in which the telephone rings with demands being made by kidnappers, and her having to phone Nicholas' father and ask for ransom money... just as the old man was coming out of open-heart surgery.

At that moment she was jolted back to full consciousness by the sound of a door banging. She hurried out and knocked on the door to Nicholas' adjacent apartment. When he answered, she found herself blurting out, "Oh, Nicholas, thank goodness you are safe. I was so worried about you. What happened?"

As he invited her in, he put his right index finger to his tightly closed lips, then handed her a sheet of paper taken from his jacket. "It was a complete waste of time," he answered. "I think I am going to abandon this reward business."

"You can't be serious!" Regina exclaimed.

"I am quite serious," he replied, at the same time shaking his head and pointing to the paper he had given her. Again he put a finger to his lips.

This time, Regina got his meaning. She remained silent, and read the message neatly handwritten on the back of a menu:

The police were at the Obregón Monument BEFORE you arrived. This confirms what I had suspected: that your apartments are bugged, and no doubt your telephone lines as well.

Let's try something else. If possible, attend tomorrow's lucha libre at the Arena México. It starts at 2030 hours. I will leave a ticket in your name to be collected at the front box office. Don't worry about being followed, but be prepared to move fast when you are contacted.

Before she could react, Nicholas said breezily, "If you are not too tired, Regina, why don't we go out for a drink? A little farewell celebration to mark the end of this business."

"A good idea. I could do with some fresh air. I'll just get my coat."

As they were about to leave, Nicholas turned back to fetch a half-size bottle of Southern Comfort from the drinks cabinet. Regina saw him slip it into the left pocket of his safari jacket. She wondered if the pressure was driving him to booze, but said nothing.

"Wait here a minute," said Nicholas when they reached the outside steps. Then, to her further surprise, he crossed the street, and tapped on the window of the police surveillance car. The uniformed driver wound down the window, and Nicholas reached in with the whisky bottle.

"*Buenas tardes,*" he said cheerfully. "We're just going out for a drink, and I thought that you might need some refreshment, too."

The driver grinned. "Very kind, *señor*. Can't drink on duty, but perhaps I could save it for later."

Beside him, sat another man dressed in a dark-brown suit. He scowled at his companion disapprovingly.

"By the way," said Nicholas helpfully. "We're going to *Il Pirata* if you are interested."

He had chosen *Il Pirata* because he had previously noted that it had a narrow annexe, with separate cubicles where customers were profitably encouraged to take a preprandial drink, while waiting for their table. As they turned off Hamburgo into the passageway leading to the restaurant, he observed that the man in the dark-brown suit was less than twenty yards behind.

He grinned at Regina. "Our police friend is still with us. For our protection, of course. But where was he earlier when we went to Plaza Garibaldi?"

"See what you mean," said Regina. "Didn't need to follow you because he already knew where you were going."

"Exactly. So much for their crap about protection." He laughed. "Anyway, it's nice to know where we stand."

Regina looked at him quizzically. "You seem remarkably cheerful tonight, Nicholas. Can't see why. This bugging business means that no one can give you information in confidence. The police will know your every move."

"Ah, but at least we are making progress."

"We are?"

"Certainly. It's like my father always used to say when pushing for some big business deal: You get no action without reaction. The way people respond to things you say or do can tell you a lot. If they don't openly react at all, then you can be left in the dark.

"This reaction gives a positive signal. If people feel a need to have our apartments bugged, then it follows that they have a real interest in what we are doing, and that suggests there must be something to be discovered. At least I know now that I am not completely wasting my time.

"Also, we know who is responsible for the bugging. There has been only one time when someone could have got

271

into our apartments without us knowing. And that was when they insisted on you accompanying me to police headquarters, for apparently no useful purpose. Ah, here we are."

In the small foyer of *Il Pirata*, they were immediately approached by the maitre d'. "*Buenas tardes, señor.* You have a reservation?"

"No. We are just here for a drink." Simultaneously, anticipating rejection, Nicholas pulled out his wallet and extracted a 100-peso bill. "Perhaps you could find us somewhere quiet and intimate."

The head waiter grinned knowingly. "Of course, *señor.* If you will follow me." He took the bill and led the way to a cubicle at the far end of the annexe. "You won't be disturbed here. I'll send someone to take your order immediately."

The neighbouring cubicles were occupied. And the brown-suited shadow had not yet entered the restaurant. "I think we can talk freely here," said Nicholas after the wine had been delivered and ceremoniously uncorked.

He had ordered 'a bottle of your best champagne'. Now he raised his glass and made a toast. "Here's to you, and a great success in Washington."

Regina thanked him, then went straight to the question that had been troubling her ever since they left the apartments. "You weren't really serious, were you, when you talked about abandoning your offer of a reward?"

Nicholas smiled. "Of course not. That was just to give out misinformation. It's the way it will be from now on. Anything I say in the apartments will be just for effect. Confuse the enemy and all that."

"You could always try getting rid of the bugs."

"Maybe. The trouble is that I have never been technically minded. I might find some, but I could never feel certain that I had traced every single one. "He grinned boyishly. "That was always Yasemin's complaint about me: that I wasn't a good handyman."

It was the first time that Regina had heard him mention his wife's name. And almost at once, she noticed that his manner suddenly became more formal.

He paused, seemingly collecting his thoughts. "But I was serious about one thing I said in the apartment, about this being a kind of farewell celebration. There is no sense in you getting more deeply involved. A pity, because I have greatly appreciated working with you."

There was a certain warmth in his voice that heightened Regina's sense of loss. She countered, "You realise, of course, that messages are likely to flood in tomorrow when your ad' appears in the newspapers. You are going to need help."

"Perhaps. But that matters much less - now that the telephones are being tapped. Meanwhile, I have two promising leads: the taxi driver Mazquiz, and this mysterious man I didn't meet at the Obregón Monument."

"If that message about being bugged is right, the police will already know about the taxi driver."

"You are absolutely right. But they won't know about the other lead. Tell me: what do you know about Arena México and this thing called *lucha libre*?"

"Can't help you much there. I have never been to Arena México. As for *lucha libre*, I can only tell you what I have been told. It means 'free fighting', and it's the Mexican version of professional wrestling. It's become really big, perhaps the most popular sport in the country.

"Many years ago, a wrestler— an American, I believe— went into the ring wearing a mask. Now many of them wear masks, and a few of the great wrestlers are kind of folk heroes who do a lot of valuable charity work. You know, I'd quite like to go."

"Forget it, Regina." He reached across the table and took her hand. "Believe me, you are well out of it. You know, everyone I care about in this world seems to meet with tragedy. And I like you too much to risk anything happening to you. So tomorrow it's over. *Punto!*"

She felt her heart tremble at his first touch. Then, just as suddenly, he withdrew his hand and picked up his glass. "Hey, this is meant to be a celebration. Drink up. Would you like something to eat as well?"

"No thanks."

Briefly, there was an awkward silence. It was broken by Nicholas who calculatingly began to probe Regina about her plans for breeding horses.

He was good at drawing her out. She even found herself talking about her secret dream of Maryland Hunt Cup glory. "It's the greatest, toughest steeplechase in all America, you know. Four miles and over twenty-two solid timber fences, some of them five feet high. It demands absolute precision when jumping at racing speed.

"Two winners have even gone on to win the English Grand National. But, of course, I'm not going to get a horse in that class. But it would be great just to have a runner."

"My goodness! You are really into this thing. I've just had a thought: my father has had business dealings with the Maktoums. Maybe he could put you in touch with them when you come to buying a mare."

She laughed hollowly. "That's rather out of my league, Nicholas. Anyway, that's a silly idea. Their speciality is flat racing."

For the first time, he was beginning to irritate her. He might mean well, but he was not talking about things that he understood or really cared about. And he irritated her still more when he went on to raise the subject of money with his reassurance that, as agreed, she would be paid a full month's salary.

"That's absurd," she snapped. "I've only been with you a single day."

"Nicholas smiled. "Please, I want you to have it. Really. You must realise the money is just a drop in the ocean for me."

"That's not the point. In my world, people expect to earn what they get. It's a matter of pride. You should understand that."

"Not in this case. The terms were agreed. And I have never ever welshed on an agreement. You see, it's a matter of pride for me, too."

Regina continued to argue the point, then finally relented. "I'll tell you what: I'll take the money, on condition that you at least let me put in a full day's work tomorrow, when all the phones are likely to be busy."

The suggestion did not fit in with Nicholas' plans. But he was willing to offer a compromise. Regina could work most of the morning, manning one of the telephones and, where it was justified, printing out any serious messages left on the computers. But then she had to take a taxi back to her own flat.

By the time they left *Il Pirata*, Regina had got Nicholas to outline clearly his programme for the next day. Early in the morning, he would ring *Radiotaxi Reforma,* and hopefully book Muzquiz to pick him up at eleven o'clock. Another taxi would be ordered for 1115 hours to take Regina home.

"If, as seems likely, there are police and reporters outside, they are certain to follow me. This should leave the coast clear for you to get home unobserved. With luck, you won't be bothered by anyone after that. But I would suggest that you fly off to Washington as soon as possible."

"Couldn't I help you lose anyone following you - like we did before?"

"Too complicated. Remember the police already know about Mazquiz. And even if I use a public booth to call him, they are likely to have him tailed.

He grinned. "Anyway, I *want* to be followed. I couldn't ask for better protection than to have a pack of news hounds snapping at my heels."

"Okay. But what about Arena México in the evening? Anyone might be following you then. The place will be packed, and anything could happen to you when you are lost among the crowds."

"That's a chance I will have to take. But I'm optimistic. Don't worry about it."

Regina looked at him intently. "Sorry, but I am worried. Can I ring you late tomorrow night to see how you got on? I promise to be discreet. We could make up our own little code."

Nicholas leaned across the table and stared at her coldly. "Let's get one thing absolutely clear, Regina. After tomorrow morning, we will have no further contact. None whatsoever. Under no circumstances are you to phone. You understand? Quite simply, it will be goodbye."

CHAPTER 21

"We must have a story for this week's issue," said editor Miguel Ramos. "If he won't give an interview, follow the *cabrón* wherever he goes. And be sure to get some pictures."

It was shortly after nine o'clock on Tuesday morning, when Emiliano Vargas left the editor's office to tackle his new assignment. In his hand was an advertisement cut from the early edition of *Excelsior*. Within five minutes, he had traced the advertiser's address via his contact on the Mexico City central telephone exchange.

He then surfed the files of microfilmed press cuttings to re-familiarise himself with details of the Chapultepec Park killings. On his notepad, he jotted down ideas for possible interview questions. Underneath he wrote large, *VIUDO GRIEGO RECIBE SU RECOMPENSA.*

Grinning, he circled the words with a flourish. Part-time pimp, more fixer than reporter, Vargas liked to tackle his work in reverse: starting with a caption to an eye-catching picture that had yet to be taken. In his mind's eye, he saw a front page picture— his manufactured picture— of a startled Nicholas Stephanopoulos being passionately embraced by a busty Mexican hooker: *the Greek widower receiving his reward.*

Like all reporters on *El Informador*, Vargas was expected to double as a photographer. The weekly scandal sheet, operating on a tight budget from cramped offices north of the Zócalo, employed only one specialist photographer, and he had been sent to Cancún, hopefully to snatch revealing beach pictures of delegates attending the economic summit.

After a call to his live-in prostitute, telling her to meet him outside *Apartamentos Orleáns,* Vargas set off in his yellow VW Beetle, heading west to Reforma, then southwest to the Zona Rosa. It was the beginning of what he would later describe to friends as the craziest experience of his journalistic career.

From 8 a.m. onwards— following the appearance of Nicholas' $10 million reward in press advertisements— the scene on Hamburgo was one of mounting disorder. Within an hour, more than fifty photographers, reporters and foreign correspondents were gathered outside *Apartamentos Orleáns*. Swelled by inquisitive onlookers— drawn like moths around a flame by the presence of three television satellite trucks— the crowd spilled off the pavement, adding to the traffic congestion created by double-parked cars.

When Vargas drove into Hamburgo shortly before ten o'clock, he found that the police had sealed off a section of the street, forcing him to park two blocks away from *Apartamentos Orleáns*. His busty hooker was nowhere in sight and entrance to the apartments was barred by six police officers.

Inside, Nicholas was in negotiation with Coronel Salvador Hernández. The officer-in-charge had requested that perhaps the Greek could make a personal statement to the media. Thereafter, the police would compel the crowd to disperse.

"What kind of statement?" Nicholas asked.

"Have you anything important to say?"

"No. Only that the reward remains on offer and that I would welcome new information."

"That's it then. Keep it short and simple. But no long session of questions and answers, you understand. We can't have you holding a press conference on the street. The security risk is too great. They can just take their pictures and clear off."

"Okay. But could we delay my appearance until eleven o'clock? I've got a taxi coming at that time. That way I could make my statement, and leave immediately afterwards. Then you'll be saved the trouble of having to break up the crowd."

Hernández thought about it, then nodded. "All right, *señor*. Meanwhile, I will instruct my men to let your taxi through. We will, of course, be giving you a police escort."

Nicholas noted that the officer did not ask for the name of the taxi service or for details of where he would be going.

In the adjacent apartment, Regina had spent two hours manning the telephones, personally taking individual calls at random. There had rarely been a break in the succession of calls, and by now her initial enthusiasm for the work had faded into total disenchantment.

Nicholas joined her immediately after the departure of Hernández. "Anything of interest?" he asked.

"Absolutely nothing. A dead loss. Everyone in this country seems to be looking for a handout or trying to sell you something. I think maybe you don't need my services after all."

Nicholas smiled. "Thanks, anyway, for all your help. Now leave those bloody telephones, and come and join me for a drink. We've got just under an hour to spare. Have you got all your things packed?"

Regina nodded and pointed to her suitcase. As he picked it up and led the way back to his apartment, she noted that he was immaculately dressed in a dark-blue, tailor-made suit. It fitted his slim figure too well for him to be carrying a gun.

Jaime Muzquiz cursed when he turned into Hamburgo and confronted a police-mounted roadblock. The man offering a ten-million-dollar reward had promised that any information would be treated in strictest confidence. Now it looked like he was going to be arrested.

He wanted to turn back, but with cars parked either side, there was no room to manoeuvre. Then, as he neared the roadblock, two policemen closed on his green-and-white VW Beetle. "Sorry, officer," he blurted out. "I think I have taken a wrong turning."

One of the policemen looked at the cab's side door bearing the logo, *Radiotaxi Reforma.* "You are booked to pick up a passenger from *Apartamentos Orleáns?*"

Muzquiz thought about lying but lost his nerve. *"Sí. "*

"You are in the right street. You can carry on."

His arrival was perfectly timed. At that moment, facing TV cameras and a battery of hand-held tape recorders, Nicholas was saying that he had no time to answer questions because he had to leave at once.

Then he concluded, "However, you are all welcome to join me. I am hoping to find a suspect who left Chapultepec

Park immediately after the crime."

Hernández, standing beside him, was about to say that everyone must now clear the street. But his words were pre-empted. Immediately, as the taxi pulled up, there was a mad stampede towards parked cars.

"Pinche hijo de puta," exclaimed Vargas as, clinging to the shoulder-strap supporting his camera, he began to run the two blocks back to his car. However, such was the traffic congestion on Hamburgo, that he had no difficulty catching up with the convoy, which was heading towards Reforma, led by Muzquiz's taxi with a police motor cyclist on either side.

Some fifteen minutes later, to his utter astonishment, a blaspheming Vargas found himself on República del Perú, within walking distance of the offices of *El Informador*. He was right back where he had started, and all hope of snapping the Greek with his Mexican hooker was lost.

By the time he reached the entrance to the offices, it had been sealed off by the police. And when he tried to gain entry, arguing that this was his place of work, he received the same short shrift as all other protesting reporters. "No one goes in until Señor Stephanopoulos comes out."

At that precise moment, Regina Marke was stepping into a taxi outside *Apartamentos Orleáns*. Two policemen remained on duty there. But, just as Nicholas had anticipated, all the news hounds had seemingly departed. She never noticed the black BMW that trailed behind at a distance, then closed up in heavy traffic as they crossed over *El Angel* on Reforma.

It took only ten minutes to reach her destination on Rio Rhin Street: a characterless four-storey building— dwarfed by nearby foreign embassies— that had been shattered by the 1985 earthquake, then redesigned like a wine rack to create the maximum number of pigeon-hole apartments.

As the taxi pulled away, Regina bent down to pick up her suitcase. Simultaneously, the black BMW took the vacated space, its onside rear door swinging open before it had stopped.

"Hey, watch out!" said Regina, as the open door missed her by no more than an inch. Then, before she knew what was happening, a large, swarthy man had got out of the car and grabbed her left arm. *"Súbete,"* he snarled, at the same time forcing her towards the back seat.

279

She grabbed onto the doorframe. A savage blow to the wrist forced her to let go. Then, as she was bundled into the car, she saw that another man was seated on the far side. In his left hand he held a .38 revolver.

It had all happened in no more than four or five seconds, and unobserved by a single passer-by. The last thing Regina could remember was a sudden sharp pain as something plunged into her left upper arm. Thereafter, all was a total blank.

"There is a Señor Stephanopoulos outside. He insists on seeing you. And he has a policeman with him."

The announcement by his flustered young secretary prompted Miguel Ramos to raise his bushy eyebrows, nothing more. The chain-smoking editor of *El Informador* was too old and too hard-bitten to be surprised by anything this late in his career.

"Really? Show the gentlemen in."

He stood up as three men entered his smoky, paper-strewn office. He immediately recognised Stephanopoulos from his recent television appearance. He had also seen the accompanying police sergeant before, but he couldn't quite place him. The third man, dressed in a grubby open-neck pink shirt and clutching a cloth cap, was a complete stranger.

"Well, *señores,* this is a great honour! Do please take a seat. Marta, could you please bring in an extra chair. Now how can I be of service to you?"

Nicholas began by introducing himself, and then the third man who had been left standing. "This is Señor Muzquiz of the *Radiotaxi Reforma*. On January 25, shortly after members of my family were killed in the *Bosque de Chapultepec*, he picked up a passenger outside the park. He delivered him to this address. I want to trace this man, and I am wondering whether you might be able to identify him."

Ramos paused thoughtfully before replying. "That was a Sunday, as I recall. Our offices would have been closed." He smiled. "It is one of the luxuries of usually publishing only once a week, on a Thursday."

"This man, as I understand it, was middle-aged, fat and balding, and carrying some kind of duffle bag. Isn't that right, Señor Muzquiz? Señor Muzquiz!"

But the taxi driver wasn't listening. "That's him!" he

cried out. "That's him! I'd remember that fat face anywhere. "Muzquiz had moved to one side of the small office, and was stabbing his index finger at a staff picture on the wall.

Ramos got up to join him. "Ah, *sí.* That's Alfredo Gómez. Used to write our main gossip column. But he ain't with us anymore."

"So where is he?" asked Nicholas.

"Last I heard he was in Cancún, working on some tourist rag. Just about right for him, the sonofabitch."

"Why do you say that?"

"I should have thought you would have known. The *hijo de puta* had exclusive pictures of the killings in the park. But he kept them for himself. Tried to make a TV deal, and didn't even give us some stills for a follow-up. Everyone knew about it."

"Everyone?"

"Well, certainly the police knew about it." He looked towards the sergeant who had been delegated to accompany Nicholas."They took him in for questioning. Soon after that, he quit our paper. Wouldn't talk about it, and we never did know what happened to his pictures."

"That's very interesting," said Nicholas. "But how did he happen to be in the park at such a critical time?"

Ramos lit a fresh cigarette from his smouldering stub. "Good question, *señor.* Afraid I don't know the answer. Must have had a tip-off. But he always kept his sources to himself. Gómez was that kind of motherfucker."

The veteran editor grinned, his voice unwavering as he lied through his nicotine-stained teeth. He had no liking for Guillermo Velázquez. But he had no intention of naming a contracted informer, and risking his job this late in his career.

"Is there anything else you can tell me?" Nicholas asked. "Perhaps something about this man Gómez. Who were his close friends, for example?"

Ramos paused. "Can't help you there. In fact, I can't imagine Gómez having any friends at all. If you want to know any more, I would suggest that you ask the police. They must know all about the *cabrón.*

"Oh, but there is one thing that might help. I believe my secretary has a forwarding address for Gómez's mail. Let me check with her."

As they prepared to leave, Ramos handed Nicholas his business card, with a Cancún address scribbled on the back.

281

"Here it is, *señor*. In return, I wonder if you could answer a few questions about your private investigation. Firstly..."

Nicholas cut him short. "Sorry. It's too soon to say anything. But thank you for your help."

"My pleasure. But before you leave, *señor*, could you please at least allow us to take a photograph?"

Nicholas shrugged. "Okay."

The picture was taken by a reporter, artfully with an *El Informador* advertising poster visible in the background. It showed Ramos shaking Nicholas by the hand, and a widely grinning taxi driver looking directly at the camera. Muzquiz still cherished real hopes of collecting the ten-million-dollar reward.

Outside, Nicholas was again besieged by reporters and photographers. With the help of his police escort, he pushed his way through to Muzquiz's cab. Then, to the confusion of reporters, he parried shouted their questions with one parting remark: "We have a suspect. If you want to know more, talk to the editor of *El Informador*."

No one took up his suggestion. Instead, everyone piled into cars to trail him back to *Apartamentos Orleáns—* everyone, that is, except Vargas. The nonplussed reporter went to check with his editor on the latest developments.

Ramos enjoyed the moment. "What the hell are you doing back at the office, Vargas?" he shouted. "I told you to follow that bloody Greek wherever he goes. Get your fat arse out of here."

Regina Marke thought she had been dreaming. But then, as she looked around, reality slowly dawned on her. She found that she was lying on a plain wooden bunk, her head resting on a grubby white mattress, her body covered by a black-yellow-and-red striped blanket. High above, in the centre of a timber-beamed ceiling, a single light bulb glowed, vaguely outlining a large, bare room.

Physically, she felt fine: indeed, unusually refreshed. But the surroundings were totally foreign. Except for the bunk, the room was unfurnished, a dank, gloomy place with a cement-coloured stone floor and unwashed adobe walls. In a far corner she saw a metal bucket - presumably for bodily functions. Otherwise, all was empty space.

Her first instinctive act was to check the time. She

discovered that her wrist-watch was gone, along with her silver bracelet. At the top of the far wall, some twelve feet high, she saw the room's solitary window: a small square of dusty, cobwebbed glass, fronted by two iron bars. No light filtered through, and she surmised that it must be after seven o'clock dusk. It meant that, since her arrival at her apartment on Rio Rhin, at least seven-and-a-half hours were unaccounted for!

Regina's next impulse was to seek a way out. Five stone steps led up to the only exit, a sturdy wooden door without a lock. She turned the handle, then pushed against the door with her right shoulder. It would not move. Thereafter, she kept hammering with her fist, repeatedly shouting, in both Spanish and English, "*Socorro! Hay alguien ahí?* Help! Is anyone there?"

For a full minute, she beat on the door and shouted. There was no sound from beyond. Finally, she sat on the bunk and tried to rationalise her situation. When being bundled into a car— her last memory— she had had a suitcase, and was carrying a shoulder bag and tweed jacket. The suitcase and bag were missing, together with her watch and bracelet. But apart from a slight soreness in her upper left arm, she felt completely unharmed. Her clothing— red skirt and white cotton blouse— was badly creased, but undamaged. The tweed jacket lay at the foot of the bunk.

Where was she? And why had she been abducted? Her surroundings suggested a basement or large cellar. It could be anywhere. To the latter question, she could think of only one logical answer: she had been kidnapped to seek a ransom from Nicholas Stephanopoulos, whose wealth had been so widely publicised.

"*Señor*, why you not go to Cancún and find this *hombre* Gómez?"

"Maybe later," replied Nicholas. "But first I want to see this *lucha libre*."

Unlike Jaime Muzquiz, so anxious about pursuing the $10 million reward, his mind was not focused on tracing Alfredo Gómez. It might be a useful lead, but obviously the man could not have been directly involved in the killings. His gut feeling was that the mysterious gringo at the Obregón Monument would be more useful.

Also, he had something else on his mind as he settled

in the front seat alongside Muzquiz. Indeed, he did not even trouble to look back as they pulled away from *Apartamentos Orleáns*. If he had done so, he would have seen that they were followed by a police car, while a second police car had pulled across the street, blocking the path of persistent reporters.

It was 8 p.m. and Nicholas was thinking that just about now his father would be going under the knife again at Papworth Hospital. They had promised to call him on his mobile as soon as the six-hour operation was over.

Two hours earlier, Stavros Stephanopoulos had sounded remarkably cheerful on the phone. "No big deal, Nikki. Like I always say: been there, done that. When it's all over, I'm thinking of taking the *Prometheus* to the Mexican west coast. Could meet you off Zihuatanejo. It's great down there."

He was feeling fine, he said. "Only trouble is that they have shaved my bloody chest again. That's the penalty for being so hairy. But it has its advantage, too. When it grows back, it will hide the fucking great scar again. Ha, ha!"

But Nicholas knew his father too well to be fooled. It was typically Greek bravado. The odds of his heart withstanding this second operation were no better than 50-50. The life-loving old man must really be shit-scared.

As he thought about it, Nicholas instinctively felt inside his left-hand pocket to double-check that he had his mobile with him. Once again, for convenience, he was wearing his fawn safari jacket over a yellow polo-neck sweater. Deep in the right pocket lay his snub-nosed Smith and Wesson.

Having largely followed his Athenian routine, Nicholas was now fully keyed-up for whatever the evening might bring. From 1 to 3 p.m., he had taken his siesta. After a shower had come the *apogevmataki,* or "little afternoon", a one-hour period of gradually getting back into the full working swing, followed by the *apogevma,* afternoon proper, when he had ploughed through the wholly disappointing messages left on the answering machines.

Back in Athens, he would now be out for a gentle jog in the *vradaki,* the "little evening", before embarking on the *vradi*, the evening proper, which usually began around 9 p.m. with a leisurely dinner. *Nichta* (night) came at some undefined time after midnight, and in spring and summer it was not unusual for his day to end around 2 a.m., taking coffee with friends in Kolonaki Square. Thus every weekday was split into two distinctly separate parts of work and pleasure.

"What you mean, *maybe later*?" Muzquiz persisted, as they turned off Hamburgo, heading towards the main artery of Arcos de Belen. "Don't you think my information is valuable, *señor?*"

Nicholas was beginning to wonder whether he had made a mistake in booking the driver again. "Of course, I do, Jaime. It could be an important clue. But I just don't want to talk about it now."

The calculated switch to first-name terms seemed to have done the trick. Muzquiz turned his head and grinned. "Okay, *señor*. As you wish."

"Tell me about this Arena México, Jaime. Can I get something to eat there?"

"Eat? No, *señor*. They don't sell food - and no hard liquor. I always take my own, some tacos and a few cans of *cerveza*. Should we stop off, and get something at a takeaway?"

"No. It's not important. I can always go to a restaurant afterwards. What time does this *lucha libre* finish?"

"Oh, could be near midnight. It depends. There are usually six or seven bouts, each lasting around thirty minutes or so. But you can never tell how much fighting there will be in-between. You have not seen *lucha libre* before?"

Muzquiz, it emerged, was a true aficionado of the sport. "I go to fights all over Mexico City. Arena Coliseo, Pista Arena Revolución, Arena Nezahualcoyotl, Arena Apatalco, Toreo, Arena López Mateos... been to them all, seen all the greats of the past twenty years.

He went on to list a catalogue of curious names: El Santo, Fray Tormenta, Aguila Solitaria, El Misterioso, Los Villanos, Médico Asesino, Superbarrio..." 'Course, it's not what it used to be. Too many team bouts, too many preliminaries between females, dwarfs, hunchbacks and the like. Getting too much like a circus. But then that's what packs them in. So many women and children want to go now."

"How about tonight?" asked Nicholas. "Will there be any good fights?"

Muzquiz grunted. "Huh! Tonight doesn't count. We don't normally have *lucha libre* on a Tuesday. This is a one-off, a special charity night. They have put up the prices, but it's all joke or exhibition stuff, no serious bouts for a championship."

"So you don't fancy going? I thought maybe I could buy you a ticket."

"Ooh, *señor!* That would be great. *Muchas gracias.* I just want to see the main attraction: El Nuevo Santo versus Médico de la Muerte. It's only a friendly, but El Nuevo Santo is always worth seeing. He's a middleweight, only eighty-seven kilos. But ooh, so fast! Runs circles round much bigger guys. *Magia!*

"Course, he will never be in the class of the original Santo. He was the greatest of them all. You know, I actually cried when he died of a heart attack. Funny thing. It shook me up more than the big earthquake that came soon after."

"Must have been quite a guy. What was his real name?"

"Rodolfo Guzmán Huerta. But not many people remember that. He will always be El Santo, Enmascarado de Plata, because he always wore a silver mask. Even kept it on when he was bonking girls in the movies. And he's still wearing it now, you know. In his tomb!

"I'll tell you something: if I could choose to be anyone in the world, I would be another El Santo. Bugger being *Presidente* or *El Papa.* Think about it. El Santo was the most popular sportsman in all México. Yet he could walk down the street completely unrecognised. When he took off his mask, then he really was masked. Invisible! Ha, ha!"

"Is it like that for the guy wrestling tonight, this Nuevo Santo?"

"Sure. Even more so. Nobody even knows his real name. Not like El Santo; you see, he had started fighting under his real name before the craze for wearing masks began. He was *un rudo* then, and no one took any notice of him. No mystery, you see."

"What do you mean '*rudo*'?"

"Oh, *señor!* You really don't know *lucha libre!* That's what it's all about: the bad guys against the good guys, *rudos* versus *técnicos.* You'll see what I mean tonight. Now this Médico de la Muerte, he's a true *rudo,* an ugly, hairy fucker in a black mask, and he can fight real dirty.

"It will be an interesting fight. But it's still only an exhibition match. Now, when they fight for real— for the championship— that will be really something. They'll make millions out of the television rights. And one of them is going to need it. For the loser will be stripped of his mask and can

286

never wear it again. And that means curtains for his career. No more big pay days. *Se acabó!*"

They were joining heavy traffic now as they turned off Arcos de Belen into Colonia Doctores. Muzquiz advised that they park down a side street, and walk the rest of the way. As they did so, Nicholas noted that a police car had pulled up some twenty yards behind.

Outside Arena México, a long line of men, women and children were queuing for the cheaper seats. Nicholas went directly to the main box office, and asked if they had a ticket left in his name. The woman behind the grill went away to check, then returned with a brown envelope marked *Para el Señor Stephanopoulos*. It contained an orange cheque-shaped ticket, numbered B17 and over-stamped: *apartados*.

Nicholas asked if perhaps he could buy a seat nearby - *para mi amigo*. The lady shook her head. "No chance, *señor*. All the best seats are reserved. Your friend will have to get in the line. Have a good evening."

"Sorry," said Nicholas, turning towards Muzquiz. He pulled out his wallet and handed him two 100-peso bills. "Will this be enough to cover the fare, and get you a ticket?"

The driver beamed. "Ah, *sí, señor*. More than enough. Should I meet you here after the fights?"

"No, *mi amigo*. I don't know when I'll be leaving. But thanks again, and here's another hundred for all your help so far. I promise to let you know what happens if and when I catch up with that Gómez fellow. *Buenas noches!*"

At 8.15 p.m., there was a call on Nicholas' private line at *Apartamentos Orleáns*. Automatically, the answering machine announced, "I am not at home at the present time, but if you will leave your name and number I will get back to you as soon as possible. Please leave your details and message after the bleep."

The caller spoke in a cultured Spanish voice, slowly and deliberately, as though reading a prepared statement:

Señor Stephanopoulos, ee have your Señorita Marke in our custody. At this moment, she is unharmed. But if you wish for her to remain alive, you will obey the following instructions.

At the earliest possible time, you will announce on

287

television that you no longer see any purpose in pursuing your inquiry into the Chapultepec Park killings. You are therefore withdrawing your offer of a reward, and returning to Greece at once.

Tomorrow morning, Señorita Marke will be given an injection of heroin. The dosage will be increased every day until you have made the above announcement, and have departed from México.

For your guidance, Señorita Marke will be fully addicted in four days, and one week from now, she will have died of an overdose, So do not delay.

CHAPTER 22

Arena México is a square, 16,402-seater auditorium, comprising two floors with the ring set in the centre. The front rows— predominantly reserved for long-term debenture-holders— are at ground level; thereafter, rows are tiered, the sections becoming progressively cheaper the higher you go. Nicholas was ushered to a second row seat beside the main aisle, and for the first time in his life he felt positively under-dressed. Around him were men in tuxedos and women in evening gowns. In the adjacent seat, on his right, sat a large, middle-aged woman wearing a sable coat and flashing chunky jewellery on both wrists and hands. Cigar smoke filled the air.

In contrast, the scene further back was a riot of colour and disorderly activity: people standing up to wave and shout to recognised friends, families dispensing tacos and colas as though out for a picnic, men popping beer cans from their six-packs. Nicholas was surprised to see so many children in the audience. Those under nine had got in free; also, a large number of unescorted elderly women.

He looked all round perchance to spot his anonymous gringo contact. But the crowd appeared to be wholly Mexican. The woman next to him certainly was. In a loud voice, she was telling her female companion about the trouble she had had with her new maid from Yucatán. "I couldn't believe it. Used one of my best bathroom towels when she had her period. *India mugrosa*! Of course, I had to get rid of her."

Then, to Nicholas' surprise, Señora Sable suddenly turned her head towards him. "*Buenas tardes, señor*. I have not seen you here before. You are *un turista* perhaps?"

"*Sí, señora.*"

"Ah, I thought so. Let me guess : *un americano?*"

"*Sí, señora.*"

She smiled, revealing deep powdered-over laugh lines. "I can always tell. It's the way you *americanos* dress. So nice and casual." Unprompted, she went on to explain that she didn't like dressing formally for *lucha libre*. But her husband

289

expected it. "He would have been here tonight, but at the last minute he was called away to Veracruz on some urgent oil business. He won't be back for at least a week."

Nicholas couldn't be sure but, from the way she fixed him with a bright-eyed look, he suspected that there was some hidden message in her words. He simply smiled back. At that moment the arena lights dimmed. There was a roll on some distant, unseen drums, and then spotlights flooded the ring where a tuxedoed master of ceremonies proceeded to welcome fans to Arena México, and thank them - inaudibly - for supporting a most worthy charity.

Cries of "*No se oye!*" came from the gallery. After adjusting his microphone, he continued, "As you know, all profits from tonight's meeting will be going to the Iztapalapa Orphanage Fund founded by El Nuevo Santo. Moreover, all the leading contestants have generously agreed to waive their usual fee - all, that is, except Médico de la Muerte."

Grinning, he raised his hands to both ears while the crowd responded with a cacophony of jeers, boos, and foot-stamping, plus blasts by a few who had brought their own trumpets.

"*Miserable hijo de puta,*" said Señora Sable, again smiling at Nicholas. "He's not really a doctor, you know. Just a bloody dentist. I hear he makes a bomb by wearing his mask when he's pulling teeth."

Another roll of drums, and seemingly out of nowhere a group of midgets in purple or yellow mini-shorts came bounding down the centre aisle, the leader cartwheeling past Nicholas, and then grabbing onto to the middle rope to perform a prodigious somersault to enter the ring.

"A warm welcome for our old friends, *Los Munchkins,*" the master of ceremonies exhorted. "And for their new challengers, all the way from Guadalajara: *Los Enanos.*"

The ensuing five-a-side battle— a chaotic display, more of acrobatics than wrestling— left Nicholas totally bemused. Midgets were flying everywhere, hurled both around and out of the ring. Two were rolling in the aisle where, to the loud approval of the crowd, a jockstrapped Munchkin was deprived of his skimpy shorts. And once, when an Enano was pinned to the floor, his four comrades threw themselves on the referee as he knelt down to begin the count to three.

After thirty minutes of mayhem, the referee blew a

whistle, raised his arms and proclaimed that somehow the Munchkins had been adjudged the winners. Immediately, the Enanos began prancing about the ring, taunting the Munchkins with shouted insults and crude fist-in-the-armpit gestures, at which point, uncontrolled fighting broke out for another three minutes.

The next two bouts, though featuring only two and three wrestlers to a side respectively, were no more comprehensible to Nicholas. One moment the contestants were engaged singly, the next minute collectively. They performed awesome feats of strength and agility, but— as with European professional wrestling he had seen on Greek television— it all seemed too well choreographed, the cries and expressions of agony a little too contrived.

He wanted to leave, and in the short intervals between each subsequent bout he looked around, hoping and praying that someone would make contact with him soon. But no one came, and now it was past eleven o'clock. Two heavyweights— one black-masked and self-evidently the villain— were entwined on the canvas. Meanwhile, the loudest cheers rose from the rear of the auditorium, where plain clothes officials were forcibly frogmarching some drunks to the nearest exit.

Then it came: the referee's verdict in favour of the man in the mask, and all at once the entire arena erupted with boos and catcalls. The despised victor responded by advancing to the ropes and jerking his right arm in a fuck-you-all gesture.

"*Baje la cabeza*!" Señora Sable shouted. And Nicholas automatically obeyed, ducking down just before one of several beer cans flashed over his head, and into the ring.

The lady was not amused. "They should not allow people to bring in their own booze. My husband says that one day someone is going to get badly cut... and it could lead to someone using a gun or a knife in reply."

Then she smiled, simultaneously brushing back her hair on one side in a positively provocative manner. "Never mind. Now it's time for the big one. El Nuevo Santo. Oooh! He's lovely!"

The lights dimmed again, and a few minutes later a fanfare of trumpets sounded. Nicholas turned to look up the main aisle. Then he noticed that the eyes of the hushed crowd were fixed not backward, but upward. Suddenly a lone spotlight focussed on the upper gallery, and there, from out of the darkness, came a seemingly ethereal figure - bright silver and white, and floating gently downwards as though on gossamer wings.

Some sixteen thousand voices cheered and chanted in unison: *Santo! Santo! Santo!* Now, as the spectral being drew near, Nicholas could see that a man was hanging by a waist harness from a cable and pulley that must have been artfully fixed into position during the brief semi-darkness. He wore a billowing cloak, shorts, kneepads and boots— all brilliant white— and, above his silver-masked head, was a snow-white halo.

Everyone was standing now. And the tumultuous ovation went on for a full five minutes as El Nuevo Santo gracefully landed ringside, unbuckled his harness, neatly propelled himself over the ropes, and then paraded, arms aloft, to each side of the ring in turn.

Nicholas looked towards Señora Sable. The lady was waving her bejewelled hands, and screaming with orgasmic abandon.

In his corner, El Nuevos Santos removed the halo supported by wires from his white bandeau; then, aided by two bikini-clad young ladies, he shed his white cloak to reveal a swarthy, finely muscled physique. Señora Sable's screams proclaimed her climax.

Now came a slow, steady beat of drums, *basso profondo*, doom-laden. This time the entrance spotlight was turned to the head of the main aisle, and there emerged the antithesis of El Nuevo Santo: a burly, hairy-chested figure who, in his open jet-black cloak and matching mask, positively exuded evil and menace. He carried a doctor's bag, and was succeeded by a big-busted woman dressed as a nurse.

All the way to the ring, they booed and hissed at Médico de la Muerte. On arrival, he strode directly across to his opponent and eyeballed him mask to mask. Then, retiring to his own corner, he had his black cloak removed by his "nurse". In contrast to El Nuevo Santo, he looked a veritable behemoth, muscle-bound and overweight.

Doctor Death now held up his hands at chin level, extending his thick fingers in the posture of a surgeon about to be gloved before performing an operation. Then he fixed his eyes on his opponent, and drew his right hand across his own throat as though wielding an invisible scalpel. The

292

announcer's microphone picked up his words: "Time, *mi amigo*, for your tracheotomy. And no anaesthetic."

Señora Sable's dark, expressive eyes were glaring daggers now. "*Cerdo asqueroso!*" she screeched.

Her subsequent insults— and the formal introductions— were drowned by a deafening roar of outrage when Médico de la Muerte, not waiting for the starter's bell, swung a rabbit punch to the back of his opponent's neck. It was the most effective blow he landed that evening.

After a delayed start, allowing him to be attended by his cornerman, El Nuevo Santo side-stepped the bull-like charge of Médico de la Muerte, and proceeded to dance around the ring in the style of an agile boxer, but here using open hands, not fists, as he regularly slapped his opponent across the face, and each time ghosted untouched away.

Señora Sable was vigorously applauding and screaming encouragement. "See that?" she said to Nicholas. "He's doing his Muhammad Ali shuffle. That clumsy oaf will never catch him." And for two minutes more, she was proved absolutely right.

But the crowd was thirsting for action. They began slow hand-clapping, and in the third minute they got the bodily contact they wanted. Following another derisory slap in the face, Médico de la Muerte screamed that he had been blinded by a thumb poke in the eye, and couldn't go on. At the referee's signal, El Nuevo Santo stood back to allow his opponent to be examined, and at that moment, instantly and miraculously, the Doctor regained his sight. He lunged forward and embraced his opponent in a bear hug, lifting him clean off the floor.

The silver mask of *el santo* concealed any agony in the face, but his gasping for air sounded real enough, and when the *rudo* released his vice-like grip, the *técnico* slumped to the canvas like a sack of *papas*. At once Médico de la Muerte launched himself into the air, his black boots directed at his opponent's head.

With only a split second to spare, El Nuevo Santo rolled to one side, grabbed a descending ankle with both hands, and twisted it so vigorously that Médico de la Muerte screamed out in pain before crashing face-down to the floor beside him. *El santo* was on top of his adversary now, pulling back his head, and at the same time, pressing his right knee into the small of his back.

293

"Kill him! Kill him," screeched Señora Sable.

Since Médico de la Muerte had both shoulders pinned to the canvas, the referee slowly began the mandatory count. "*Más rapido!*" shouted the crowd, and after at least five seconds had elapsed, the count of three was reached to register an official fall.

Thereafter El Nuevo Santo resumed his slap-and-run approach, once eluding a charge by grabbing the bull's shoulders, and performing an extraordinary overhead somersault worthy of an Olympic gymnast. The fans began laughing at Médico de la Muerte. He responded by standing still in the centre of the ring, beckoning and shouting for *la bailarina* to come and get him.

The onus was on *el santo* now. This time, hurling himself into the air, he led with his feet, striking the *rudo* so forcefully in the stomach that he was sent reeling backwards with his head and shoulders protruding through the ropes. El Nuevo Santos grabbed both his ankles, and propelled him clean out of the ring.

Next, to the delight of the crowd, their hero vaulted over the ropes to land on the villain outside the ring. Nicholas never knew precisely what followed.

He saw two sweat-soaked masked figures rolling entwined on the floor, only a few yards away. He watched in wonder as a woman in front of Señora Sable began jabbing her umbrella in the direction of Médico de la Muerte's groin. And he physically felt the proximity of fans, who were spilling down the main aisle to get a clearer view.

At that moment, amid the total confusion, a stranger grabbed his left arm and rasped, "Mr. Stephanopoulos, follow me. NOW." It was the same burly, crew cut man who had been clubbed by the police after he had thrust a business card into his hand outside *Apartamentos Orleáns.*

Unhesitatingly, Nicholas followed the man as he forced a way up the aisle. Thirty rows back, beyond a group of brawling fans, they turned into a deserted corridor, and the stranger led him towards a door marked *Salida de Emergencia.* The black Honda outside already had the engine running.

Within five minutes of witnessing the fracas in Arena México, Nicholas found himself in the back seat of a car heading east on Dr Río de la Loza. He looked out the rear window, more curious than anxious.

His back-seat companion spoke in English. "Don't worry, buddy. No one is following you now. Relax. You are with friends. Let me introduce myself. The name's McClellan, Brad McClellan. Nice to meet you at last." And he shook Nicholas by the hand.

Outside Arena México, a man in a dark-brown suit sat in a police car with his head tilted back, and a bloodstained handkerchief clutched to his nose. Meanwhile, his uniformed driver was on the radio to headquarters, reporting that they had lost contact with Stephanopoulos.

"Let's cruise around," said the man with the nosebleed. "Maybe we can spot the taxi he came in." But he already knew it was virtually hopeless, and he was cursing his luck in somehow getting caught up in the brawl between fans.

His only hope now was that nothing had happened to the Greek *hombre,* and that perhaps they would find him safely back at *Apartamentos Orleáns.* Otherwise, as he well knew, he would be back on traffic duty, once again having to depend on *la mordida* to make a living wage.

The black Honda made so many turns down ill-lit side streets that Nicholas was totally disorientated. "Where are we going?" he asked.

"To a friend's house," said McClellan. "Not too far now."

"So, exactly who are you, and who is this friend?"

"Later. All will be explained in good time."

"The message on your business card said you could help me? Is that right?"

"Absolutely. But this friend of mine may be able to help you even more. Just be patient. Don't know about you, but I'm famished. As soon as we get there, I'm going to attack a nice juicy steak."

Something about the stranger's manner made Nicholas feel totally relaxed. He released his grip on the gun in his right-hand pocket. "Can you make that two steaks? I haven't eaten properly all day."

"No problem. Tell me, Nicholas: You don't mind if I call you, Nicholas; do you? How did you enjoy the fights?"

"Interesting. But not exactly my idea of sport."

"Yeah! You can say that again. But I thought the fighting outside the ring was pretty good. Those brawling fans certainly made sure that we weren't followed."

"Yes, that was a bit of luck."

"Luck, my fucking foot!" McClellan grinned broadly. "It took quite a few pesos to get those guys to become supporters of Médico de la Muerte. They did it well."

For the second time now Nicholas looked at his wristwatch, and when McClellan asked him why he was so interested in the time, he explained that his father was undergoing a heart bypass operation, and that he was awaiting a call from the hospital in England.

McClellan exploded. "My God! Heaven protect us from amateurs! You mean to say you are actually carrying a mobile? Let me have it at once. Rodrigo, stop the car!"

He then went on to explain that the Mexican police could track mobile phone users through the telephone company computer. "Bloody hell! You might as well go around with a beeper or an implanted transmitter. Tell the whole bloody world where we are!"

"Sorry," said Nicholas. "I didn't know. But at least no harm has been done. I haven't used it today."

"Bollocks! Don't matter whether you are using it or not. They emit signals automatically every half-hour. We've got to get rid of the thing... NOW!"

After being assured that he could ring the hospital from their destination, Nicholas reluctantly handed over his mobile. McClellan got out, placed it under the front wheel of the Honda, and ordered the man he called Rodrigo to drive on.

Some five minutes later the Honda turned down a cul de sac, passing by warehouses in what seemed to be an industrial estate. There were no streetlights now, but directly ahead, in the beam of their headlamps, Nicholas saw a large wooden board with graffiti scrawled around the large printed words "*METALMECÁNICA JERÓNIMO.*"

"I'll do it," said McClellan as they halted before a broad iron-barred gateway topped with barbed wire. After removing a padlock and chain, he swung the gate open; then, speaking for the first time, the driver called out, "*Muchas gracias.*"

A few yards beyond the gateway, McClellan pushed open two barn-like doors, and Rodrigo drove on to park inside. The American closed the doors behind them, and seconds later he hit a light switch to reveal a cavernous, disused workshop.

"Better lock up, Rod," he said, handing the driver a key.

"Follow me, Nicholas. We'll get you to a telephone right away."

He threaded his way through a vast array of dust-covered workbenches and rusted machinery. Then, in a far corner, he mounted a spiral, wrought iron staircase leading up to a heavy, oaken door. Again, he produced a key and turned the lock.

Within, Nicholas was surprised to see an area that looked positively pristine in contrast to the scene below. Strip lighting set between slanting beams flooded an enormous, open-plan room with bare, whitewashed walls and polished parquet flooring. The room was partially divided by a wicker screen: one side forming a lounge furnished with a contemporary four-piece suite, several pouffes, a coffee table, drinks cabinet and television; the other side occupied by a dining table and four chairs, a long walnut sideboard, and, incongruously, a cork-matted corner section with an exercise cycle and assorted weightlifting equipment. The place, he noted, was totally functional— not a single decorative item in sight.

Almost immediately, Nicholas moved towards the sideboard on which there was a telephone. "Not that one," said McClellan. "I expect you'd like some privacy. There's another phone in the study. This way."

From the dining area, a corridor led off at a right angle to a kitchen, three single bedrooms, a bathroom, and, at the end, a small room with a desk, computer and telephone.

"You can ring from here. Just one small point. I'm afraid I can't give you our number so that you can have the hospital call you back. Too risky. But you can always ring again from here whenever you like. Okay?"

Nicholas didn't see the need for such security, but he was not going to waste time seeking an explanation. He nodded and took out his Filofax to get the Papworth Hospital number.

"I hope it's good news," said McClellan, and he closed the study door behind him as he left.

Alerted by the sound of bolts being drawn back, Regina Marke sprang to her feet. For nearly two hours, she had remained seated upright on a mattress which she had removed from its bunk and laid against a wall, directly alongside the five stone steps leading up to the door. Within reach of her left arm, strategically placed in readiness, stood an empty tin bucket.

The heavy, wooden door opened inwards and away from her. Seconds later, Regina saw a blue denim trouser leg reach the third step that was level with her waist. Instantly, according to plan, she swung the bucket by its handle.

Propelled with all the strength she could muster, the bucket caught the entrant on a kneecap, and brought him crashing to the floor below. Ahead of him flew a wooden tray, a plate, two tacos and a plastic cup of orange juice.

At once, Regina stepped round the prostrate figure, and made a dash up the steps. But the doorway was blocked by a second, much older man. Towering over her, he grabbed her two-handed by the hair, forced her to her knees, and then propelled her backwards.

By now, the other man had got to his feet. As Regina sprawled on her back in front of him, he cried out, "*Pinche puta,*" then savagely kicked her in the ribs.

"That's enough, Francisco," said the man on the stairs. "Just leave her there. If she wants her supper, she can scrape it off the floor."

The man called Francisco glared at Regina, and he gobbed on her dress as he limped his way towards the steps. The other man stepped back to let him pass, then reappeared in the doorway.

"I came to see whether you had fully recovered," he said. "Obviously, you have. Don't bother to get up. That pose will do fine."

Having struggled into a kneeling position, Regina noticed for the first time that the man had a camera in a leather case hanging on a strap around his neck. Now he lifted it from his waist and lined up the lens. The camera flashed twice. "That will do fine."

"You are wasting your time," said Regina, grimacing with pain as she tried to stand upright. "No one is going to pay a ransom for me."

The man smiled. "Sleep well, *señorita.*" And then he

298

was gone. The heavy door slammed behind him, followed by the sound of bolts being drawn back into place.

Finding it too painful to stand, Regina dragged herself over to the mattress and lay there, gently cradling her bruised ribs. Then, as she tried to rationalise her situation, her anxiety swelled to deep foreboding. Why had her captors not troubled to mask their faces? Why had one even been mentioned by name? Did they not fear that she might identify them when she was eventually released?

She could remember them well: the man called Francisco with a distinctive rat-like face and a Zapata moustache; the other man, perhaps in his sixties, tall, wiry, smartly dressed, and speaking with a markedly upper-class accent. And the latter, most strikingly, was completely bald.

The questions led her to only one logical and appalling conclusion: they had no intention of ever releasing her. And this, in turn, led her to the ultimate question: Why, once the ransom had been paid, should they keep her alive?

Returning from the study, Nicholas slumped in an easy chair and cupped his head in his hands. McClellan felt no need to ask about the news from the hospital. He turned off the television, went over to the drinks cabinet and poured a large brandy. "Here, drink this. I'll leave you alone for a while. We can talk later."

Nicholas dropped his hands. "It doesn't matter. There's nothing to talk about. I don't see how I can go on with this business - not now."

McClellan touched him on the shoulder. "I understand. It must be a terrible shock. I guess you'll need to get to England as soon as possible. Let me at least check the flights for you."

"England?" Nicholas looked up at the American, and then read his mind. "No, you don't understand. My father is okay - at least for the time being. He's in intensive care, on a ventilator machine. They will know more after forty-four hours. No, it's my assistant. Regina Marke. They've got her. Whoever *they* are."

Nicholas duly explained that, after calling the hospital, he had rung his private line at *Apartamentos Orleáns* to listen to any messages that had been left on the answering machine. There was only one, and he recalled it almost word for word.

"So you see. My hands are tied. *Christos*! I didn't think anything in the world could stop me. But this! If I let Regina die, I guess I will be no better than they are. There's no way out. I'll go on television tomorrow."

McClellan poured himself a Scotch, pulled up a chair, and sat facing Nicholas across the coffee table. "Yeah! You may be right. On the other hand, what is the guarantee that they will release her once you have made your announcement, and left the country? They might want to keep her indefinitely - just to make sure that you don't come back."

"I still don't see that I have any choice. Their demands are clear, and, in any case, I have no way of contacting them to discuss how and when she will be released. It's hopeless. I should never have got her involved."

McClellan smiled gently. "Relax. It's too late for you to do anything until the morning. In the meantime, you might as well enjoy a good meal. I'll put the steaks on now."

Nicholas' patience snapped. "Fuck the steaks! I want some facts... NOW! You have talked about a friend who might help. But who the hell is he? And who, for that matter, are you? Somehow, I don't believe you are a reporter with this— what do call it?— *Central Press Agency.*"

"You are absolutely right. But I was hoping to leave the explanations until my friend arrived. Anyway, as I have told you, my name is Brad McClellan. And no, I am not a newspaperman. Until two months ago, I was employed by the CIA. Now— officially at least— I am retired.

"The point is that my last assignment was to observe the PGR's investigation into the Chapultepec Park killings. I was one of two CIA men assigned to give what assistance we could. The FBI was represented, too, and, as you probably know, it was they who uncovered the Armenian connection.

"But that was a load of crap! We already knew the real reason for the killings, but we couldn't say anything.

"Ah! Did you hear that? Our friend has arrived home. Might be better if he helps me to explain the rest. Won't be a minute."

McClellan unlocked the oaken door, left it open and returned to his chair. A few seconds later, a swarthy, track-suited man entered the room, followed by Rodrigo, who locked the door behind him. Slipping off the large sports holdall that hung from his right shoulder, the stranger immediately strode

300

over to Nicholas and extended his right hand. "Señor Stephanopoulos, I presume. I am most pleased to meet you."

Nicholas shook hands, all the while studying the man's features. He did not recognise the face, a striking face, heavily pock-kmarked, with a strong square jaw and dark, expressive eyes that were somehow accentuated by what he took to be deep laughter lines. Yet something about the man's whole demeanour seemed vaguely familiar.

At once his unspoken question was answered. "In fact, *señor,* to be precise, we have met briefly before, though in rather undignified circumstances." Grinning, he walked over to his holdall lying on the floor, pulled back the zip and reached inside to produce a bright silver mask and a white halo.

"Remember these? Not so long ago I was wearing this mask, and rolling almost under your feet. So now, *señor*, you are a member of a very small, select club: the handful of people who have met El Nuevo Santo face to face.

"But let me introduce myself properly. My given name is Ramírez. Julio Ramírez. My kid brother, Manuel, is supposed to have killed your wife, your son and your father-in-law."

CHAPTER 23

Looking out through the dark-tinted windows of the white Mercedes, Nicholas saw a sign that told him they were bypassing Cuernavaca, heading south on Highway 95. They could not be far, he thought, from the home of Doña María Dolores Castillo de Tunaman, the reclusive stepmother-in-law whom he had never actually met. And with that thought came a tinge of guilt. Might the tragedy have somehow been averted if he had accompanied his family on their ill-fated visit to Mexico?

It was, he immediately realised, a pointless question, and he put it out of his mind. It was useless looking back. He had to think more positively, more rationally. Better still, for the moment, he should not be thinking at all; he should be getting some rest to be fully alert for the challenge ahead.

McClellan and Ramírez had the right idea. After their late-night session— talking into the early hours and consuming rather too much red wine— they had fallen asleep on the long drive south. But Nicholas could not switch off. His mind was still racing: a computer suddenly loaded with a mass of new data that required sorting and analysing as he sought to adjust to his new situation.

Overnight, his circumstances had totally changed. No longer was he in command of his own one-man mission of vengeance. He was now taking orders, trusting in the judgement of two strangers, who seemed to be far ahead of him in seeking out whoever was responsible for the killings in Chapultepec Park.

But was he doing the right thing agreeing to join them on the drive to Acapulco? After all, what did he really know about these characters? His gut feeling was that they were both honourable men. He believed everything they had said. And he had been impressed by their assurance that they were not interested in his reward money. Julio had added that, if they were successful, Nicholas might care to make a donation to his Orphanage Fund.

Yet the nagging suspicion remained— especially with McClellan— that they knew rather more than they had told him, that their motives were not exactly the same as his own. And he remembered his father's last words: *Don't trust anyone.*

The crew cut American was seated directly in front of him, alongside Rodrigo, who was now wearing a chauffeur's uniform, though for this stage of their journey he had discarded his cap and jacket, and had loosened his tie. To Nicholas' left, casually dressed in white flannels and an open-neck green silk shirt, his head resting on a cushion propped up against the rear side window, was the enigmatic Julio Ramírez.

Could he really trust them? Most importantly, was he right in not immediately returning to the *Apartamentos Orleáns,* and then meeting the demands of Regina's captors?

If his companions were correct— and they were so dogmatic about it— only direct, independent action offered any hope of saving Regina's life. And such action, they had argued, would become impossible if he returned to his apartments, and came under police surveillance again.

On the other hand, if he did not return, the kidnappers could not be certain that he had received their demands. And that uncertainty could buy them some extra time. Forty-eight hours. That was all they asked for. If they had not gained Regina's release in that time, then he still had the option of going on TV, and withdrawing his offer of a reward.

But what if they were wrong? What if the kidnappers immediately went ahead with their threat of injecting Regina with heroin? Could he afford to take the chance?

Now, in reconsidering his position, he thought over everything they had told him the night before, trying to evaluate the mass of information, and to see if he had overlooked some vital point, some critical flaw in their plan.

He closed his eyes. *"You won't like it."* Again and again, those words of McClellan echoed in Nicholas' mind as he thought about the big American, and all that he had said earlier in explaining the Chapultepec Park killings... And it was true. He didn't like it.

That previous evening, as he recalled, they had begun their discussion over drinks, while Rodrigo busied himself in the kitchen, preparing steak sandwiches. And, right from the start, he has raised the two questions that had haunted and driven him for the past eleven weeks: *Who was responsible for*

303

the killings of his wife, son and father-in-law? And why?

Unemotionally, the American had replied, "If you mean, who actually pulled the trigger, then I can give you a straight answer. The evidence conclusively shows that the killer was Jesús Moreno, a sergeant in the corps of Presidential Guards, and the commander of the fifty men responsible for patrolling Chapultepec Castle by day.

"There's no doubt about it. I've seen all the evidence gathered by the chief investigator, Comandante Barraza. He's a smart cookie, this Barraza; very efficient. And, believe me, we are greatly in his debt.

"Anyway, it's like this. Manuel Ramírez - Julio's brother - he was just a patsy, the fall guy. In fact, we believe that he was the first of five people to be killed in the park that day - shot between the eyes, at point-blank range, by Moreno.

"We may never know the precise details. But, as Barraza sees it, Moreno killed Manuel shortly before noon, using his .38 handgun, presumably fitted with a silencer. Then, after using the sniper's rifle for the other killings, he hurried down the stairs in time to pretend that he had been the first to arrive on the scene.

"Having met another guardsman, who does not appear to have been an accomplice, he then went back up the tower, fired a single shot in the air, and returned to claim that he had killed the assassin.

"It's Barraza's theory— strictly a theory— that Manuel and the rifle were smuggled into the tower at the end of Moreno's day shift the previous evening. Somehow, the guard commander then had the tower closed with a sign saying that it was under repair. This sign mysteriously disappeared immediately after the shootings. So, maybe Moreno did have an accomplice. We just don't know. But we are satisfied that he was the killer.

"Unfortunately, Nicholas, you can't make that bastard pay for his crimes. As you may have seen on TV, or read in the papers, Moreno was killed in a so-called car accident on the Toluca highway.

"But who was truly responsible for the killings... and why? Now there the answers are not so simple. I cannot yet say for certain who masterminded the killings.

"As for why: Well, I have my own theory about that. It remains to be proven, but really there is only one answer

304

that fits all the knows facts. And I'm afraid you won't like it."

There was a long pause. Nicholas stared at McClellan intently. "I want to hear it."

"Okay. In my opinion— and I feel absolutely certain it is right— the target in the park was not ambassador Tunaman at all. The aim, all along, was to kill the Finance Minister, Roberto Martínez."

"How can you be so certain?"

McClellan looked at him, grim-faced. "I should not be telling you this, but I'll risk it in strictest confidence. The fact is that Secretario Martínez was working for us. The CIA, that is. He was recruited for us long ago, by one of his professors— an ex-company man— when he was at Harvard.

"Martínez was not a paid agent, you understand. He was far too idealistic ever to have accepted money. It was simply that he shared our loathing of drug trafficking - a trade that is creating chaos in both the U.S. and Mexico.

"Unfortunately, involvement in the drugs trade now extends so high up in Mexico that Martínez could not realistically hope to expose the key criminals in his own country. At best, we hoped that he might unearth information that would identify Mexican drug barons who had fortunes stashed away in U.S. bank accounts. Then we could take it from there.

"I was Martínez's contact in Mexico City, and the last time we met— several weeks before he was killed— he said that he soon expected to have some very important information for us. The conclusion is obvious. Somehow, someone learnt of this, and had him eliminated.

"It fits an all too familiar pattern. In the past year, in Mexico. three undercover agents of the DEA— that's the U.S. Drugs Enforcement Administration— have completely disappeared, presumed killed."

"I see," said Nicholas. "So you are saying that the killing of my son, wife and father-in-law was just an unfortunate accident, the result of wild shooting by the man Moreno?"

McClellan's lips tightened. "I am afraid not, Nicholas. And this is the part you won't like. The fact is, I agree with Barraza's opinion: that the killings were quite deliberate. Moreno was a top marksman, you see. And he bloody well had to be to hit anything at the distance involved in Chapultepec Park.

"The M-21 he used is a highly sophisticated weapon. It needs real expertise to get it zeroed in correctly, let alone to fire it accurately at long distance. And, as Julio says, it is impossible to imagine his brother having acquired the necessary skill and self-control.

"Incidentally, though it was never disclosed, Barraza discovered that the arsenal of the Presidential Guards near Los Pinos has no fewer than six M-21s, part of a consignment officially obtained from the U.S. Army. But he could find no record of how many of the guns had originally been delivered."

"I don't understand. Why then should this assassin kill completely innocent bystanders?"

"Well, Barraza put it to me rather oddly, like this: *Say, for example, you wanted to hide a cube of sugar that had some special value. Where better to hide it than in a bowl of sugar-lumps?*"

Nicholas clenched his fists and his face contorted with rage. "*Christos*! Are you saying that my family was slaughtered just to cover up another crime? It's monstrous!"

"As I say," McClellan replied. "It's only a theory. But it fits the facts. And it certainly worked. All the attention was focussed on the killing of the ambassador. No questions asked about why the Finance Minister should have been killed. It was automatically presumed that— like your son and wife— he had the misfortune to be hit when moving across into the line of fire."

At that point, they had been joined by the man called Rodrigo, who was bearing a tray laden with four plates and a small tower of steak sandwiches. He placed the tray on the coffee table, and with his right foot pushed up a pouffe, and sat down.

He was a muscular-looking man, much the same build as Julio, but with a squarer face that was framed with greying sideburns. Nicholas, still visibly fuming, eyed him suspiciously, and wondered whether they should be talking in front of him.

Julio read his mind. "Ah! I don't think you have been properly introduced. Nicholas, this is my *compadre*, Rodrigo Monteagudo. We go back a long way, and he knows all about this business. In fact, if it wasn't for Rodrigo, I wouldn't be here today. You see, he introduced me to *lucha libre*. Taught me everything I know."

As he went on to explain, Rodrigo's so promising

career in *lucha libre* had been cruelly cut short by an opponent who had twisted his left leg so violently that his cruciate ligament was severely torn.

"We first met in a Mexico City gym, where he was assigned to me as a cornerman. Later, I was sponsored to fight in *El Norte*. And you know what? I couldn't afford to pay Rodrigo at the time, but he had such faith in me that he came along at his own expense. What a guy!"

Rodrigo looked impatiently at Julio, but said nothing because he had a mouthful of sandwich.

"Anyway," Julio went on. "To cut a long story short, Rodrigo was with me when I had my first defeat in Chicago, being cut so badly around the eyes that the referee stopped the fight. I could have returned to boxing after a six months' rest. But, like Rodrigo said, I cut too easily. It was liable to happen again and again.

"It was his idea that he should coach me in *lucha libre*. And his idea that I should keep my identity absolutely secret. Quite simply, he made me. He became my manager as well as my trainer." He grinned. "Yeah, and my cook and chauffeur, too.

"Rodrigo has a brother who sometimes deputises as my cornerman, like last night at the Arena México. But otherwise no one else has been allowed to know my identity. Not even members of my own family. I feel bad about that. But it's just too risky. Certainly my father could never be trusted to keep the secret... and to make big money in this business it's really important not to reveal the man behind the mask.

"According to Rodrigo, it's even too risky hiring extra help." He grinned again. "But, of course, that's his way of justifying his outrageously high salary!"

Rodrigo chuckled, and reached out for a second steak sandwich. "Oh yeah? I tell you, these *pepitos* are so good, I am thinking of putting in for a raise."

As Nicholas so clearly remembered, their light-hearted banter had greatly irritated him. All he could think about at the time was McClellan's explanation of the killings. Somehow, it made the slaughter seem all the more diabolical, and at this point, he was resolved more than ever on vengeance, even at the risk of Regina's life.

Unable to contain his inner rage any longer, Nicholas had glared at McClellan and shouted, "Bugger all this talk.

307

What I want to know is what we are going to do about the killings. Or don't you care any more, now that the gunman is dead?"

For a few seconds there was silence. Then Julio, speaking softly, responded. "My sincere apologies, *señor*. Of course, we care. Deeply. It's just that we've had rather more time to adjust to the situation. We should have remembered that it's all new to you, and it must come as an enormous shock.

"If you will permit me, I will explain what we have done so far, and then perhaps Brad will say something about what action we might take next."

Briefly Nicholas was distracted from his review of that first meeting. Feeling a slight draught of air, he opened his eyes.

"Is that too much for you back there?" asked Rodrigo, who had opened his offside window a fraction. "I thought a whiff of fresh air might do us some good. No smog here. We must have dropped more than four thousand feet from Mexico City."

"No. That's fine," said Nicholas.

He looked across to Julio for a reaction. But the Mexican— like McClellan— still seemed to be sound asleep. It was more than an hour since they had dozed off, and he wondered at their ability to relax when so much was at stake. *Did they really care about the killings in the park?*

Then he thought back to what they had said the previous evening, and concluded that his doubts were perhaps unreasonable. McClellan, after all, cared enough to pursue the investigation, even though he was officially retired - or at least, so he claimed.

Nicholas still had nagging doubts about the American's motives. He could understand how the man felt indirectly responsible for the death of Martínez. But was that sufficient reason for continuing to seek the killers in his own time and at his own expense?

On the other hand, he could readily empathise with the Mexican. Like himself, Julio Ramírez was personally motivated. *Philotimo,* family honour, was at stake. He had lost a brother. Also, his desire for vengeance had become all the greater after McClellan's suggestion that drug traffickers might be involved.

"You okay back there, *amigo?*" chirped Rodrigo, looking in his rear-view mirror.

"Why don't you get some sleep?"

"Will do," said Nicholas.

Once again Nicholas closed his eyes, and this time he made a conscious effort to sleep. But it was useless. Still the mind would not stop working. Now it was tracking back over all that Julio had said; remembering how, at great length, the Mexican had convincingly explained his hatred of anyone involved in the drugs trade, a hatred going back to the death of his baby brother, Alfredo.

"Poor Alfredo!" Julio had began. "Just ten years old he was when he started sniffing that bloody glue. It was only Resistol 5000 cement, you know, the stuff that shoemakers use. But the principle is the same. It's just the first step towards harder drugs.

"That glue shouldn't be sold to kids. I was stupid enough to try it once myself. When you inhale it, you feel a tickling in the nose, like when you are about to sneeze. But instead of coming down, it goes up until you feel your brain is shrinking.

"You know how when you stay a long time in a hot bath, and your hands are all wrinkled? Well, I felt like my brain was wrinkled. After a while, there was a pleasant sensation, a bit like being drunk. But you lose all sense of time and distance. And that's what happened to Alfredo when he walked out in front of that fucking car.

"You can easily spot the glue-sniffing addicts in Mexico City. They walk around like zombies. Ask them where they are going and they say things like '*I am going to meet my destiny,*' and they have to keep on inhaling every five minutes or so just to keep feeling high. But eventually they come down to Earth with a bloody awful headache and sense of nausea. Then they vomit, and find they don't want to eat or sleep. It's a depressive, totally addictive.

"Of course, glue-sniffing is the least of our problems now that cocaine has flooded the market. How I detest those drug-pushers! Quite deliberately, they brought down the street-price of coke so as to get more and more people hooked, and now the bastards are pushing up the price again. I tell you, they are systematically destroying our country, and turning this city into a stinking sewer. Do you know that three-quarters of all crimes in Mexico are drug related? And that at least four thousand people are murdered every year in drug turf wars along the northern frontier, many of them mutilated, tortured and beheaded before being dumped in mass graves?

"Anyway, to start at the beginning, I was absolutely shattered when I heard on TV that my brother had been named as the assassin. I never believed it for a moment. Not little Manuelito. If you knew him as I did, you'd know that he was quite incapable of doing anything like that.

"Sure, he was easily led astray. But firing a rifle in those circumstances! Well, that's absolutely ridiculous. Why, the kid couldn't even snatch a woman's handbag without running chicken scared.

"That shooting. It must have required a degree of skill, plus nerves of cold steel. And Manuel just wasn't like that. Too emotional, too highl-strung; hopeless at anything of a practical nature.

"So you see, Nicholas, I saw him as much a victim as the members of your family who were killed. Like you, I swore to find out who was responsible. And the first step, it seemed to me, was to trace his movements between leaving home, and ending up in that tower five months later.

"The only thing I had to go on was my knowledge of Manuel's way of thinking. I tried to put myself in his position. Where would he go when— after his humiliating serenade of Consuelo— he was desperate to escape from everyone?

"I remembered how, one year earlier, after some petty-thieving had gone wrong, he had made himself scarce by hitching a lift down to Acapulco. There, for a while, he made a living by working the beaches— you know, peddling trinkets and sometimes— though he hated it - picking up extra cash for servicing some sex-starved, matronly tourist.

"Well, I went down there, and struck lucky almost straight away. On Condesa Beach, I showed a picture of Manuel to a young guy selling silver bracelets. But I didn't need the picture. He remembered my brother well... and not very happily. Said Manuel had invaded his patch, and had undercut his prices.

"So when had he last seen Manuel? According to him,

it was about three months earlier. And did he know where he went after that? The guy grinned and said, 'Not far. The cops grabbed him for selling stolen goods. They should have kept him locked up longer because I hear he turned into a killer.'

"At that point I seemed to have struck a dead end. I wasn't going to risk asking questions at the police station. They would probably have hauled me in as well.

"I didn't know what to do next. But then I had another bit of luck. I met Brad. Or rather he met me. And he agreed that I should go back to Acapulco to do some more digging. Anyway, let him tell you about it. It's a curious story."

It had been Barraza's idea. At the time the Comandante had abandoned hope of making progress with his own investigation. However, in casual conservation with McClellan, he had remarked that he was unimpressed with the FBI's search for Julio. It was a long shot, he said, but there was always the possibility that the missing brother had returned to Mexico - in which case it might just be worthwhile keeping a close surveillance on Manuel's funeral.

McClellan agreed, and, even though the funeral came after his retirement from the CIA, he chose to carry out the surveillance unofficially. Like the FBI agents in Miami, he had a photograph of Julio in boxing pose. And at the *Panteón de Dolores,* using high-powered binoculars, he kept watch from behind a huge Siqueiros monument, more than a hundred yards from the funeral scene.

He spotted no one remotely resembling Julio. Then, after the mourners had departed, he ranged his binoculars over the cemetery, and was attracted by an extraordinary tombstone that was covered with tiles, each decorated with bright-coloured, cartoon-like images.

"It was so weird," McClellan explained. "And purely out of curiosity I went over to take a closer look. I was studying the strange pictures when a cemetery attendant passed by. I stopped him and asked him about the tomb, why the large headstone had a portrait of an old woman while all the tiles had comic scenes featuring a man.

"He then told me a long story: about Conchita Jurado, an eccentric Mexican woman who had spent many years masquerading as a Spanish multi-millionaire called Don Carlos

311

Balmori. This was her tomb. The tiles, he explained in detail, depicted scenes from her life - how, wearing a false moustache and goatee beard, she had hoaxed and humiliated scores of fortune hunters - women hoping to find a wealthy husband, and businessmen seeking the tycoon's financial support.

"Anyway, the point is that it was another twenty minutes or more before I left the cemetery. It was then, on the way out, that I chanced to look back and noticed there was a man standing alone beside Manuel's tomb. Using the binoculars again, I judged that the man could well be the missing brother.

"I didn't risk running towards him, but kept out of sight, and followed him at a distance to the main exit. There I saw him get into a most distinctive white Mercedes.

"I couldn't quite make out the licence number, but I didn't need to. Painted on the near side was a matchstick figure with a halo standing between the words *EL SANTO*. When I asked around, I found that the car was commonly known to belong to a famous wrestler called El Nuevo Santo."

At that point, Julio took up the story. "It was one hell of a shock. Two days later, I was in the American Bookstore on Avenida Revolución, signing copies of a *lucha libre* picture book to raise money for charity. As usual, when making a public appearance, I was in masked disguise. And suddenly this stranger comes up and says, 'Could you please sign it,' to Julio Ramírez?'

"Well, I nearly fell out my chair. But at least he was discreet. After I had signed his copy, he just presented me with a business card, which had a message telling me to visit him at his apartment in the evening.

"And that's how we got together. Once I had convinced Brad that I knew nothing about the killings, we agreed to work together in finding out who was responsible. Actually, I didn't have much choice if I was going to keep my identity secret.

"Anyway, I told him about my trip to Acapulco. It surprised him because he had seen Manuel's police file, which had no mention of his having been arrested down there. In turn, he told me about this *hombre*, Guillermo Velázquez, assistant manager at the Esmeralda Hotel, and how he had tipped off a gossip columnist about the birthday party in the park.

"That Acapulco connection seemed significant. So we

312

agreed to start from there. Brad would make inquiries at the police station while I would make contact with Velázquez.

"As expected, the Acapulco police denied all knowledge of Manuel having been arrested. Interestingly, however, Brad discovered that the local *jefe*, Teniente-General Ernesto Torres, was a brother of Ignacio Torres, assistant to the Mexico City police chief, General Delgado.

"Unfortunately, I had a lot of fund-raising engagements in Mexico City, and it was not until last week that I could get away to Acapulco. Then I booked into the Esmeralda under the name of Señor Carlos Jurado. Brad suggested the phoney name. The idea was that I should pose as the manager of El Nuevo Santo, and say I was there to make arrangements for his holiday, and then perhaps a local fight.

"As it happened, I never did manage to make contact with Velázquez. He had suddenly left for the United States. But the trip wasn't wasted. Indeed, it turned out to be hugely profitable.

"We have a saying in Mexico that luck and death— *la suerte y la muerte*— are much the same; that they can come unpredictably at any time. Well, at the Esmeralda, *la suerte* seemed to be very much on my side. I learnt so much from Señora Esperanza Valázquez, not least the fact that her husband was a close personal friend of police chief Torres. And that gave me the first notion of a plan that has been redesigned and much improved with the help of Brad's expertise."

"*Cabron*," shouted Rodrigo, just before he gave three loud hoots on his car horn. Then he muttered, "Okay! If you want to play games."

Nicholas looked up to see ahead of them a dust-covered half-truck that had veered across into the fast lane. On the left wing of its tailboard, crudely fingered in the dust, were the words *Lado de paso*. On the right wing, the message *Lado de moribundo*.

The half-truck began to wander erratically between lanes. Without hesitation, Rodrigo put his foot down hard and the Mercedes, accelerating in a few seconds from 100 kph to 130 kph, zoomed through a narrow gap on the passing side.

Both McClellan and Ramírez were wide-awake now. "Very good," grunted the former. "But let's slow down before

313

we get a speeding ticket."

Julio looked across at Nicholas and grinned. "As you see, we have some really loco drivers in this country. Even so, there was no real point in our overtaking because we've got to get off the highway soon."

He estimated that they were no more than half an hour from Acapulco, and so they took the next turn, pulling off the side-road to park on a dirt track. There, Rodrigo donned his chauffeur's cap and jacket, and adjusted his tie. Meanwhile, Julio went to the trunk to fetch out his white cloak and silver mask, plus a white baseball cap with the name El Nuevo Santo inscribed in blue above its peak.

As they moved back onto the highway, Julio smiled at Nicholas and said, "It's like what that Conchita Jurado always said after she had hoaxed someone, and revealed her true identity: *Nothing is exactly as it seems to be. Nothing is real. The truth is always hidden.*"

Bypassing the central sweep of Acapulco Bay, the white Mercedes turned onto Avenida Almirante Horacio Nelson, and then followed the Scenic Highway on its steep serpentine route towards the airport. High above the town, they passed the unique, luxurious hotel complex of Las Brisas with its 250 pink-and-white *cassitas* and 200 swimming pools. At that point, Julio telephoned ahead to alert the Esmeralda of their imminent arrival.

Around the great loop of East Bay, some nine miles from the town centre, they passed the 777-room Acapulco Princess, composed of two sixteen-storey buildings, one shaped like an Aztec pyramid, the other like a Mayan pyramid - and arguably the most lavish hotel in all Mexico. Nearby was its sister hotel, the smaller Pierre Marqués, with which it shared an 18-hole championship golf course.

Unlike the Princess, the Esmeralda, a quarter mile beyond, was wholly futuristic in style: a great hexagon with a twenty-four-storey, glass-fronted tower block rising from each angle. The top floor of each tower was designed to form an opulent penthouse suite with its own roof garden above; and, within the hexagon, a vast lobby was laid out atrium-style: a marbled, sky lit central court rising through five storeys, with galleries of boutiques, bars and guest rooms opening off at each level.

The majority of its five hundred fifty guest rooms, however, were sited within its six tower blocks, all with floor-to-ceiling sliding glass doors opening on to private terraces, and balconies planted with colourful flowering shrubs. The main interior of the hotel was styled to give a maximum sense of spaciousness, an effect most striking in its twenty-thousand-square-feet lobby, which had been planted with sixty-foot tall coco palm trees, and laid out with a flowing lagoon and two wooden bridges leading to its Laguna Bar on an island in the centre.

The Esmeralda was not for the average tourist, nor was it well geared for young couples with small children. Essentially, it catered for wealthy North Americans seeking a truly luxurious holiday in terms of service, facilities and security, and usually content to remain in a self-contained complex that included a private beach, two large swimming pools, tennis courts, gourmet restaurants, shops, nightclub, gymnasium and sauna baths.

Before entering this cocooned environment, guests were required to check in at the security gate at the head of the main driveway. But Julio's white Mercedes was automatically waved through, and on arrival in the forecourt, it was met by the newly appointed assistant manager, Señor Javier Zavala. He had four porters standing by, plus an attendant to park the car.

As requested by Julio, the local media had not been informed of the visit of El Nuevo Santo. However, for publicity purposes, the hotel's resident photographer was there to take pictures of the figure in silver mask, white baseball cap and long, flowing white cloak.

Señor Zavala escorted the arrivals to the nearest tower block, and accompanied them in the elevator to the penthouse suite. Two porters followed behind with the luggage, though Rodrigo insisted on carrying a large sports holdall, explaining with a grin that it contained training weights that only a real macho man could lift.

Zavala, full of chat about the hotel's amenities, was eager to show the new arrivals around the penthouse. But Julio dismissed him curtly. "If you don't mind, *señor*, we need to rest after our long journey. Leave the bags. We'll unpack them ourselves."

As soon as the assistant manager and porters had left, Nicholas exclaimed, "*Christos!* Julio. I don't know how you manage to fight with this infernal thing on. It's so damned hot."

Then, flopping into an easy chair, Nicholas unstrapped the silver mask and tossed it on to the floor, along with his sweaty baseball cap.

"Sorry about that," said Julio. "But you should not have made your face so familiar on TV. Let me get you an ice-cold drink."

Now, for the first time, it could be seen that Nicholas was barefoot beneath his hitched-up cloak. He had needed to leave off his shoes to conceal his inordinate height.

A few minutes later, the doorbell rang. Nicholas sprang out of his chair, grabbed the mask and cap, and hurried towards the nearest of three bedrooms. "Hang on," said Julio, and he opened the front door a fraction. Then he added, "It's okay."

The door was opened wide to reveal a raven-haired woman, pencil-slim and of moderate good looks that were hugely enhanced by her perfect grooming and exquisitely-cut designer suit. Everything about her— so tastefully understated— exuded coolness, chic and class; all, that is, except for the large, darkly expressive eyes with their hint of nervous intensity.

Then she entered the room, and the image of stylish restraint was quickly dispelled. Effusively, she embraced Julio and called him *querido,* and, not waiting for introductions, she moved on to approach the still white-cloaked Nicholas. "Ah! And you will be Señor Stephanopoulos. I am very pleased to meet you."

She extended a handshake. "Welcome to *La Esmeralda.*" Then, turning to Julio, she said, "If it's not too soon for you, I have ordered a cold buffet supper to be served in my suite at eight o'clock. Is that all right?"

Julio nodded. "That will be fine, Esperanza."

CHAPTER 24

The penthouse suite of Señora Esperanza Velázquez—
like the five others at the Esmeralda— comprised a large
living room with a built-in bar, three bedroom units with
velvet wall coverings, a fully equipped kitchenette/breakfast
room, an onyx-tiled bathroom with two shower units, and a
large sunken double-bath in the shape of a heart, and a spiral
staircase leading up to a private roof garden. Unlike the other
five, however, this penthouse also had a boardroom-cum-
dining room furnished with a long, hand-carved mahogany
table, tweny chairs and film projection equipment.

It was in this boardroom, at eight o'clock in the
evening, that five people— Brad McClellan, Julio Ramírez,
Rodrigo Monteagudo, Nicholas Stephanopoulos and Esperanza
Velázquez— gathered to finalise plans for what McClellan had
named Operation Terror. His long-shot scheme had two prime
objectives: the exposure of the person or persons responsible
for the murders in Chapultepec Park, and the rescue—
hopefully within the next twenty-four hours— of Regina
Marke.

But first they helped themselves to a self-service
buffet supper— assorted cold meats, seafood, salad and
savouries, plus a choice of red and white wines— that had been
laid out at one end of the long conference table. Then, soon
after they were seated, Julio tapped his wine glass with a
spoon, and stood up to make an announcement:

"*Señores,* before we get down to business, I would like
to propose a toast: to Esperanza Velázquez, our beautiful and
generous hostess, without whose co-operation we would not be
here today, and certainly not able to go ahead with the drastic
action now being planned."

While Señora Velázquez remained seated, the others
stood up and, raising their glasses, declared in unison, "To
Esperanza."

As the toast was being made, Julio and Esperanza
exchanged knowing smiles. Only they could appreciate the

humour of the situation, remembering that it was exactly one week, almost to the hour, since they had enjoyed a rather different supper in that same penthouse suite.

Julio had already recounted to Brad and Rodrigo, and later to Nicholas, the outcome of his first meeting with Señora Velázquez. Discreetly, however, he had chosen to omit the more intimate details of that unforgettable encounter.

It had happened on the day that Julio had booked into the Esmeralda under the name of Señor Carlos Jurado. At the time, he had no clear-cut plan beyond seeking to contact the assistant manager, Guillermo Velázquez, initially on the pretext of making advance preparations for the visit of El Nuevo Santo.

By the same token, he had no idea where this ploy might lead, only a vague hope that perhaps, in the process of discussing publicity and security arrangements, he might learn something useful about Velázquez's contacts with the media and the local police. Lurking at the back of his mind, there was also the dark thought that, if necessary, he might have to resort to strong-arm tactics in questioning the man.

Unfortunately, or so it seemed at the time, Julio learnt that Velázquez was no longer the assistant manager. Currently, he was in the United States and— according to his successor, Señor Zavala— no one quite knew when he would be returning to Acapulco.

Pressed further, Zavala lowered his voice almost to a whisper. "In fact, between you and me, I rather doubt that he will ever be coming back. Some family trouble, I believe."

Frustrated, Julio expressed again how much he had been hoping to meet Velázquez in person. And at that point, Zavala suggested that perhaps he should talk to Señora Velázquez. "She has recently taken over as manager, you know."

"Fruitful" was the adjective Julio had used when first describing his encounter with Señora Velázquez. It was more appropriate than Brad and Rodrigo would ever realise.

They had first met in the manager's office. There, the lady had enthused at the possibility of El Nuevo Santo staying at the Esmeralda; indeed, without prompting, she proposed that special concessions might be made if the visit could be used to publicise the hotel.

318

"I very much look forward to meeting your famous fighter. I have seen him on television, of course. But what's he really like, this Nuevo Santo? Behind the mask, I mean."

Julio smiled. "Oh! Very handsome and absolutely charming. But you'll have to take my word for it. He never takes off the mask, you understand."

"Never?"

"That's right— except, of course, when we are completely alone."

"How fascinating! You must tell me more about him."

The lady seemed very friendly and relaxed, and so Julio ventured to ask about her husband. "I was very much hoping to meet Señor Velázquez, but I gather that he is in *El Norte*, and may not be coming back for a while."

Esperanza's face hardened, and she reached for a cigarette. "Are you a personal friend of his?"

"Not at all. In fact, we have never met."

She lit the cigarette and drew on it hard. "Good. Then you may as well know that we are separated, and he certainly will not be coming back here."

There was an awkward pause. And then, all of a sudden, her manner changed. Smiling warmly, she said, "I have an idea, *señor*. Why don't you join me for dinner this evening. Then we can discuss arrangements for the visit in more detail."

Julio said he would be delighted.

"Splendid. Shall we say eight o'clock... in my penthouse suite? You see, I have a four-year-old son, and this is his nursemaid's evening off. I could easily get a substitute, of course. But really, I would prefer to be there myself. I hope you don't mind."

Julio never did meet Jaime, her four-year-old son. When he arrived at the appointed hour, the boy had been put to bed, and Josefina, the live-in *niñera,* had already left. There were no servants on hand, and, on entering the spacious living-room, he saw that a cold buffet supper had been laid out on a long sideboard.

Señora Velázquez, looking radiant in a simple, V-necked aquamarine dress, was holding a cocktail glass when she welcomed him into her suite. Almost at once, she said, "Let me get you a drink. I'm having a White Russian myself. But perhaps you'd like something stronger."

"Thank you, *señora*. A whisky and water— no ice—

would be fine."

As she went over to the corner bar, he looked around the room: brilliant coloured carpets scattered about highly polished parquet flooring, marble pillars on either side of partially curtained-off balcony doors, two sofas, three easy chairs and a pair of coffee tables hand-carved in mahogany with inlaid travertine marble tops. But it was the wall paintings that automatically caught the eye, and in particular, a huge landscape depicting the Valley of Mexico.

"Ah, you have good taste," said Esperanza, as she handed him his drink. "That's an original Velasco. I'm afraid the other penthouses have nothing in that class. But otherwise we can provide your Nuevo Santo with a suite much the same as this one.

"What do you think? Of course, it's much better in daylight. Then you have a fine view of the Pacific from here."

"Señora, it's quite magnificent."

"Oh, please, call me Esperanza. How's your drink... *Carlos*? Not too much water, I hope?"

By nature, Julio Ramírez was not a conceited man. But even he could not help sensing the message being given out by the lady's fetching smile, and distinctly warm tone of voice. It surprised him greatly. Esperanza had a real touch of class; also some indefinable quality that he found strangely, compellingly attractive.

The soft lighting in the room added to the suggestion of intimacy, and this was positively reinforced when— after they had selected food from the buffet— she chose to sit close beside him on the smaller of two sofas.

Esperanza had replenished her glass from what looked like a jug of milk, and she was so animated that Julio began to wonder how many White Russians she had had before he arrived.

"Now then," she said. " I want to know all about your Nuevo Santo. Is it true what they say: that he even keeps his mask on when making love?"

Julio laughed. "My goodness! Do they really say that? I would think it most unlikely."

To her subsequent questions, he replied that, yes, he had taken part in *lucha libre* before becoming a manager; no, as far he knew, fights were never fixed; yes, most fighters exaggerated or simulated pain, and no, El Nuevo Santo was not— and never had been— married.

Deliberately seeking to switch the conversation to more pertinent matters, Julio expressed his sympathy regarding the Chapultepec Park murders. "It must have been a terrible shock for you."

"*Si*, it was." And then, to his surprise, she grinned wryly. "You know what's funny? Two of my three sisters lost a good husband that day, and there is me, married to a complete shit, and he survives. Ironic, isn't it?

She emptied her glass, and lit a cigarette. "Oh dear! You must excuse me. I do believe I've had rather too much to drink."

Julio wanted to follow up on her earlier remark. But he was forestalled. Esperanza picked up his empty tumbler and moved away while saying, "Let me get you another drink."

On returning from the bar, she remained standing. "I'm just going to check that my son is sleeping all right. Why don't you come with me, and I'll show you around the rest of the penthouse."

The quick tour ended in the sumptuous bathroom, all gleaming onyx marble, with two full-length mirrors, and a sunken, heart-shaped double-bath bath in the centre. "I hope you like this," said Esperanza. "It's the main feature of all our penthouse suites."

Then she gave Julio a wicked smile. "You know something. I feel like taking a bath right now." She immediately switched on a tap, kicked off her shoes and turned her back to him. "Would you mind helping me with this zip?"

The request was made so casually that Julio automatically complied. He had moved the zip no more than an inch when Espernaza flipped the dress off both shoulders. It dropped to her ankles and, as she stepped out of it, she spun around.

"Thank you, *caballero*," she said smilingly.

Julio just gaped in wonder. The lady was totally naked. She had a wonderfully athletic figure: powerful-looking shoulders and hips, and a narrow waist. Above all, his eyes were riveted on her breasts. Though only marginally developed, her breasts had a fetching firmness that was somehow accentuated by the prominence of her nipples, and the spread of their areolae, so ample and enticingly dark.

Unabashed, Esperanza now unpinned her swept-up

321

black hair, and let it tumble around her shoulders. In the process, she raised her arms, stretching her small breasts in a way that Julio found sexually provoking beyond belief.

Indeed, he was so surprised and stimulated by her drink-induced brazenness that later he would have no clear recollection of how subsequent events developed. But somehow, after responding to an irresistible dare, he found himself sharing the bath with his giggling hostess.

She entirely took the initiative; at one point, on the pretext of groping to retrieve a bar of soap, she contrived to end up cradling Julio's genitalia, and achieving his instant arousal. The outcome was inevitable. Soon afterwards, they were sharing Esperanza's double bed, their entwined bodies writhing in ever-quickening spasms of sexual abandon.

The passion of Esperanza was unlike anything Julio had experienced before: a symphony of sensual pleasure artfully composed, and orchestrated with varied pace and power. There was no subtlety in the first movement: an opening burst, without foreplay, of frenzied, uncontrolled copulation. But then followed an interlude of gentle tenderness as she caressed and coaxed his instrument into a more prolonged and meaningful performance, one so neat in tempo that they climaxed in a synchronised orgasmic eruption.

Julio slumped back into a state of contented exhaustion, and yet still, this most demanding maestro was not done. After much kissing and stroking, she mounted him once again and, to his amazement, he found himself responding - at first with only semi-tumescence, but soon, lubricated by her natural juices, with maximum rigidity. Esperanza, thrusting down with awesome pelvic power and controlled muscular contractions, did the rest.

His physical resources now completely spent, Julio lay back gasping with all the desperation of an athlete who had just completed his first sub-four-minute mile. Meanwhile, Esperanza slipped out of the bed, saying, "Don't move. I'll be back in a moment."

In the bathroom she douched herself on the bidet, then returned wearing nothing more than a fresh spray of anti-perspirant deodorant. As she padded across the bedroom, Julio stared in admiration at her splendid physique, and thought to himself how large breasts— so much favoured by Mexican men— were highly overrated.

Esperanza curled up on the bed, resting her head beside him, and stroking his sweat-soaked hair. Julio's heart was still pounding. "Jesus, Esperanza," he said. "With your stamina and agility, you could be a champion in *lucha libre.*"

She laughed, and used the edge of a sheet to wipe his brow. "Ah, *mi querido*, you are the champion, not me. Now I know what I have been missing all these years."

For a few minutes, they lay silently locked in each others arms, both feeling totally content and secure, both instinctively aware of a strange chemistry between them, of some invisible force that drew them together in both body and soul.

Finally, Esperanza broke the natural silence. Raising herself on one elbow and, grinning mischievously down at him, she said, "Well, you have certainly answered my earlier question."

"What do you mean?"

"About El Nuevo Santo. Whether or not he takes off his mask when making love."

"I don't understand."

"Oh! Come off it, Carlos, or whatever your real name is. I'm not stupid, you know. I have seen El Nuevo Santo fight on television. And earlier today I looked up a picture of him in a magazine.

"Forget the masked face. I'd know that physique anywhere. What do call them? Pectoral muscles? Whatever, yours are wonderfully developed. I suggest you keep away from the hotel swimming pool if you want to remain anonymous."

Grinning wickedly, she now slid her left hand down his stomach, and gripped his limp penis. "And that's not all that's wonderfully developed."

She then rested her head on his chest, and looking down inquisitively, she gently pressed down on his foreskin, all the while increasing her grip until the exposed, blood-trapped dome of his member had swollen to a glossy purple.

"Hey! Steady on," said Julio. "I can't take any more punishment. I concede. You're the winner!"

She snuggled up to him, and lightened her grip. "I'll tell you what," she said. "Let's play the Truth Game. You answer my questions, and I'll answer yours. Okay?"

"Okay."

"*Bueno*. As the declared winner, it's my turn first. So

what's your real name? I promise not to tell anyone. And why are you here, pretending to be your own manager?" She removed her hand from his half-swollen organ.

Julio was now able to think with his head. "That's two questions." He levered himself up into a sitting position, resting his back against two raised pillows. Esperanza followed his example, at the same time drawing a semen-stained bed sheet across their legs, and just high enough to cover his genitalia, and her own profusion of pubic hair.

"If you don't mind," Julio continued. "I'll just answer your second question at this stage. It's not that I don't trust you, Esperanza. But what you don't know can't hurt you."

He then went on to explain that, for reasons of his own, he was investigating the murders in Chapultepec Park, and in this connection he wanted to question her husband about his dealings with a certain Alfredo Gómez of *El Informador*.

"I see. So you think that my husband may have somehow been involved with the killings?"

"Hey! It's my turn to ask a question. First of all, what is your husband doing in *El Norte*, and why is it that you are not expecting him to come back?"

At that point, Esperanza reached across for a packet of cigarettes and a lighter that lay with an ashtray on a small bedside table.

"That's two questions also," she said after lighting up. She inhaled deeply, and blew out a cloud of smoke. "Never mind. I want you to know all about it."

As Julio later told Brad and Rodrigo, Esperanza was reluctant to talk about her husband "but I eventually managed to win her confidence". Exactly how this had been achieved, he never explained. It was not mere gallantry on his part. It was because experience had taught him to be guided in life by one fundamental principle: never to reveal more of one's private self than was strictly necessary.

The magician who reveals the secrets of his wizardry is never regarded in the same awe, and, again and again, he had seen how a *lucha libre* giant was reduced to mere mortal stature when he was stripped off his mask. *Familiarity breeds contempt* might be a cliché, but it was nonetheless true for all that.

Esperanza, in contrast, held nothing back. In answering Julio's questions, she was releasing her innermost feelings, and expressing a profound hatred that she had not even related to her priest in the confessional.

With refreshing honesty, she stressed how she had been a fool from the start. Her older sisters had warned her in no uncertain terms about the folly of becoming involved with her tennis coach, Guillermo Velázquez. He was, they said, a no-good womaniser and gold-digger, and he would be incapable of being a faithful husband.

"It was funny. The more they spoke badly about him, the more fiercely I defended him. I must have been mad. But then I was totally besotted with him, you see. He was so devilishly handsome, and oh, he could be so charming when he wanted.

"Not that I was completely blind to his faults. Even I could see that he might go astray from time to time. But I so wanted him, and like so many young Mexican girls, I went into marriage falling back on that common prayer - you know the one? - *Please, God, let not my husband cheat on me / And if he does, please let me not know about it / And if I know, please let me not care about it.*

"Unfortunately, I *did* get to know about it. And I *did* care. I don't just mean his little flirtations. I could live with that. But what happened last November was something else. I can never forgive him for what he did then. Never!"

That November, as she recounted, one of the Esmeralda's penthouse suites had been occupied by the family of Garfield Saunders Jr. who had recently run successfully for the U.S. Senate in Massachusetts. "It was the most valuable booking we ever had. As you may know, they are right up at the top of the social register in the States, rivalling the Kennedys as one of Boston's oldest and most celebrated families.

"Old man Saunders is a billionaire banker, and I understand that he was the biggest contributor to President Carmichael's campaign fund. Anyway, as you can imagine, we gave them the full VIP treatment. They were big spenders, and I thought it had all gone really well.

"God! How blind I was! Two months later, the truth came out. I had only just come back from Cuernavaca after a terrible time trying to console my widowed sister, Dolores. Soon after we were supposed to be attending the funeral of

325

poor Roberto. And then it happened.

"After receiving a phone call, Guillermo told me that he could not go to the funeral. He said he had to leave at once for the United States on important business, and he could not be sure when he would get back.

"Now what possible business could he have in the States? He wouldn't say, and so we had the most almighty row. Finally, I dragged it out of him. I couldn't believe it at first - it seemed so disgusting. I became hysterical, and started throwing things, and told him to get out immediately.

"I have never seen or heard from him since, and, for his sake, I hope I never do. Because I think I would kill him if I had the chance."

She drew hard on her cigarette, then vigorously stubbed it out in the ashtray. Julio took her hand, and waited patiently for her to be more explicit.

There was now real emotion in her voice as she revealed the reason for her husband's sudden departure. The Saunders party, it emerged, had comprised the senator, his wife and their two sons and daughter. The latter, named Samantha, had had daily tennis coaching from Guillermo.

"I thought nothing of it at the time. After all, the girl was only SEVENTEEN! But that didn't stop Guillermo. Oh, no! That phone call, I learnt, was from her father. Unbelievably, the girl was pregnant, and the senator was demanding that my husband go to Boston at once.

"They are strict Catholics, you understand," she said tremulously. "And it was especially awkward for Saunders because he is a well-known anti-abortionist."

She moved to reach out for another cigarette, but Julio pulled her back and put an arm around her shoulder. Then, as she nestled against his chest, he gently stroked back her hair. "*Querida,* don't talk about if you don't want to."

Esperanza kissed him on the cheek. "No, it's all right. In fact, I am just beginning to realise that I am so much better off without him. It's that child, Samantha, I feel sorry for. She can't know what a real *hijo de puta* he is."

"So what happens next?

"Oh, no doubt, with all their influence and money, they'll find some way of covering it up. All I know is what Guillermo told me before he left: that there was a plan to send the girl to a finishing school in Switzerland, and later to have the baby secretly adopted. But apparently Samantha was refusing to go, and now they were hoping that my husband would be able to persuade her.

"Since then, Guillermo has telephoned several times from Boston. But I have refused to take his calls. Let him sweat. I can guess what he wants: some kind of quick divorce."

"Is that possible?"

"Normally, no. But anything's possible for people like the Saunders. Think of all the scandals that the Kennedys have survived. At least twice, they have got round the laws of the Church to get an annulment."

She became tight lipped, her eyes blazing more with hatred than pain, and again Julio stroked her hair. "At least, *querida*, you will be well rid of him. The man seems about as loveable as a rattlesnake."

"Don't flatter him," she snapped. "At least a rattlesnake gives a warning before it strikes."

Esperanza looked at her watch. "It's getting late. Let's get up, and have some coffee before Josefina gets back."

After sharing a shower, they had their coffee in the kitchenette, now both fully dressed, and with Esperanza more composed and businesslike. "Well, *Carlos*," she said. " I have answered all your questions. Yet I still don't even know your real name. And you haven't explained why you are so interested in the Chapultepec murders? Are you a part-time detective or something? I think you owe me some answers."

Julio reached across the breakfast table and took her hand. "*Mi reina*, you are absolutely right. You do deserve some answers. But first, could we just clear up this business of your husband, and the man Gómez of *El Informador*. Did you know that he told him about the birthday party in the park?"

"No. But I can quite believe it. Guillermo liked to boast that he had good contacts with the Press, and I do know that he got regular cheques from *El Informador*."

"Is there nothing else you can tell me? Nothing, for example, about his reaction to the murders?"

"Not really. I think he was as shocked as we were. He was scared, too. He said we needed greater security at the hotel, that perhaps all members of our family were in danger.

"Funny thing that. I agreed with him, and suggested that perhaps we should ask the police for special protection. Yet he didn't like that idea at all, and said he would rather hire some *guaruras.*"

"What's funny about that?"

"Nothing really, except that our police chief, Torres, was a personal friend of his. He could easily have asked him for police protection, and saved us some expense. But he refused to contact Torres; said it would be better if we made our own arrangements."

Julio remained silent, deep in thought. Meanwhile, Esperanza poured herself a second cup of coffee, lit another cigarette and then puffed out impatiently. "That's it. I've talked enough. It's time you answered *my* questions."

"You are right," said Julio.

In his heart, he wanted no secrets to come between them. But it was his head that persuaded him now. He needed to take a calculated gamble. For already a vague, desperate plan was formulating in his mind, and for that plan to succeed, it would be essential to have Esperanza's help. He had to trust her.

And so he proceeded to tell her everything, including his secret identity.

As he expected, Esperanza readily agreed to help him in any way she could. She owed that much, she said, to her sisters. But she had one precondition. "Whatever happens, if you find my husband was in any way involved, I want the bastard publicly exposed; destroyed."

Her eyes blazed as she spoke, and Julio silently reflected that *Hell Hath No Fury...*

"So how can I help you, Julio?" she asked.

In answering her question, he stressed that first he would need to return to Mexico City, and confer with Brad McClellan. "Then, if he agrees, we will come down after my fight next week. I'll give you a ring when we are ready to leave."

At that point, they heard a door being closed. Josefina was back.

It was now almost midnight. Esperanza accompanied Julio to the elevator, and there they spontaneously embraced. For both of them, the feeling was based on infinitely more than just physical attraction.

It had been a curious opening to the meeting in the boardroom. From the start, Julio had focussed all the attention on Esperanza. He had proposed a toast to her, and he had gone on to remind everyone that it was their duty to make

328

absolutely certain that no one ever knew of her involvement in their plans.

"As you all know," he said. "Esperanza has already taken a risk on our behalf. Now, whatever happens tomorrow, we must be consistent in our stories. Señora Velázquez is to be seen as an innocent victim, completely fooled, like everyone else, into believing that she was dealing with the real El Nuevo Santo."

Brad McClellan concurred. "That goes without saying, Julio. We are already agreed on that point." And he swiftly directed the conversation in a different direction. Though he did not express it directly, his main concern was not the welfare of Esperanza, but the role in their plans of Nicholas Stephanopoulos.

Everyone present was feeling great sympathy for Nicholas. Only one hour earlier, he had received the dreaded news: that his father had passed away peacefully, having never recovered consciousness while still in intensive care.

Julio had suggested that, in the circumstances, they would fully understand if he immediately left to prepare for the funeral in Athens. Meanwhile, he could rely on them to pursue his family's murderers with ruthless and relentless vigour.

But Nicholas had insisted on staying. It was what his father would have wanted, he said. Indeed, vengeance for his family's honour had been his father's dying wish. And now, more than ever, Nicholas was resolved on seeking retribution. Without doubt, in his mind, his father was the fifth victim of the Chapultepec Park killings, condemned to death by the heartbreaking stress of it all.

Understandably, the Greek now seemed somewhat remote and introverted, and accordingly the others were at pains not to intrude on his grief. Nevertheless, there was no mistaking the fact that McClellan's anxieties were directed towards Nicholas.

Taking command of the conservation, the CIA man declared, "I think we are all now sufficiently familiar with the plans for tomorrow. There's really no need to go over the details again. But I must stress the importance of getting our priorities right.

"Of course, we all want to find out who was responsible for the Chapultepec murders. But we cannot afford to go off at half-cock for the sake of some personal

329

vendetta."

"What do you mean?" asked Julio.

"Simply, that we are taking an enormous gamble, and on nothing more than a hunch. There is no telling how it will turn out, but— depending on the outcome— we must be prepared to adjust our action as the situation demands."

McClellan turned his head towards the man seated beside him. "Nicholas, let me ask you a question. Just suppose that tomorrow we hit the jackpot straight away, and find the person who planned the killing of your wife and son? How are you going to react?"

The Greek fixed him with a cold, steely gaze. "You know my position. I can't rely on Mexican justice. If we find the bastard, it's my duty to kill him... and the more he suffers in dying the better. It may sound barbaric to you. But what they did to my family was barbaric. There can no other way. It is the way of *philotimo.*"

"I appreciate that," said McClellan. "I just want to be sure that you understand *our* position: that it might become necessary to *delay* your vengeance until we have found a way to rescue Miss Marke. Also, I may need time to get other information out of the person or persons responsible. After that, you can do what you will. Agreed?"

Nicholas nodded. "It won't be easy. But yes, I agree."

CHAPTER 25

There was a positive spring in the step of Teniente-General Ernesto Torres as he strode briskly down the main corridor of the Acapulco police headquarters. The duty officer on the front desk moved quickly to hold open the central glass door for his chief. Outside the front entrance, another officer was standing by, ready to open the near-side rear door of the *Jefe's* black, customised Lincoln Continental.

Before stepping into the limousine, Torres paused to unbuckle his wide patent leather gun belt with its holster and the pearl-handled Colt .45 revolver he carried primarily for show. He wrapped the belt around the holster and gun, then handed it to the attendant officer who duly stowed it on the back seat of the car.

Next, the police chief unbuttoned and removed his gold-braided jacket. As he did so, the attendant officer automatically produced a coat hanger from inside the car, took the neatly pressed jacket and hung it from a strap above the far side rear window. The officer then stood back to close the door after Torres— invisible behind dark-frosted, bulletproof windows— had taken his seat.

Corporal Jorge Barrientos had been well trained. Too well trained for his liking. His reward for finishing top in marksmanship and unarmed combat at the police academy had been immediate promotion... and seemingly interminable duty as driver, bodyguard and general factotum to the man they called *El Emperador de Acapulco*.

For three years Barrientos had dutifully served his emperor, never for a moment giving a hint of his secret contempt for the man. He found his subservient role all too demeaning; he hated the long, undefined hours of work; above all, he despised his *Jefe* for his unpredictable mood swings, and his colossal vanity and fastidiousness.

But there was one huge consolation. Once or twice a year, when seized by a rare fit of *bonhomie*, *El Emperador* would hand his long-suffering servant a fat wad of pesos -a

331

tax-free gift surpassing his miserable annual salary. For Barrientos, with an almost permanently pregnant wife, it was a bonus of crucial importance.

From experience, the corporal could judge that his *Jefe* was in unusually good spirits this morning. Absent was the customary growl. Instead, as they moved off, Torres spoke softly. "No hurry, Jorge. We're well ahead of time."

He was in good spirits because a routine week had been enlivened unexpectedly by a welcome social engagement. The previous evening he had received a telephone call from Señora Velázquez, inviting him to the Esmeralda hotel to attend a special reception she was giving for El Nuevo Santo.

The opportunity to meet Mexico's most celebrated wrestler was attractive enough. But no less appealing to Torres was the prospect of renewing his acquaintance with Esperanza Velázquez.

There was very little that happened in Acapulco's tourist-geared society without the knowledge of its omnipotent police chief. His network of informants embraced all the major hotels and nightspots, and thus he had been advised almost immediately of the arrival of El Nuevo Santo. More significantly, he had known for weeks that Guillermo Velázquez had left the country, and was not expected to return.

Though married, and with a long-established *casa chica,* Torres still regarded Señora Velázquez as a highly desirable target— physically attractive, well-connected, and so wealthy in her own right that she need never be the financial burden that his current, tiresomely demanding mistress had become. Now, with Guillermo out of the way, seemed a good time to make his first move.

As the Lincoln Continental neared the summit of the Scenic Highway, Torres looked at his Rolex watch. "Not quite so fast, Jorge," he said. "You know I like to arrive exactly on time: not a moment too soon, not a moment too late." It was 10.45 a.m.

In Mexico City's police headquarters, Coronel Ignacio Torres, the younger brother of Ernesto, was seated in front of his chief's enormous mahogany desk, patiently awaiting General Delgado's reaction to his latest report.

El Jefe was puzzled. An entire day had elapsed since his men had lost contact with Nicholas Stephanopoulos at the

332

Arena México. Subsequently, the bug-monitoring unit had not recorded a single sound from within the Greek's apartments; only insignificant telephone messages left by assorted reward-seekers.

Early this Thursday morning, Delgado had felt justified in ordering his men to enter the apartments. "Turn the place upside down, if need be," he had told Torres. "We must find some clue to the *cabrón's* whereabouts."

But *El Robot* had nothing of value to report. There was not a scrap of evidence to suggest where the Greek might have gone. All his clothes were still there, as well as various personal belongings, and two suitcases. Moreover, all the bugs were still in place, and operational. And that message left by the kidnappers was still on the answering machine.

Delgado doodled on his notepad as he considered his options. Finally, he responded, "There's nothing for it. We'll have to put out an *orden de arresto* for him. Have his picture circulated to all patrol units, and have men on special duty at the main bus depots, and the airport. Orders are to detain him on sight, to take him into protective custody, forcefully if necessary.

"I want this given top priority, you understand, Torres? Don't involve the media at this stage. But find the Greek *cabrón* - and fast."

At precisely 11 a.m., the Lincoln Continental pulled up in the forecourt of the Esmeralda hotel. Corporal Barrientos quickly got out, opened the rear door for his chief and subsequently helped him on with his uniform jacket, giving it a few cursory flicks with his gloved right hand.

After fetching out the *Jefe's* gun belt and holster, Barrientos made a move to get the chief's cap and gloves, which were lying on the back seat. But he was forestalled. "I will not need those," said Torres. Having strapped on his gun belt, he pulled out a comb and stroked it twice over his centrally parted, sleeked-back hair, then, very precisely, using both hands, he donned a pair of gold-rimmed shades taken from his breast pocket.

"General! How nice to see you again! I am so glad you were able to come."

He looked over the roof of the car to see Señora Valázquez approaching down the marble steps of the hotel's front entrance. He moved round to meet her, then took her extended hand, sandwiching it in a two-handed grasp.

333

"Ah! *Querida señora,*" he gushed. "Thank you so much for inviting me. I am not too early, I hope?"

"Absolutely not, General. You are right on time. The other guests have not yet arrived, but that is because El Nuevo Santo especially wants to meet you first, and discuss security arrangements for his coming fight.

"Now, what about your driver? The reception will last at least an hour-and-a-half. Would he perhaps like to wait in our Laguna Bar? We could lay on a lunch for him there."

Torres smiled. "That's very kind of you. But I would prefer him to stay with the car, just in case there are any urgent police messages on the radio. Then he can contact me on my mobile."

"As you wish, General. I'll have someone show him where he can park."

"Please! We don't need formalities any more. Do call me Ernesto... *Esperanza.*"

Esperanza now led the way to the nearest tower block, and they took the elevator to the penthouse suite occupied by Julio and his three companions. Rodrigo, dressed in a business suit, opened the door when they rang. Beyond him, in the centre of the living-room, Torres saw a figure wearing a white cloak and silver mask.

He did not wait to be ushered in. Immediately, he strode past Rodrigo and went up to the masked man. "Ah! El Nuevo Santo. I'd recognise you anywhere," he joked. "Let me introduce myself: Teniente-General Torres. Chief of police. At your service."

He extended his right hand. In response, the masked man drew out a hand from beneath his cloak. In it, looking rather like a TV remote control, was an Air Taser stun-gun. He pressed the trigger button with his thumb.

Powered by a single nine-volt battery, the weapon immediately released compressed air that fired two wire-guided darts into Torres' chest. The probes stuck to his jacket, simultaneously emitting a high-voltage electrical impulse that attacked the neuromuscular system.

The police chief crumbled to the floor in a daze. Operation Terror was about to begin.

Regina Marke gave out a piercing scream as the man called Francisco straddled her waist and leant over to pin her arms behind her head. She spat in his face.

"Give him a hand," said the tall, smartly suited man who stood at the end of the bunk on which she was lying. A third man promptly crouched down behind her, putting a hand over her mouth, and holding her down by the forehead.

Regina squirmed, and registered wide-eyed alarm as she saw that the tall man was approaching her with a hypodermic needle in his hand. He spoke softly, in the matter-of-fact style of a professional medic.

"Now then, *señorita,* this is not going to hurt, provided that you keep absolutely still. In fact, you may soon find it to be rather pleasant."

Accepting her fate, she stopped struggling, and braced herself as the needle penetrated a vein in her right arm. It was neatly done, only a mild pricking sensation.

Francisco eased himself off her body, but before releasing his grip on her wrists, he spat back in her face.

Regina wiped her face with a sleeve. Then, glaring at her assailants, she shouted, *"Cerdos asquerosos!"*

The tall man smiled. "Don't blame us, *señorita.* Blame your Greek friend. All this would have been unnecessary if he had done what we told him."

Regina sat up, clutching her violated right arm. "What have you put in me?"

"Only some top-quality heroin. Just enough to give you a taste for it. We'll see how you feel tomorrow."

"Wait," she called out as he followed the other men up the steps. "I must have something to drink." There was no reply, only the sound of bolts being drawn after they had closed the heavy wooden door behind them.

As he slowly regained consciousness, Teniente-General Torres was first aware of a severe soreness in his wrists. He straightened his legs to take his body weight, and immediately the pain eased.

Within a few seconds, all his senses were restored, and the full horror of his situation dawned on him. He was strung up between two marble pillars, his legs and arms stretched out diagonally, and bound by ropes. Something was strapped across his mouth, making it impossible to speak. And he was totally naked.

The view directly ahead alarmed him even more.

335

Seated on separate chairs were three men wearing black masks, and standing to one side of them was a white-cloaked, silver-masked figure, the man he had recognised as El Nuevo Santo. In his right hand was a three-foot-long, silver-bladed machete.

In a panic, Torres tugged violently on the ropes, but he could move his hands and legs no more than half-a-metre from the pillars.

Then one of the black-masked men stood up and approached him. As they had planned, all the talking was to be left to Julio. Schooled in the tough back-street vernacular of the Tepito jungle, he was best equipped to speak in a voice designed to convey savagery and menace.

He stood in spitting distance of the police chief, stretched his mouth in a wide, teeth-flashing grin, then spoke slowly and deliberately, "Welcome to hell, shit-head. How terrible this hell will be is going to depend entirely on you. I suggest, for a start, that you stop squirming. You will only tighten the ropes."

There was a long pause as he turned away, and took a few paces with head bowed, as though composing his thoughts. Then he again stood directly in front of Torres, his arms folded across his chest.

"Right, General arsehole. Now listen very carefully to what I am going to say. We don't have time to screw around. We want answers *at once*. There will be no second chance. Your miserable life will depend on how far you co-operate in the next ten minutes or so.

"But first let me introduce you to someone. Just so that you fully appreciate your position, I want you to meet the *real* Nuevo Santo."

He nodded to the white-cloaked figure who immediately came forward, his machete held in two hands across his chest. The figure then stood perfectly still as Julio reached behind his head to unstrap and remove his silver mask.

Julio turned back to face Torres. "Well, scumbag, I am sure you will recognise our friend. Anyway, let me introduce you. Meet Señor Stephanopoulos. The man who had his wife and son killed in cold blood in Chapultepec Park."

Nicholas stared at the police chief, his eyes glaring with genuine hate. Meanwhile, Julio continued, according to plan. "As you can see, there is no El Nuevo Santo. But don't blame yourself. Señora Velázquez made the same mistake.

And, like you, she is now safely tied up.

"Okay, Señor Stephanopoulos. What shall we do with this *culero*?"

Nicholas, still glaring, said nothing. Instead, he moved in close to one pillar and then, gripping the black hilt of his machete in both hands, placed its cold blade against the base of Torres' genitalia.

"Oh dear!" said Julio. "How interesting!" He moved still closer to Torres, confronting him eyeball to eyeball. "Tell me, scumbag, have you ever seen a picture of a Chinese eunuch? I have. Nothing there at all. And very painful, they tell me.

"With one quick swipe they would remove the entire scrotum and penis. The agony is intense, and that was using a very sharp knife. I'm afraid this machete may not do the job quite so neatly.

"Afterwards, for the rest of your miserable life, you will have chronic infections. It will be painful just having a pee. And no more sex, of course. But the good news is that you could still live like that to a very great age."

Nicholas pressed the blade more firmly against the chief's genitalia, and Torres froze in terror. "Don't do it, *señor,*" said Julio. "Maybe, this *culero* can help us."

He turned again to the petrified Torres. "Sorry about that. But I am not sure I can control this gentleman. He is very temperamental, and he has got it into his head that you are responsible for killing his wife and son. I can only suggest that you keep absolutely still."

He paused deliberately. "It's really up to you, General, whether you keep or lose your manhood. Now then. I am going to ask you a few simple questions. For this purpose we will remove your gag. But one scream, just one wrong word, and you will be a desexed chicken. Understand?"

Torres nodded frantically.

"*Bueno,*" said Julio. "But remember this. We are desperate men, and we are in a hurry. No questions will be repeated. We want straight answers... and nothing else. Just one unsatisfactory answer, just the faintest hint that you are lying and..." He swung his right hand in a chopping motion. "Whoosh!"

Julio turned, and nodded towards another man in a black-mask. Rodrigo promptly left his seat, and came forward to remove the wide strip of adhesive tape that had sealed the police chief's mouth. Torres let out an uncontrollable yelp as the tape was ripped from his thin moustache.

Then he felt the machete pressing still more firmly against his genitalia. He looked at Nicholas goggle-eyed.

"Right," said Julio. "Question one. And be very careful how you answer. Remember we know quite a lot already.

"Here it comes. Did you know in advance that the birthday party was going to be held in Chapultepec Park?

"*Sí.*"

"How did you know?"

Torres' voice trembled. "Guillermo Velázquez told me."

"*Bueno.* You see, we can tell when you are telling the truth. So don't risk telling a lie. It would mean instant castration.

"Now another question: What did you do with this information from Velázquez?"

"I don't understand."

At once there was pressure on the machete blade. Torres gasped, his eyes and mouth open wide. Though he could not see it, a small trickle of blood had begun to ooze from the innermost part of his groin.

"Wrong answer, arsehole," said Julio. "That's your very last warning. Just give straight answers. Nothing else.

"I repeat. What *exactly* did you do with the information?"

"I told Doctor Zaragoza."

"Oh yes. And who is Doctor Zaragoza?"

"He runs the Miguel Alemán Clinic, here in Acapulco."

"Why did you tell him?"

"I knew he wanted to know about anything involving Secretario Martínez."

"Why did he want to know?"

Torres paused, looking anxiously towards Nicholas, then taking a deep breath.

"He was planning to assassinate Martínez."

"I see." Julio broke off, briefly pacing to one side as he collected his thoughts. In that short interval, Nicholas rested the point of his machete on the floor. Torres closed his eyes as though in prayer. But in seconds Julio was resuming his questions, and once again the blade was poised to deliver the dreaded amputation.

338

As before, Julio spoke with his arms folded across his chest. "Now then, shit-head, I am going to ask you several questions. And this time I want a *full* explanation. But be sure to keep it to the point. Understand?"

"*Sí.*"

"Right then. Explain this. Exactly what is the role of Doctor Zaragoza in all this? Why should he want Martínez killed? And what was your part in the assassination plan? Think carefully before you reply. Remember we can easily know if you are lying."

Torres took another deep breath. Then, in a tremulous voice, he began:

"Zaragoza is a key man in distributing drugs throughout México, and his clinic is a cover for his operations. I understood that he wanted Martínez killed because he had uncovered details of the drugs network. My part was only to provide someone who could be blamed for the crime."

He looked desperately towards Nicholas. "Please, *señor*. Believe me, I had no idea that anyone else would be killed. What happened to your family was unforgivable. I..."

"Enough!" Julio shouted. "No speeches. Just keep to the facts. So who did you provide?"

"Just a common thief. The man who has been named as the assassin. Manuel Ramírez."

Julio gritted his teeth. "Then what happened?"

"To Ramírez? I don't really know. We just took him to the clinic. My guess is that they got him hooked on drugs, and somehow persuaded him to take part in the assassination plan. Really, I can't tell you any more."

Following renewed pressure, more blood oozed from the minor wound to his groin. "Please, please," Torres begged. "That's all I know. Truly. I couldn't ask Zaragoza too many questions."

"Why not?"

"You just didn't, that's all. Zaragoza is very secretive - and dangerous. He has friends in very high places, and powerful Mafia connections."

"Like who?"

"Truly, *señor*. I don't know. And I never dared to ask. Everyone is frightened of Zaragoza. All I know is that he works for the New Gulf cartel, and is a kind of paymaster, responsible for handing out bribes. Through him, they have

339

control over top officials in the government, the police and the military. Everyone takes bribes from them, even officers of our anti-narcotics agency, and the coastguard service."

"And how about you? Are you in their pay?"

Torres swallowed hard. "*Sí.* "

At that point, the third and tallest of the masked men left his chair, and whispered in Julio's ear. Julio nodded to McClellan, and then resumed his interrogation.

"Be sure to answer this next question truthfully. Exactly how did Zaragoza know that Martínez had information about the drugs cartel racket?"

Again Torres looked pleadingly towards Nicholas before giving his answer. "Truly, I swear on my mother's life that I do not know. Zaragoza never explained that sort of thing."

McClellan returned to his seat, alongside Rodrigo. Then, for the first time, Nicholas spoke. But before doing so, he leaned across Torres, stooping to place his left hand against the blunt side of his machete's blade. It was as though he was preparing to make one clean, decisive cut.

He looked upwards, hatefully into Torres' face. "I have just one question for you, *cabrón*. Do you know what has happened to my assistant, Señorita Regina Marke?"

Torres did not hesitate. He nodded frantically. "*Sí, sí, señor*. I do know that. I heard that she has been taken to the Miguel Alemán Clinic."

Nicholas maintained his firm grip on the blade. "Are you sure? How do you know?"

"I have an informant inside the clinic - one of the *guaruras*. He told me that the *señorita* was being held prisoner there. But truly, I know nothing more than that."

Nicholas pulled the blade away, and stood up straight. Torres was crying now, the tears dripping down his flushed face. "Please, *señores*," he said in a croaking voice. "Could I have a drink of water?"

Julio signalled to Rodrigo. Accordingly, he fetched a glass of water, and then held it to the police chief's parched lips. Frantically, Torres gulped the drink, much of it spilling down his chin, and on to his bare chest.

At that point Nicholas threw his machete onto the marble floor and, fist clenched, stormed out of the room. Julio and McClellan promptly followed him into the kitchenette. There they found the Greek removing his white cloak.

"I can't take any more of this charade," he snapped. "Another minute with that slimy creature, and I swear that I will kill him."

Julio sympathised. "I don't blame you. But I think I have first claim on the *cabrón*. After all, he was the one who sacrificed my brother."

McClellan fixed them with a stern look. "For God's sake, stop and think. No one is going to kill Torres... not yet. If we are going to save Señorita Marke, we need to keep him very much alive."

It was 11.35 a.m. when Corporal Jorge Barrientos, responding to a call on his mobile, left the Lincoln Continental and made his way up to the penthouse suite. He was puzzled. Why should his *Jefe* want to see him? And why had his voice sounded so hesitant and slurred? Could it be that his chief was the worse for drink?

But the message was clear enough. "Jorge, I need to see you at once. Come to the penthouse suite in tower block D." He did not hesitate to obey.

On entering the suite, Barrientos never saw Rodrigo standing behind the door. Like his chief, he was immediately greeted with twin darts fired from an Air Taser stungun, though this time the shots struck him in the back. The next thing he knew was that he was lying in what seemed to be a broom cupboard. He had been stripped to his underwear, and he had been bound up with ropes, and gagged with masking tape.

By this time, Torres, though still naked, was seated on a settee. Julio was alongside him, holding a knife to his belly.

"You did that last call well," said Julio. "But now comes the *real* test. You are going to make the most important call of your life. I leave it to you what to say. But think carefully about it. We have told you what we want. And if your call doesn't get the required result, I promise you - you will be butchered meat."

The police chief breathed deeply, trying to compose himself before he picked up the telephone, and dialled a number. Several seconds passed before anyone answered. Then he spoke with as much authority as he could summon.

"This is Teniente-General Torres speaking. I wish to speak to Doctor Zaragoza... urgently."

CHAPTER 26

It was noon, just one hour since Teniente-General Ernesto Torres had arrived at the Esmeralda hotel. And now, for the first time, the police chief was able to think clearly about his situation. Following his two phone calls, they had awarded him a measure of dignity by allowing him to put on his trousers and shirt. Then they had left him alone, bound only at the wrists, which were roped around the back of a single pillar.

To be sure, he remained profoundly frightened. Most especially he felt threatened by the Greek, whose eyes had blazed such pent-up savagery and hatred. But he was no longer completely paralysed with fear. He was thinking ahead, trying to anticipate future events. And uppermost in his mind was the need to remain alert at all times, to be prepared to act instantly, if circumstances offered a chance of escape.

Both their questions and their demands had already given him a shrewd idea of what his captors were planning. In the final interrogation session, the tallest of the masked men had questioned him at length about the Miguel Alemán Clinic - its location, its layout and security system, including the number and weaponry of its *guaruras*. Then they had compelled him to request an appointment with Doctor Zaragoza that afternoon.

The conclusion was obvious: they were planning to use him in order to gain entry into the fortified premises, probably for the purpose of rescuing Regina Marke. And from this, he derived a morsel of comfort. If his theory was correct, then they would need to keep him alive, at least until their objective had been achieved.

And a lot could happen in that time. Perhaps Zaragoza would be on his guard. Maybe he would have been alerted by the nervous tremble of the voice that had asked to see him so urgently... on a matter so important that he could not safely discuss it on the phone. Perhaps...

Eventually, being unable to think further ahead,

Torres' thoughts wandered back over his interrogation. What exactly had he told them? That the clinic was sited some seven miles inland, high up in the hills behind Acapulco; that it was an isolated hacienda approached by a long driveway through dense woodland, and set in some twenty acres that were surrounded by high stone perimeter walls topped with barbed wire.

With a shaky hand, he had sketched them a rough picture of the overall layout. There was only one entrance, via a main gate near the head of the driveway. This was permanently guarded by plain-clothed *guraras,* who were based in the adjacent lodge. Beyond, the woodland eventually gave way to open grounds that provided no cover, and were scanned by closed-circuit TV cameras.

Across these grounds, the driveway led, via an archway, into a large courtyard at the heart of the hacienda. This area was always floodlit at night. On the northern side were the two-storey private quarters of Doctor Zaragoza, and directly opposite was a huge hangar-like building, which had replaced a complex of treatment rooms and a swimming pool.

Another side of the courtyard was lined with a single-storey row of luxury apartments once reserved for the clinic's exclusive clientele. Here, until three years ago, the rich and the famous came for prolonged health treatment, most commonly to combat alcoholism or drug addiction. Subsequently, potential clients had been told that the clinic was closed for extensive redevelopment.

The private apartments, Torres had explained, were now occupied by *guraras.* Altogether, there were some twenty of them, and those on guard duty were armed with .38 Special revolvers and 9 mm. Uzi submachine-guns.

He had not been inside their quarters, nor had he been inside the great hangar. However, he had been told that the latter was a storehouse for drugs, primarily cocaine shipped in from Colombia. It also garaged a fleet of two-ton army trucks which, driven by uniformed "soldiers", were used to bring in the drugs, and later to transport them to safe house distribution centres throughout the country.

Next, he remembered, his inquisitor had asked him about the layout of Doctor Zaragoza's quarters. He explained that he had never been upstairs in the main colonial-style building where the doctor had his private apartments. On the ground floor, however, he recalled that an inner gallery extended along the entire front of the building, and led to a large livingroom, which had a full-sized billiards table in the centre. It was the only room he had seen, and, as far he knew, there were no security devices there.

Throughout the questioning, Torres had been too terrified to deliberately hold anything back. He had answered spontaneously, as fully as his panicky thinking would allow. Most importantly, hoping to curry some favour, he had volunteered the suggestion that Regina Marke might be held prisoner in the cellars below the main building.

But now, on reflection, he realised that he had neglected to tell them what he had heard about the upstairs rooms. There, so it was rumoured, the doctor had a large study crowded with precious *objets d'art* and valuable paintings.

And here he had one other slightly comforting thought. He had neglected to tell them that the doctor's inner sanctum— so he had been told— was protected by a most unusually sophisticated security system.

While Torres was left alone to ponder his fate, his captors were gathered in the master bedroom, where Brad McClellan had taken charge of planning their next moves. Laid out on the double bed was an array of weaponry that had been unloaded from the sports holdall that had been carried into the hotel by Rodrigo.

This small arsenal, collected by McClellan from a CIA safe house in Mexico City, included three strange-looking shotguns, which had a pair of tubular magazines mounted atop a full-length barrel that extended almost to the end of the shoulder butt. In addition, there were four pistols, three tear-gas canisters, cardboard boxes containing ammunition, a couple of hand grenades, plus four gun belts and special shoulder holsters.

In Mexico City, McClellan had not troubled to familiarise his companions with these weapons. "It's unlikely that we will have occasion to use them," he had said. "But we have to be prepared, just in case we should strike lucky, and see a way of rescuing Miss Marke."

They had struck lucky. And now everyone was agreed that they needed to act swiftly and independently. As McClellan observed, "It's useless trying to seek official help. There is absolutely no one we can trust. Corruption is just too

344

widespread."

In the bedroom, McClellan was demonstrating how to handle one of the shotguns. None of the other men had fired a gun before. But, as he stressed, no great skill was needed to use this weapon. "You don't have to be a good shot to handle a Neostead shotgun. In fact, its recoil system is so good that it can be held and fired with one hand."

He held the South African-made gun with two hands, the butt pressed hard into his shoulder as he peered down the raised sights. "This way it can be used like a rifle, and with great accuracy over a hundred metres or more. It can fire thirteen rounds in rapid succession, and it is powerful enough to stop a light tank in its tracks.

"On operations in Colombia, we found it most effective when fired from the hip and used like an old-fashioned blunderbuss to spray advancing troops with hundreds of lethal ball bearings.

"The joy of this weapon is that it can be loaded with at least two different types of ammunition at the same time. As you can see, it has two tube-shaped magazines, and you can alternate between them automatically, or select just one, as you wish.

"For our purposes, I suggest we load just one tube with ball bearings. The other can be used, as need be. For example, we could use the spare tube to fire teargas canisters through windows from a distance of one hundred feet or more.

"Then again, by loading specially designed cartridges, we could use it to blast down a door without hurting anyone in the room beyond. The FBI have found that especially useful in hostage rescue operations."

He pointed to the two grenades. "And these can provide a valuable backup. They are special magnesium-based concussion grenades. We call them 'flashbangs'. On exploding, they just dazzle and stun people temporarily, without doing them any lasting harm. They were first used successfully in rescuing hostages in a hijacked German aircraft at Mogadishu, way back in the 1970s, and again in the Iranian embassy siege in London in 1980.

"Right. Take up a shotgun, and get the feel of it. They are not as heavy as they look, and they are small enough to carry in a concealed shoulder holster."

After answering questions about loading procedures, McClellan put down the shotgun, and picked up one of the

345

pistols. "Now this is something special, too. A Belgian-made Five-Seven. It may look ordinary enough, but it has twenty times the range and penetrating power of commonly used police pistols. It uses the same 5.7mm. ammo as a sub-machine-gun, and yet it has sixty percent less recoil than a .44 Magnum.

"Until a few years ago, our special anti-terrorist units were using the Browning 9mm. pistol, which fires eight-gram bullets at a speed of three hundred fifty metres per second. Well, this pistol is far superior. It fires bullets weighing only two grams, at a muzzle velocity of six hundred fifty metres per second. In other words, nearly twice as fast."

Nicholas looked at him impatiently. "Okay, we have got the point: these weapons are the best. But, hell! We haven't got time for one of your training lectures. Let's get a move on. We are losing valuable time, and heaven knows what they may doing to Regina."

"Patience," snapped McClellan. "You're forgetting that all our plans depend on precise timing. We have to synchronise every move we make, and at the moment we are right on schedule. And, Nicholas, let me remind you of one other thing: at all times, you take orders from me. No one fires without my say-so.

"If we are lucky, and everything goes according to plan, we may not need to use these weapons at all. On the other hand, we must always be prepared for the unexpected. And remember this: whatever happens, if it is humanly possible, I want this Doctor Zaragoza taken alive."

"And what about Torres?" asked Julio. "Do you want him kept alive?"

McClellan shrugged. "I leave that to you. As far I am concerned, he is expendable - at least once we have got inside the hacienda. There is just one other thing."

He turned to Rodrigo. "Everything has gone smoothly so far. But from now on, we are putting our lives on the line. We are facing a real combat situation. I understand why Nicholas and Julio want to take the risk. But this is not really your fight. Are you sure you want to be involved? No one would blame you if you backed out."

Rodrigo feigned horror. "How can you ask such a thing? Julio is my *compadre*. His fight is my fight." He grinned. "Anyway, I have to protect my interests. El Nuevo Santo is— how do you say it?— my meal-ticket."

McClellan smiled. "Okay, Rambo."

But he was not really amused. He admired the resolve of his companions, but he still harboured serious doubts about the wisdom of going into action with such complete amateurs. Also, as he had told them, he would normally regard the wearing of body-armour essential in an operation of this kind. Unfortunately, he had been unable to get hold of protectors in time.

"Right then. Let's get ready. Everyone, sychronize your watches precisely. I make it exactly 1255 hour... Okay? Good. Now, Nicholas, it's time for you to make that phone call."

For the second time that day, Nicholas dialled the number of the Greek embassy in Mexico City, and asked to be put through to the cultural attaché. He spoke in his native tongue. "Viktor, we are just about to leave as planned. Stay by the phone, and be ready to act when you get our call in about half an hour. We are all depending on you."

Teniente-General Torres was feeling almost human again. He had donned his full-dress uniform, and he had even been allowed to strap on his broad leather belt and gun holster, complete with his cherished pearl-handled Colt .45 revolver, albeit with the bullets removed.

All his captors were now unmasked, and he studied their features carefully for the purpose of future identification. The slim, darkly-handsome Greek he already knew by name. And he had already concluded - from his ponderous Spanish accent, his fair complexion and crew-cut hairstyle - that the tall, burly McClellan was an *americano*. The other two were unmistakably Mexican, and in the case of Julio he felt certain that he had seen him somewhere before.

Three of the men were now dressed in identical, dark-blue tracksuits and sneakers. The other was wearing the uniform of Corporal Barrientos, and it fitted him perfectly. Torres wondered whether or not his driver was still alive, but he was too afraid to ask.

It was shortly before 1330 hours.when Rodrigo, in corporal's uniform, started up the Lincoln Continental. Teniente-General Torres, wearing his peaked cap and gold-rimmed shades, was seated alongside him, and the prodding of a pistol muzzle in the back of his neck reminded him that Brad McClellan was seated directly behind him.

As they moved off, McClellan leaned over so closely that Torres could feel his breath. "You may be thinking," he whispered. "That I can't afford to kill you. And you are right. There will be no quick death for you. Just one false move, one wrong word, and I'll shoot off one of your ears. Then maybe the other. I promise. You can count on it."

Torres' compliance was quickly put to the test. At the end of Esmeralda's driveway, they were surprised to see one of the security guards waving them down. Rodrigo pulled up and wound down his window. "Is something wrong, officer?" he asked casually.

"Not at all. But I had orders to give you this when you left." He handed Rodrigo a pink envelope. Then, seeing Torres beyond the driver, he saluted. "Have a good day, General."

Driving on, Rodrigo glanced down at the envelope, then passed it over his shoulder to Julio. "It's addressed to you, *compadre.*"

Inside the envelope, Julio found a note written in a neat, artistic longhand. It read:

Beloved,

For the first time in years, I have remembered a little poem that my mother taught me as a child:

> The sun lights up a drop of dew.
> The drop of dew soon dries.
> You are the light of my eyes, my eyes.
> I'm brought to life by you.

God speed, querido. And please, PLEASE, come back safely.

Love,
Esperanza."

"Any trouble?" asked McClellan.

Julio folded the note carefully and, unzipping his tracksuit, slipped it into the breast pocket of his shirt. "No.

Everything is fine. Just a note from Esperanza wishing all of us luck."

At 1400 hours, assistant manager Zavala hastened from his office to the penthouse suite of tower block D. He had been feeling miffed at his exclusion from the reception for El Nuevo Santo, though this had since been tempered by the surprising discovery that Teniente-General Torres had been the only guest.

Now he felt only alarm. Señora Velázquez had sounded almost hysterical on the phone. "Come at once," she had cried. "Something terrible has happened!"

Responding immediately to Julio's call on his mobile, Esperanza was playing her prearranged part to perfection and on time. When Zavala arrived, he found the door open, and his boss seated in a distressed state on a settee. Her dress was torn, and some ropes were scattered on the floor.

"Oh! Thank God, you are here," she said. "It was just awful. They had guns, and they tied me up. I have only just managed to get free." Then, burying her head in her hands, she began to sob.

Zavala sat down beside her, took hold of one of her hands, and tried to calm her. "It's all right, *señora*. It's all right now. You are safe. Try to tell me what has happened."

Esperanza straightened up, and seemingly composed herself. "I don't really know. They must have been terrorists or something. All I know is that they took the General away."

"But what about El Nuevo Santo and his friends? Didn't they help?"

"You don't understand. They were the ones who did this. The man who called himself El Nuevo Santo seemed to be one of them. Perhaps he wasn't the great wrestler at all."

Zavala stood up. "I'll call the police at once."

"Wait," said Esperanza. "I have just remembered something else. They got the General's driver up here. They tied him up, too. I think they put him in the broom cupboard. You had better check."

Zavala checked. He found Corporal Barrientos gagged and trussed up like a chicken, his legs doubled behind him and roped to his hands so that he could not move or make a sound.

Barrientos needed several minutes to get back full

349

mobility in his limbs. Then, after downing a whisky provided by Zavala, he began to take command of the situation.

"We must act quickly. How long have these men been gone?"

"I don't know," said Zavala. "I have been working in the office. I didn't see them leave."

"I know," said Esperanza. "It must have been about half an hour ago."

"Any idea where they were heading?"

Esperanza smiled. "I know that, too. I heard one of them say something about the Miguel Alemán Clinic. I think, maybe, they were taking the General there as a hostage."

Bueno," said Barrientos. And he picked up the telephone.

The Lincoln Continental had pulled off the road and was parked in woodland, some one hundred yards from the turnoff into the driveway leading to the Miguel Alemán Clinic. While Rodrigo remained in the driver's seat, keeping a gun— Barrientos' .38 revolver— trained on Torres, the others had got out to unload the sports holdall from the trunk.

All were now armed with a Neostead shotgun, and wearing a gun belt with a Five-seveN pistol in the holster. In addition, McClellan had the two stun grenades in pouches attached to his belt.

Julio had laid down his shotgun while making a call to Esperanza at precisely 1355 hours. Now he passed the mobile to Nicholas, and they checked their watches, and waited. Then, at 1410 hours, exactly as scheduled, Nicholas rang the number of the Greek embassy. Again, he got through to the cultural attaché. "Okay, Viktor," he said. "You should start phoning now."

Ten minutes later, the Lincoln Continental turned into the long driveway. Again, McClellan prodded his pistol into the back of Torres' neck. "It's up to you now, General. If we don't get in, I will be shooting to kill."

At police headquarters in Mexico City, General Juan Delgado received a call on his private line. It was Isabel del Río of Channel 13 TV, and her opening gambit took him

350

completely by surprise.

"*Buenas tardes*, Juan. Sorry to trouble you, but I wondered if you would like to make any comment on the Acapulco crisis."

"Crisis? What crisis?"

"You mean you don't know about it?"

Delgado was getting irritated. "No, Isabel. I don't. Why don't you tell me about it."

"Well, we have just had this tip-off from the Greek embassy. I thought that you might be interested because Señor Stephanopoulos is involved. It seems that he went down to Acapulco following up information about the Chapultepec Park murders. Anyway, I don't understand how or why, but we are told that the Greek, and Teniente-General Torres, the Acapulco police chief, are being held hostage at the Miguel Alemán Clinic."

Delgado took a deep breath. "I can't believe it. It doesn't make sense."

"Maybe not," said Del Río. "But they are taking it seriously in Acapulco. I have just phoned the police down there. They tell me that they have already called out a team of Zorros to storm the place. They are treating it as either a kidnapping, or some kind of terrorist operation."

"*Dios mío!* Are you reporting this on the news?"

"You bet we are. In fact, I am covering it myself. We are leaving by helicopter as soon as possible. Should be a great story. Pity it's not an exclusive."

"What do you mean?"

"Just that. This guy from the Greek embassy said that he was telling me about it first. But he added that he wanted maximum coverage, and that he would be ringing all his media contacts - the other TV channels, as well as CNN, *Time* and *Newsweek.*

"Sorry, Juan. They are calling me. I've got to go."

Delgado lit a cigar, leant back in his swivel chair, and thought for a while. Finally, he summoned Coronel Ignacio Torres on his buzzer, and told him all that del Río had said.

"He's your brother, Torres, so you may want to check with Acapulco headquarters. But you can leave me out of it. I can't cover up for these arseholes any more."

Then, after Torres had left, he got on his direct line to Los Pinos.

CHAPTER 27

It was 1416 hours when Coronel Carlos Rivas personally took the emergency phone call from Corporal Jorge Barrientos. As the acting deputy to the Acalpulco Chief of Police, he found himself in a quandary. It was only hearsay that terrorists or kidnappers had taken his *Jefe* as a hostage, possibly holding him prisoner in the Miguel Alemán Clinic. How should he respond to such an improbable report?

He could be in deep trouble with the chief if the report was correct and he did not react quickly. By the same token, he could equally be in trouble if it was a false alarm, and he authorised an unjustified police raid on the clinic.

To add to his confusion, Rivas had heard the rumours that the clinic was a centre for illegal smuggling. Still more rife were rumours it was a base for the development of top-secret biochemical weapons - hence the unusual movement of army vehicles in and out of the complex. On the other hand, his *Jefe* had firmly dismissed such stories, insisting that the clinic was merely undergoing major redevelopment before reopening in a few years' time.

Thus various ideas entered his head. He could phone the clinic to seek confirmation of the report. But if the report was correct, then he would be revealing to the terrorists that their position was known. He could alert the *Zorros,* and have the paramilitary police force standing by for action. Or he could do nothing, and wait for the abductors to make their demands.

It was another telephone call— received only a few minutes later— that spurred Rivas into making a decision. Isabel del Rio, the celebrated television presenter, was on the line. She had heard that Señor Stephanopoulos and the Acapulco police chief were being held hostage at the Miguel Alemán Clinic. Could the Coronel confirm this? And if so, what action would he be taking?

"Who told you this?" he asked.

"I can't tell you that," she replied. "But I can say it is a fairly reliable source. Are you saying our information is wrong?"

"Not necessarily. We just don't have all the facts yet. And anyway, who is this Stephanopoulos?"

"Oh! Surely you must have heard of him— the Greek billionaire who is offering a reward for information about the

Chapultepec Park murders."

"I see. That Greek."

"You mean, you didn't know he may have been kidnapped?"

"No."

Del Rio persisted. "So then how about your police chief. Is he missing?"

"*Sí.*"

"So what are you doing about it, Coronel? Are you just going to wait till you hear from the kidnappers?"

Rivas reacted defensively. "Of course not. We have our *Zorros* standing by. I cannot say any more at this stage. Now, if you will excuse me, I must get on."

The Coronel was still pondering his position when he received a succession of similar inquiries from the Mexican media, plus *Time* and *Newsweek*. This resolved the issue for him. The eyes of the world were on him, and he could not be seen to be dithering. He would alert the *Zorros* to be ready to move on the Miguel Alemán Clinic, with the backup of the newly formed police helicopter unit.

It was now beginning to make some sense. Kidnappings of wealthy businessmen had become commonplace in Mexico. Maybe the clinic was a base used by kidnappers, and maybe the police chief had just got caught up in a snatching by accident.

That would explain the puzzle, which had already prompted a joke circulating among his staff: *Why should anyone kidnap the Jefe? Because they are going to demand a big ransom for NOT releasing him.*

Subsequently, by phone, Rivas discussed the options with Comandante Luis González, the *Zorro* commander. He mooted his idea of making a preliminary phone call to the clinic. But the experienced commander opposed the suggestion.

"If there are terrorists or kidnappers in the clinic, we do not want to alert them. It would lose us our greatest advantage: the element of surprise. Also, it could lead to a long-drawn-out siege situation.

"Our first objective must be to seal off and secure the area. If, in the meantime, you receive demands from the kidnappers, we may have to negotiate with them. On the other hand, if demands have still not been made when we have our men in position, then I recommend we take the initiative,

353

and make a lightning strike before they are put on their guard."

Rivas agreed. "Very well, Comandante. Draw up what plans you think necessary. But I will be personally taking overall command of the operation. How soon can your men be ready to move?"

González could scarcely conceal his disgust. "Coronel, we are *always* ready. We can move off just as soon as you are ready to join us."

It was 1435 hours when the Lincoln Continental pulled up in front of the barrier at the head of the long driveway into the Miguel Alemán Clinic. The entrance was blocked by an electrically operated wooden boom wrapped in barbed wire. And immediately they were approached by a *guarura* who emerged from the adjacent lodge. He wore jungle green denims, and had an Uzi sub-machine-gun slung over his right shoulder.

Félix Calderón, like so many *guaruras*, was an ex-policeman who, out of financial necessity, had turned to work in the private sector. Instinctively, on seeing Torres, he gave a smart salute.

"*Buenas tardes*, General," he said. "You are expected."

Normally, Calderón would inspect any unauthorised vehicle before having the boom lifted. On this occasion, it never occurred to him to look in the back where McClellan, Ramírez and Stephanopoulos were seated behind tinted closed windows.

But he did observe one routine. After signalling for the boom to be raised, he stepped onto the running board. "I will escort you to the hacienda," he said.

Ricardo coughed, and Torres got the message. "That will not be necessary," he said. "We know the way well enough."

"But, General," Calderón protested. "I have my orders to accompany all visitors."

Torres turned to him and snapped, "I said it will not be necessary. Corporal, drive on."

He spoke with such authority the *guarura* automatically stepped back, and as the boom went up Rodrigo let out the clutch.

McClellan leaned forward, stroking his pistol across Torres' neck. "You did well, General. Keep it up, and you

354

might still come out of this alive."

Torres said nothing. His thoughts were focussed well ahead. He had already decided on the moment when he hoped to be able to make his move.

Within five minutes of Coronel Rivas' call, Comandante González had assembled his *Zorros* in the briefing room above the old fire brigade station in downtown Acapulco. Below, the depot that had once housed fire engines was now occupied by five armoured cars equipped with 3.5-inch rocket launchers, six jeeps and eight Kawasaki ZX-12R superbikes fitted with bulletproof visors and leg guards.

His élite paramilitary group - originally modelled on a U.S. SWAT team - comprised only 40 men, but they were highly trained specialists: all sharpshooters, expert in handling sniper rifles, sub-machine-guns, pump-action shotguns, and automatic pistols; all familiar with a variety of explosives and with techniques for disarming booby traps.

Unlike their American counterparts— most notably those attached to the New York PD— they rarely indulged in a prolonged siege situation, during which a bore-them-to-death psychological approach was adopted. More often than not, the Mexicans favoured a gung ho approach, a quick full-frontal assault. It was an uncompromising tactic not always in the interests of hostages, but one designed to serve as a sharp deterrent to would-be kidnappers. In this respect, as the latest crime statistics indicated, it had had considerable success.

Most commonly, when kidnappers had been located, *Zorros* would launch their attack without prior warning: blasting locks from doors with Remington shotguns, firing in cartridges of CS gas and then, wearing protective masks and flak jackets, bursting into a building or room, and instantly firing shots from their thirteen-round 9mm. Browning pistols.

As close-quarter marksmen, they were specially trained to storm a room in pairs, each man being given a separate arc of fire, each moving continually and, if necessary, rolling over and over on the floor while still shooting. The aim was to hit each target with two shots to the chest; also, they were trained to fire a precise head shot at a kidnapper holding his hostage in front as a shield. In some cases, unfortunately, there was not always time to distinguish between the kidnapper and the kidnapped.

When Coronel Rivas arrived at the *Zorros* depot, he was impressed to see that they were already lined up to move off. It was 1445 hours, only fifteen minutes since he had phoned the commander; and he had driven over in his squad car at breakneck speed, with sirens screaming, to clear the downtown traffic ahead.

Besides his regular driver, Rivas was accompanied by Corporal Barrientos, who had been ordered immediately to take a taxi from the Esmeralda hotel to police headquarters. No sooner had he arrived, than the still-confused corporal found himself back on duty.

He had stressed that he could not identify the men who had kidnapped the General. But Rivas was adamant. "You were responsible for the *Jefe's* safety. He would expect you to be involved in his rescue."

At the depot, Comandante González was standing by a jeep with an ordinance survey map spread out on the hood. He saluted the Coronel, then drew his attention to the map.

"I have already gained a good idea of the layout by going to Google Earth and zooming in on the hacienda. Of course, for really detailed images we could ring Denver and order high-resolution pictures from the NAFTA intelligence 'spy' satellite. Amazing. They can get pictures of objects as small as a metre in diameter. But that could take too much time. I don't think we should delay; and I don't want to alert anyone in the clinic by sending in a helicopter to take aerial photographs.

"Luckily, we have this very detailed map of the area, and I have more information about the layout from one of my men, whose father worked there years ago, when the place was a mezcal-processing plant."

Rivas grinned smugly. "I can do better than that, Comandante." And from his inside pocket, he produced a folded leaflet. "We dug this up from our records department. A brochure promoting the clinic. It's only three years old. It has a map giving directions there, also photographs of the main building, the various treatment rooms, and a large swimming pool."

González flipped quickly through the brochure. "Excellent, Coronel. However, it does not tell us if or how the place is guarded." He pointed to an armoured bulldozer. "I propose taking this along, in case there is a barrier at the entrance."

Drawn up behind the bulldozer were four standard armoured cars, a second jeep with a radio transmitter in the back, and eight motorcycles with their riders— helmets in hand— standing alongside them. Stored in metal containers at the rear of each bike were two CS canisters, a protective mask and first-aid kit. Each rider— a member of the so-called flying squad— wore a bulletproof vest over a black leather zip-suit, and had a sub-machine-gun slung diagonally across his back, plus an automatic pistol and knife in a holster strapped around his right and left calf respectively.

"If you agree, *Coronel*, the plan is to move in on the hacienda at maximum speed, and without giving any advance warning. There is only one route in and out, so we propose the *Tránsito* police should set up a roadblock north and south of the main driveway. Then we will send in our *pelotón volante* for a lightning strike.

"The aim will be to storm the main building before any resistance can be mounted. Of course, it may all be a false alarm, and our men have orders only to shoot if they meet with opposition. But, just in case, we will have armoured cars as a back-up, and we will be in radio contact with the helicopter unit. They will already be airborne and in close striking range.

"Do you approve, *Coronel*?"

"*Sí.* It all makes sense. Just be sure your men understand their mission. The primary aim is to get the *Jefe* out alive. If he is in there, hopefully he will still be in uniform. So let's have no cock-ups like hitting him with indiscriminate fire."

Just as the *Zorro* attack force was preparing to move out of their Acapulco depot, Brad McClellan's four-man hit-squad was speeding down the long driveway towards the hacienda complex. Soon they passed plushy lawns being watered by sprinklers. Then, rounding a fountain in the centre of a courtyard, Rodrigo halted the Lincoln Continental directly outside the front entrance to the main building. Only two men were in sight. They were wearing white overalls. Both were unarmed, and apparently taking a smoke break outside the hangar-like warehouse across the way.

Almost immediately, a *guarura* emerged from the arched main entrance: a rat-faced man with a Zapata moustache. He was dressed in ordinary civilian clothes - blue jeans and a pale yellow, open-necked shirt. But he also wore a

357

gun belt with a .38 revolver in the holster.

He went directly to the open car window where Torres was seated. "*Buenas tardes*, General. The front gate told us you had arrived. Doctor Zaragoza is expecting you, and he has asked me to escort to you to the library. He will join you there in a few minutes."

He then opened the front passenger door, and stood to one side. "My name is Francisco, General. If you would please follow me."

As he spoke, he did not hear McClellan gently open the back door behind him. The next thing he knew, the muzzle of a pistol was being jabbed hard into his waist, and a voice was rasping, "Don't make a sound, *hombre*, or you are dead. Now, just move slowly, and get in the back of the car."

Francisco promptly obeyed. As he ducked down to enter the car, he felt a hand reach out, and remove his revolver from its holster. Ahead of him, two men were seated in the back, and the nearest one— Julio— had a pistol trained on him.

The other man— Nicholas— was looking the other way, out through the tinted rear window, to keep a close eye on the two men standing outside the hangar. The men were looking towards the car, but still puffing on their cigarettes, and seemingly unaware of anything unusual. About half-a-minute later, they trod their fag butts into the dirt, and went back into the building.

Meanwhile, Francisco had found himself squashed on the back seat between strangers. McClellan, who had squeezed in behind him, was now holding two handguns, one of which was being pressed into the side of his neck.

Fixing Francisco with a menacing glare, McClellan did all the talking. "Right, now. We want some answers... and fast. How many *guaruras* are here?

"About twenty, *señor*."

"Where are they... *exactly*?"

"Six are stationed at the main gate. Another six are on loading work in the warehouse. The rest, I don't know. They are on the night shift. They could be anywhere, probably in their private quarters... over there." He pointed directly ahead, to a single-storey row of apartments at the far end of the courtyard.

For a moment, as he looked ahead, Francisco wondered why the General was just sitting there, so still and silent. He could not see that Torres, too, was being held at gunpoint. Then, momentarily, he summoned up a morsel of courage. "Just who are you?" he asked. "And what is it you want?"

McClellan jabbed his second pistol deep into the man's flabby midriff. "Shut up, arsehole! And listen carefully. Who is in the main building?"

Francisco winced under the pressure of the gun. "Just the kitchen staff - and, of course, *El Doctor*."

"Exactly where is Zaragoza?"

"In his study, upstairs."

"Is he alone?"

"I think so, *señor*. But I can't be sure. He might have his secretary with him."

"And is that everyone in the building?"

"*Sí, señor*."

McClellan jabbed the .38 revolver deeper into the man's flab. "Oh yes? Then where is the woman you are holding prisoner?"

Francisco trembled. "Sorry, *señor*, I forgot about her. She is locked in the cellar. Really, that is everyone."

"Is there anyone guarding her?"

"No. She is alone."

McClellan withdrew the gun from Francisco's midriff, looked at his watch,

and then spoke to his companions. "We don't have much time to spare. A Mexican SWAT team could be arriving any time, so let's move fast - more or less as planned.

"Rodrigo, I want you to take up a firing position in that gallery looking out onto the courtyard. If any *guaruras* approach from across the way, try to keep them pinned down with shotgun fire.

"Meanwhile, Nicholas, you take this *hombre,* and get him to guide you down to the cellar. When you have got Regina out, lock him in there and join Rodrigo as quickly as possible.

"Julio and I will take the General, and try to locate this Doctor Zaragoza. Any questions? .... Good! Then let's get going."

Regina Marke was desperate. The light-headedness experienced after the first dose of heroin had long since worn off. Now the hunger pangs had returned, stronger than ever; and, above all, she craved something to drink. The huge temptation was to close her eyes, and surrender to her longing for sleep. But stubbornly, ever since dawn, she had fought against Nature, willing herself to remain awake.

Logically, she had concluded that this was the critical day. By this time tomorrow, she would no longer have the strength, nor the will, to resist. In all probability, they were going to pump into her more of that filthy heroin. So she had to remain alert, ready to take any chance of escape, however remote it might be.

The next time they opened that door was likely to be her last hope of making a bid for freedom.

At the sound of the bolts being drawn back, she moved swiftly— just as she had done once before— to the side of the stone steps. It was now or never. Once again, the door swung open, inwards and away from her. Once again, a blue denim leg appeared.

As the foot reached the second step, level with her shoulder, she reached up and grabbed the ankle in both hands and tugged with all of her strength. And, just as before, the rat-faced man called Francisco was brought crashing to the floor.

Rushing around him, Regina mounted the stairs, again only to find a second man blocking her path. Instinctively, she stretched up with her arms, her fingers— extended like claws— aiming to scratch the man in the face.

And then she saw the face. "Oh Nicholas," she cried out. "Thank God! Thank God you are here!"

In his right hand, Nicholas held a pistol, which he had trained on the prostrate *guarura* below. But now, Regina moved so quickly that his line of fire was impeded. All at once she was on him, reaching up to clutch his waist, and bury her head against his stomach.

Looking over her, Nicholas now saw the *guarura* pulling out a knife that had been concealed in his lower trouser leg. In an instant, the man was on his feet, lunging forward with the dagger held above his head.

"Look out," Nicholas cried. But Regina could not move in time. As the assailant swung the knife towards the small of her back, the Greek reached down to block the flashing blade. He took the full force of the blow on his left forearm.

Almost simultaneously, he pushed Regina to one side, and squeezed the trigger of his pistol. There was no time to take aim. The high-velocity 5.7mm. bullet struck the *guarura* full in the face, virtually obliterating his features.

Regina reacted with extraordinary presence of mind. She saw that the left arm of Nicholas' blue tracksuit had already turned crimson, soaked in blood. And within seconds, fearing that an artery had been severed, she was taking emergency action.

Hurrying back down the steps, she bent over the mutilated corpse of the *guarura,* and removed his leather belt. This she now twisted as tightly as possible around Nicholas' left arm, just above the gaping wound. Then, having stemmed the blood flow with her makeshift tourniquet, she took the loose ends of the belt and buckled them around his neck to form a high sling.

Next, she wrapped her silk headscarf around the wound. "We've got to get that properly bandaged," she said. "I'll get the knife, and cut up some material."

At that moment, they heard the piercing, high-pitched sound of sirens, and seconds later, came the sound of machine-gun fire..

"There's no time," said Nicholas. "Can you get my shotgun out of its holster? Do it now. QUICKLY."

He spoke so commandingly Regina obeyed without thinking. Awkwardly, she pulled out the shotgun from his shoulder holster and, though in obvious pain, he grabbed it in his right hand.

"Thanks. Now, whatever happens, I want you to stay here until I get back. You are not to move. Understand?"

This time Regina did not obey. "Nicholas, I'll go crazy if I stay in this place a minute longer. I am coming with you."

Like Nicholas, McClellan and Julio had entered the main building unobserved, both fully armed, and with a "guide"— Torres— to lead the way at gunpoint. To their left, at the far end of the gallery, they could hear faint sounds of life coming from the kitchens. While Nicholas was being led to the right and down cellar steps, they were guided up a wide, central staircase leading to Dr. Zaragoza's private quarters.

At the top of the stairs, Torres turned right and led them towards an archway at the head of a long corridor. "I can't be sure," he said quietly. "But I think the doctor's study

361

is at the end of that corridor." And then, suddenly, he slumped against the nearest wall, clutching his chest and giving a groan as he slid down to the floor. "Help me," he gasped. "I think it's my heart."

"Bloody hell," said McClellan, who was carrying his shotgun at the ready. "Keep an eye on the bastard while I go ahead."

McClellan was just moving off when the alert Julio detected the faintest hint of a smirk on the General's face. "Hold it, Brad," he called out. "Something's not right here."

Julio jabbed his shotgun into the General's throat. "Get up, arsehole, or you are going to die *now*... from lead poisoning."

Torres struggled to his feet. "Really, I don't think I can go on."

"We'll see about that," snapped Julio, and he pushed the General towards the archway. "Let him go first, Brad."

Torres braced his feet like a racehorse reluctant to enter the stalls. "No, no!" he pleaded. At once McClellan grabbed him by the collar and propelled him through the archway.

Instantly, a security system was triggered off by the metal of the General's unloaded Colt revolver. Alarm sirens started screaming. Simultaneously, a sheet of steel descended from the ceiling like a guillotine, making it impossible for McClellan and Ramírez to follow the General.

Though they could not see it, another sheet of steel had descended at the far end of the corridor. Nor could they hear the roaring of an engine, which was now spewing a colourless, odourless, toxic gas into the chamber formed by the two metal sheets.

McClellan slammed the butt of his shotgun into the wall of steel... to no effect. Then he heard the sound of rapid gunfire below." Shit," he cried. "We've got to get back and help Rodrigo."

Within three minutes of setting up a roadblock south of the hacienda, the *Tránsito* police had their first customers": a private car, followed soon after by another car and a satellite truck with ACAPULCO TV written large on either side. In each car, there was a photographer and a stringer, representing *Time* magazine and *Newsweek* respectively. All were told the road was closed indefinitely to traffic. They said they would wait.

Meanwhile, without giving any warning, the *Zorros'* armoured bulldozer had been driven directly into the boom-barrier at the entrance to the driveway, smashing it like a matchstick and then immediately halting just beyond the adjacent guardhouse lodge.

From inside the vehicle, over a loudspeaker, a voice boomed, "You are completely surrounded. Drop your weapons, and come out with your arms held behind your head."

There was no resistance. Seeing a rocket launcher trained on the lodge, six *guaruras* meekly came out to surrender.

At that moment, the guardhouse resounded with the screeching of sirens that had been relayed automatically from the hacienda. Seconds later, the *Zorros* could just make out the distant crack of machine-gun fire.

Comandante González did not trouble to consult with Coronel Rivas. He immediately decided a change of plan was necessary. There could be no surprise attack. And he was not going to expose his flying squad to a shooting match. He would go in first with the armoured cars, and call on the helicopter unit to give overhead support.

Responding to the scream of sirens, the *guaruras* working in the warehouse had immediately buckled on their gun belts. Then they had slid back the great hangar doors, and moved out with their .22 Uzi sub-machine-guns held at the ready.

Rodrigo, crouched behind the gallery wall on the opposite side of the courtyard, did not hesitate. He opened fire with his Neostead shotgun, unleashing a wide-ranging spray of lethal ball bearings that sent the *guaruras* scurrying back inside the hangar for cover.

Then, glancing to his left, he saw another threat. Six armed *guaruras* had emerged from the block of apartments at the far end of the courtyard. However, they were totally exposed, without any kind of cover to aid their advance; and again, one long burst from his shotgun was sufficient to make them retreat.

Thereafter, when the *guaruras* in the warehouse returned fire, it was only through a narrow slit in the hangar doors that greatly limited their arc of visibility, and allowed only one gunman to operate at a time. The others, in the single-storey apartment block, had taken up firing positions in

363

front windows. But their angle of fire was too obtuse for them to be effective.

Rodrigo realised he was now most vulnerable to any attack from the rear. But fortunately, there was none. In the main building, the domestic staff had chosen to barricade themselves in the kitchen until the danger had passed. Downstairs, at the other end of the building, Dr. Zaragoza's secretary had locked herself in the library.

For several minutes, ever conscious of the need to conserve his ammunition, Rodrigo restricted himself to firing in short, sporadic bursts. Then he found himself joined by McClellan and Ramírez, and almost immediately afterwards by Nicholas and Regina. All had made their way to his position on their hands and knees, so keeping cover behind the gallery wall. Nicholas did so with great difficulty, but refused help. "I'm okay," he insisted. "And I can still handle a gun."

McClellan quickly summed up the situation. "With four shotguns, you should be able to keep all of them pinned down long enough for help to arrive. Stay here. I'm going back to see if there is any other way into the doctor's quarters."

Shortly after he had left, armed only with his Belgian pistol and two stun-grenades, the others saw the armoured cars approaching down the driveway, and heard the whirring of three choppers overhead. Their insurance policy was paying off just in time.

At the head of the stairs, McClellan arrived just in time to see the archway on the right opening up, as the curtain of steel disappeared back into the ceiling. Simultaneously, another sheet of steel was rising near the far end of the corridor; and somewhere overhead he could hear the dying, whirring sound of what he later discovered to be an extractor fan.

A few yards beyond the archway, Teniente-General Ernesto Torres lay motionless on the floor. Keeping an eye on the corridor ahead, McClellan stooped to feel the pulse in the General's neck. There was no trace of a beat.

Proceeding down the corridor, his pistol held at the ready, McClellan came to a single door on the right. It was slightly ajar. He kicked it open, immediately ducking back behind the wall to take cover.

When there was no reaction, he removed a stun-grenade from a pouch in his belt. He was poised to toss it into the room, but then changed his mind as a distinctly cultured voice called out, "Do come in, whoever you are."

Cautiously peering round the doorway, McClellan saw a tall, wiry gentleman standing at an open window behind a desk. He was completely bald and looked like an elderly business executive - bespectacled and neatly attired in shirt and tie, the jacket of his mauve worsted suit being draped over his desk chair.

No one else was in the room, and so McClellan advanced with his pistol trained on the man. "You are Dr. Zaragoza, I presume," he said.

The man's reply was immediately drowned out by a booming announcement coming from the courtyard below. Over a loudspeaker on one of four armoured cars, a voice was saying, "Your position is hopeless. You have one minute to put down your weapons, and come out with your hands behind your head." Then another sound could be heard: the roar of helicopters directly overhead.

The man turned to look down at the scene beneath his window. "You are just in time to see the show. Have a look."

His relaxed, casual reaction surprised McClellan. Keeping his gun pointed at the stranger, he rounded the desk. "You are Dr. Zaragoza?"

"That's right. And you, if I am not mistaken, are Señor McClellan of the CIA. I recognise you from television... at a press conference held by the Procurador General."

He again looked out of the window. "Ah! Here they come. Our brave *guaruras!* Never slow to surrender. The show's already over." Then he pointed to McClellan's pistol. "You really don't need that, you know. But you have done well. My security system was supposed to keep all weapons out of my study."

"So I have seen," said McClellan. "What did you release into the corridor? Some kind of poison gas?"

"*Sí.* To be exact, hydrocyanic gas, a mix of sodium cyanide and diluted sulphuric acid. Anything metallic triggers off the release mechanism, and it can kill within seconds. It didn't stop you, of course. But at least it bought me valuable time to prepare."

"What do you mean?" asked McClellan, who was finding the doctor's relaxed manner highly suspicious.

The doctor pointed across the room towards a wall

365

safe, which was wide open. "I presume you are working with the DEA. You will find all the evidence in there: names, dates, all my payroll records for the past three years. I was keeping it as insurance. But it doesn't matter now. Nothing matters any more. But if I'm going down, I will at least be in good company."

At that point, the doctor reached out to a coffee mug on his desk. "You don't mind if I finish my drink, do you?"

Before McClellan could think, the doctor had picked up the mug, and gulped down its contents in one long swig. Then, ignoring the threat of McClellan's gun, he sat down in his swivel chair, and tilted it back so he was looking up at the ceiling. "I'm afraid, *señor*, I am getting too old and too weak to face all this shit."

Zaragoza closed his eyes, and McClellan took the opportunity to glance out of the window. Below, he saw six *guaruras* lined up at gunpoint against the hangar. *Zorros* on motorcycles were roaring down the driveway, and a helicopter was setting down in the courtyard.

"Just stay exactly where you are," said McClellan. Then, out of the doctor's line of vision, he went over to the wall safe, removed the contents and laid them on the desk. There was a CD and two books, one of which he saw at a glance was a thick ledger recording details of payments. The other book, thin and rectangular, was a personal diary.

Before he could examine them further, he was distracted by the sound of footsteps down the corridor outside. He moved swiftly to the doorway, still holding his pistol and keeping a watchful eye on the doctor. Outside, he saw three black-leathered *Zorros* approaching, their sub-machine-guns held ready for action.

Immediately, McClellan returned to the desk, laid down his pistol, and slipped the diary and CD inside his tracksuit top. "Don't shoot," he called out. "Everything is under control."

As the *Zorros* entered, he held up his hands to show he was unarmed. Meanwhile, there was no reaction from Zaragoza. One of the *Zorros* shook him by the shoulder. Still he lay back in his chair, eyes closed and breathing heavily. And then, to everyone's surprise, he began snoring loudly.

Subsequently, no one was able to rouse the doctor from his deep slumber. In fifteen minutes, he would be dead.

CHAPTER 28

Five days after the storming of the Miguel Alemán Clinic, Coronel Carlos Rivas was still basking in the reflected glory of the drugs coup of the century. Already, hanging behind his desk in the former office of Teniente-General Ernesto Torres, there was a framed picture of the double- page centre spread taken from the current issue of *Time* magazine. And already well-worn was the videoed recording of his appearance on TV.

Beneath the *Time's* banner headline— *Drugs Coup of the Century*— was a photograph of Rivas standing between wide-open hangar doors. Behind him, stretching far into the distance, were rows of wooden crates. The caption read: *Acapulco police deputy uncovers twenty-five-metric-tons of nearly pure cocaine with a street value— when diluted— of $14 billion.*

He could still scarcely believe his good fortune. At present, he was the acting Acapulco Police Chief. But his promotion to *Jefe* now seemed inevitable. Nationwide publicity had surely assured that. The government, desperately needing to restore public confidence, was unlikely to bypass him with a political appointee.

It was ironic, he reflected, because his first impulse on that fateful day had been to restrict press coverage. True, he had eventually allowed the representatives of *Time, Newsweek* and *Acapulco TV* to pass through the roadblock. But, on arrival, they were strictly limited to taking shots in and around the warehouse.

He had posed for them before the crates of cocaine, and alongside a heap of confiscated weaponry: "Enough arms to have started a small war." He had confirmed that Teniente-General Torres had been killed. But he had refused to say anything more, stressing that a detailed statement could only come later, after he had had an opportunity to assemble all the evidence. Meanwhile, everyone found on the premises was being held incommunicado, pending the arrival of transports to take them to police headquarters for questioning.

That was normal procedure. But then Isabel del Rio had arrived by helicopter and, succumbing to her persuasive charms, he had allowed her access to his prisoners. And that, Rivas now recognised, had led to crucial developments.

Del Rio's high-profile reporting had indeed worked in his favour. But, above all, as he thought back on it, the more he realised how much he owed to the strange *americano*. It was McClellan, so he understood, who had been responsible for the timely arrival of the media people; McClellan who had drawn his attention to the now-famous ledger that had exposed the high-ranking officials involved in the biggest drug-trafficking bust ever known.

Within twenty-four hours— before its contents were made public— that ledger had been confiscated by the Procurador-General who, at the President's command, had been put in charge of a special investigation. At the time, in view of the high-level officials involved, Rivas had anticipated a major cover-up. But such action had been forestalled, and again that had been entirely due to the enterprise of McClellan.

When Del Rio and her film crew landed in the forecourt of the Miguel Alemán Clinic, it was just twenty minutes since the *Zorros* had taken complete control of the hacienda complex. The American stringers and local television people were already on the scene. But that competition did not concern her. What mattered was that she was ahead of her CNN rivals, so giving her a national TV exclusive.

Del Rio was quick to take the initiative. Having congratulated the Coronel on camera on 'a brilliantly executed operation', she drew him to one side, and suggested she might be of useful assistance. She had personally met Señor Stephanopoulos and if, as reported, he was in the clinic, she could positively identify him.

Rivas agreed. To the chagrin of other reporters, she alone was allowed to enter the heavily guarded main building - though without her film crew, and on the clear understanding she was not to interview anyone.

Inside, Comandante González had sealed off three areas: the cellar and the upstairs corridor where the bodies of

Francisco and Torres respectively had been found, and the study in which Doctor Zaragoza had died, despite the efforts of *Zorros* to revive him. None of the bodies was to be removed until forensic experts had arrived and examined the crime scenes.

Meanwhile, everyone found on the premises had been herded into the large downstairs livingroom where they were held under armed guard. At one end of the room, eighteen *guaruras* were seated on the floor. At the other end, some seated, some standing, were five members of the domestic staff, together with a smartly suited young lady, Doctor Zaragoza's personal secretary.

From the doorway, Del Rio spotted Stephanopoulos immediately. He was on a sofa in the centre of the room. Regina Marke was seated beside him and, with the aid of McClellan, she was fixing a sling to support his freshly-bandaged left arm. Julio Ramírez and Rodrigo Monteagudo were standing nearby.

"That's him," she said. And, without seeking approval, she swept past two armed guards, and approached the Greek. Rivas, raising a hand for the guards to stand their ground, hurried after her.

"*Buenos días*, Señor Stephanopoulos," she chirped. "Oh, my goodness, you have been injured."

Nicholas smiled. "It's nothing, *señorita*. But I would like to thank you for coming here so promptly. May I introduce you to my friends? This is my assistant, Señorita Marke, who was being held hostage here. And this is Señor McClellan..."

Rivas cut him short. "Alto! We strictly agreed to no interviews. I must ask you to leave, *señorita*. You have identified Señor Stephanopoulos. The rest will have to wait until we are back at headquarters."

At that moment, McClellan interjected. "Excuse me, *señor*. But before you leave, there is just one thing you should know. Upstairs, on the desk in Doctor Zaragoza's study, you will find a ledger detailing all his drug-dealing transactions. I wouldn't like it to be lost."

The Coronel deliberately ignored him and immediately had del Rio escorted from the building. He did not accompany her. As she left, she looked back, and saw him hurrying up the main staircase.

Outside, Del Rio gave instructions to her cameraman

and soundman. The trio trooped off to a distant corner of the courtyard, and there she scribbled a few notes for an updated news report. A consummate professional, she did not need a script chalked up on an idiot board. Instead, she relied simply on a few headings as a guide.

"Okay, Ed. I'm ready," she said. And then, standing in the shade of a palm tree, she began her report, which was successfully completed with the first take.

It's now less than half an hour since the Acapulco Zorros stormed the heavily guarded Miguel Alemán Clinic and discovered an enormous horde of illicit drugs. As we reported earlier, our information is that the raid was initiated in the belief that terrorists were holding hostage the Acapulco police chief, Tteniente-General Ernesto Torres, and the Greek billionaire, Nicholas Stephanopoulos.

This has still not been confirmed. Coronel Rivas, in command of the operation, has refused to make any statement until all the suspects have been questioned. We do know, however, that Teniente-General Torres has been killed. And now I can report exclusively on more dramatic developments.

A few minutes ago, I met Señor Stephanopoulos. He has suffered a wound to his left arm, but otherwise he's very much alive and well. He was not permitted to make a full statement. However, he did reveal that his assistant, a Señorita Marke, had been held hostage at the clinic. I saw her, and apparently she is unharmed.

Why these hostages were taken remains a mystery. Could it be connected with the fact that Señor Stephanopoulos was offering a ten-million-dollar reward for information regarding the killings of his family in Chapultepec Park?

This seems a distinct possibility. Because I can reveal that among those present in the clinic is the americano, Señor McClellan. Señor McClellan, it may be recalled, was the CIA representative assisting in the official inquiry into the Chapultepec Park murders.

Was he also being held hostage? We still do not know. At present, the only certainty is that the Miguel Alemán Clinic, under the direction of Doctor Antonio Zaragoza, was being used as the base of a massive drug-trafficking operation.

We still don't know the whereabouts of Doctor

Zaragoza. But I can reveal, exclusively, that the police may have detailed evidence of his drug-running network. According to Señor McClellan, they can find in Zaragoza's study a ledger containing records of all his drug transactions.

We will bring you further bulletins on this extraordinary affair, as soon as more information becomes available. This is Isabel del Rio. Channel 13 News. From the Miguel Alemán Clinic, Acapulco.

Her report arrived just in time for the four o'clock news round-up. It went out nationwide. Its repercussions were immediate.

It was 1645 hours when Coronel Rivas arrived back at Acapulco police headquarters. Within five minutes, he learnt by telephone that he was no longer in charge of the biggest case of his career.

On the private line, awaiting his arrival, was the Procurador-General, José Rodríguez. He came directly to the point. "I am calling, Coronel, on the direct orders of *El Presidente*. He congratulates you on your action at the Miguel Alemán Clinic. However, he regards this affair of such national importance that he has put me in full command of the investigation. I am leaving for Acapulco immediately. Meanwhile, I need a rundown of the present position. Have you questioned anyone yet?"

"No, Señor Procurador. Everyone found at the clinic is being brought to headquarters. They should be here any moment, and I will begin interrogations immediately."

"Now hang on, Coronel. Let's get our priorities right. First of all, you should make sure that everyone is properly searched and their possessions confiscated. To save time, you can begin taking statements. But don't get involved in detailed interrogations. I will personally be questioning the main witnesses.

"Now tell me. I understand that your *Jefe* was killed at the clinic. Were there any other casualties?"

"Just two, *señor*. One is a man who has yet to be identified. Someone had shot him before we arrived, blowing much of his face clean away. The other victim has been identified by his secretary as Doctor Zaragoza, the head of the clinic. We found him in a coma, and he died soon afterwards."

371

"I see. Was the doctor able to talk?"

"No, *señor*. He never came out of the coma."

"And what about his ledger that has been mentioned on the TV news? Does it exist?"

Rivas responded with a touch of pride. "Ah, *sí, señor.* That is safely with me at headquarters. But I haven't had time to examine it yet."

"Excellent, Coronel. You have done well. Now you are to keep that ledger under lock and key. It could be vital evidence. No one— not even you— should touch it until I have arranged to have it properly examined. Is that clear?

"*Sí, señor.*"

"Now, one other thing. I understand from the TV news that the people found at the clinic include a Señor Stephanopoulos and an *americano* called McClellan. Is that correct?

"*Sí, señor.*"

"Well, you are to be very careful how you handle them. We don't want any complaints about ill-treatment. The Greek embassy has been on to us about Stephanopoulos. And the American ambassador has even contacted *El Presidente* about McClellan. Seems he was at one time the ambassador's personal bodyguard You can expect them to send down a lawyer. Well, that's it. Any questions, Coronel?"

"Um... *sí, señor.* The *americano* has with him two Mexican friends, as yet unidentified. Should I deal with them separately?"

"No. Leave me to question them. Anything else?"

"*Sí, senor.* What about the media people? They are screaming for a statement. What do I tell them?"

"You are to tell them absolutely nothing. Meanwhile, everyone is to be held in custody until I arrive. Understand?"

"*Sí.* Oh, and there is just one other thing, Señor Procurador, What about the casualties? Can we go ahead with autopsies? I have already sent forensics to the clinic."

"That's all right. Go ahead. But do nothing else until I get there. I should be with you in two hours. There will be three of us; and my secretary has booked us in the Condesa del Mar. We will need a car at the airport to meet us."

"Very good, *señor.*"

The Procurador General hung up, and Coronel Rivas spat into his dead chief's spittoon.

372

It was, in fact, just under two hours before the Procurador General arrived in Acapulco by private jet. Accompanying him were Emilio Ortega, his effeminate young personal assistant, and Luis Enrique Montaño who, to the mortification of Subcomandante José Ibarra, had been chosen as successor to Comandante Barraza.

At the airport, they were met by Corporal Jorge Barrientos. For the second time that day, he had driven out of town via the Scenic Highway. But this time he was at the wheel of Coronel Rivas' black Mercedes. The customised Lincoln Continental that had been the pride and joy of his late *Jefe* was still at the Miguel Alemán Clinic, awaiting examination by forensics.

Sending Barrientos had been a deliberately mischievous ploy on the part of Rivas. Remarkably, the Procurador General had not troubled to ask him about the circumstances in which Torres had been kidnapped. He felt no desire to volunteer the information. Nor did he give Barrientos any instructions to do so.

They were only a few minutes out of the airport when they passed the turn-off to the Esmeralda hotel complex where both Torres and Barrientos had been knocked out by a stun-gun. The corporal's passengers were busy talking among themselves. It was not his place, he judged, to break in on their conversation.

Then, for the first time the Procurador General chose to address the driver seated beside him. "Could you drive a little faster, corporal? We are in a hurry."

"*Sí, señor.*" Barrientos inwardly smiled, remembering how, on that same stretch of road, *El Emperador* had told him to slow down.

Now he was exceeding the 100 kph speed limit. But for the Procurador General, it was already too late.

In the interim, Coronel Rivas had followed his orders to the letter. The Zaragoza ledger was locked in his office safe. He had ensured that all detainees were searched. He had stood firm against vociferous news reporters, insisting that no statement could be made, and no questions answered, until after the Procurador General had arrived. And he had extended special privileges to Stephanopoulos and McClellan.

The Greek and the American were now comfortably confined to the private lounge adjoining the former office of

373

Teniente-General Torres. There, at the request of Stephanopoulos, they had also been joined by his assistant Señorita Marke and his two unidentified friends, Julio Ramírez and Rodrigo Monteguado.

They had been together for no more than ten minutes before they had a visitor: Ms. Julia Philpotts, a lawyer attached to the U.S. Consulate which operated from Acapulco's Plaza Continental Hotel. She had insisted on being allowed to see McClellan and Marke. "I have also been asked to represent Señor Stephanopoulos until the Greek embassy can arrange for their own lawyer to get here."

Coronel Rivas had judged it expedient to comply.

After a private interview with the two American citizens and the Greek, the lawyer aggressively confronted Rivas in his office. "It is an absolute disgrace, Coronel. Señorita Marke is very weak, and obviously dehydrated. She should be given medical attention at once, and whatever food and drink that she needs."

Rivas looked suitably contrite. "My sincere apologies, *señorita*. I will see to it immediately."

After he had given instructions by phone, Ms. Philpotts returned to the attack. She wanted to know if her clients were being charged with any offence, and if not, how soon they were to be released. "May I remind you, Coronel, that under Mexican law, you may not detain anyone for more than forty-eight hours, before presenting that person before a judge."

She added a special plea on behalf of Regina Marke. "This young lady has already spent three days in captivity as a hostage. She has suffered a terrible ordeal, and it is unthinkable she should be detained here overnight."

"I do sympathise with her situation," Rivas replied. "And you are welcome to have the *señorita* examined by your own doctor. But at present we cannot release anyone without the authority of the Procurador General. I am afraid my hands are tied.

"As for any charges, that again is a matter for the Procurador General. Meanwhile, the official line is that they are not under arrest but are simply here to assist in our inquiries."

"I see. And how about Señor Stephanopoulos? He is wounded. Will he be getting proper medical attention?"

Rivas waved his hands. "Ah, we have already offered

to have him seen by our doctor. But he has refused any treatment. Says it's okay because the knife missed his arteries. We cannot force him. Perhaps you can have a word with him."

"I will. Now, about your inquiries. My clients wish to be as helpful as possible. And they are prepared to make formal statements. But I must insist on being present when you interview them."

"Of course, *señorita*. We would not wish it any other way."

In his dealings with the Press, Coronel Rivas struck a similarly sympathetic note. He appreciated their need for more information, but stressed that he could not make any statement without the authority of the Procurador General. They would just have to wait for his arrival.

In this instance, his stalling had significant repercussions. The reporters were not prepared to wait. With at least two hours to kill, they turned to seeking information elsewhere. Talking to junior police officers, they quickly discovered an intriguing lead. Teniente-General Torres had last been seen leaving for the Esmeralda hotel to attend a reception for El Nuevo Santo. He had been driven by Corporal Barrientos.

Barrientos was under orders not to speak to the Press, and in any event, he was currently driving back from the airport. So their next line of inquiry was obvious.

This time, Del Rio did not steal a march on her rivals - even though she phoned ahead to request a private interview with the manager of the Esmeralda hotel. "I will be delighted to see you," said Señora Velázquez. "But no, I cannot talk to you exclusively. As I have just told the Acapulco TV people: *all* the Press are equally welcome."

McClellan and Julio had briefed Esperanza well. Above all, she remembered the words of the *americano:* "We cannot get too much publicity. It is our only effective weapon. Corruption is so endemic in Mexico, we can only force change by exposing the dirt to the full light of day."

At 1920 hours, Procurador General José Rodríguez and his companions arrived at Acapulco police headquarters. They found Coronel Rivas in a high state of excitement. Without formalities, he went directly to the point. "I realise, Señor Procurador, that you must be tired after your journey. But there really is something you must see at once. It could

375

change everything."

After they had taken seats in his office and had been provided with drinks, he signalled for his secretary to switch on the video recorder. It was a replay of the seven o'clock news on Acapulco TV. The presenter announced that they were now going over to the Esmeralda hotel - "where, a short time ago, the manager, Señora Velázquez, held a press conference. This has revealed sensational new facts about this afternoon's raid on the Migel Alemán Clinic."

The conference, held in the Laguna Bar, was recorded in full. It began with Señora Velázquez making a formal statement from carefully prepared notes. She opened by saying that she had a confession to make. "Today, I deliberately lured Teniente-General Torres to this hotel on the pretext that he was to meet the *lucha libre* star, El Nuevo Santo. My main purpose was to help Señor Stephanopoulos to discover who was primarily responsible for the murder of his family in Chapultepec Park.

"Why should I wish to do this? You might think I was seeking the reward money he has offered. But this is not so. I am not interested in any financial reward. No, my reason was personal." She paused, and looked grimly at her audience. "I wanted to help, because I believed my treacherous husband, Guillermo Velázquez, had played a part in making those terrible murders possible.

"I had already learnt that— in return for money— my husband had told *El Informador* about the birthday party that was to be held in Chapultepec Park. And I had reason to suspect he also gave this information to the police chief, Teniente-General Torres.

"This has now been confirmed. But, before I say any more, I would like you to listen to a tape-recorded confession made by Torres earlier today. After that, I will be pleased to answer any questions you may have."

She signalled to her assistant manager, Zavala, and he switched on a tape recorder. In this recording, which had been carefully edited by McClellan, Torres stated that Guillermo had told him about the party in the park, and that he had passed on the information to Doctor Zaragoza.

He had done so because he knew Zaragoza was interested in the engagements of Secretario Martínez, whom he was planning to assassinate. Zaragoza wanted him killed because he had discovered details of his drugs network. To this end, Torres provided him with a man who could be framed for the crime: a common thief named Manuel Ramírez.

Torres further confessed that— like many officials in the government, police and military— he was in the pay of Zaragoza. And finally, he revealed that Señorita Marke was being held as a hostage in the Miguel Alemán Clinic.

The tape recording abruptly ended, and for a few seconds, there was stunned silence. Then came the barrage of questions.

"Señora, the police chief sounds terrified. How did you get him to make this confession?"

"I can't say. I wasn't there at the time. The interrogation was organised by Señor McClellan. Afterwards, he devised a plan to rescue Señorita Marke from the clinic."

"Is that the americano who represented the CIA in the inquiry into the Chapultepec Park murders?"

"That is correct. But before the murders, Señor McClellan was working with the DEA, and he had been hoping to get information from Secretario Martínez about drug-smuggling in México."

"What was the part of El Nuevo Santo in all of this?"

"Ah, he was magnificent. In fact, he made it all possible. And now, with his approval, I can reveal his true identity. His name is Julio Ramírez, and he is a brother of Manuel Ramírez, the man who has wrongly been blamed for the murders.

"It was Julio who discovered that his brother had been arrested in Acapulco a few months before the murders. And that led to suspicions that Torres might have been involved."

"So how was the rescue operation carried out? Who was involved, and who killed the Jefe?"

"Oh, you will have to ask Señor McClellan about that. I wasn't there. All I can say is that they decided to act on their own, because they did not know who they could trust in the police."

"What has happened to Dr. Zaragoza? Has he been arrested?"

"I have no idea."

"You mentioned your husband's part in the killings. Where is he now?

"I don't want to talk about that Judas. And that, *señoras* and *señores*, is really all I have to say. Any other questions, you had better put to the police."

"Just one last question, señora: what happens now to the $10 million reward offered by Señor Stephanopoulos?"

"Ah, *sí*. That I can tell you. Señor Stephanopoulos had decided that the reward money should go to Señor Julio Ramírez. In turn, Señor Ramírez has decided all the money should go the Iztapalapa Orphanage Fund."

"Thank you all for coming, and please feel welcome to order drinks from the bar. Compliments of the Esmeralda hotel."

The video picture switched back to the studio. There, the news presenter shuffled his papers and said: "Unfortunately, we have been unable to obtain official comments on these extraordinary revelations. But we hope to bring you a special bulletin at eight o'clock. And now for the rest of the news..."

At a signal from Coronel Rivas, his secretary switched off the television, and everyone looked towards the Procurador General. But there was no immediate reaction. For several seconds he just stared at the blank screen, apparently dumbfounded.

When he finally spoke, it was not to make any comment. Grim-faced, he turned to Rivas. "I need to make a phone call. Have you somewhere I can talk in private?"

"Certainly, *señor*," Rivas replied. You can use my secretary's office. I'll show you the way."

During his absence, Emilo Ortega did most of the talking. When the Procurador General returned, he heard his assistant saying, "It's outrageous. That woman should be arrested along with the others. We can't have people taking the law into their own hands in this way..."

Rodríguez glared at him. "Right, everyone out," he snapped. "I want to talk to the Coronel alone."

Subsequently, he pulled up a chair, facing Rivas across his desk. He looked at him sternly. "We've got a very delicate situation here, Coronel. All this media coverage is getting out of hand. And I don't want any more surprises. We have got to take complete control.

"Now, before we start taking statements, is there anything else I should know? Anything at all. I don't want to hear any new information from the Press."

Rivas opened a folder. "We do have information from forensics, and preliminary reports from pathology."

"Let's hear it."

"Firstly, the *Jefe*. His death was by asphyxiation following inhalation of a lethal nerve gas. They have yet to do a full autopsy, but all the evidence and symptoms point to hydrocyanic gas which can kill in seconds. Whatever it was, the gas was released from a cylinder, which was found to be part of a security system installed by Dr. Zaragoza.

"Then there is Dr. Zaragoza. Analysis of a coffee cup found in his office has revealed traces of KCN— potassium cyanide— dissolved in water. They say such a mixture— water with as little as one gram of KCN— would render a person unconscious in a minute, and result in death in fifteen to forty-five minutes, depending on the physical strength of the person and whether his stomach was full or empty. We know the doctor died fifteen minutes after he was found to be in a coma.

"In addition, we have the testimony of his secretary, a Señorita Orozco, who identified the body. She described it as "a happy release". According to her, Zaragoza had been undergoing unsuccessful treatment for cancer of the colon. We expect to have the results of a full autopsy very soon. But obviously all the evidence points to suicide.

"Finally, there is the body found in the cellar. This has been identified as Francisco Domínguez, the chief *guarura* at the clinic. It is confirmed that he was killed by a 5.7mm. bullet fired at close range from a Five-seveN pistol. Four such pistols were among the weapons surrendered when we raided the clinic."

"What else?"

Rivas turned to a second file. "So far, we only have statements by McClellan, Stephanopoulos and Señorita Marke, all made in the presence of an American lawyer. They more or less bear out everything you have just heard on TV. The *señorita,* it seems, was being held hostage at the clinic in an effort to get the Greek to stop his inquiries into the Chapultepec Park murders. McClellan, in his statement, takes full responsibility for organising a rescue operation.

"There is one new fact. The Greek says he shot the *guarura* Domínguez to prevent him killing Señorita Marke. And her statement supports his evidence: that the *guarura* was attacking her with a knife."

"Hmm! And what about El Nuevo Santo? Is he really the brother of Manuel Ramírez?

"We haven't interviewed him yet. But, *sí,* it certainly

379

seems so. The man said to be El Nuevo Santo matches a picture of Julio Ramírez that was circulated by the PGR when they were searching for him. This is also confirmed by McClellan, who says in his statement that Ramírez took part in the rescue operation, along with his driver, a Rodrigo Monteguado."

The Procurador General paused to light a cigarette, then spoke very slowly and deliberately. "Now, Coronel, I am going to tell you something in strictest confidence. And if you breathe a word of it to anyone else, it could seriously jeopardise your career. You understand?"

Rivas nodded.

"*Bueno*. Now, the fact is, that I have spoken directly to *El Presidente* about this. He has seen the Velázquez press conference on Channel 13, and he is deeply disturbed about the way things are developing. He feels it is seriously undermining the forces of law and order, and that it is encouraging people to think they can take the law into their own hands."

Rivas jumped in. "I could not agree more, *señor*. This business is bordering on anarchy. Perhaps we should arrest Velázquez for her part in the affair."

Rodríguez glared at him. "That is exactly what we should *not* do. You are missing the point, Coronel. The last thing we want is to have these people made into martyrs. With El Nuevo Santo involved, they will already have massive public sympathy. What we have to do is play down their rescue operation and concentrate attention on the success of your prompt police action.

"We have to recognise that your *Jefe* was corrupt, and deplore the fact. But that is as far it goes. The point is that the force as a whole - a Mexican force - acted swiftly and efficiently, and seized the biggest haul of drugs ever known."

Rivas smiled. "So, what do you want me to do, Señor Procurador?"

"Sometime or other, you will have to talk to the Press. Just bear all this in mind when you do. Play up the role of the *Zorros,* and stress that the private rescue action— however romantic it may appear— could have ended in tragedy but for police intervention."

"There's just one problem, *señor*. This Zaragoza ledger. For all we know, it may expose other corrupt officials, maybe even in the police."

"That brings us to another crucial point. The contents of the ledger will remain strictly confidential until a new Presidential Anti-Drugs Commission has completed a full investigation. *El Presidente* has asked me to head this special committee, and it will be conducting the most exhaustive inquiry of its kind ever made. I will be announcing this very shortly."

"What about the people we are holding in custody? At the very least, we can charge McClellan and his friends with unlawful possession of arms."

"Not even that, Coronel. Everyone who was employed at the clinic is to be held in custody and charged with offences under the Anti-Drugs Act. But we are not going to boost public sympathy by charging the others.

"I will be telling the Press they are being released immediately on two conditions: that they remain available to appear before the Anti-Drugs Commission and that, in the meantime, they do not communicate with the media, or say anything that might prejudice our inquiries."

Rodríguez looked at his wrist-watch. "It's getting late. I want you to set up a press conference for nine o'clock.

"I propose that you speak to them first. Give them all that autopsy and forensic stuff, and the Greek's statement about shooting the *guarara*. Then I'll wind up with the news about the special Anti-Drugs Commission.

"With all that information, they'll be wanting to catch deadlines, so we should be able to keep questions to a minimum.

"One more thing, Coronel. Arrange for McClellan and his friends to be released while the press conference is in progress. Perhaps their American lawyer can pick them up. If not, then lay on transport to take them wherever they want to go. Just get them away with a minimum of publicity. We don't want a media circus."

Mark Hellman, the CIA station chief, was back in Mexico City, relaxing in his stylish Las Lomas apartment when he received the phone call from Washington. It was 8.45 p.m. He had anticipated the call, but he had not expected it to come from the DDO in person. Now he feared the worst.

William J. Stanleigh, Deputy Director (Operations), was calling from his Savile Lane home close by the Langley headquarters. He had seen the Esperanza press conference on CNN television, and he was furious.

"Damn you, Hellman. Why wasn't I consulted about this McClellan operation in advance? Have you taken leave of your senses down there?"

Hellman paused for thought. Maybe it wasn't as bad as he feared. He took a deep breath. With luck, he could talk himself out of this one.

"Hellman! Are you still there? Can you hear me?"

"Yes, sir." Masking his nervousness, he spoke in his usual authoritative manner.

"About McClellan. The fact is that I am as appalled as you must be. I had no prior knowledge of the operation. In fact, I didn't even know that McClellan was still in the country."

"What the hell do you mean?"

"Didn't you know, sir? He retired from the Company five weeks ago. If he was involved in this Acapulco business, he was acting entirely independently."

"Are you serious? Do you realise I have just had a call from the President congratulating us on this drugs bust? I was really embarrassed. I could hardly say I didn't know anything about it."

"I am sorry, sir. What would you like me to do?"

"If this gets out, it could seriously damage the CIA's reputation. We're in enough trouble already. There's only one thing to do. Get in touch with McClellan, and see if it's not too late to hush up his retirement. We need his co-operation. If necessary, tell him we can extend his service by six months... and increase his pension."

"Yes, sir. I'll get on to it right away."

Subsequently, Hellman put through a call to his paid contact at Acapulco police headquarters. The officer advised him he was too late. "The *americano* has just been released. I don't know where he is now."

"Find out," barked Hellman. "I'll be flying down first thing in the morning. I've got to handle this personally."

Ms. Julia Philpotts had a sense of style. She hired a chauffeur-driven stretch limousine to collect her three clients on their release. They were accompanied by Julio and Rodrigo: and after Julio had phoned ahead on a mobile she was advised they would be staying overnight at the Esmeralda hotel.

The lawyer did not accompany them, but issued a warning, "If you leave the hotel, you must let me know where I can reach you. I have given my guarantee to make you

382

available for interview by the Anti-Drugs Commission at any time. And remember that, meanwhile, you are forbidden to discuss this case with the media."

Fifteen minutes later, they were being welcomed back by Esperanza Velázquez. Again, they were accommodated in the penthouse suite of tower block D, though without Regina Marke. She was totally exhausted, and accepted the suggestion that she should rest in Esperanza's private suite.

Meanwhile, a magnum of champagne was being uncorked in the penthouse. Esperanza was in celebratory mood. She had started drinking after her press conference.

"What a day it has been!", she exclaimed, as she handed glasses around. "I can't believe it went so well. You have all done marvellously, and, thank God, you have all come back safely."

"You have done magnificently well yourself," said Julio. "Anyway. Here's a toast to all of us."

After the toast, McClellan turned to Stephanopoulos, who was seated on a sofa. "Yes, it's certainly gone well. But now let's see what we've got."

Nicholas understood. He slipped his left arm out of its sling, and Julio helped him remove the top layer of bandages. Beneath it was a slim pocket diary with a CD protruding from inside its bloodstained cover.

CHAPTER 29

Brad McClellan was grinning from ear to ear as they watched the start of the *24 Horas* programme on Channel 13. "Well, *mi amigos*— as we say in my country— the shit had really hit the fan."

"Yeah," said Rodrigo, who was on his second large whisky after the long drive back from Acapulco. "In this case, enough excrement to have come from a herd of elephants."

The shit— discovered on Dr. Zaragoza's CD— was a record of the millions of U.S. dollars paid out in the course of drug-network operations in Mexico over the past three years: dates, sums and, most sensational of all, the names of recipients.

The fan was the most powerful of its kind in the world. Before leaving Acapulco, McClellan had put the entire record on the World Wide Web.

Technically, as the American had stressed, they were not breaking the conditions of their release. Via Esperanza, the Press had been notified of the website address. But they themselves had not made any comment to the media. Instead, they were letting Zaragoza speak for them... and to devastating effect.

From the grave, Zaragoza— apparently the treasurer, if not the Paymaster General, for the New Gulf Cartel— had incriminated one hundred fifty-seven public officials who, according to his bookkeeping, were on the payroll of the drug barons.

Meticulously, he had recorded modest sums paid out as *mordida* to scores of low-ranking police and customs officers. At the other end of the scale, five names stood out as recipients of six-figure sums: Brigadier-General Antonio Cordero Reyes, commander of the army garrison in Acapulco, Jorge Flores, a former Director of the National Institute for Combat Against Drugs; Gregorio Rebello, chief of the Federal Prosecutor's office in Tecate, Baja California; Pablo Silva Fuentes, the District Judge of Tijuana; and José Francisco

384

Cuellar, the commander of the Anti-Narcotics Federal Judicial Police in Tijuana.

But all these names paled into insignificance when measured against that of the leader in the pay-out stakes. If Zaragoza was to be believed, payments totalling a staggering $250 million had gone to a former attorney general who, until his recent retirement, had been in charge of his country's campaign against drug trafficking and had been credited with the smashing of the notorious Juárez cartel.

His name was Gastón Alfonso Pérez, the elder brother of the President of Mexico.

On the day after the raid on the Miguel Alemán Clinic, McClellan, Stephanopoulos and Marke had left the Esmeralda hotel for the nearby Acapulco Airport. They took an early morning flight to Mexico City, having first advised their American lawyer that they would be staying at the *Apartamentos Orleáns* on Hamburgo.

There, in the late they afternoon, they were to be joined by Julio and Rodrigo, who drove back in the white Mercedes, storing it at Julio's warehouse retreat and then switching to Rodrigo's less conspicuous Honda saloon.

It was during the flight to Mexico City that McClellan and Stephanopoulos took the opportunity to review the evidence they had obtained— namely, Dr. Zaragoza's recorded accounts, and his small pocket diary.

McClellan had a fifty-page printout of the CD. As he pointed out, it was disappointing in one major respect. "It deals exclusively with operations inside Mexico. No details about the foreign suppliers and distributors. And though all the bribes are paid in U.S. dollars, there's not one fucking word about their American collaborators. Someone else must have handled all the pay-outs over the border.

"Of course, the Mexican government will be forced to take drastic action. There will be arrests and prosecutions, though I fancy that Gastón Pérez will be out of the country by now. But we have seen all this before. New drug bosses will emerge in Mexico to link up with the suppliers and the U.S. distributors, and eventually they will be back in business - on as big a scale as ever."

Nicholas, for his part, had no real interest in the contents of the CD. All that mattered to him was the entry in Zaragoza's diary for Saturday, January 24. Every other day in the diary was either blank, or simply had a note of a particular appointment: a time and a name. The names were of Mexicans, some already mentioned in his financial accounts, the others unknown.

But on January 24, Zaragoza had simply scribbled: *Jupiter has flown. I think he is mad - paranoid! Isn't one death enough?*

The date was significant. It was the day before the killings in Chapultepec Park.

"Who the hell is Jupiter?" Nicholas asked. The question was to prey on his mind to the exclusion of everything else.

"That's what I want to know," said McClellan grimly. "It could be the key to smashing the cartel. Let's hope something develops from the Internet release. Maybe that will give us a clue."

He did not mention he already had a hunch— and a vaguely— formed plan that might expose the mysterious Jupiter.

At seven o'clock, they were all together in *Apartamentos Orleáns* to witness the first reaction to the revelations on the Internet. As presenter Isabel del Rio had just announced, the entire *24 Horas* show was to be dedicated to 'Mexico's greatest scandal since the Salinas Affair'.

With the aid of film footage from Acapulco, she swiftly reprised events of the day before. Then she went on to announce that there had been a "sensational new development", the publication on the Internet of accounts, purportedly kept by Dr. Zaragoza, and naming prominent Mexican figures as having received payments from the New Gulf drug cartel.

"Most sensationally, these accounts allege that $250 million were paid to Gaston Pérez, the elder brother of *El Presidente*, and a former attorney general, in charge of combating the traffic in drugs.

"Unfortunately, Señor Pérez is not available for comment. It is believed he and his wife are presently abroad. Meanwhile, these allegations have already had dramatic repercussions, both here and in the United States.

"In this context, we will be showing you a recording of the White House press conference held by President Carmichael earlier in the day. And later distinguished guests will be joining us in a studio discussion about the significance of these developments. But first we are going over to *Los*

386

Pinos for a special presidential broadcast."

Ricardo interjected with a loud guffaw. "Oh, this should be a laugh! Let's see how our great leader wriggles out of this one."

The screen now showed *El Presidente* seated at his desk in front of the Mexican flag. His face was frozen in solemnity, and he spoke in a funereal monotone:

Compatriotas, I am speaking to you this evening with a heavy heart, at a time when this great nation of ours is under grave attack from within. As you will know, evidence has emerged of a great cancer in our midst, of a pernicious drug-trafficking network operating on a scale that is seriously undermining law and order, and creating corruption on an horrific scale.

Firstly, however, I wish to congratulate our brave Acapulco police. Thanks to their promptness and efficiency in carrying out a bloodless emergency action, we have now secured what appears to be the main control centre of drug-running activities in Mexico. This is a major breakthrough, of which we can be proud.

Secondly, and most importantly, I wish to reassure you that your government will see that this is just a beginning - the first step in waging a great new war against the drug menace, and against corruption in general.

I have already appointed a special Anti-Drugs Commission to be headed by Procurador General José Rodríguez. And this committee will conduct the most exhaustive investigation ever undertaken. No one— absolutely no one— will be immune from their inquiries.

Beyond this, I can tell you that I am taking immediate action to introduce a wide-ranging package of reforms to reduce corruption and promote professionalism among federal police and prosecutors. This reform package will include new training and recruitment procedures for law enforcement officers, and a reorganisation of the PGR's structure. Newlyappointed officers will have to undergo a comprehensive vetting process, including polygraph and drug testing, as well as financial and personal background checks.

All too often, in the past, we have discovered that police officers dismissed in one state contrive to find law enforcement employment in another. Again, to counter this, I am establishing a national security register to keep track of censured police officers. Furthermore, we will be keeping a more thorough check on judges, who have sometimes been guilty of reinstating corrupt police officers after their dismissal.

Now, in closeup, the face of the President noticeably hardened. At the same time his voice became more stern and aggressive in pitch.

All these actions emphasise how seriously your government regards the new evidence that has emerged from Acapulco. But this brings me to an equally disturbing aspect of these developments. We recognise our duty to put our own house in order. But we do NOT approve of foreigners taking reckless, independent action, and conducting private witch-hunts on our sovereign territory.

Nor will we accept the new invidious practice of trial by Internet, of trial by denunciation— that is, blackening the reputation of public officials before they have had an opportunity to answer charges before a legally constituted body. Such action is wholly irresponsible and unjust. It makes a mockery of our judicial procedures. And it presents an unsavoury image of our great nation to the entire world.

For many years now, our country has recognised the importance of U.S.-Mexico co-operation in the war against the drugs trade. But both governments must recognise the need to work with absolute deference to national laws and institutions, and with full respect for the dignity and sovereignty of each nation. In this respect, we are deeply disturbed by the trend towards U.S. government agents and their collaborators taking unilateral action on our territory.

Indeed, this government has never tolerated, and never will tolerate, armed DEA and CIA agents operating on Mexican soil.

More shockingly still, I am advised that there is strong evidence to suggest that a foreign vigilante may have resorted to torture in order to extract a so-called confession from the late police chief of Acapulco.

However well-intended, there can never be justification for such action. Our Constitution categorically prohibits torture. And any statements made under such extreme duress are unacceptable in a court of law.

388

At that Rodrigo let out another huge guffaw. *"Dios mío!* Is he kidding? *Qué hipocresía!"*
"Shush," said McClellan. "I can't hear."

... so let us not imagine that only Mexicans have a case to answer. The United States government may hold us responsible for flooding their country with illicit drugs. But it is their complete failure to introduce tougher gun controls, which allows lethal weapons to floodsouth across the border, and make us the victims of so many violent crimes. Also, drug-trafficking on such a vast scale would not be viable without such a voracious demand for cocaine in the United States.

It is at home that the Americans need to wage their war on drugs, not by interfering abroad— whether operating covertly on our soil, or spending billions of dollars on military aid to Columbia, supporting operations that only result in fuelling civil war and pushing up the prices of cocaine and heroin.

But let us not despair. Here, at least, we now have a great opportunity to win the war against the evil forces that are responsible for so muchof the crime and human suffering in our country. And rest assured, this government is determined to succeed in that aim. Thank you... and buenas noches.

"What a load of horseshit! What a windbag!" said Rodrigo. "No mention of his bloody brother, you notice. And I'll bet a lot of that drug money went into the President's election campaign fund."

"True," said McClellan. "But he is smart in seeing attack as the best form of defence. Smart, too, in not giving anyone a chance to ask questions. But it should be different now."

Del Rio was just announcing that they were going to screen part of the press conference held at the White House earlier in the day. The screen now showed President Carmichael standing on a podium. Beside him was a man whom McClellan recognised as George Mansfield, Director of the National Drug Intelligence Centre.

The TV coverage cut to the President's reply to a reporter's question about his view of the latest revelations on the Internet.

Now, Henry, you know better than that. I am not going to prejudge unsubstantiated information. But I will say this: our intelligence agencies take recent developments in Mexico very seriously indeed. To such a degree that we may have to review the extent of our co-operation with the Mexican authorities.

You may recall that long ago, during the Clinton Administration, the House of Representatives voted to censure Mexico for failing to collaborate in the war on drugs. But the President rejected pressure to decertify Mexico under the provisions of the Drug Free America Act, a move that could have led to cutting off U.S. aid.

Mr. Clinton then became the first U.S. President to visit Mexico in forty years, and he and President Zedillo duly signed a declaration against drug-trafficking and illegal immigration.

Well, this administration will be taking a tougher line. Indeed, we cannot readily dismiss the possibility of withdrawing aid to Mexico.

For more than two decades, we have recognised the importance of our two countries working closely together to combat the drug menace. But recently, there has been disturbing evidence that such co-operation— the exchange of intelligence and technical expertise— has been counterproductive. I can say no more than that at this stage.

"Mr. President, how will this effect the NAFTA Agreement— bearing in mind that Congress is due to consider a proposal for legislation that would require re-negotiation of— or even withdrawal from NAFTA if the agreement does not meet required standards, including anti-drug co-operation and trade balances?"

I am afraid I cannot anticipate what will happen in Congress. But again, the situation is so serious that we may find it necessary to renegotiate the NAFTA Agreement.

Of course, NAFTA has become a powerful drive for our economy, and it has established Mexico as our second-largest trade partner. But this does not automatically justify its continuation, In pursuit of a healthy economy, we must beware of confusing "standard of living" with "quality of life". They are not necessarily one and the same.

Quite simply, the drug war has become the greatest threat to our country since the ending of the Cold War. For this reason, I now propose to convene— as soon as possible— a hemispheric Anti-Drug Summit to be held in Washington. In the meantime, Congress will be discussing the law mandating the annual preparation of a list of countries that should be denied U.S. aid, on account of their deficient co-operation in the anti-drug struggle.

"Mr. President, can you confirm that the CIA was responsible for initiating the raid in Acapulco which has uncovered the nerve centre of the Mexican drug network?"

I am sorry, Dorothy, but for security reasons I cannot make any comment on that. However, our Drug Intelligence Director, Mr. Mansfield, does have a statement to make about events in Mexico. Meanwhile, ladies and gentlemen, if you will excuse me, I have a pressing engagement to attend. Thank you.

As President Carmichael left the podium, the camera closed in on Mr. George Mansfield, who now read out a prepared statement.

I regret to say that it is too early to evaluate the sensational allegations, which have just been released on the Internet. At the same time, we do have reason to suppose they may be well-founded. I hope to have more information for you on this after I have received a report from Deputy Director Stanleigh of the CIA.

However, I can now confirm that, immediately prior to his murder, the Mexican Finance Minister, Mr. Roberto Martínez, was working closely with the CIA and the DEA on anti-drug intelligence. In the light of subsequent events, we firmly believe he was the main target in the Chapultepec Park killings last January, and that the New Gulf cartel was responsible for the shootings.

At a time when there is much dissatisfaction with Mexico's anti-drug co-operation, I would like to pay a special tribute to Mr. Martínez's noble sacrifice in risking— and finally giving— his life in the war against illegal drugs. He was a very brave man, a true friend of our country.

Hopefully, his sacrifice will not have been in vain, and we will at last see real progress in fighting this greatest threat to our nation. The sad fact is that some ten million Americans are now chronically addicted to illegal drugs, and we estimate that at least ten million more use cocaine with some regularity As a result, drug abuse is now killing more than one hundred thousand American citizens each year, roughly twice the number of casualties suffered in Vietnam.

The main source of this problem is clear. Mexican drug lords have long since supplanted the Colombian cartels they once served. Our latest estimate is that eighty percent of all cocaine entering the United States, and forty-five percent of all heroin, is coming in via Mexico.

It is the judgement of DEA intelligence that Mexican drug lords are now spending in excess of $600 million a year to bribe corrupt Mexican police and military officials. At the same time, we must recognise our own shortcomings, largely arising from inadequate searches of incoming traffic. On average twenty thousand Mexican trucks cross the border everyday, and...

At that point, the recording was cut short, and live coverage in the studio was resumed. From behind her desk, Del Rio announced that she would now be discussing the significance of the new drugs crisis with her three special guests.

"We are pleased to welcome General Juan Delgado, Mexico City's Chief of Police, and Señor Sebastián Fidel Barraza who, until his recent retirement, was the PGR Comandante in charge of the investigation into the Chapultepec Park murders.

"Unfortunately, the government has declined to send a spokesman. Also, we are prevented by legal restrictions from interviewing anyone involved in the raid on the Miguel Alemán Clinic in Acapulco. However, we are pleased to have with us tonight a gentleman who has a very special and personal interest in the Chapultepec murders and events in Acapulco..."

As she spoke, a second camera picked up three men sitting at a table facing Del Rio. "Oh! *Dios mío*, Julio," exclaimed Rodrigo. "They've only roped in your old man. This could be chaos."

Julio grinned and leaned closer to the screen. "On the contrary, Rod. This could be deadly dull. You're forgetting what time it is. *Papá* always gives up the booze for Lent."

In the ensuing discussion, no one was more surprised

392

than Barraza. He had expected Fernando to launch into a tirade, but now the ex-boxer bore no resemblance to the violent, opinionated demagogue he had interviewed two months before.

A pale shadow of his normally inebriated self, Fernando was nervous, tongue-tied and sometimes barely coherent. Mostly, he was content to answer questions with a single syllable. Del Rio tried to draw him out by suggesting that his son Manuel was probably framed for the killings in the park. He just shrugged, and mumbled that it was fate.

He only came to life when asked about Julio. No, until now, he had never known that Julio was the masked wrestler, El Nuevo Santo. "But I am not surprised. Nothing that boy does surprises me. He is a born winner, a great character... and character is your destiny. I am very proud of him. He should be made *Presidente.*"

Everyone in the apartment looked at Julio to see his reaction. He had buried his face in his hands to hide his amused embarrassment.

Barraza, too, was uncomfortable on television. Indeed, only the opportunity to promote his forthcoming memoirs had persuaded him to appear. Wearing dark shades to hide his bulbous eyes, he cut a menacing figure. But at least he was fluent.

He had never accepted the conclusion that Manuel Ramírez was responsible for the Chapultepec Park murders. He would be naming the real killer in his memoirs, and detailing evidence of a major conspiracy to conceal the truth.

"As for the internet information, I do not doubt that many high-ranking officials have accepted bribes from drug cartels. Corruption is rampant among our law enforcement agencies, and I only hope I am called to give evidence before the Presidential Commission.

"One other thing. We have heard our *Presidente* speaking critically of the activities of CIA and DEA agents in Mexico. But, on the Chapultepec Park investigation, I worked closely with a Señor Madison and a Señor McClellan of the CIA, and I found their co-operation most constructive."

Del Rio turned to Delgado. "What do you think about that, *Jefe*? Do you think there has been a conspiracy to hide the truth about the Chapultepec murders? And more especially, do you accept there is widespread corruption among our police?"

The General, ever the consummate TV performer, smiled and replied in a totally relaxed style. "Ah, Isabel, how we all love conspiracy theories! It could be John Wilkes Booth and Lee Harvey Oswald all over again. Whenever an alleged assassin is killed before being put on trial, everything becomes possible. Now we can expect all manner of crackpot conspiracy theories... and who is left to refute them?

"I am not saying there was not a conspiracy. But who knows, maybe this whole thing has been set up by the CIA to make them look good.

"As for corruption in our police forces: so what else is new? As long as our officers remain grossly underpaid, there will always be some rotten apples in the barrel. But at least I am proud to see that no high-ranking officers in my Mexico City force has been named on the Internet."

Del Rio interjected. "But *Jefe*, what about Teniente-General Torres, who has confessed to being involved with the New Gulf Cartel? Wasn't he once on your staff? And isn't his brother now one of your chief deputies?"

"Oh, Isabel, the question is unworthy of you. Have you forgotten Cain and Abel? Are you going to tar the reputation of a long-serving officer with the deeds of his brother?

"No, let us await the findings of the Presidential Commission before we begin to cast any more stones."

Curiously, it was left to Fernando to have the last word. "Do you want to say something, Señor Ramírez?" asked Del Rio, seeing his hand raised like a schoolboy in class.

"*Sí, señorita*. I just wanna give a message to Julio. If he is watching, I ask him to get in touch with me, and we will have a big party when Easter is over. Um, that's all."

Del Rio smiled. Quite so. "Well, it only remains for me to thank you, *señores*, for appearing here at such a short notice. Clearly, tonight, we have only just touched on what promises to develop into a major scandal. Doubtless, we will learn much more when we can talk to the Procurador General, and to the key figures involved in the Acapulco raid. In the meantime, thank you, and *buenas noches*."

"What a load of crap!" said Rodrigo. "I hate that smug *cabrón*, Delgado. What a pity he was not named on the Internet. They should have asked him where his private fortune comes from."

"That's easy," said McClellan. "His pay-off comes

from the President direct. Of course, that's probably drug money, passed on by Gaston Pérez in the form of contributions to the party's fund. But you'll never prove it. That Delgado is sitting pretty. He's a born survivor."

"You're right," said Julio. "In the final analysis, all we have done is the work of the picadors. We have weakened the enemy, and the authorities will now perform a lot of fancy passes. But no one is going to deliver the *coup de grace.*"

Regina Marke was exhausted. She has barely been able to keep awake during the *24 Horas* show and now, at 8 p.m., she took her leave. "You must excuse me, gentlemen. But I am going to get an early night."

As she moved to leave for her adjacent apartment, Nicholas sprang to his feet. He felt guilty. Opening the door for her, he apologised. "Please excuse me, Regina. In all the excitement, I completely forgot that you had so little sleep in captivity."

She smiled. "That's all right, Nicholas. I'll be fine in the morning. How is the arm?"

"Feels okay, thank you. We are sending out for some pizza. Shall I bring some into you?"

"No, thanks. I couldn't eat a thing. I just need some sleep. Good night."

Five minutes later, Nicholas was tapping gently with his foot on her apartment door. On answering, already in her nightgown, Regina saw that he was carrying a tray in his good right hand.

"Sorry to disturb you, Regina," he said. "But I thought you might like a mug of hot milk. There's some biscuits, too, if you want them."

"That's very thoughtful of you. Milk would be nice. Won't you come in for a minute? I'd like to talk... help me to unwind."

"Are you sure? I really don't want to keep you up."

"No, please. There's something I want to ask you about - alone."

Nicholas placed the tray on a coffee table and sat beside her on the sofa. Though she looked tired, her green eyes were as arresting as ever, and for the first time, by the generosity of her low-cut nightdress, he was able to appreciate the firmness of her well-rounded breasts.

He deliberately averted his eyes. "What did you want to talk about?" he asked.

"First of all, I want you to know that I have decided to go back to the States, as soon as our lawyer can get clearance. And tomorrow, I will be moving back to my own apartment."

"That's good," said Nicholas. "There's nothing more you can do here. I'm just sorry you have had such a terrible ordeal. You have been wonderfully brave, and I can't thank you enough for all you have done."

"So what happens next?"

"You mean immediately? Well, Brad is staying here tonight. The others are going to stay at Rodrigo's apartment off Insurgentes."

"No, I mean about your investigation. Will you be going back to Athens as soon as you have appeared before the Commission?

"That depends."

"On what?"

"On whether I have found the person who ordered the killings in the park."

"You mean you are still going on with this business? Whatever for? You know the killer is dead. And Torres and Zaragoza are dead. Isn't that enough?"

"No, Regina. It is not enough. Nothing has really changed. There is still someone out there who ordered the killings. And, whatever it takes, I've got to get the bastard."

"But that could take forever. And suppose you do find the man. What then?"

"Let's not talk about that now. You need to get some sleep. We'll talk tomorrow." He stood up and, before moving towards the door, he leaned over and kissed her gently on the lips.

His impulse was to take her in his arms and lift her onto the bed. But with his left arm in a sling that was never an option. Instead, he whispered softly, "One day, all this will be over, Regina, and perhaps I can invite myself to your place in Maryland. Sweet dreams."

As he reached to open the door, she called out, "I would love to see you in Maryland, Nicholas. But not if you go on with this *philotimo* obsession. It's time to let go."

"Oh, Regina," he replied. "If only you were Greek. You would understand. There can be no compromise with *philotimo.* Julio feels the same. It is our duty. We must go on."

"Goodbye, Nicholas."

They ate their pizza in the kitchen. Not because they preferred its informality, but because this was the only room that McClellan, after thorough inspection, had judged to be bug-free.

Julio opened a bottle of Californian Cabernet Sauvignon, and, as they raised their glasses, McClellan made a toast. "Here's to you guys. I want to thank you all for your help. You've done a really great job. We may not have smashed the drug cartel forever. But, my God, we have made life difficult for them."

He looked towards Julio. "So, my friend, what are you going do now? I guess your wrestling days are over now that you've lost your mask."

"Hey! Steady on," exclaimed Rodrigo. "Are you trying to put me out of a job? El Santo still hasn't lost his mask in the ring. And anyway, with all this publicity, he'll have more fans than ever."

Julio smiled. "Maybe. But let's face it. Without the mystery, you lose the magic. In any case, I'm not getting any younger, and I'd sooner quit while I am at the top. But don't worry, Rod. Whatever happens you won't be without a job. I promise you."

Rodrigo laughed. "That's big of you, *compadre*. On the other hand, I might just find myself another fighter. After all, I've made one great champion. I could always do it again."

The light-hearted banter irritated Nicholas. "*Christos!* You are talking as if our mission is all over. Have you forgotten the original objective? I was never interested in the drugs war. I just want to get the bastard who ordered the killings."

He glared at McClellan. "So, who the fuck is this Jupiter? I get the distinct feeling you know more than you are saying."

McClellan took a sip of wine and paused for thought. "Hmm! I was afraid you'd get round to that. I was hoping to tackle that question alone. But I guess I owe you an explanation.

"The truth is I don't know for sure who Jupiter is. I have my suspicions, but they are entirely based on circumstantial evidence. I need something really incriminating before I am prepared to accuse anyone.

"Anyway, let's consider the facts. We have Zaragoza's diary entry: *Jupiter has flown. I think he is mad... paranoid. Isn't one death enough?* And then there is that date: the day before the shootings.

"Jupiter. Chief of the Roman gods, the largest of the planets. The code-name suggests he is Zaragoza's boss... at least as far as security operations are concerned.

"*Jupiter has flown.* Let's take that literally. We could be looking for someone who left the country immediately before the killings."

Rodrigo jumped in. "That might be Gastón Pérez. It's rumoured he is out of the country."

"I doubt it," said McClellan. "Why would Zaragoza use a code-name for Pérez when he often names him in his ledger? Anyway, if the President's brother is out of the country, my guess is he only left after we exposed him on the Internet.

"No. My theory is we are looking for someone who was in a position to know that Martínez was working undercover for the CIA and DEA. That really narrows the field."

"You suspect someone inside the CIA or DEA?" asked Julio.

"It is a distinct possibility. Why do you think I have been working alone on this? Three DEA agents have gone missing in Mexico in the past year. There has to be a leak somewhere. As a result, I don't trust anyone in our agencies - no one, that is, except Arthur Madison.

"Madison and I go back a long way. He has never worked with the DEA, and he was certainly in no position to know about Martínez. After our talks with Barraza, he agreed that I should stay on and snoop around independently. He knows all about our operation, and if he was the mole he could have tipped off the cartel before our raid on the clinic."

"So who do you suspect?" asked Nicholas impatiently.

"As far as I know, only three people besides myself knew I was working with Martínez as an agent. One is a DEA official who has since been moved from Mexico City to Miami. He's working undercover, and I don't know how to contact him. The other two are in the CIA and, between us, Madison and I are going to try to check them out."

"How?" asked Nicholas. "And what can we do to

help?"

"Well, it's a long shot, a bluff to draw out the mole. The thing is, this Jupiter fellow cannot know what's in Zaragoza's diary. If he feels threatened he just might break his cover.

"Madison is going to try that bluff in Langley. On the other hand, for all we know, this Jupiter could be in Mexico City. And if he is going to be drawn out, it will have to be a very convincing threat... and, ideally, from someone he doesn't know."

He looked towards Rodrigo. "It's asking a lot, Rod. But would you be willing to act as a decoy? It could be dangerous."

Rodrigo didn't hesitate. "I'm your man. Just tell me what you want me to do."

McClellan eyed him thoughtfully. "First of all, tell me about this apartment of yours. What's its layout?"

"Oh, it's nothing special. The top apartment in a narrow three-storey building on Villalongin Street. That's off Insurgentes and close by the Jardín del Arte Park. There are just two bedrooms, a small living room and a tiny kitchenette. No dining room. I usually take my meals on the rooftop garden."

"How do you get in?"

"From the ground floor entrance there's a single narrow staircase— very steep— leading up to the third floor. Then a few steps up to a black metal door that leads onto the *azotea.*"

"Nothing else? No other way in or out?"

"Not really. There's an old fire escape running down from the roof garden. But that's just a rusty ladder fixed to the wall. Don't know if it's safe for use."

"How about the ground floor entrance? Does everyone in the building have a key to the main door?"

"No. That door is never locked. Each apartment has it own lock."

"Who else lives in the building?"

"The ground floor apartment is unoccupied at present. Otherwise there's just two women who share the apartment below. They both work in the local chemical bank."

"Excellent. Now here's what I propose."

After outlining his plan, McClellan got Rodrigo to write a letter in Spanish.

It was headed with his home address and read as follows:

To Jupiter,

Through a friend of mine, who until recently worked as a guarura at the Miguel Alemán Clinic, an interesting little book has come into my possession. It is the pocket diary of Dr. Zaragoza. In it, he names you as helping to operate a drug network under the name of Jupiter.

We have not shown this diary to anyone else. We think it might be valuable, worth at least $100,000. If you want to buy it, bring the money— cash only— to my third-floor apartment at 7 p.m. today. I'll be waiting in the roof garden. After 7.15, the deal is off, and we start lookingfor another buyer.

Come alone... and don't get any fancy ideas. My friend has a photocopy of Zaragoza's entry in the diary. If anything happens to me, he knows what to do.

Rodrigo Monteagudo

"That's good," said McClellan. "If we've got the right man, it won't matter if he checks you out in the phone book, or with your neighbours. Of course, it's just possible that he could have got your name from the Acapulco police. But then that might help to explain how you got hold of the diary."

He then sealed the letter in a pre-addressed envelope. "We'll deliver this to the U.S. embassy first thing tomorrow morning."

400

CHAPTER 30

It was only a brisk ten-minute walk from the Villalongin Street apartment to the U.S. embassy on Reforma. Rodrigo, posing as a messenger, dropped off his letter at the reception desk, and then joined Julio for breakfast in the nearby Continental restaurant.

He found Julio poring over the morning papers. *HERMANO DEL PRESIDENTE EN ESCÁNDALO DE DROGAS,* screamed the front page of the *Excelsior,* and similarly, the other dailies focussed primarily on the role of the President's brother as Mexico's "biggest drug profiteer". According to some reports, Gastón Pérez and his wife were now in Switzerland, where they had stashed illicit millions of dollars.

Rodrigo flipped through the tabloids, taking special interest in one centre page spread that featured pictures of El Nuevo Santo and reprised his career.

"Hey, Julio, this one's great! They rate you the greatest champion of the people since Superbarrio. And look at this cartoon. They've picked up on what your father said on TV. There's you wearing the presidential sash and handing over your mask to President Pérez."

Julio glanced at the drawing and, mimicking John Wayne, drawled *"That'll be the day."*

"I'll tell you one thing for sure," said Rodrigo. "You can make a small fortune selling your story to the papers. I'll bet they're out with their cheque-books hunting for you right now."

After a second cup of coffee and his third doughnut, he looked at the menu. "I'm still hungry. I think I'll have the *huevos con jamón.*"

"Forget it," said Julio. "There's no time. We've got to get back and get ready. Remember, if we have found Jupiter, we can't count on him keeping that seven o'clock appointment. Who knows, he might choose to jump the gun and send in some thugs."

It was almost 10 a.m. when they got back to Rodrigo's apartment. They had expected Brad and Nicholas to be there waiting for them. But another hour passed by, and still they had not arrived.

"Something's wrong," said Rodrigo. "Maybe we should give them a ring."

Julio shook his head. "You know what Brad said. No calls to *Apartamentos Orleáns.* They may still be bugging the phones there. We don't want the police tracing a call, and we certainly can't risk Jupiter finding out that you are not working alone."

As he took the elevator to the seventh floor of the CIA's Langley headquarters, Arthur Madison mused over the curious coincidence of events. That Friday morning, just when he was about to request a private interview with the new DDO, he had received a call summoning him to the DDO's office.

In advance, he had worked out very carefully what he was going to say. Now, conversely, he found himself wondering what the DDO wanted. He could think of only one reason why the chief should wish to see him, and he was right.

William J. Stanleigh, the Deputy Director (Operations), came straight to the point. "I've got a problem, Arthur. It's about this guy McClellan. I learn that officially he left the Company two months ago. Yet now, he pops up leading some gung-ho drugs bust in Acapulco. Entirely without our authority.

"It's all very embarrassing. On one hand, I have the President praising the CIA's smart work. And ambassador Henderson has even suggested that his former bodyguard should get some kind of medal. On the other hand, if it gets out that we knew nothing about the operation, we're going to be a laughing stock."

Madison chewed thoughtfully on his empty pipe. "I see what you mean, sir. A pity. And just when we could use some good publicity."

"Exactly, Arthur. Now, the thing is this. You must know McClellan pretty well after working with him in Mexico City. What's your personal assessment of the man? Is he an irresponsible loose cannon? Or d'you think he might co-operate, and keep quiet about having worked on his own?"

"Well, sir..."

"Hey, cut out the *sir* shit. You can call me Bill. Now give it to me straight. Is this guy a nut or what?"

"Well, Bill, I can only say I found him a very intelligent and highly responsible colleague. Have you tried contacting him?"

"I've got the station chief Hellman working on that right now. But he missed him in Acapulco, and now time is getting short. We need to get hold of him quickly - before any real damage is done. I was wondering whether you had any ideas."

Madison decided it was time to play his bluff.

"I have a confession to make - *sir*. I am in regular contact with McClellan, and I have known all along about his activities."

Stanleigh glared at him. "Are you serious? What the hell is going on?"

Madison explained in detail - how they had felt the need to operate in secrecy after the disappearance of so many undercover agents; how they felt sure there had to be a mole inside one of the intelligence agencies. "We just couldn't trust anyone, you see."

"Christ," exclaimed the DDO. "That's all we need - another fucking Ames! Now listen, Madison. I can't approve of your action. It's inexcusable. You should have discussed this with me beforehand. I shall have to consider disciplinary action. Meanwhile, if we have got another rotten apple in the barrel, I want him sorted out - fast. Have you got any notion who he may be?"

"Well, sir. We do have an important clue. We think he goes under the code-name of Jupiter. We got this from the personal diary of Dr. Zaragoza - you know, the guy who was running drug operations in Acapulco."

"Is that all? Just a code-name?"

"Not quite, sir. Zaragoza used some kind of elaborate code when writing about Jupiter. McClellan is working on it right now. He thinks he can crack it, and get his real name."

"Really! Is he an expert code-breaker, too?"

"No, sir. Strictly an amateur."

"That's not good enough. What's the good of our having highly skilled cryptographers if we don't use them. I'll have one assigned to you, and the two of you can get down to Mexico City right away."

"Would you mind, sir, if I picked my own

cryptographer— someone I feel I can trust."

"Not at all. Whatever you need. Just get results... and report back only to me. At the same time, see if you can get McClellan to keep quiet about having operated independently. And I expect you to keep quiet about it, too."

"Absolutely, sir." Madison smiled enigmatically and paused. "I am afraid, sir, that I have one more confession to make. There is a diary and a reference to Jupiter. But no coded message. I made that up. I just wanted to see your reaction, hopefully to eliminate you as being the possible mole."

"Bloody cheek!" exclaimed Stanleigh. And then, unpredictably, his stern face dissolved into a broad grin. "Well, are you satisfied that I am not your mole?"

"Yes, sir. Quite satisfied."

"Good! Then no more jerking me off. So what other crazy ideas do you have about who this Jupiter might be?"

Madison explained McClellan's theory that it must be someone who knew that Martínez was an undercover agent. "If his hunch works out, it could be that he will trap the mole tonight."

After he had heard the plan of entrapment, Stanleigh looked to one side as he composed his thoughts. Then he spoke softly. "Do you realise, Arthur, what this could mean for the CIA? Another Ames case after all the other scandals going back to that costly bombing of the Chinese embassy in Belgrade. It could swing the balance in the Bureau's bid to take us over completely.

"As for Mexican co-operation in fighting the drug war – well, you can guess what their reaction would be. It's just the kind of excuse they need, and the price will be more demands for financial aid."

"I appreciate all that, sir. But I really don't see that we have any choice. We've got to get this mole."

The Deputy Director leaned across his desk. "There is a choice, Arthur," he said, almost in a whisper. "It would be better for the country, for all of us, if we could avoid another big show trial."

"How do you mean?"

"I mean, Arthur, it would be better if this Jupiter could somehow just mysteriously disappear - just like those brave agents the DEA has lost in Mexico. Vanish without a trace. As if swallowed up by a black hole."

It was 11 a.m. and McClellan was cursing himself for his lack of foresight. He should have anticipated the problem. The Press had been buzzing Nicholas' apartments since dawn and, despite getting no reply, they had camped on the doorstep, their numbers swelling by the hour.

Two hours earlier— at McClellan's suggestion— Nicholas had confronted the media, explaining that they were wasting their time. By the conditions of his release, he was not permitted to discuss events in Acapulco while he was still under investigation.

It was to no effect. "Who else is with you?" shouted one reporter. "Where is El Nuevo Santo?" shouted another. Nicholas ignored them, and retreated to his apartment.

By this time, two television crews had joined the gathering vultures. It seemed to McClellan they were trapped. They could not hope to get to Rodrigo's apartment without being followed.

Next, in desperation, he had got Nicholas to phone General Delgado's office. The *Jefe*, they said, was not available. Instead, he was put through to Coronel Hernández.

Nicholas duly explained that he and Señorita Marke were under siege by the media, but were bound by law not to speak to them. Also, his assistant needed complete rest after the trauma of her kidnapping ordeal. Could the police perhaps disperse the Press and TV people?

Hernández said he would see what could be done. In fifteen minutes, two squad cars had arrived. Subsequently, the police duly manned the main entrance to *Apartamentos Orleáns*. But they took no other action beyond booking and moving-on vehicles that were illegally parked on Hamburgo.

At this point, Regina decided she had had enough. She was leaving. Soon afterwards, shielded by the police, she got into a taxi that had been booked to take her to her own apartment on Rio Rhin Street. Only a couple of reporters chose to follow her.

Now, at 11 a.m., McClellan resorted to one last, desperate ploy. Using his mobile phone, he made a call that linked him via a private line direct to U.S. ambassador James Henderson. "Boss," he chirped in a familiar style. "This is McClellan. I've got a problem. And I need a very big favour."

"Brad, just name it. By the way, congratulations on your great drug-busting work in Acapulco. Where are you now?"

Coincidentally, at this hour, another call was being made to the U.S. embassy on Reforma. From Langley, Arthur Madison got through on a scrambled line to Wade Hellman, the CIA's station chief in Mexico City. He was speaking, he explained, on behalf of the DDO. "He wants to know if you have contacted McClellan yet."

"I've got a problem," Hellman replied. "I missed him in Acapulco, and now I find he's holed up in an apartment block on Hamburgo. The place is teeming with press and TV people. If I tackle him there, I'm going to be recognised, and there could be some awkward questions asked. What do you suggest?"

"Leave McClellan to me," said Madison. "I'm flying down today. Meanwhile, there's another problem, and the DDO wants you handle it personally. How well do you know Barraza, who used to be the PGR Comandante?"

"Not well. I've met him several times on official business. But he's retired now."

"I know that. But our information is that he has been actively working with McClellan. He may not have been involved in the Acapulco operation. But he certainly knows McClellan has retired and has been operating on his own."

"So what?" said Hellman.

"So, there's a real danger of him spilling the beans. I think I can get McClellan to co-operate, to keep quiet about his retirement. But Barraza's another matter. He's already been on television. Also, we know he is writing his memoirs."

"I see what you mean. What do you want to me to?"

"Go and see him. Explain why we would rather he didn't mention that McClellan has left the Company."

"Okay. He's living in Cuernavaca now. I'll make an appointment to see him tomorrow."

"Not tomorrow, Wade. The DDO wants him checked out *today*."

"Oh shit! I'll have to leave right away. I don't fancy that drive back in the dark."

"Excellent."

"Just one question, Arthur. What if he won't co-operate? Do you want him taken out?"

"Absolutely not," said Madison. "Another killing could get us into deeper trouble. But the DDO says you are authorised to offer him a cash inducement. If necessary, you

406

can go up to $20,000."

It was just after midday when another taxi pulled up outside *Apartamentos Orleáns.* Police cleared a passage and, with flashbulbs popping on either side, McClellan and Stephanopoulos made their getaway.

Inevitably, a convoy of press cars set off in pursuit down Hamburgo. But within six minutes, their journey had come to a dead end. Shortly after rounding the Angel Independence Monument, the taxi pulled up outside the U.S. embassy. Four U.S. marines, waiting kerbside, promptly escorted the fugitives inside.

Half an hour later, waiting pressmen saw ambassador Henderson leaving in his distinctive car, which flew the American flag. He waved to them as he drove by. Behind him sat two men wearing U.S.marine uniforms, and dark shades beneath their peaked caps.

They had travelled only half-a-dozen blocks when the car stopped just beyond the Cuauhtémoc statue. Unnoticed, the "marines", having removed their uniform jackets and caps, got out and headed on foot towards nearby Villalongin Street.

Both men had a haversack slung over their right shoulders. As they took their leave, the ambassador called out, "Good luck, Brad. And watch your back."

By eschewing the old scenic route in favour of the purely functional toll highway, Wade Hellman took only an hour to reach the congested centre of Cuernavaca. He then headed south on Boulevard Juárez, and eventually turned off into an upper-class residential area where single-storey, ranch-style houses, predominantly white or pink, were set amid spacious grounds, almost invariably with a swimming pool and a liberal blaze of bougainvillaea.

Many elderly Americans had chosen to end their days in this salubrious hill resort, some becoming members of the golf-and-country-club set, others preferring to be reclusive devotees of gardening, and perhaps painting. To Hellman, however, it was an anathema, a grotesque departure lounge of life.

At foryt-six, he was already planning to take an early retirement... after perhaps three or four years in his imminent new position as Deputy Director Chief of the Latin American section at Langley. And not for him any quiet, geriatric environment. He loved big cities for their access to theatre, gambling and night spots; and he loved San Francisco best of all.

San Francisco was his idea of paradise, the place on Earth where he most felt at home and able to be himself, without fear of disapproval or discrimination. The wonder was that, for career purposes, he had effectively masked his natural proclivities for so long, restricting himself in Mexico to one discreetly supported catamite.

Hellman could not get back to Mexico City soon enough, and now, he was thankful Barraza's house was easy to find: a white adobe bungalow, simply identified by a street number sign, unlike neighbouring residences with names like *Shangri-la,* and *Avalon.*

At the end of a short, gravelled driveway, he found that Barraza— alerted by a security device— was there to meet him. He was standing outside the house, in the shade of a jacaranda. He was wearing gardening gloves and had secateurs in one hand.

For a moment, Hellman failed to recognise Barraza as the smartly suited Comandante he had met some six months ago. His first thought was that this man, wearing baggy shorts, open-necked shirt and a floppy sunhat hanging over sunglasses, looked remarkably like Mr. Magoo.

On the other hand, Barraza's firm and direct manner of speaking was unmistakable. *"Buenas tardes,* Señor Hellman. You are earlier than I expected."

Hellman forced a smile. "Your directions were very good, *señor.* Thank you very much for agreeing to see me at such short notice."

"Quite! Well, if you'll follow me, we can talk in my study. I expect you would like a cool drink after your drive. What can I get you?"

Left alone in the study, Hellman looked out the French windows and saw there was no swimming pool, only a small, well-manicured lawn with immaculately kept herbaceous borders.

After a few minutes his host returned, carrying a pint glass of pineapple juice, with lemonade and ice. "Sorry to keep you waiting. But I don't have any servants here - just a cleaning lady who comes in twice a week."

Taking a seat behind his desk, he removed his floppy hat, and then rummaged in the right-hand drawer at ankle level. "Oh dear. I was hoping to offer you a cigar, but I seem to be out of them."

"That's all right," said Hellman. "I don't smoke."

"Good. Then let's get down to business. What can be so important you couldn't talk to me about it on the phone?"

Hellman explained the CIA's concern about McClellan. "As you will appreciate, *señor,* we would sooner not have it known that he was acting independently."

"I see. So you want me to say nothing about his retirement?"

"Exactly."

"Well, young man, I shall have to think about that very carefully. As you probably know, I am writing my memoirs at the moment."

The somewhat condescending *'young man'* did not disturb Hellman. He was used to it; in the Company, his boyish looks had brought out jokes about his having a portrait in the attic. Nevertheless, the man's tone was suggestive. He sensed that the ex-Comandante was fishing— as was to be expected— for the usual *mordida.*

"I understand, *señor.* We would, of course, be prepared to offer you some compensation for any loss to the contents of your memoirs."

"Are you offering me money?"

"*Sí.* If you wish. Though strictly off the record. And tax-free, of course."

"How much?"

Hellman found his bluntness disconcerting. "Um, I really don't know, *señor.* Shall we say $5,000?"

Barraza replied only with a derisive puffing sound.

Hellman grimaced. He had no time to engage in lengthy bargaining. He went straight to his limit. "I can offer you $20,000. That's the tops. And very generous, I am sure you will agree."

To his surprise, Barraza suddenly pushed back his chair and stood up. Inscrutable behind his dark glasses, he said sternly, "I am afraid, young man, you have had a wasted journey. Look around you. I am not exactly living in luxury. If you were smart, you would have deduced that I was that rarest of creatures: a policeman who has *never* been for sale. I wish you good day."

As he sped back on the highway, thankful to be ahead of the rush-hour evening traffic, Hellman cursed the ex-Comandante. *What a repulsive-looking lizard of a man! It would be a service to humanity to have him taken out.*

Meanwhile, Barraza had returned to his desk. There he switched off the tape recorder in the bottom right-hand drawer. He had, he reflected, an interesting little anecdote to add to his memoirs.

CHAPTER 31

"Like I said before, we've got to be prepared for the unexpected. Remember it was only Julio's quick thinking that saved us from Zaragoza's booby trap. So stay alert, and, if necessary, be ready to improvise. You all know what you have to do, but let's go over it one more time and see if there is anything we might have missed."

It was 5.45 p.m., and in the small rooftop garden of Rodrigo's apartment they were seated round a wrought-iron table as McClellan reviewed their plan.

"Basically", he went on," we have everything worked out on the premise that our man will show at 7 p.m. - hopefully alone. But, as I have said, there is always the chance - if he is desperate enough - that he might come earlier, and with armed accomplices.

"Either way, Madison should be able to alert us on his mobile. He left the embassy five minutes ago, and any time now, he should be calling to say he's in position.

"But don't forget what Zaragoza wrote... about Jupiter being a mad paranoid. If, as we believe, he ordered the killings in the park, then he's capable of anything, however extreme. So let's be prepared for the worst."

McClellan paused. "As I see it, the worst scenario is that he might choose to fire-bomb the place... trying to destroy the evidence, and anyone here in the process.

"The good thing is he has hardly had time to plant an explosive device in advance; also, we know our suspect cant get here before 6 p.m. On the other hand, there's always the chance that Madison will be unable to alert us in time. For example, if a bomb was thrown from a fast-moving car.

"Luckily, we know the fire escape is reasonably secure, and in the event of a bomb that's our best bet of getting out. So Nicholas, if there is an explosion, you and Rodrigo should get up here as quickly as possible. But we won't be waiting for you, because it's safer that we don't all get on that ladder at the same time. Agreed?"

411

They nodded.

"Okay. Now does anyone see any problem that we haven't covered?"

"What about the women downstairs?" asked Rodrigo. "I know what I have to do if they arrive back soon. But suppose they go shopping or something after work, and get back later than usual."

McClellan sighed. "That's an awkward one. I'm afraid we're going to have to leave it to chance. We can't risk Madison coming out to warn them off. Jupiter could be watching, and everything needs to look normal."

"Anything else?"

"Just one thing," said Nicholas. "What if no one shows up? Have you got any other plan?"

McClellan shook his head. "In that case, we're at a dead end. Full stop. But don't think about it. We must presume someone will come. Right. Let's get ready. It's going to be a long next hour."

From a haversack, McClellan handed each of them a Walther P88 pistol, plus a 15-round box magazine which snapped into the butt. Nicholas and Rodrigo, who were also given walkie-talkies, then went down to the livingroom - the only third-floor room with a door opening onto the staircase. They locked the door behind them.

Meanwhile, Julio helped McClellan to move the wrought-iron table to one side of the small patio, leaving room for one chair between the table and the section of stone wall leading directly onto the fire escape.

Twilight was closing in fast now. McClellan switched on just two of the patio lights so that Julio, seated against the parapet, would soon be only a shadowy figure.

It was just after 6.p.m. when Madison first called on his mobile to confirm that he was in position behind park bushes, almost directly across the street from Rodrigo's apartment. Fifteen minutes later, he called again. Two women were approaching... and yes, they were now turning into the building.

Instantly, McClellan alerted Rodrigo on his walkie-talkie, and immediately the Mexican hurried downstairs, meeting his neighbours just as they were about to unlock the door to their second-floor apartment.

"*Buenas noches, señoritas,*" chirped Rodrigo. "Excuse me, but I've a small problem. I wonder if I could come in for a minute." He spoke as casually as possible, not wishing to alarm them.

"Of course," said Manuela, the older and far plumper of the two women. She rather fancied Rodrigo, her interest in him being heightened by the certain mystery that surrounded him. She had never discovered exactly what he did for a living, and why he was so often away from home.

On two occasions, she had asked him about his work. Each time, he had quickly changed the subject, saying only that he was involved with boxing promotion, and that it was much too boring to talk about.

"Can we get you a drink, Rodrigo?" Manuela asked, after he had entered their livingroom.

"*Muchas gratias*. But thank you, no. I really don't have much time."

"Oh! Anyway, do sit down. Eugenia, I'd love a coffee. Would you mind?"

The younger woman smiled coyly at Rodrigo, then left for the kitchen. "Well now," said Manuela. "So what's the problem? And how can we help?"

Rodrigo looked suitably contrite. "I have a favour to ask. But I don't know quite how to put it. The thing is, you see, it's rather embarrassing and personal."

Intrigued, Manuela leaned forward on her easy chair. "Please, don't be afraid to ask. I would be only too glad to help."

"Well, it's like this: anytime now I've got this man coming to see me. The fact is, he's a heavy drinker, and sometimes he can get extremely violent. I wouldn't want you to be disturbed. So I was wondering if, for the next hour or so, you could stay inside, and keep your apartment door locked and bolted."

"*Dios mío*! How terrible! Who is this man, and why are you seeing him? Shouldn't we be calling the police?"

"Absolutely not. It's too personal."

"Really?" said Manuela, her wide eyes begging for an explanation.

Rodrigo shifted his chair a little closer, and spoke softly. "Can I talk to you in complete confidence, Manuela? Just between you and me?"

"Of course."

"Well, you see, this man has somehow got it into his crazy head that I've compromised his daughter. It's quite

413

untrue, of course. I don't even like the girl. But she keeps ringing me. I think she must have said something to her father, probably trying to trap me into marriage."

"How awful for you," said Manuela. "I still think we should call the police."

"No, please. I am quite strong enough to handle him myself. But, just in case, I would like you to keep to your apartment." He grinned. "I wouldn't want him to fall on you if I had to knock him down the stairs."

She smiled back. "Very well, Rodrigo. We'll do you as you ask. But promise me one thing."

"What's that?"

"That when he's gone, you'll come down for a drink, and tell me how it's all turned out."

"Of course, Manuela. Now I really must go." He reached out and patted her hand. "And thank you for being so understanding."

Her large expressive eyes lit up, and she followed him to the door. "Now remember," he said. "Keep this locked until I come back. Don't open it to anyone else. It's just possible he could knock on your door by mistake."

Alone, outside, Rodrigo leaned against the corridor wall and breathed a great sigh of relief. Then he hurried upstairs to join Nicholas in the livingroom. Like Manuela, he locked the door behind him.

The long wait ended at 6.55 p.m. Madison was on the line to McClellan, and he had unexpected news. "A police car has just pulled up outside. The light's bad, but as far as I can make out, there are two uniformed officers in the front.

"Yes, that's right. I can see them now. An interior light has gone on, and someone's getting out at the back. Yes, it's our man. He's talking to the officers... oh, and now he's heading for the front door. What do you want me to do?"

"There's no time to talk," said McClellan. "Use your own judgement. I've got to go." He switched off his mobile, alerted Rodrigo on the walkie-talkie, and then climbed into his position.

With one ear pressed against the living-room door, Rodrigo could clearly hear the man approaching. The wooden boards of the uncarpeted staircase creaked every step of the way. Briefly, there was silence, as the man paused outside the door. Then he moved on, up the seven steps that led through an open black metal door onto the *azotea*.

The man became clearly visible as he stepped under the main patio light: darkly handsome and immaculately dressed in a pinstriped suit. He was carrying a small briefcase, and was apparently unarmed.

He looked around, and noted that the rooftop garden was deserted, except for someone seated in the shadows behind a wrought-iron table. "Señor Monteagudo?" he asked.

"*Sí,*" said Julio. "You're right on time, señor Jupiter. I trust you've brought the money."

The man came forward, and laid the briefcase on the table. "It's all there. Count it if you wish. Now let's see exactly what I'm paying for."

Julio pulled out the diary from the breast pocket of his denim jacket. Then he switched on a table lamp, and opened the diary at a folded-down page. "The entry for January 24th is especially interesting. Zaragoza seems to think you're mad because you ordered more than one killing in Chapultepec Park."

The man glared down at him. "Look, I didn't come here to talk. Just hand it over, and let me see for myself."

At that moment, he was horrified to see the outline of a second man looming large above and behind the man in the chair. From the fire escape, McClellan clambered down, and stepped into the light. He had a Walther P88 in his right hand.

"YOU," exclaimed the man called Jupiter.

"Yes, Wade. It's me. You fucking traitor! You wanted to see the diary. Well, sit down and read it. Just that entry for the twentieth… and read it aloud."

Hellman sat down and, momentarily confused, took the opened diary and mumbled the two lines. Then he looked up at McClellan, who was towering above him. "Shit! This doesn't prove a thing." He started to flip frantically through the diary. "I can't see my name anywhere. What kind of stupid game are you playing, McClellan?"

"No game, Wade. I'm afraid this is curtains for you. We don't need written proof. Your presence here is enough."

Hellman's eyes blazed with hatred. "Damn you, McClellan. You can go to hell. I'm not standing for this a minute longer. I'm leaving now. Shoot me in the back if you like. The police are outside, and they'll be coming in if I don't appear in the next five minutes."

He stood up and turned to leave. And then he stared

reality in the face. Ahead of him, in the archway opening onto the stairs, was the menacing figure of Nicholas Stephanopoulos. He, too, had a gun in his hand.

McClellan grabbed Hellman by the shoulder. "Sit down, shithead," he barked. "You aren't going anywhere."

He returned to the parapet, and looked down onto the street below. There was no sign of a police car.

Use your own judgement. Pondering on McClellan's words, Madison had taken out his pipe, and then started to chew as he tried to assess the situation. Assessment was his business; what he did best. But action was something else. He had not handled a gun since those far-off days in the CIA training school at Cape Peary, Virginia. He had an encyclopaedic knowledge of international terrorism, and yet, absolutely no firsthand experience of active duty in the field.

Now, disconcertingly, his assessment was that the situation demanded immediate action. Why were the policemen waiting there? He could think of only three explanations: they were waiting to assist Jupiter in a quick getaway, they were standing by in case he summoned their help, or they were under orders to investigate if he did not reappear in some predetermined time. Whatever the explanation, they constituted a threat to McClellan's plan.

He drew out the Walther P88 that bulged in a shoulder holster beneath his sports jacket, pushed home the box magazine, and then tucked the weapon into the back of his corduroy trousers. It was time for the academic to prove himself as a man of action.

After lighting his pipe, Madison proceeded to break cover, and walk nonchalantly across the well-lit street, directly towards the police patrol car. The officer in the passenger seat saw him approaching. Madison promptly smiled, and gave a friendly wave with his pipe-holding left hand.

"*Buenas noches, oficial,*" he called out. "What a lovely evening!"

The officer lowered his half-open window, resting his right hand on his .38 revolver.

Madison puffed on his pipe, then spoke again in broken Spanish that failed to mask his languid South Carolina drawl. "Excuse me, *señor,* but I wonder if you could help me. Stupidly, I've got lost. I am looking for Rio Marne Street."

His manner was so normal that the officer took his

416

hand away from his gun and began to give directions. "It's only a block away. You keep going straight, then take the first right..."

"You're too kind," said Madison with an avuncular smile. "I must give you something for your trouble."

Casually, he reached into his back pocket and, instead of the expected wallet, drew out his P88, swiftly thrusting it through the open window.

"One wrong move, and you're dead," he snapped. "Look straight ahead. Now, very slowly, both of you pull out your hand-guns and toss them over your shoulders."

When they had complied, he climbed into the back seat, picked up one of their .38 revolvers, and held two guns to the back of their necks. "Right. Start the engine and move off slowly. Don't touch the horn, and don't make a turn until I tell you."

Thirty minutes later, the police car pulled off the Tolcua Highway into a designated picnic area surrounded by towering fir trees. It was pitch black when they got out of the car. And there, at Madison's command, the officers removed their uniforms and boots, and threw them onto the back seat.

"Okay, *mi amigos*," said Madison. "Start walking into the woods, and don't look back." As the two figures in white underwear disappeared into the darkness, he started up the car and headed back to the city.

En route, he called McClellan on his mobile, and recounted his actions. "I plan to dump the car in some dark alley off Reforma. It'll take some time for those cops to get back, and then they're going to have some awkward explaining to do. Is that okay, Brad?"

McClellan chuckled. "Excellent, Arthur. You did well. I suggest you get back to the embassy now. We can take it from here, and I won't contact you again unless I need you. Cheers!"

He then looked across the table at Wade Hellman. "Bad news, I'm afraid. Your cop friends won't be coming, after all. Seems they've gone on a picnic."

Hellman didn't react. He was busy examining his red-stained white silk handkerchief, confirming that his nose had stopped bleeding at last. He was already a broken man.

Twenty minutes earlier, McClellan had attempted to cross-examine Hellman in an orderly fashion. "Let's start at the beginning," he said. "Just when and how did you come to be involved with the New Gulf drugs cartel? And why, for God's sake, when you had so much going for you?"

The CIA station chief simply looked up at the night sky, ignoring the questions. His wrists were handcuffed behind his chair. Julio and Nicholas flanked him, sitting marginally behind.

McClellan leaned across the table and barked, "Look at me, you bastard. I don't want to have to resort to violence but, by golly, I'll beat the shit out of you if I have to. Believe me, your own mother won't recognise you when I've finished."

Hellman faced up to him. "Now see here, Brad, this has gone far enough. I know it looks bad - my being here. But the fact is that I got this curious letter and I decided to play along with it. If this diary existed, it might be valuable to the Company. Why do you think I brought the police along?"

"Are you kidding?" snapped McClellan. "Let's cut the crap. You're this character Jupiter, and I hold you responsible for the deaths of at least three DEA agents, plus those victims in the park."

"What makes you so sure? Doesn't it occur to you that I might just be telling the truth?"

"Oh! I'm sure all right. Remember those words in Zaragoza's diary: *Jupiter has flown*? And the date, January 24? Funnily enough, that was the very day you left Mexico."

"But you know why. My father was critically ill in Stockton. I had to see him before he died."

"Bollocks! I checked that out with one of our agents in Stockton. He traced your father and found him extremely fit and well. And you know what? When the agent said he knew you, your father complained that he hadn't heard from you for more than ten years. Not even a postcard, he said."

Hellman looked flustered. "I suggest", McClellan went on, "that you wanted to be as far away from Mexico City as possible, just in case anything went wrong with your plan to eliminate Martínez."

"Suggest what you like," said Hellman. "I don't know anything about those stupid killings in the park."

It was at that point Nicholas suddenly lost control. He stood up and, without warning, swung his right arm in a great loop to crash his fist into Hellman's face.

The blood gushed down in a torrent, soaking Hellman's white shirt and grey tie, and dripping onto his crotch. He let out an almighty yelp, and squirmed in a vain effort to free his hands.

"Christ!" exclaimed McClellan. "Couldn't you have waited?"

"No," said Nicholas. "I've had enough of this crap." He took out his wallet, and extracted a photograph. "See this?" he said, thrusting the picture in front of Hellman's crimson face. "That's my wife and son. Just nine-years-old he was. And you had to kill him, you fucking shit."

With a mouth full of blood, Hellman was in no state to reply. McClellan turned to Julio. "Take off the handcuffs, and let him clean himself up."

As Hellman tried to mop up the mess, McClellan stood over him. "You've only yourself to blame. You should have stopped bull-shitting us. I suggest you make it easy on yourself and give us straight answers."

Hellman nodded, tearfully. "Okay. Anything you want. Just keep that animal away from me."

Nicholas clenched a fist, as though about to strike again. But Julio grabbed his arm. "Leave it, Nick," he said softly. "Our time will come."

From that point on, Hellman answered McClellan's questions with extraordinary candour, beginning with a confession about how he'd been 'sucked in' to work with the New Gulf drug cartel. It had happened four years ago, not long after his promotion to CIA station chief.

"Things were going really well. We were doing a good job, helping Gastón Pérez's anti-drug units to combat the Juárez cartel. I had no idea then that they were just using us as a means to take over the Juárez operation.

"Well, later on, when I was on leave in Acapulco, the police arrested me. Can you believe it? They said I'd sexually abused an under-age beach boy. I still think I was set up. The kid looked at least seventeen. Anyway, the scandal would have finished my career. I was desperate. But they never pursued the paedophilia charge. Instead, I was offered a deal by Torres, the police chief. He would drop charges in exchange for information.

"Stupidly, I thought that one tip-off would let me off the hook. But it only got me in deeper. There was no escape, you understand. In the end, I was running their security operation, not to protect their interests, but to save myself from discovery. I was terrified of that."

He spoke plaintively, as though expecting sympathy.

"Tough," growled McClellan. "So you betrayed our agents, condemned them to death, just to save your own miserable skin. Nothing else? No pay-offs?"

Hellman hung his head. "Yes, they did eventually pay me. I got it direct from Pérez. But I only took money to prepare for a way out. I was going to quit, as soon as I moved to Langley, and then take an early retirement."

McClellan, now seated, leaned across until their heads were almost touching. "So what about Martínez? He was my contact. Why did you have him killed?"

"It was on orders from Pérez. He found out Martínez had been investigating his bank accounts. The whole operation was in danger... only weeks before I was getting away from it all."

"That doesn't explain all the killings in the park. Was that your idea, killing so many innocent people?"

Julio forcefully held Nicholas back as Hellman replied. "That was terrible," he whined. "Again, it was Pérez's plan; and he rushed into it when he heard about the birthday party. He thought shooting the Turkish ambassador would take attention away from the death of Martínez, confuse any investigation."

McClellan reached out and grabbed Hellman by his blood-soaked tie. "I don't believe you. I suggest you panicked, and that *you* ordered a massacre, just like Zaragoza says in his diary."

Hellman looked anxiously towards Nicholas. "No, really. It was all a mistake. Only Martínez and the ambassador were supposed to be killed. That poor boy and his mother! They must have just got in the way."

As a wild-eyed Nicholas struggled to move, Julio held him firmly in a half-Nelson grip. "Leave it!" he rasped. "I've told you what we can do."

McClellan moved on to asking questions about the cartel's operations. Hellman confirmed that Gastón Pérez ran the network with Zaragoza as his second-in-command. As far as he knew, the President wasn't directly involved, but he was compromised by the fact that his brother had made huge contributions to his election campaign funds. "I can't be sure, but I think he paid General Delgado to cover up his brother's tracks."

Hellman insisted that he had never met Zaragoza in

person. "We spoke only by phone. It was my job to advise him if I knew of any threat by the DEA to his activities. But my information was of minimal value. He always seemed to know more than I did about border security.

"I think he had some valuable contact on the American side: someone who handled all bribes to U.S. customs officials. But I never knew who it was."

Then he brightened slightly. "However, I can give you one useful tip. All that coke discovered at the clinic. What do you think's going to happen to that junk? Check it out. I happen to know that more than half of all narcotics seized by the Mexican police finds its way back onto the market."

At this stage, as he talked, Hellman seemed to become more relaxed, more sure of himself. Then he revealed his line of thought. "I suppose, Brad, that you're wired and are getting all of this on tape."

"Really?" asked McClellan.

"Yeah. Just like you did with Torres. But the thing is, all this— what I've been saying— under duress— will be inadmissible in a court of law. The days of trial by ordeal went out with the Middle Ages."

McClellan looked at him deadpan. "What trial? What court of law?"

Hellman was still digesting that enigmatic response when McClellan stood up and looked at his watch. "It's time we got moving. Sooner or later those cops are likely to come back."

Julio turned to Nicholas, who had been remarkably quiet and subdued since his last explosion. "Are you all right, *amigo?*"

Nicholas nodded.

"Right then," said Julio. "It's back to my place. I'll get this creep ready. Meanwhile, perhaps you could fetch Rodrigo. We'll need to use his car."

Throughout the interrogation of Hellman, Rodrigo had squatted on the stairs below, keeping a lookout for any intruders. Now he appeared, carrying the remains of his six-pack of *cerveza*. "All quiet down there," he chirped. "Who'd like a drink? Only two cans left, I'm afraid."

Nicholas declined. Julio and McClellan took up the offer. Meanwhile, Hellman, now back in handcuffs, watched them intently, waiting for some clue to their next move. To his relief, there was no hint of anger in Nicholas' face. The

Greek seemed completely composed.

But then McClellan spoke, and the subsequent conversation set alarm bells going off in his head. "Well, guys," said Brad. "I guess this is the end of the road. It's been great working with you, and I want to thank you one last time."

"What will you do now?" asked Julio.

"Dunno exactly. I'll have to see what Madison says. Anyway, I'll be staying at the embassy until I get clearance from the Anti-Drug Commission. If you need me, you can reach me there."

In turn, they all shook McClellan's hand. Then he drained his can of beer and stowed his gun and the two walkie-talkies in one of the haversacks.

Meanwhile, Julio was talking to Rodrigo. "What do you want to do now, Rod? We need your car, but really there's no reason for you come with us."

"You're right," said Rodrigo. "I think I'll stay here." He grinned. "I had better chat up those *señoritas* before they start asking questions. I won't need the car. Bring it back when it suits you."

McClellan, with his haversack slung over his right shoulder, was now moving towards the stairs. "Take it easy, guys," he called out. "If I don't see you again, good luck."

At that point, Hellman exploded in terror. "Brad," he screamed. "Where you are going? Don't leave me with these nutters. Brad! Brad!"

But by now, McClellan had disappeared down the stairs. "Shut up," said Julio. He picked up the bloodstained handkerchief and, with a struggle, he stuffed it into the American's mouth.

"Okay, Nicholas. Let's get going."

CHAPTER 32

The *Cerro de la Estrella*— Hill of the Stars— rises like a giant pyramid above the township of Iztapalapa in the southeast of Mexico City. Here, at the end of every cycle of fifty-two years, the Aztecs of Tenochtitlán assembled in trepidation to await the beginning of a new cycle, or the end of their world.

It was all because the Aztec calendar did not exactly accord with the annual cycle of the sun. Thus, every fifty-two years, it was necessary to observe a twelve-and-a-half-day period of adjustment marked by fasting and penitence, and by the extinction of all flames. The limbo ended at midnight with a "new fire" ritual being performed by their priests. If they failed to rekindle fire, the Earth would remain forever in darkness.

In their hilltop temple, the *teocalli*, the priests, sought to avert Armageddon by rubbing sticks together on the naked chest of a sacrificial victim. When the sparks began to fly, a priest opened the victim's chest with his obsidian knife, tore out the palpitating heart, and threw it into a newly made fire. Then a great bonfire, built on the corpse, signalled far and wide that the world was saved for another half-century.

The "new fire" ceremony was last performed in 1507, twelve years before the Spanish conquistadors marched into the Valley of Mexico to subjugate and plunder the empire of Moctezuma II, destroy all temples and idols, and impose on all Indian peoples the "true religion".

Subsequently, an entirely different ceremony evolved in its place: a mass ritual now acknowledged to be the most spectacular of its kind in Mexico City; a religious enactment organised every year by a committee of Iztapalapa residents and played out before an audience of tens of thousands.

And this year— as the principal benefactors of the projected, multi-million-dollar Iztapalapa Orphanage— Julio and Nicholas were to be the chief guests of honour.

The heat was oppressive that afternoon when they

took their seats, alongside local dignitaries, in a makeshift stand on the crown of the *Cerro de la Estrella*. But now a cooling wind was getting up, and far away a black storm cloud was beginning to creep menacingly across the bright-blue sky.

Looking down through binoculars, Nicholas scanned the great mass of humanity that was approaching the base of the hillside. There, by the roadside, he could see a long-bearded, red-cloaked man swinging by the neck from a solitary tree, his tortured face lit by the intermittent flicker of forked lightning, his tongue hanging grotesquely from his gaping mouth.

And not far beyond, another man— barefoot, stripped to the waist, and carrying a giant wooden cross— had fallen down on bloodstained knees, and was grovelling in the dust while two Mexicans in the uniforms of Roman centurions lashed him with leather whips.

It was 4.30 p.m. on Good Friday, and now— following an enactment in the town centre of the arrest and trial of Jesus— the Iztapalapa Passion Play was nearing its climax.

They say that only the bullfights in Mexico start consistently on time. So there was no surprise that the proceedings were running an hour behind schedule. But the delay meant they caught the brunt of the promised storm which now unleashed gale-force winds that whirled blinding, choking dust into mouths, nostrils and eyes.

Torrential rain followed, and in a few minutes the temperature plunged by some 20 degrees Fahrenheit. There was no cover. Everyone— participants and spectators alike— was drenched and chilled to the bone.

Meanwhile, struggling up the hillside, through the wind and the rain, came two columns of purple-robed volunteer penitents called Nazarenes: two hundred youths of Iztapalapa, mostly in their teens, each wearing a crown of sharp-pointed thorns, each dragging from his right shoulder a black cross that varied in size and weight, according to how much the penitent chose to punish himself.

For more than two hours, the Nazarenes had been shuffling barefoot over the sun-drenched cobbles of the town's narrow streets; now some were in acute distress and needed a helping hand. And between their two columns, Nicholas could see the agonised figure of Christ, staggering under the weight of his cross.

On either side were Roman soldiers, resplendent in

424

their homemade togas, shining breastplates and plumed helmets. A few had improvised incongruously, one sporting a T-shirt emblazoned with "Star Wars", another with a flowery tablecloth draped over his shoulders. But all clearly relished their villainous roles, flourishing their swords or whips with alarming vigour while others, on horseback, rode so recklessly that nearby spectators needed to leap back to safety.

Julio, who had seen it all before, guided Nicholas through the action. He explained that Judas Iscariot, swinging so realistically from a tree, was well-supported by a hidden harness, and that his bloated tongue was an artful prop. As for Carlos Garcia, the eighteen-year-old garage mechanic cast in the role of Christ, they had used make-up and paste to provide him with whiplashes, cuts and bruises.

"Mind you, it's still quite an ordeal. The guy playing Jesus spends a year training for the part, and today he will have humped that huge cross for nearly three miles. I've tried lifting it and, believe me, it's tough. Eight-feet high and a hundred sixty-five pounds of solid pine.

"What's more, not all the cuts and bruises are faked. Some of those whiplashes really connect with his bare back. He can't keep falling down without cutting his knees. He also gets blisters on his feet, and real scratches on his head from wearing that crown of thorns."

Nicholas passed him the binoculars. He wasn't really listening. In his mind, he was some seven thousand miles away, thinking back to the last Holy Week he had spent with his family in Athens. How different it was from this noisy, chaotic scene.

Good Friday in Athens was then, as always, a day of great solemnity; a day when the entire city was plunged into deepest sorrow. Flags were flown at half-mast, *evzones* carried their rifles reversed, and church bells everywhere tolled a funeral knell. The main spectacle came at 9 p.m. when, in churches all over the capital, candlelit processions formed to escort the flower-decked bier of Christ through the streets of every parish.

On this day, a year ago, Nicholas and Yasemin had taken Georgios to Syntagma Square where thousands of Athenians held glowing candles as they watched the principal procession: a funeral cortège led by the silver-helmeted National Guard, and including two military bands and contingents of soldiers, sailors, and Boy and Girl Scouts.

425

Towards the rear, preceded by an empty cross, came the funeral bier of Christ borne shoulder-high by white-robed priests. As it passed by, the people knelt and then, shielding their candles, fell in behind to follow the procession back to Athens Cathedral.

But it was the following day— and the scene on another hill— that Nicholas was remembering now. On that Easter Saturday, just like his father before him, he had taken his son to the summit of the 886-foot high Mt. Lycabettus for the unforgettable experience of the midnight Resurrection Service, which is the climax of Holy Week in Athens.

There, outside the minuscule chapel of Aghios Georgios, they had joined thousands of Athenians who stood shoulder-to-shoulder, surrounding the church and spreading out in a great serpentine chain down the hillside; everyone holding an unlighted candle, and silently awaiting the moment of universal rejoicing.

Shortly before midnight, the dimly lit church was plunged into total darkness, symbolising the blackness of the grave. Then, exactly on the magic hour, the incumbent priest emerged from the chapel, and proclaimed, *"Christos anesti!"* (Christ is risen!)

"Christos anesti!" Under his breath, as he thought back to that day, Nicholas repeated the words which, one year before, he and Georgios had shouted aloud, joining in the triumphant cry that was taken up by the multitude. And subsequently, everyone had lit a candle from his neighbour, passing on the light until the summit wore a halo of flickering flames, and then forming a great zigzagging chain of light as they spiralled down the hillside. Above, rockets flashed across the cobalt sky; below, church bells everywhere proclaimed the Resurrection.

But now, on the *Cerro de la Estrella*, the memory of that joyous scene turned sour as his mind flashed back to another night on Mt. Lycabettus; the night when his entire world had fallen apart with the devastating news that his beloved wife and son had been murdered in Mexico. He gritted his teeth, and thereafter thought only of his *philotimo*-driven duty: to avenge their deaths with equal cold-bloodedness.

"Nicholas! Are you all right?"

Julio looked concernedly at his companion. The Greek was just staring blankly into space, seemingly oblivious to the rain that was dripping down his face.

426

"What? Oh, yes. I'm fine," said Nicholas. He wiped his face with his bare hand. "Shouldn't they be stopping in this storm?"

Julio didn't need to reply. At that moment, a voice boomed over the public address system, "Don't move away. Never mind the weather. You're supposed to suffer on this day."

Two condemned "robbers", wearing only loincloths, were now being roped to crosses on the summit. Meanwhile, the Jesus of Iztapalapa was drawing near, struggling to haul up his huge cross while being driven on like a burro by whip-waving centurions.

When he had reached the open ground between the two crucified men, Roman soldiers set up his cross and then, after splashing his hands and feet with blood, attached him to the cross by iron rings with simulated nails.

Julio turned towards Nicholas and grinned. "The kid's lucky. In the Philippines they have been known to hammer real nails, clean through the palms, to fix their Jesus to the Cross."

At that point, as though timed for Wagnerian theatrical effect, the storm produced a drum roll of thunder followed by forked lighting. A horseman was almost thrown as his mount reared up in fright. Then he bellowed his scripted line, "He will be crucified because he is a traitor to our empire."

For fifteen minutes, young Carlos Garcia remained crucified, all the while lashed by icy rain. Meanwhile, the amateur actors played their parts. Speaking into a microphone, artfully concealed in the head of a decorated pole held aloft by a horseman, one robber pleaded with Jesus to save him. The second robber said that he would accept whatever fate Jesus thought fit.

Some thirty yards down the hillside, Mexican police had linked batons to hold back the vast gallery of spectators. Owing to faulty microphones, the onlookers were unable to hear the words spoken by Jesus and by Roman centurions. But many of them booed at the proceedings, and one old woman screamed out, "*Pontius Pilate, es un cabrón!*"

The climactic scene then ended curiously with the appearance of a long-haired actor, white-robed, and fitted with huge artificial wings, climbing up a stepladder behind the Cross, and looming over Jesus of Iztapalapa in the role of a

427

consoling angel sent down by God.

Miraculously, as it seemed, the storm now passed as suddenly as it had begun. Clouds dispersed, giving way to a clear blue sky, and a sun that burned down so intensely that everyone's rain-soaked clothes quickly began to dry.

The show was over and, in a disorganised mass, players and spectators alike began to stream down the hillside. Meanwhile, the half- frozen Carlos was taken down from the Cross and draped in a shroud. Six disciples carried him back to town where, discreetly, he was spirited away to receive pain-killing injections and a medical checkup. It would be several weeks before he recovered completely.

It was shortly before 7 p.m., when the local dignitaries assembled in the Iztapalapa town hall to attend a formal dinner to be held in honour of Julio and Nicholas. And there the honoured guests were joined by three others: Señora Esperanza Velasquez, Rodrigo Monteagudo and Julio's father, Fernando.

The dinner was scheduled for 8 p.m. But first, one more ceremony had to be performed. Darkness was rapidly descending on the Valley of Mexico and— at Julio's suggestion— it was planned to stage a modern version of the Aztecs' 'new fire' ritual to placate the gods, and hopefully ensure the return of the sun.

In the floodlit *zócalo*, overlooked by the Church of St. Lucas, a vast crowd had gathered to witness the ceremony and, more importantly, to salute their great hero and benefactor. And now, in the fading light, they had taken up a deafening chant.

"El Santo! El Santo," they chorused incessantly. And eventually, Julio responded by appearing alone on the balcony of the town hall and raising both arms aloft to acknowledge their resounding cheers.

Almost a full minute passed before the cheering subsided. Then, with the aid of a hand-held microphone, Julio addressed the festive crowd.

"*Mi amigos*, thank you all for your wonderful welcome. But really, I do not deserve your cheers. The real credit today belongs to a young man— a stranger to our land— who has suffered the most appalling personal loss in Mexico City; a man who nevertheless, with extraordinary generosity of spirit, has made it possible for us to start building in Iztapalapa the greatest orphanage our country has

428

ever known."

He signalled for Nicholas to join him on the balcony and, after a short delay, and a friendly push from Rodrigo, Nicholas emerged from behind the French windows.

"*Compatriotas,*" Julio continued. "Let me introduce you to Señor Nicholas Stephanopoulos, my eternal *compadre* and your greatest servant, the noble gentleman who has donated a staggering $10 million to our great social project."

From somewhere in the crowd a mariachi sounded a joyful fanfare on his trumpet; and Nicholas duly waved as everyone cheered and applauded. But he declined Julio's offer of the microphone. "No, *compadre.* I can't speak now. This is your show, your people."

Knowing the Greek's stubborn streak, Julio didn't attempt to persuade him. Instead, after raising a hand to appeal for quiet, he resumed his address which, to the amazement of Nicholas, began to sound more like a political speech:

Our dear friend is too modest to speak. But let me tell you exactly what his huge contribution means to us in real terms. Until his arrival, we had raised just over $2 million towards the Iztapalapa Orphanage. Now, overnight, that sum has been multiplied six times. We're no longer planning to build a modest institution, but a veritable mini-city for deprived children, one we hope will become a model for similar homes throughout México.

Though we originally planned for an orphanage, this development will no longer be only for orphans, but also a home for children who've been abandoned by their parents, and left to fend for themselves on the streets.

Ninety years ago, in the United States, a Catholic priest called Father Flanagan set up a Home for Homeless Boys. It began with only five boys but eventually it catered for hundreds, growing into such a huge community that it was renamed "Boys Tow"'. Now the dream of following his example— here in México— is no longer just a dream. It's a reality. Here, in Iztapalapa, we will be building a complex that will provide a suitable drug-free environment in which a thousand boys and girls can develop their individual skills and be properly prepared to take their place in society.

And this is only just a beginning. I want to see the day when similar institutions exist throughout the land. At the same time, we must continue to put pressure on the politicians to take supportive action.

"Schemes like the Iztapalapa Children's Home can only be truly effective when they're backed up by political action, by a full-scale war on the peddling of drugs that, more than anything else, is destroying our children's future; by rooting out the corrupt police officers who pressurise children to commit petty crimes, and then extort profits from them.

Above all, we need a massive reduction in unemployment, and a decent minimum wage. Without that, the law that bans child labour will remain a mockery, and more than a million children under fourteen will continue to work as street vendors, and slave away in small private workshops and on farms.

He suddenly stopped speaking and smiled. "I'm sorry, *amigos*. I'm going on too long. I'm sure you don't to want hear all my opinions. I just want to thank you all for..."

His next words were drowned out by another trumpet blast, and a single cry of *"Viva el Santo!"* that was immediately taken up by the crowd to become a prolonged rhythmic roar: *"Santo! Santo! Viva el Santo!"*

Julio held up a hand for quiet. Then, solemnly, he uttered five words, which briefly stunned the crowd: *"El Nuevo Santo es muerto."*

"I must tell you," he went on, "that El Nuevo Santo has fought his last fight. The mask has gone forever. From now on, I'm plain Julio Ramírez. But I'm not giving up fighting altogether." He grinned. "I have been persuaded to engage in my toughest fight yet. In the next elections, I will be standing as a congressional candidate for the National Action Party."

The crowd seemed to be frozen. And then, suddenly, the silence was broken by a single cry of *"Santo es muerto! Viva Julio Ramírez! Ramírez por Presidente!"*

Again, everyone echoed the cry, and the *zócalo* resounded with the mass chorus of *"Viva Ramírez! Ramírez Presidente!"*

It was 7.30 p.m, and the crowd was now in a more light-hearted mood after Julio had been joined on the balcony by Esperanza, Rodrigo and Fernando. Introducing each of them in turn, he praised Rodrigo as "the trainer who made El Nuevo Santo" and, wrapping an arm around Esperanza, he

430

announced to thunderous applause that he hoped eventually to make her his wife.

Finally, he came to Fernando and said, "For you older people, my father needs no introduction. He will be remembered as the great Quasimodo, who once fought for the light-heavyweight championship of México."

Fernando waved in response to the cheers, and Julio invited him to say a few words. The old man took the microphone and spoke only briefly, but in a down-to-earth style that delighted the crowd.

"I just wanna say how glad I am to be here today. I'm very proud of my boy Julio, though I'm sorry he's giving up *lucha libre* for the dirtier fighting of politics. And one other thing bugs me. Back inside, they've got loads of free drinks, and I can't touch a drop. What a waste! Anyway, I'll drink a toast to every one of you, as soon as these fucking forty days of Lent are over. *Muchas gratias!*"

At this point, before the laughter and the cheers had died away, the mayor of Iztapalapa, Señor Enrique Mérida, joined his guests on the balcony and took over the microphone.

"*Señoras y señores,*" he proclaimed. "Thank you all for coming to welcome our honoured guests. It now only remains to conclude the proceedings with our "new fire" ceremony. For this purpose, we will be turning off the floodlights, and I would ask you to clear a passage to the sacrificial pyre.

"Now, in recognition of his most generous support, we are pleased to invite Señor Stephanopoulos to dispel the evil of darkness and bring forth the goodness of light."

A few minutes later Nicholas, accompanied only by Julio, emerged from the town hall. Then, after being handed a flaming torch, he made his way to the centre of the *zócalo* where a huge bonfire had been constructed out of tree branches, wooden boxes and assorted debris.

High up, firmly roped to a pole protruding from the heap, was a dummy-like figure in a long-flowing red cloak, and with a sack-covered head fitted with a black wig, and a bushy false beard. He represented the treacherous Judas Iscariot who, all over Mexico, was being burnt in effigy this day.

Steely-faced, Nicholas took one look upwards, and then plunged his torch into the pile's base of straw. Within a few seconds, the fire was ablaze. A single star-bursting rocket exploded in the night sky, and the huge crowd clapped as the *zócalo* became aglow with brilliant light.

"*Judas es un cabrón,*" someone shouted, and there were cheers as flames rose up to consume the despised traitor. Only Nicholas and Julio were alert enough to detect that— behind narrow slits in the sacking— living eyes were bulging in an expression of genuine agony and horror.

Julio smiled sardonically, and whispered to Nicholas, "Who was it that said vengeance is a dish best served cold?"

Nicholas did not reply. He took a deep breath, stretching up to his full height. For the first time since that night on Mt. Lycabettus, he felt whole again, his *philotimo* fully restored.

Lightning Source UK Ltd.
Milton Keynes UK
13 December 2009

147456UK00002B/7/P